MW01050069

We Got Him

We Got Him

A novel by ELIZABETH SEARLE

American Fiction Series

©2016 by Elizabeth Searle
First Edition
Library of Congress Control Number: 201593385
ISBN: 978-0-89823-348-3
e-ISBN: 978-0-89823-349-0

Cover design by Ethan DeGree
Author photo by Mark Karlsberg

The publication of *We Got Him* is made possible by the generous support
of Minnesota State University Moorhead, The McKnight Foundation, the
Dawson Family Endowment, and other contributors to New Rivers Press.

For copyright permission, please contact Frederick T. Courtright at
570-839-7477 or permdude@eclipse.net.

New Rivers Press is a nonprofit literary press associated with
Minnesota State University Moorhead.

Alan Davis, Director and Senior Editor
Nayt Rundquist, Managing Editor
Thomas Anstadt, Co-Art Director
Trista Conzemius, Co-Art Director
Kevin Carollo, MVP Poetry Coordinator
Bayard Godsave, MVP Prose Coordinator
Thom Tammaro, Poetry Editor
Wayne Gudmundson, Consultant
Suzzanne Kelley, Consultant

Publishing Interns:
Laura Grimm, Anna Landsverk, Desiree Miller, Mikaila Norman

Book Team:
Samantha Alvers, Molly Christenson, Ashley Peck, Marie Veillette

Editing Interns:
Mikaila Norman, Luke Quanbeck

 Printed in the USA using acid-free, archival-grade paper.

We Got Him is distributed nationally by Small Press Distribution.

New Rivers Press
c/o MSUM
1104 7th Ave S
Moorhead, MN 56563
www.newriverspress.com

For Barbara Price Searle

and in loving memory of

William Deasy Searle (1930-2016)

My Parents, forever in love

Contents

We got him.

Boston Mayor Tom Menino

Twitter message, following capture of

Marathon Bombing suspect

April 19, 2013

Prologue

Someone's Son

Bomber Boy, Sarah kept silently chanting. The dark-eyed young Boston Marathon bombing suspect kept hovering, all night, on the birth room TV. Below him, Sarah lay in wait. In labor, two months too soon. Timing, intently, her own breaths.

Bomber Boy: one, two, three—

His blurred, sullen face kept mixing up, in Sarah's stunned mind, with the equally sullen face of her nineteen-year-old stepson PJ—maybe in police custody by now?—and with the big-eyed face of the little boy blown up days before at the Boston Marathon finish line.

Bomber Boy: four, five, six—

All those boy faces mixed with the fierce, fuzzy ultrasound face of the baby boy inside her. A swirly close-up seemingly taken in outer space but really in an inner space she'd never quite believed she had—until him. His unformed, creamy astronaut face. The face that she and Paul had awaited for years. A baby too late, and now tonight, too early. Where *was* Paul?—

TEENAGE JIHADIST? the TV asked, then a rush of shakily filmed gunshots. MASSIVE MANHUNT UNDERWAY.

And, Sarah told herself sadly, *he was someone's son.*

"I'm turning off the damn TV," her husband Paul announced behind her bed curtain in his deepest supervisor voice. He was back in the birth room, back from handling whatever—Sarah was scared to ask—was going on with PJ. "It's upsetting my wife."

Bomber Boy: seven, eight, nine—

"No," Sarah managed between breaths. The boyish suspect in profile in his white cap flashed yet again onscreen. She didn't want it—him—to go away. Because, she decided dazedly, he had become *it*. Her 'fixed object,' the object the birthing class instructor had told them to choose and 'focus on' in the birth room.

He did look—didn't he, in those unfocussed finish-line shots?—like Paul's son PJ. Defiant teen-boy stance; flat dark stare. So damn young. Surely he hadn't really done it.

Bomber Boy: ten, eleven, twelve—

Sarah squeezed shut her eyes, like a kid making a birthday wish. A healthy, full-term baby; the biggest, simplest wish of Sarah's thirty-five-year-long life. But nothing about getting her son—her and Paul's son—had been simple. Nothing had gone according to *What to Expect*, that battered paperback knocked off their bed earlier on this very night in the impulsive love-making they never should have dared in her seventh month. The dog-eared book, spotted with fresh blood by the time they got out the door. They drove through panicky traffic- and siren-filled streets, hearing the radio reports of BOSTON IN CHAOS, and BOMBING SUSPECTS REPORTEDLY ON THE RUN.

A siren behind their own speeding car. PJ in the backseat hoarsely urging Paul to drive faster. Sarah beside Paul, holding onto her belly. Paul steering headlong into what he'd dubbed the "Rotary of Doom." Then the jolt, the bump. Paul crashing onto Doom's central island, into its To BOSTON sign.

Blue and white Belmont Police car lights fitfully flashed on Paul's stoic profile and grey-flecked beard. His hair still curly and dark like his son PJ's, and like that of the bombing suspects: those digitally-enhanced, instantly-famous faces. Photos released by the FBI earlier this same day.

Birth day? Or would the Belmont Police somehow halt this premature birth? Behind her in the backseat, as the police car door slammed, Sarah felt man-sized PJ duck down. God, what-all *was* going on with PJ?

Protectively, Paul and Sarah faced those blaring lights together, PJ cowering behind them. Did he still have the jackknife, which only Sarah had seen, in his jacket? Would he use it this time?

Paul and Sarah stiffened like the true culprits. Both of them, Sarah sensed through her pulsing pains and the pulsing lights as the cop approached their car, bracing for the worst. *Maybe*, the unquenchable optimist in Sarah thought, *this would bring them together?*

Bomber Boy: thirteen, fourteen, fifteen—

In the beeping monitor light of the birth room, in the pulsing dark of Sarah's squeezed-shut eyes, Paul screaked open her bedside curtain and snapped off the nonstop TV news. Sarah blinked her eyes and it—he—was gone

The hovering Bomber Boy.

"No . . . I . . . I need him," Sarah managed, pointing a shaky finger to the screen. Paul gaped at her like she was losing it *Bring him back,* Sarah wanted to say. But she was panting, straining with a new contraction.

"He's fine. He's going to be fine," Paul muttered to her. Meaning PJ? The baby? The bomber?

Paul took Sarah's sweaty hand in his steady one. He squeezed Sarah's fingers, so their wedding bands pressed together. Gold, hard as bone. Sarah shut her eyes again, sucked under once more, picturing the boy face that had somehow become PJ plus the bomber plus her baby.

Bomber Boy: sixteen, seventeen, eighteen—

Past midnight now, on this marathon birth night. Mutely, Sarah squeezed Paul's hand back. Gold to gold, bone to bone. At least, this night of nights, she felt closer to him than she'd felt in months. She and Paul were braced now—pulling together like Boston, Sarah hoped—against the blast of disaster they'd awaited their whole, holy-wedlocked life.

Part One

Birth Night

Chapter One

April 18, 2013; 8:30 p.m.

Lightening

"The baby becomes you."

In bed that evening, Sarah woke to Paul's words. Setting her, setting everything, in motion. If he hadn't said those words, Sarah would later wonder, would they have made love that night? Would she and the baby have stayed safe?

"Wha—?" Sarah rolled over, their Birds of Happiness wedding afghan sliding off her bare shoulders. Her belly jutted up. She blinked in the half dark. Her tall, bearded husband stood above her, home early.

"Baby," she muttered, "becomes—?"

"You. Is becoming to you. I was just looking at you . . . " Like he'd been doing all week, ever since marathon day. Glints shone in his dark eyes.

"At me and him," Sarah reminded Paul, caressing her belly. Her son stayed motionless inside her. When pregnant women get upset, she'd read, fetuses fall into "anxious stillness." *Sorry*, Sarah told hers silently. She'd been freaked out since witnessing the marathon bombing from miles away, days before. And now today—thanks to PJ and his crazy visit—she was freaked out for even more reasons than everyone else in Boston.

"Hey, Sare?" Paul asked as if he'd heard that unspoken sorry. "You OK? You overdosing on CNN?" He set a SweetNGreek bakery bag on his nightstand with a waxy crackle. "Heard on the radio the FBI released the suspect photos. Heard they're getting all kinds of leads. There were news trucks and FBI vans blocking Memorial Drive . . ."

Paul lifted the remote and switched on their small, flat-screen TV. News voices blared forth—BACK IN A MINUTE WITH MORE UPDATES ON THE SEARCH FOR THE BOMBING SUSPECTS—

"Please, I don't want to see that." Sarah pulled herself upright in bed. She'd switched off the news around noon when she'd glimpsed PJ outside.

"And I don't want to hear *this*." Paul muted the creepy, cheery music for an ad they both hated with a sad-eyed cartoon woman walking under a cartoon cloud and the looming name of an antidepressant. This ad, Paul and Sarah agreed, was depressing in itself. The cute black hole trying to suck the woman in; the cuter little pill pulling her back from the brink.

"Like you do with me," Paul tried joking now, shrugging off the tweedy suit jacket Sarah had bought for his Center Director job.

"Hey, I'm the one who's down today, Saint Paul," Sarah murmured wryly as he settled on their bed. She seized the remote, switched off the now-smiling cartoon woman, whose oversized doe eyes remained implacably sad. "God, Paul, they kept showing that sweet, big-eyed little boy who got killed at the finish line. I kept picturing that little girl I h-held on to—"

Her voice choked; she was teary-eyed, as she'd been on and off all afternoon. All week since the marathon, every loud sound startled her, even though she'd been too far down the marathon route to hear the actual blasts.

Paul climbed into bed fully dressed, stretching his big-bear body beside hers. Sarah knew she should tell Paul right away about PJ and his surprise visit today after so many months MIA.

"GodPaul," she whispered instead like one word. She snuggled closer, shaking back her rippled, unbraided hair. "Glad you're home early . . ." She nuzzled Paul's dense, scratchy beard.

Is PJ, she wondered, *still out there, nearby?* He'd told her he hadn't meant to scare her, with his knife. But who could believe PJ?

Paul half-smiled at Sarah, meeting her eyes fully for a change.

"And yeah, I have been overdosing on news." She tugged their Birds of Happiness afghan around her like a shawl. Its once-white wool showed pale stains of wine and chocolate and semen. How long since they'd made love? "Yeah, they kept saying they're releasing those photos and all. But GodPaul, I just wanted to turn it *all* off . . ."

"What. The world?" Paul rested his long-boned arm around Sarah's shoulders. "Maybe you're finally a true-blue Stratidakis. If Grandma Stratidakis had knitted that, it would've been the birds of unhappiness."

Sarah sighed impatiently, blinking back her tears. Paul and his pessimism, his family's supposedly doomed genes. "C'mon. We've got a plan, right? Our bad genes will clobber each other." She switched to her headline voice. "Manic and depressive have a baby . . ."

"Manic had that plan," Paul grumbled as Sarah mimicked her own manic smile. At least neither of them had yet reached what Paul would call a "clinical level."

"Manic versus depressive, and guess what?" Sarah hauled herself to her knees. Her belly hung over her sweatpants waistband. "Manic *won*."

Stifling her unromantic grunt, Sarah straddled her husband's bear-sized body. Her breasts strained her stretchy maternity bra. "Makes you know life is short, what happened this week." She settled onto Paul, pinning him under her seven-and-a-half-month weight. After they'd made love at last, maybe she'd be able to tell him what happened today when PJ reappeared. "Y'know, we've been way too cautious." Sarah smoothed Paul's button-down shirt. She breathed deeply, smelling the still warm baklava. "I mean, you went and brought my favorite dessert. We could share it like we used to, if you want."

"I want," Paul breathed back, "But—"

"It's about time," Sarah cut in, surprised by her overheated body, suddenly sexed up the way it had been in her second trimester, back in their second honeymoon, over the winter holidays.

Paul shifted his legs. Sarah felt him bump her book at the foot of their bed. *What to Expect* had explained it all: "Some pregnant women experience increased sexual appetite, their vulvas engorged and ultrasensitive."

I'll say, Sarah thought. She rubbed Paul's zipped crotch through her sweatpants. Her belly curved out full and white between her and him, marked by her new linea nigra.

Paul fingered the darkened line lightly, respectfully. "Your racing stripe."

"Damn straight."

He traced the line, his fingertip steady. "You sure earned it," Paul told her, sounding tender, though he hadn't always been in their tense years of trying.

"You too." Sarah pressed his strong hand, flattening it on her belly.

His hands were what she'd first noticed about Supervisor Stratidakis. A tall, intense man with big, calm hands. In the Profound Developmental Disability Ward, he cupped wildly jerking heads. In the Center cafeteria, he tossed spilt salt over his left shoulder. Their shared superstition formed the first wordless bond between them.

"The baby does become you . . ." Paul eased his hand from under hers. "God, Sare. Monday when I heard about the bombs on the radio, knowing you were there, I damn near crashed the car . . ."

"But we're both here now." Sarah smoothed Paul's thick, curly hair—his pride. Smoothing his tangled thoughts, they always joked. Outside, leafy branches brushed their windscreen.

Paul gave his sure supervisor nod. Sarah began rocking on top of him. To hell with everything else, she felt, as she always felt when they got down to it. Their wood sleigh bed creaked its sex song. Sarah took hold of Paul's shoulders. Paul rocked with her, under her, as if the bed really was a sleigh. Starting a wild ride, Sarah held on.

✺

"Something's wrong at the finish line!"

Sarah couldn't see anything at first, could only hear the people crammed around her at the Chestnut Hill Reservoir banks, near the turn onto Beacon, shouting confused rumors. Some hunched over their cell phones urgently, and some held their phones high to catch shots of the runners slowing.

"Some are running back! *They're running* back!*"*

Like rogue waves sweeping backwards on a beach. It looked so unnatural, so wrong to Sarah as the herd of runners slowed at the turn, as the first of the reversed runners stumbled into sight, waving their arms, telling fellow runners something urgent. Everyone looked as stunned as Sarah felt. What was happening? Hadn't there been a distant sound, like muffled thunder?

She clutched her seven-month belly. The only clear fact in her own mind.

"I'm pregnant!" She found herself calling out foolishly as she pulled herself up from Evvy's folding chair. The crowd shifted; her chair knocked over. Folks on the grassy banks stepped toward Beacon Street, holding up their damn phones like flares in the hazy sun.

"A manhole exploded!" someone shouted.

"I'm pregnant!" Sarah protested, jostled by people pushing closer to see the

mass of numbered runners, halting, stumbling, bunching up. Evvy among them?

Sarah strained to see her friend, the one person in this giant, confused crowd who'd help Sarah keep her baby safe. In a blur of panic, Sarah backed toward an abandoned water bottle stand as others around her surged forward.

"Mommy! Where's my mommy?" a little girl with scared eyes and beaded braids keened. Sarah gripped the girl's bony shoulder and held on hard. Sirens whooped by.

"Stay here so she can find you," Sarah told the girl in her best mom voice.

She handed the girl a water bottle and stole one for herself, too. The two of them waited, frozen on the sidelines, until minutes later when the girl's mom, who'd run ahead to make sure her sprinter son was OK, came back and claimed her girl. She told Sarah there'd been two explosions. A chunky college girl runner appeared with a bloody arm. She'd ripped out her own IV in the hydration station, she explained hoarsely, to make way for all the injured.

"Injured?" Sarah demanded when Evvy—her short, gray-blonde hair damp, and her runner number lopsided—found her.

They'd agreed beforehand on how Sarah, in her bright green BC ALUM sweat-shirt, would sit in Evvy's folding chair to watch Evvy turn onto Beacon Street.

They wound up leaving the knocked over chair behind. Evvy led Sarah by the hand through the scared, scattering crowd to her own car, parked in a Boston College track coach's apartment lot. Sarah glimpsed a teenage girl with pasty, bloody hair crying that this wasn't her blood, not her blood. There were people screaming in the distance and more sirens than Sarah had ever heard at once. She wanted to sob like that little girl with braids. Sarah's cell beeped in her purse, but she couldn't remember what to do, how to answer.

When at last they reached the car and Sarah answered Paul's seventh call, she couldn't speak at first, could only, finally, cry. But Paul knew it was her.

"*Is* this safe, Sare?" Paul made himself ask, clearing his cigarette-rough-ened throat.

"Sure it's safe," Sarah insisted, breathless like him. Her face too pink, her olive eyes too bright.

Paul kept rocking beneath his flushed, fierce-eyed wife. Even in the dim room, Sarah's rich brown hair showed the subtle reddish glints he'd always seen once he'd first noticed them, and her. What was she up to now?

Quiet Sarah McCall, her pale, oval face almost plain, until you looked. Sarah's pregnant weight, plus the cigarettes he'd snuck, made Paul breathless. He'd been sneak-smoking extras this insane week, what with nearly losing his mind when he couldn't reach Sarah on marathon day, then having to relive it all through televised hysteria. Shaky camera shots of the sudden, giant smoke clouds that had almost eaten up his wife and unborn baby.

Paul planted his hands on Sarah's curvy hips, holding her steady. For all its weight, her belly seemed like a giant bubble. His cock was stiffening, straining through his pants. If he thrust up inside her, would the bubble burst?

"Couples do it all the time this late. We've been missing out. I've been missing . . . you." Sarah fingered Paul's shirt buttons, tickling his chest. "Don't you think our lives lately have been missing . . . the . . ." she worked the top button free, "point?"

Now she was talking. Paul shifted his legs, his cock getting hopelessly hard. How he'd missed this hot, anticipatory ache.

As Sarah unbuttoned her way down his chest, the folded paper in his shirt pocket crackled. Paul blinked. The weird email from PJ that he'd received earlier in his office and hadn't wanted to forward to Sarah at home. The printout he'd carried all day over his heart, where PJ himself damn well belonged.

His troubled son, estranged son—or maybe he only wished PJ was estranged.

Despite the crackle, Sarah smoothed open Paul's shirt. She curled her fingers into his chest hair. Thick and black, no gray like his beard.

"Hey now," Paul mumbled. "Anything inappropriate will do."

Sarah let her warm fingertips graze his nipples. "How's this for inappropriate, mister?" Clumsily, her belly bumping him, she stripped off her sweatpants, releasing her faint, wet scent.

"Careful," Paul warned her and himself. She resettled her weight on top of him. She was wearing only her maternity bra. Her belly's lower curve rubbed Paul's balls through cloth. Yes, wasn't this what he needed today? After the week they'd had? As she pulled his shirt further open, Paul again heard and felt the stiff paper in his pocket like a warning.

"What's that?" Sarah asked. He pushed her hands gently back.

"Just an email I printed out. From . . . PJ."

"Oh?" Sarah's voice and body both subtly tensed. Damn, was PJ going to break this spell between them? "When—when did it come?"

Why ask that? Paul wondered.

"This morning," he told Sarah, watching her eyes deepen in their olive green.

PJ's midnight email had greeted Paul on his office computer. He felt the jolt in his gut he always felt at PJ's emails. He'd read and reread his son's latest while smoking a forbidden cigarette for breakfast and listening to Anton Bruckner—his favorite since his dad's death. Nothing like Bruckner's eighth to take you beyond your own puny brooding. Those unearthly French horns. Listening with eyes shut was like being dead, only conscious. Black bliss.

As Paul made his afternoon rounds, tromping from the Severelies' residence hall to Moderatelies', the cool spring air soothed his smoky throat. On impulse, after his district director's phone conference, Paul locked up his office at 8:00 p.m. One thing he'd learned in years of managing his up-and-down moods: when a hopeful mood hit, he damn well had to act on it. So, he'd stopped at SweetNGreek. Post baklava, he planned, he'd show Sarah PJ's email. PJ's request that sounded like, but surely wasn't, a threat.

"We can talk about it later," Paul told Sarah now. "It's nothing so bad . . ."

Sarah was nodding slowly, as if she already guessed it *was* bad. But she'd see, Paul vowed as he unbuttoned his own last buttons, why they had to do it, try it. Taking PJ in. What the hell might PJ do or try next if they didn't?

And if she said no? Paul wondered as Sarah opened his shirt all the way. She was balanced on top of him, waiting. His hard-on waited, too.

"Hey, I got something to show you . . ." Reaching up with both hands, matter of fact as a stripper, Sarah stretched her new bra's nursing slits. Her breasts burst out, swollen in their mesh of blue veins. She breathed in as if modeling the lingerie she used to order by mail. "Is it too much, this bra, or does it work?"

Below her, Paul answered emphatically, "Both."

Sarah dared a belly-quaking laugh, rocking harder along with Paul, her bobbing breasts leaky. What had *What to Expect* promised in that sole, sexy passage? Some pregnant women experience orgasms or multiple orgasms "accompanied by streams of milk spurting from their breasts"?

Sarah leaned on Paul as she stopped laughing, her hand pressing the folded email waiting in his pocket. *PJ sent it this morning,* Sarah reminded herself. Before his surprise afternoon ambush visit to her. Before PJ stole the card she never should have kept.

Sarah straightened her back, her grin fading. God knew what the email said. *PJ was here,* Sarah braced herself to say to her grinning husband. But as she breathed in deep to speak, she felt a shift inside of her. Her belly suddenly seemed to hang lower, heavier.

"Wow. I—I think the baby's dropped a little lower into his chute. Only that can't be, not for a couple more weeks . . ." Sarah balanced on Paul, hesitating now that he was so ready. "Is this 'lightening?' I'm kinda light-headed, too. My center of gravity shifts, the book says. So I get off balance . . ."

"Damn book got that part right." Paul steadied her hips. "Christ, Sare." He was stiffening his long body under her. "Maybe we shouldn't, if you're too, too . . ."

"Big?" she filled in, scooting back, reaching down, unzipping him. "No really, I'm fine. Better than ever . . ." Sarah resettled over his unzipped crotch feeling sure, somehow, they should go through with this. Then after, she could and would tell him about today. "Look, Saint Paul, lightening is natural. It may be a little early, but it's a good sign. It's normal. It's all good . . ."

She hunched lower, weighed down by her freed, blue-veined breasts. Melons in netted sacks. Paul pressed the small of her back, easing her to him. His bristly beard scratched her skin. She gasped. The familiar yet startling feel of Paul's tongue. He licked one nipple. Milky fluid the book called colostrum.

She met Paul's gaze. "As long as it's—OK with this lightening thing." Paul's voice sounded strained. "Christ, Sare. What's the damn book say?"

"I *told* you. The damn book says that it's . . . sex is, even third trimester, usually, normally, y'know, OK . . ." Sarah stretched back one leg and groped with her bare foot. "Anyhow, fuck the book."

She kicked. *What to Expect* thudded the floor. Paul gazed up at Sarah as if he had, in fact, no idea what to expect next.

"After all . . ." Sarah shifted her weight, tugging down his briefs, "nothing in this pregnancy's gone by the book. Why should the home stretch?"

She freed Paul's hard-on and straightened with it, her breasts and belly jutting out regally. He rocked beneath her again, in earnest. Sarah rubbed his upright cock, its welcome heat. She shut her eyes against the dim, silvery bedroom, shutting out the whole horrific week.

"It's OK, Saint Paul, we'll be OK. Let's just, y'know, *go.*"

14

Sarah was four, maybe younger; she was whatever age memory begins, because this was her first. She was trying to tell a lady that her baby doll was going to have a baby, her tongue almost too young to shape the sentence. Her never-cut hair hung around her face. Her baby doll was— that word. Magic, maybe a bad word; the P-word that Sarah's big cousins knew.

"Your dollie is . . . ?" the lady friend of Mommy's prompted, fixing upon Sarah the intent, coaxing gaze she longed for from her mother, who was inside making clinky ice drinks. Barefoot, sunlit Sarah and the shaded, high-heeled lady stood outside on the pine needly patio that smelled of damp brick and moss. Sarah rubbed her foot on a secret patch of moss and squeezed her soft-bodied, hard-headed doll.

"She—she's p-p-p—" Sarah stuttered, the lady's gaze urging her toward the word Sarah felt she knew. Yet it wouldn't come, wouldn't let her speak it and free herself from its spell.

Pregnant. All her life, Sarah had longed to be pregnant. For so many reasons, but hidden among them was knowing for nine months you could do nothing, as she secretly loved, while really doing the most important thing of all.

At first, Thursday, April 18th, 2013, had been another shapeless pregnancy day, perfect in its way. She shut off the news at noon, breaking the marathon week spell. Guiltily sick of hearing about all the marathon watchers who had bravely rushed toward the explosions, the truly wounded. If she hadn't been pregnant, she would have helped more than that one scared girl, right? But being pregnant was an excuse for more than just laziness. Selfishness for two?

She and her baby were safe, Sarah told herself sternly, switching off the set. That was what mattered now. No bombers would make their way to this shady, tree-lined side street in Belmont, this comfy condo that Sarah had purchased by selling the stock shares her long-distance dad had left her. Paul, in the new director job he had taken for the higher salary, had a late meeting. Sarah spent a quiet morning cooking up Evvy's tomato basil soup recipe, and drawing an ink panther for her student Keesha's virtual zoo. With her pregnancy, she'd shifted to part-time art therapy at Arsenal Arts Center in Watertown.

Guiltily lucky, yes, in more ways than one these days. Sarah set aside her sketchpad and lay propped by pillows, stroking her belly with ink-stained fingers. All morning, she had savored the misty drizzle she and the cat sensed coming in the air from inside. She kept the bedroom window open. The borrowed black cat, her model, crouched on the sill; its tail twitched.

It would kill the thrill if they found out its name, Sarah and Paul joked. Their gardening-fanatic, bachelor neighbor didn't know that Sarah let in his cat the days she didn't work. She borrowed the cat because she didn't want Paul and her lavishing a childless couple's love on a pet of their own.

An example, Paul claimed, of Sarah trying to stage manage their life. But getting a cat, to her, would have meant admitting they'd remain childless. She'd held out against it; she'd won.

"C'mere, crazy cat," Sarah crooned from her pillows, her pre-lunch rest. The cat was spooked, Paul claimed, by the baby. A third heartbeat in their bed.

You're spooked, too, Sarah thought toward absent Paul, stretching her legs under the afghan. Before the baby, the cat lounged for hours as she sketched, purring between her thighs.

Now he stropped his head yearningly against the windscreen and meowed to get out.

Sarah scooted to the edge of the bed. She gripped the sill for balance. At the cat's purring encouragement, she raised the wood-framed window higher and unlatched the screen. The cat sprang onto the maple's leafy branches.

Sarah drew one delicious, misty breath and glimpsed—through the cat-shuddering branches, blocks down the sidewalk—a boy or man. He was too far away to see a face, but her heartbeat thickened. Broad shoulders hunched; black, curly head bowed. He headed her way.

The Boston Bomber? Or—God, no—PJ?

She re-latched the window screen and stepped back from it. It couldn't be PJ. She'd almost rather it be the bomber. PJ had been gone, except for a few curt emails and calls, ever since that last August day at Spy Pond. His last spectacular blow up.

Sarah sank back on the bed, telling herself for the hundredth time that she should tell Paul everything about that last day—Her role in driving her stepson away. PJ staying with his mom in Ohio all fall, all through the holidays. Sarah so happy at Christmas to be pregnant at last, so eager to nest with Paul.

She scanned the books scattered across the bed. Her "soft desk," Paul called their bed these days. The old *Army Survival Manual* they'd bought for military-crazed PJ and unearthed after the bombing day, *One Step*

Ahead catalogues, a *Baby Safe Your Home* book, Sarah's *Films of the '40s Guide*, her Spy Pond-stained sketchbook and, most battered of all, *What to Expect When You're Expecting*. Its pages curdled from spilled ginger ale bottles Sarah carried with her in her sickly first trimester, followed by her unexpectedly sexy second.

Sarah fingered *What to Expect* like a lucky charm. She was old-fashioned; she liked books, not screens. And this book, even just its title, always comforted her. She knew she should look out the window again. Instead, she flipped the pages she'd lingered over at Christmas in her second trimester. Surprised then by her suddenly voluptuous body, its undeniable "increased sexual appetite." All perfectly normal said *What to Expect*.

She and Paul had reconnected in every way, their holiday week a mini honeymoon. *We're stronger together now*, Sarah told herself. *We're stronger, and I'm stronger than last summer.* She shut *What to Expect*. She set it beside *Baby Safe Your Home*. My body's not a body anymore, she reminded herself. It's a baby safe. It's keeping my baby locked safe inside.

Dutifully, Sarah hauled herself up. She stood like a guard in her SPECIAL OLYMPICS sweatshirt and sweatpants, facing the window, her belly chilled by the breeze. She spotted him again, closer, through the tree branches.

PJ. Paul Jr. Only a couple blocks up now, standing soldier-still. Sarah stood rigidly, too, her doubled heartbeat thudding her throat and chest. PJ's curly black hair; PJ's dramatic black brow and bulging eyes. His worn denim jacket. The unmistakable bulky shoulders with their hidden tattoos.

Paul Stratidakis Jr.: a.k.a. 'PJ,' a.k.a. 'PS,' as Paul Jr. used to sign his painstakingly printed letters. Your son, Sarah had told Paul, sees himself as a mere postscript. Back then, Sarah was sure that she, with all her untapped mother love, could change that. Our practice son, Sarah secretly deemed Paul's scruffy child who visited Boston twice a year from Ohio. Playing spy and soldier. Admiring Paul and adoring Stepmommy Sarah with his unmistakable mother hunger.

Sarah pressed one hand to her belly, her son. Outside, PJ shifted from foot to foot like he'd done since he was five. Hyper PJ. She'd introduced him to karate, encouraged him to invent stories instead of tell lies, to write down his vivid, violent song lyrics. She'd pretended the card he'd sent her was song lyrics, too—her first big mistake, followed by even bigger ones that final day at Spy Pond.

Down below, Paul Jr. scuffed a sidewalk puddle. Stocky and

square-shouldered, man-sized now. His Greek-Armenian hair thick and solid black the way Paul's used to be.

The stepmom part of Sarah felt weak-kneed with relief to see him out there, alive and well. But she backed away from the window, shakily. TROUBLED STEPSON STALKS PREGNANT STEPMOM; MISSING STEPSON RETURNS TO—what? If he raised his head, would he see her through the trees? He stood stiff like the young soldiers on TV, raising their tremulous weapons, set to strike. PJ ducked his head. In a neat karate move, he sidestepped behind the neighboring double-decker, a shingled wall of dove gray, like theirs. The shaded sidewalk was deserted; the traffic rumble of Pleasant Street was muffled. The dogwoods were blowing, branches clawing the sky.

Sarah shoved the window down in one glass-rattling thump. Breathlessly, she crept around the bed, lifted her phone, punched in Evvy's number. As it rang, she glanced at her sketchbook askew on the bed, its algae-green Spy Pond stain.

"'Lo." Evvy picked up on ring six, breathless like Sarah. Evvy Elfman, as light and offhandedly graceful as her name.

"It's me." Sarah hugged her belly with one arm.

"Not little ol' Mommy Me," Evvy murmured in her caustic Carolina drawl.

"Try big ol'." Sarah pictured Evvy's cynical pixie face, sun-lined. Evvy in her Arlington apartment, flipping her fingers through her hair—feathery short, ashy gray plus dirty gold.

"I was thinkin' of stopping by, after orange belt. You freakin' out again, hon? Still having nightmares about the bombs? God, I'll never forgive myself for bringing you to cheer me on in that goddamn race—Hey, lemme get my tea."

Evvy's phone clunked. Anti-stress green tea. Evvy'd been drinking cup after cup lately when she and Sarah poured over Evvy's sperm bank catalogues, Evvy ruling out with an airy wave any potential donor who misspelled words on his *About Me* fact sheet.

It was Evvy who'd sat at Sarah's side through all those depressing, exhilarating One Way Or Another meetings that Paul wouldn't attend, saying he didn't want to falsely raise "our," meaning "her," hopes. For the baby that Evvy—with her steady hand, with the first LHRH injection to clear Sarah's Fallopian tubes—had helped create.

The baby safe, for now, under Sarah's tensed hand.

"You do sound downright freaked, Sarah sweetie. What's up?"

"You won't believe, but . . . PJ. I saw him out on the sidewalk. Unless

I'm totally seeing things. Just standing out there. God, at least he's alive."

"Oh, that boy's alive all right." Evvy slurp-sipped. Evvy was the only one who knew about what-all, or almost all, had gone on with PJ.

"Oh Evvy. He's a good kid at heart, right? But you know how crazy he got last summer. And now he's *here,* back from Cleveland or God-knows-where, wanting God-knows-what . . ."

"Shoot, hon. I want to come over and try an' knock some sense into him."

"You can't, Evvy. You've gotta teach your orange belts in—what? Half an hour? Besides, I've always been able to handle PJ."

"Lookie, how about I check up on you later, stop by with some kale soup?"

"Got my own soup going—your recipe. You take such good care of me."

Always cutting short any expression of the affection she seemed to crave, Evvy hung up.

Shakily, Sarah set down her phone. She didn't look at the window. She lifted her sketchpad, a floppy paper shield. Tensely, she flipped pages. Her old charcoal action drawings of PJ and Evvy practicing karate moves. PJ's scrawled lyrics. Sarah was always so eager to find peaceful outlets for PJ's energies, to practice art therapy techniques on the stepson she'd imagined saving. But hadn't she screwed him up worse?

Sarah let the sketchpad flop shut. Still standing, she lifted her remote and flipped on the corner TV—CNN: BOSTON POLICE AND FBI TO RELEASE PHOTOS OF BOMBING SUSPECTS—

Sarah flipped it off again, somehow scared to see those shots. She turned toward the window and craned her neck. No PJ visible outside now. Had he moved closer?

⌇

Go, Paul thought as they lay together panting, then breathing evenly, Sarah maybe half asleep. Paul stroked her hair, head resting on his chest. He kept picturing her saying "go" above him, her face heedlessly happy, pale skin glowing in the room's half dark.

Paul's mouth still held the milky oyster taste from her breasts. The warm, liquid trace alive on his tongue. Maybe that, plus sex, was the drug he'd needed. He scorned the antidepressants his doctor once tried to push. How long had it been, what with the baby and his own crazi-ness? When the mood hits, you have to act—quick, before it vanishes.

Right? Paul had thrust up into Sarah carefully, gripping her smooth, curvy hips. Struggling to hold his glowing bubble of a wife steady, everything silenced for Paul in the deepest silence and flesh folds of her.

The beautiful room inside her; where his new son was cocooned. *My son*, Paul had reminded himself as he'd thrust deeper. *Mine, mine.*

With PJ, at first, Paul hadn't known for sure. When pregnant, Adina had confessed to simultaneous affairs. Even with Sarah, Paul's paranoid side had fleetingly wondered how his borderline sperm count had produced this so called miracle baby.

But—Paul stroked Sarah's hair slower, his own breaths slowing—Paul knew he could trust Sarah, if no one else.

Her soft mouth half-opened as she slept. Christ, Paul had to keep Sarah safe, doubly safe. From everything outside their home, from poor, screwed-up PJ soon to be inside. Paul slid his hand down Sarah's shoulder to the curve of her back, her warm bare skin.

Her body, with all its pregnant weight, had felt so solid on top of his. Paul had gotten to like having her on top. Even before she got pregnant, she'd stopped lying on her back during the months of infertility injections—those bruising needles Paul had refused to administer at first. Evvy stepped up in Paul's stead and gave Sarah the first injection right here in this bedroom, so he'd been shamed into it.

Led into it, he'd secretly thought, *by the balls*. But wasn't it, as Sarah said, all good now? Paul could feel the baby now, so close. *My son*, he'd been thinking as he'd come. Sarah gasping too, her face shining with her deepest pink flush.

"Paul?" Sarah sat up, startling him, bare-breasted and breathless. Looking not at Paul but at her bulging, brown-striped belly. *Aftershock*, Paul thought, gazing at Sarah's stilled, dazed face. Like she'd just been through an earthquake, only she *was* the earth.

"GodPaul," she mumbled, one word. "GodPaul, something's happening . . ."

Paul was startled to see movement. He sat up beside her, snapping on the nightstand light, staring, too. A protrusion—a heel, a hip?—moved like a shark's fin under the pale, stretched stomach skin. Sarah was holding her belly with both hands, a globe she was struggling to contain. Helplessly, she turned her head and locked her gaze with Paul's.

What the fuck have we done?

Spring, 2000

"*Mommy?*"

Sarah jolted awake, thinking for a half-conscious moment that the baby she'd been dreaming had materialized overnight. She stirred in Paul's arms on their newlywed bed. She reminded herself that six-year-old PJ was visiting and sleeping on the fold-out couch.

"*Mommy Sarah?*"

His quick steps muffled through the wall. The door creaked. Barefoot, PJ charged across the bedroom. Slap slap, his feet against the wood floor.

His brash, husky voice. "Time to hug me!" PJ dived onto the bed and squirmed between sleeping Paul and laughing Sarah. She breathed the musky boy smell of his mussed black hair.

Smelling a baby's head is supposed to increase fertility, so maybe smelling a boy's is double strength. PJ seized a handful of her own hair, sniffed it.

"*What're you doing?" Sarah gasped in her usual stepmommy tone: mock-aghast, genuinely delighted. PJ buried his face in her loose hair, snuffling.*

"*Smellin' you," he mumbled into her hair, sounding delighted with himself.*

Sarah laid back, hugged PJ closer, and stretched out her legs in the prim cotton nightgown she wore for PJ weeks. She sighed, struggling to contain his strong-limbed boy body in her arms.

"*Help me watch," she whispered to still his squirms. He raised his ruddy face, widened his bullfrog eyes. Sarah nodded toward the open window; spring morning air drifted in.*

"*If you see a squirrel, you'll get your wish!" She and PJ fixed on the branches outside. In a blink, they both gasped; a squirrel appeared. Meaning, Sarah decided, she would get her wish, get pregnant. The squirrel quivered, its tail curved in a furry question mark.*

Chapter Two

April 18, 2013; 9:10 p.m.

Bloody Show

"What's wrong? What is it, Sare?"

"It's OK; I'll be OK—"

They both spoke at once. Something was tightening inside Sarah's belly, inside her groin, like menstrual cramps only bigger. Plus, she felt her crotch still pulsing from her come. Plus, the baby was stirring in there, waking, doing the Watusi. Sarah braced her hands on her belly.

Her belly a mountain Paul had climbed, she thought dazedly. But of course he hadn't. He hadn't climbed on her. She'd been on top the whole time, the whole ride.

"Does it hurt? Was I too rough? Did I hurt you? Christ, did I? Sare?"

"It's . . . it's not that. It can't be. It's—you know what? I've heard . . . I've read that sometimes coming—the mother coming—it triggers contractions. Not birth contractions but practice contractions." Sarah lay back and faced the ceiling, hearing herself babble. "And those come-contractions make the baby move is all. I'm all stirred up, so the baby gets stirred up, too. I feel so—funny." She couldn't stop talking, trying to convince herself. "But that's OK, that stillness. That's part of lightening, what the baby's supposed to do. Only, we sure woke him up. Woke me up, too, Saint Paul. Felt like I was *coming* for two. Plus, God, I'm starved . . ."

"You sure, Sare? That's all you're feeling—him moving?" Paul reached for the bakery bag, maybe eager like her to eat, not talk.

"I'm not sure of anything this crazy week," Sarah mumbled, reminding herself with a fresh heartbeat of dread that she needed to tell Paul PJ had been here today. And Paul needed to tell her what was in PJ's email. Plus, what was to stop PJ himself from stomping into their home, blurting out God-knew-what?

But Paul beside her seemed companionable, like the pre-baby Paul, so the email couldn't be bad, could it? Paul unrolled the wax paper bag, releasing the sweetly greasy aroma.

"My mouth's watering for two," Sarah announced, reaching.

"Women and children first." Paul tilted the honey-steeped bag her way.

She seized two sticky pastry diamonds, weighted with dates and nuts, slick with honeyed grease. Outside, a distant siren sounded.

"Guess we should turn on the TV. See what's up. Though I bet Evvy would call me if any big news breaks—" Sarah nibbled sweet, flaking crust. "She thinks we're cut off from civilization 'cause we're not on Facebook . . ."

"I don't care if she practically was the one to impregnate you with those damn shots. Don't go signing onto Facebook to please Evvy. That would be the ultimate marital betrayal." Paul shook his head, taking on his old, gruffly joking tone.

Sarah grinned as Paul fingertip-lifted his own baklava diamond. She enjoyed his not-quite-joking jealousy. What had Evvy told her last summer?

Sarah's problem, Evvy had drawled, was discovering, mid-life, her "terrific, terrible talent" for making everyone fall in love with her.

Luxuriantly slow, Sarah bit her baklava. Paper-thin layers of crust, then the rich inner mix of date paste and nuts and achingly sweet honey. Sarah felt happy despite everything. The first time she'd felt so relaxed since the bombing. She struggled to chew it all, her mouth brimming with honeyed saliva. Sex and baklava. Couldn't she savor that combo a little longer?

If her baby was OK, that's all that mattered. And wasn't her baby OK? Hadn't the crampy sensation subsided?

Sarah wiped her mouth. "Doesn't your body just feel so . . . happy?"

"All over." Paul allowed, chewing. He swallowed and cleared his throat, a professor introducing a difficult new topic. "Listen, Sare . . . this email." Sarah nodded, her eyes wide and her mouth bulging with food. "PJ's back in Boston, or so he says. Sent me a crazier-than-ever message . . ." Sarah felt another crampy sensation. She heard the siren outside rising.

"God—" Sarah wiped her greasy fingers on the sheet and reached for the remote. She'd been so afraid of PJ today she hadn't been thinking, like a real mother or even stepmother should, of his safety. "If PJ's out there, we gotta find out what's up."

She flipped on CNN. The screen bloomed into life. Sarah popped one last bite of baklava into her mouth. BOMBER SUSPECT PHOTOS RELEASED, the crawl read. Floating above were two fuzzy but digitally-enhanced photos. The news commentators were babbling about 'the black hat and the white hat' because the two suspects each wore baseball-style caps.

The younger white hat suspect, shown in profile with his curly dark hair and sneaky smirking face, was the one Sarah fixed on. Beside her, she felt Paul fix on him, too.

"Christ," Paul breathed. "That white hat one . . . Jesus Christ, he could almost be . . . he can't be—"

Before Paul could say "PJ," Sarah breathed in sharply. She choked, rich sweetness clogging her throat. Tears flooded her eyes, the blurred faces onscreen blurring further. Sarah gasped for breath but none came.

After she had glimpsed PJ all-too-clearly through the window then lost sight of him, Sarah had paced the bedroom, avoiding that window.

I gotta get away from here, from you, or I'm gonna . . . I don't know *what I'm gonna do!* Hadn't those been PJ's last shouted words that hot August day at the pond? How could she have let PJ flee? And never told Paul the whole story, only Evvy, who was there to see it all. Or almost all. What kind of stepmother did that make her? Shouldn't she call Paul immediately?

To calm herself, Sarah had switched on her TV, flipping away from CNN to a shrink show, Dr. Phil only sleazier, and muted it. No sound needed since the faces were captioned.

An elaborately made-up, perversely proud mother face showed now onscreen. SHE SEDUCED HER DAUGHTER'S BOYFRIEND. What would Sarah's worst secrets be reduced to if she had the gall or guts to lay it out on TV? STEPMOM DROVE VIOLENT STEP-SON TO—what?

With a spastic thumb jerk, Sarah snapped it off. Any shrink show crowd would judge her guilty. Familiar, secret guilt twisted her gut. Hadn't she triggered it all?

PJ's crazy impulses last summer, his abrupt disappearance in August. Adina's mother, PJ's Nana, had let Paul know only that he was in Ohio. PJ barely spoke to Paul on Thanksgiving or Christmas. Finally in January, PJ had emailed terse, cryptic words, claiming he was in Cleveland in an apartment near his Nana's house, was considering joining the US Army.

Who could believe him? He'd been in trouble all his young life for lying, exaggerating, telling tales, claiming to his grade school teachers he really was a spy, that his lunchbox held deadly glue sandwiches. Then later, bragging in high school about the heavy-duty jackknife he'd bought at a military cutlery shop in Elyria, Ohio. The same knife he'd pulled out, to Sarah's horror, the last Spy Pond day. Now today, with PJ back, what next?

The phone buzzed. "Hey, little momma. Just checking in on you." Evvy raised her voice above the karate class clamor. "Did PJ come calling or what? Maybe I oughta powder some lovage roots to keep him away . . ."

Sarah gave a nervous laugh. How irrationally gleeful she had been to discover Evvy Elfman practiced for real what Sarah had pretended to practice during her solitary childhood: witchcraft. A Wiccan, Evvy called herself. Paul scoffed, but who knew if the coriander seeds Evvy had crushed into a glass of white wine after that first LHRH injection had helped?

"Wish it were that simple with PJ. Oh Evvy, I saw him again, even clearer. He's out there on our street, but he hasn't come in. I'm almost afraid for him to . . ."

"Sweetie, that boy loves you. Loves you too much. And maybe he'd like to clock Paul, but he'd never hurt you. You know that, right?"

"Wish I felt so sure. Maybe it's just the whole bombing thing. I turned off the news; I didn't want to see the photos they're releasing . . ." Sarah felt her baby's foot flutter. She sat on the bed, her own foot twitching, wagging like a teenager's. They'd have to drive a stake through that foot, Paul said, before they could bury her.

Something thumped through the open window. Someone on the porch below?

"Evvy, I gotta go." As Sarah clicked off the phone, the door buzzed. Sarah pulled herself off the bed. A second, punishingly long buzz. The duplex's downstairs door. That door led to the shared entry hall, the stairway up to her and Paul's condo. The rude, extended buzz ripped through the afternoon's layers of peace.

The floor creaked under Sarah's feet. Cautious as a burglar, she crept barefoot on the polished wood floor into the living room. Its shelves were piled with books, Paul's classical CD collection, and small, framed paintings, some Sarah's, some gifts from students. Its walls glowed with the new paint she'd chosen when they'd deleaded for the baby.

Soft pumpkin, Sarah reminded herself as she reached the wall receiver. She pressed one stiffened finger to the *talk* button.

"Who is it?" Her voice came out shaky but loud. She lifted her finger, pressed *listen,* and stiffened all over, though the answer was no surprise.

PJ's hoarse, boy-smoker voice deepened by the static to the depth of his Dad's. "Da Bomber. Your very own—" He paused in a staticky blur of heavy breaths. "*Terror*-ist."

She released *listen* before he could say more. Surely this was another sick PJ joke. She leaned her full weight onto *talk.* "PJ, God, is it you?"

No answer, but through her door she could hear the clack as he unlocked the downstairs door with his own keys—of course he still had his own. She stood back, half wanting to bolt the upstairs door, but telling herself she couldn't lock him out—Paul's son.

PJ thudded up the steps and thumped open the door. He filled the doorway with his bulky shoulders, wider than ever, and his doggy, sweaty boy smell, stronger than ever. He shook his curly head, hair short. He stared Sarah up and down, his bulgy eyes all pupil, doubly dark.

Same black brows and lashes, same sullen, darkish lips he hated. Frog face, he'd been taunted before he learned karate. Frog face, fag face.

Sarah faced him for the first time since that day on Spy Pond Beach, behind the feverishly green bushes when he'd pulled out that jackknife, staring at it himself as if he didn't know how it got in his hand. For months Sarah had wondered, *would he actually come after her?* She couldn't believe he would, but she could imagine him stabbing himself if she betrayed him in his twisted teenage mind. But of course she was betraying Paul by not telling. All fall and winter she'd wondered and worried and tried to reach PJ on her own; she'd secretly signed up for Facebook but not found him there. Not telling Paul, or even Evvy, about the knife.

Sarah drew a deep, shuddery breath now, taking PJ in. He'd gained muscle since summer, his body stocky but strong. Eyes bright but not overly bright like they'd been that last day.

"Stepmommy." PJ straightened and mock-saluted her.

Sarah answered, a tense attempt at her old gushy stepmom style: "*PJ*."

"Call me Paul," PJ told her, curt as his dad.

She stood before him, tongue-tied. As a boy, PJ had tackled her with his hugs. Now he stayed back a few feet, as if from a force field.

Sarah stood stiff and still. She let PJ take in her seven-and-a-half-month belly, outlined by her sweatshirt and sweatpants. She held still, as if that belly would halt any further craziness. PJ's knitted brows and intent dark eyes made him seem like Paul more than ever, but his pouty, pronounced mouth was his sexy, melodramatic mother's.

"Your hair," Sarah began again. "Looks good, Peej, looks . . ." She fluttered her fingers around her own braided hair. "Shorter. Hey, you didn't really, like you said in that email in January, sign up? For the, you said—army?"

"I might." PJ heaved a big-shouldered shrug. "Think I'm a big enough boy?" Their old joke, Sarah always assuring him he was getting tall like Paul.

But he wasn't. His mom's petite genes held him back. Sarah couldn't make herself nod now, eye to eye with PJ. She pictured TV images of fallen, untended, boy-faced soldiers.

"You grew, too." PJ nodded at her, her body. He bounced on his boot heels. Nineteen now, college age. He had surely been high that final day at the pond. Did he even remember what-all had happened?

"Anyhow." PJ stared straight at Sarah's swollen breasts. "What you got for me to eat?"

PJ? Paul was thinking in dumbstruck horror, facing the blurred, digitalized profile onscreen. Thinner and sharper-nosed than his son's, but who knew if PJ had lost weight in the months he'd been gone? Lost weight and lost his mind?

Paul turned to Sarah to share his wide-eyed shock. His wife was coughing—hard. Her hands flew up to her throat. Universal symbol for choking, Paul had intoned in many a Center training seminar. Christ, was she?

"Sar-*rah*." An earthquake in the bed, baklava bag spilling, Birds of Happiness lumped aside. Paul slapped Sarah's tensed, bare back.

"THE WHITE HAIR—I MEAN WHITE HAT SUSPECT," a TV news voice was stumbling over itself to say. "YES, WHITE HAT, THE YOUNGER SUSPECT. AND THE BLACK HAT IS—"

Sarah bent over her belly, spitting up, shooing Paul off with one hand.

"I got you!" He jerked himself sideways so he could reach around her, clasping his clenched hands above her belly. Heimlich for pregnant or obese victim instructions leapt into focus in his brain.

"BLACK HAT, WHITE HAT," TV voices kept nightmarishly repeating. Sarah jabbed her elbows backwards, breaking Paul's awkward hold.

Let her, his trained brain said. She was coughing; that meant she could do it.

"Don' hurt . . . th' *ba*-by," she was able to gasp. Chin wet, she twisted to face Paul indignantly over her hunched shoulder.

"—AS POLICE IN BOSTON CONTINUE THEIR MANHUNT, RESPONDING TO THOUSANDS OF CALLS FROM BOSTON RESIDENTS WHO MAY RECOGNIZE THE FACES IN THESE JUST-RELEASED PHOTOS . . ."

Paul, shaking with relief, muttered that of course he wouldn't have hurt their baby. He knew the right way. Back at her Center orientation, Paul had stood behind Sarah in the Heimlich demonstration and curved his body around hers—their first touch. Sarah, trembly too, shook her head as if to clear it.

She wiped her wet-lipped mouth. She told him, "Sorry. Sorry," trying to wipe her stickily streaked belly, too. Then she wadded up the stained Birds of Happiness, dropped it overboard onto the floor. Her belly looked smeared, glazed with honey. She hugged herself, her arms still as strong as in the days when she'd lift adults onto Center changing mats.

Paul rubbed his arm where she'd elbowed him. He lifted the remote, muted the TV, and stared harder now at the floating televised face that could've been—yet wasn't—PJ.

Sarah, reading his mind as always, used her first breaths to put it into words. She pointed weakly at the screen, her voice scratchy but clear. "God Paul . . . that nose, come on. Too long, too bony. Yeah, the hair is PJ but, but—PJ, he's not *thin* like that. You know that. Not crazy like that, either. *I* know that, I mean. I . . . see, today . . ." Sarah shook her head as if overwhelmed, swallowing hard.

"Today, yeah. PJ's email. That's what I've been trying to—meaning to tell you." Paul gathered crushed, sticky baklava halves, remembering names, old Somerville pals of PJ's who might know where he was now.

"So you got . . . got that email this morning, Paul?"

"Yes. I already told you. PJ sent it last night." Paul switched off the ceaseless CNN. They had their own emergency to attend to. He reached in his shirt pocket, drew out the folded paper, and handed it to Sarah gently. "To my work email. I . . . I didn't want to forward it to our computer, didn't want to worry you. Didn't want anyone at work seeing it either, so I printed it out and deleted it."

Sarah lifted it from him shakily. She leaned back on her pillows. She had pulled her bra back on over her breasts. "God, what now?"

Paul leaned close so they could read it together.

DAD: YOU'LL BE OH-SO SORRY TO HEAR
I'M HERE, BACK IN BOSTON 2 DROP MY
OWN BOMB ON U, HAHA
STEPMOMMY'LL BE SORRY TOO
WAIT&SEE HOW SORRY
WAIT&SEE WHAT PJ DONE NOW
CAUSE, FOR STARTERS, SEE, I NEED $$
PLUS PLACE 2 STAY
YOUR PLACE THIS TIME, 2 HIDE ME
YOU CAN'T LET ME DOWN THIS TIME,
DADDY
—YOUR (REMEMBER ME??) #1SON PAUL

Christ Almighty God, Paul thought as Sarah dumbly contemplated the note. *Is this going to push her over the edge?*

"Not surprised the kid sounds mad at me, as per usual," Paul muttered over Sarah's shoulder, "But for him to sound that way, almost threatening, to *you* . . ."

Tick, tick, tree branches tapping the screen. Yet more distant, or not so distant, sirens. Paul felt Sarah beside him sitting heavily silent.

"Anyway." Paul drew a husbandly, high-dive breath, wondering if hormone-dazed Sarah even got what PJ's note meant. PJ wouldn't be sharing an apartment with other guys like last summer. PJ wanted to stay here this time, baby or no baby, to hide from who knew what. Christ, could PJ be connected to the marathon mayhem in some way? What kind of dad would even think such a thing? "So, Sare, see? We've gotta track him down. Sounds like he's in some kind of trouble. Sounds like PJ wants to—needs to—stay with us."

"Y-you're right, Saint Paul. We've gotta track PJ down. That's for sure, for starters. And we need to talk." Sarah pressed her belly like it was hurting again, yet she kept talking away in her manic mode. "But

I . . . I've gotta calm down first. I feel . . . funny."

"Me too, Sare. Jesus, that damn Bomber Boy photo on TV—it's not—it can't be PJ. But Christ, if the cops are looking for dark and curly-haired troubled kids his age, and he's running around out there . . . I can't let him down one more time."

"Oh Paul—"

"Halt." Paul held up a traffic cop hand to ward off her usual *you've tried, long-distance parenting sucks, your ex is crazy, it wasn't all your fault.* "Don't. I don't know what the hell's up with PJ, but I gotta find out, find him. I owe him."

"You do. We do," Sarah mumbled. "I . . . I'm sorry. I just can't think right now. I just feel so—" She rolled off the bed. Standing up naked except for her black bra, she opened her arms. "God, look at me." She displayed it to him and to God: her voluptuous, swollen body, her racing-striped belly stained with the glazed streaks she'd spit up. "Lemme get clean. Then we'll talk about this PJ thing, figure out how to find him."

"I'm on it," Paul assured her, shifting to supervisor mode. "First, I'll call those guys from last summer. Maybe he's with them. You take a bath, OK? That always calms you down. Don't worry. You're dirty-sweet, and you're my girl," Paul added, singsongy. The old rock song he'd declared was hers, in their long-gone courtship days.

She laughed, albeit a bit hysterically. "Don't *you* worry, Saint Paul." She hesitated, then shook her head and turned her creamy, white back on Paul. She padded naked toward their bathroom, moving stiff-legged, like something still felt strange inside. He watched her bare, rounded ass, each slow step.

Christ, Paul exhaled as the bathroom door shut. She'd be the death of him yet.

✦

A fever, Sarah McCall told him the first day he drove her home from her late shift. "I got a fever. My head is all hot, and my hair hurts."

"Your hair?" He turned slowly, hunched in his swivel chair. There stood shy Sarah McCall, hidden in her big pullover sweater. Her usually pale, oval face was flushed, her dark hair pulled into its heavy-looking braid.

And it hurt? The brown hair in which Paul saw, as he pulled himself up to Supervisor height, glints of dark red. Sarah's olive gaze caught his, her eyes even more starey than usual, glassy bright.

"Doesn't your hair hurt when you have a fever?" she asked like young PJ.

"Haven't noticed." Paul patted his own coarse, curly hair. "Look, I can tell you're not faking it."

Words he'd repeat in a much different way weeks later, lying beside her.

But that first night, to save feverish Sarah from taking the 11 p.m. bus, Paul spread his overcoat in the backseat of his car so she could lie down. He drove her home, her voice behind him pleasantly slowed, dreamy with fever.

She kinda liked fevers, she told him. Kinda liked lying in bed reading and sketching, her body the best temperature for her arthritic cat to curl up against.

"So even being sick is a pleasure to you?" he asked. He'd noted to himself the grave pleasure she seemed to take in Center students, in their slow-motion pace.

"Mmm," she murmured from the nest she'd made in his backseat.

The next week, after Sarah McCall came back to work, Paul started studying her. This girl who, her employment application told him, had a BA in art therapy. She was not so different from any of the sweet, down-on-their-luck, Liberal, artsy-type girls who worked, usually briefly, at the Center, but something about her held Paul.

Quiet, slow-moving Sarah, with the almost-auburn hair and subtle half-smile and lit-up eyes, held some secret. Some instinct for how to be—Paul had never understood how in this world anyone could be—happy.

Christ, Paul thought as he straightened the sheets on their sex-messed bed, if it could be just him and her. No grown or unborn sons coming between them. His hands still felt shaky from the choking, the shock of those FBI photos onscreen.

What was wrong with them—him and Sarah, and PJ himself—that they'd think for a second the bombing suspect was PJ? The poor kid hadn't actually done anything violent in his short life. Well, anything more violent than his occasional fights at school. Plus, whatever it was that happened at that graveyard last October with that cow tongue which had almost earned PJ an arrest record in Ohio. A misdemeanor fine, anyhow.

But nothing worse that Paul knew about. Not yet.

Listening to Sarah run her bath, Paul picked up the Birds of Happiness. Sarah had insisted on arranging their bed next to the window so she could see *her* trees. Paul spread the afghan over the sheets, noticing on its formerly-white wool new, sticky, dark stains—her spit-out baklava.

But was that a spot of red mixed in, too? Of blood from their sex?

He lifted the afghan, sniffed the brownish stain, smelled only sweet. Of course not blood, Paul told himself as he re-arranged the afghan, his fingers still sticky. He was light-headed like Sarah. Panicked by the bomber photos, by PJ's YOU'LL BE OH-SO-SORRY message.

Paul lifted and re-folded the email printout, creasing it. Damn kid had dropped out of sight, save for emails, vamoosing back to his mom in Ohio after royally screwing up his summer Center job. Paul rested PJ's folded email on the dresser. He lifted his address book, flipped to the number of the apartment PJ had shared last summer with that guy, that Ben.

Paul dialed the cordless phone. What would he say if he did reach his son?

That tense, hot 2012 summer with PJ lingering around, even though he lived in Somerville with Ben and Ben's friends. PJ sometimes swimming with Evvy and Sarah at Spy Pond. Paul was caught up in the multiple tensions of his new suit-wearing job as Center director and with his dad's drawn-out death. Then PJ disappeared in late August, and Sarah unexpectedly turned out to be pregnant in mid-October. She hadn't been herself since. Paul hadn't been himself. Now, Christ, they both better rally some new selves, proper parent selves. Paul sat on the edge of the bed, his body still post-sex relaxed in its bones. He listened to confused mechanical clicks. A voice told him the number was no longer in service.

Before he could stop himself, Paul punched in another number, long distance—Nana in Ohio. Paul hadn't talked to PJ's Armenian grandma since his calls last fall, when PJ was almost indicted over what the Ohio police dubbed the Cow Tongue Incident. Paul had offered to drive out to Ohio, but Nana had told him no. No, PJ did not wish to see him.

Outside, wind was picking up, the branches *scratch-scratching* the window. Adina's mother's home phone rang. What if, for once, languid Adina answered?

Paul tightened his grip as the rings buzzed. He fought the urge to hang up and dial 911, notify the police that his own son was threatening him and his wife. That he was a nineteen-year-old, dark-haired, dark-eyed male.

You know, kinda like the guy in the bomber photo.

The phone was still ringing in Nana's house. How often had Paul pictured PJ arrested, PJ going off big time. Only months ago when the

Newtown Elementary School shooting filled the airwaves, Paul had felt worried sick that PJ, with all his soldier toys and spy lies, might somehow become the next Adam Lanza. Paul reading over and over the news accounts of Lanza and his gun-loving Mom. Paul telling himself no matter what, he couldn't beat that bad parenting prize.

"Yah? Who is there?" Nana answered, brusque as ever. Her harsh, accented voice as hard as ever for Paul to understand. Did Nana know where PJ was?

"He go to *you*," Nana answered in belligerent near-shout. "He say to *you*, and I see about the *bombs*," she added, as if Paul had set them off himself.

"Yeah, the marathon bombs, the photos of the bomber suspects," Paul found himself saying nervously, and adding, "But that's not him, not PJ—"

"Not *him*! Not him no *bomber*!" Nana exploded. For once, when he least wanted her to, understanding him perfectly. "Not PJ! But you do not know where he *is*? If he is *her*?"

"If he is 'her'?" Paul repeated, feeling as if his ears were being boxed.

"*Hurt*! I try to call PJ and to see is he *hurt*?"

"Hurt by the bombs? The marathon bombs? I just got an email from him today. I'm sure he's fine, Nana. But I just . . . just wanted to see if you know where he's staying—"

"You *not know*. Not know is he hurt, not know where is he. You have *lost him*."

The line went dead. She'd hung up on him, not for the first time. *The old lady's right*, Paul thought as he clicked off his phone. Old-World right. Like his mom, when she used to yell at him, throwing in Greek words her mother had yelled at her. So PJ had told Nana he was going to see Paul. Yet he hadn't. Could something have happened to PJ today? Since sending that email?

What could Paul do? What would a good Dad do, in Nana's book? But hadn't it been domineering Nana more than drifty Adina who'd kept Paul from PJ?

Paul dialed PJ's cell number but got no answer, voicemail full. Not that it was unusual for PJ to shut everyone out. Should he drive around looking for PJ, checking bars?

Inside the bathroom, Sarah was filling the tub so she could soak. Paul shoved the cordless phone back on its charger. What had he done, thrusting his cock up into his pregnant wife, giving her cramps? Other couples did it, sure. Other dumb, lucky couples who got pregnant right away, who tempted fate regularly and won.

What had come over them? Paul wondered, re-buttoning his shirt. Sarah had said they'd talk more about PJ after her bath. Did she know something he didn't know? Was that why she'd been so agitated? Paul paced the bedroom. At least he felt energized, buoyed by sex with Sarah, better for him than any antidepressant. Paul stuck with his up-and-down moods, like the Boston weather he'd endured all his life. At least they were real, were his.

So yes, he sometimes dragged round his dinosaur tail of depression. Yes, he spent many nights on the couch brooding over his dead dad and his absent son. Listening, this marathon week, to an electronic music piece called "Isolation Part One" that Paul had discovered years ago around 9/11. Eerie minimalist chords that made Paul picture people jumping from the World Trade Center and falling, each alone.

Paul halted his steps, deciding to brew coffee for what he sensed was going to be a long night. He heard Sarah slosh in the tub, in her own spell. Yes, black coffee would clear his head for confronting Sarah, finding out what she knew. He turned to head for the kitchen, glancing at the bed. Wondering as he left the bedroom, *Was that blood, one spot of blood, on the Birds of Happiness?*

Da Bomber. It's your very own terrorist.

Sitting submerged in warm but not hot water, her belly half afloat, Sarah prayed it was just anxiety that was making her feel so strange inside. She wished she had simply told Paul PJ *had* been here today. Now she'd also have to explain why she hadn't told him right away.

PJ behind the Spy Pond bushes grabbing hold of her. Not like a boy, like a man. In old wrestling games PJ used to play with her and Paul; Paul would always warn PJ and Sarah not to get too rough, like he was their dad.

Sarah blinked in the warm bathroom, her breaths wheezing. Why had PJ stolen that birthday card today while she was in the kitchen fixing him food? PJ and his proposition. The card he never should have sent and she never should have kept. Yet another thing she should've explained right away to Paul. All of it so much harder to explain the more she put it off.

Sarah swallowed, her throat sore. She had to stay calm—get calm—no matter what. Almost choking on baklava had been the latest obstacle to her baby. A lurch in her unsettled insides, so riled up after the shock of sex, then so stilled.

And now? That odd inner pressure, like pre-menstrual cramps. Underwater, Sarah fingered her appendix scar. Her infected appendectomy had scarred her Fallopian tubes at age twenty-one. Her doctor had predicted infertility. Sarah had often slipped behind the Center's metal adult-diaper cabinets to cry. To finger her appendix scar as if it marked where her womb had been removed.

She'd taken to telling her cousins to make her an honorary 'auntie,' saying, "Looks like that'll be it for me." One day from behind the diaper cabinets, she overheard one of the female staffers praise Paul's diaper-changing finesse. He'd make, the woman told Supervisor Stratidakis, a great Dad.

I've got one son, Paul had replied flatly. *Looks like that'll be it for me.*

A sign, Sarah later believed. When she and Paul started dating, she was relieved at first to realize Paul meant it; he felt he should have no more kids. He believed Sarah's doctors. He believed there was little chance of a miracle birth when she stopped using her diaphragm, even when she started the infertility treatments that Massachusetts insurance covered so fully. Her hand circled her belly, lightly massaging it.

"All I want," she'd tried telling Evvy, "is to make a happy home."

"All?" Evvy had scoffed, "but Sarah sweetie, that's what's hardest to make."

Sarah slowed her hand. Despite her mind whirring away, her post-sex body was relaxing in the bathwater. Her baby usually liked her warm, lingering baths, his serpent curves moving like waves inside her belly. Today, he stayed notably motionless. Sarah pressed her back into the curve of the tub. She let her underwater thighs loll apart.

It rose from between her thighs, cloudy white curls of Paul's semen. Then Sarah's curved spine stiffened. Her gut jumped—a tint of red.

She stared dumbly through her stuck-up knees. Paralyzed, thinking at once: I'm bleeding; I can't be bleeding, it's post-sex spotting. No, it's the first fucking stage of labor. My God, it's my bloody show.

Sarah hauled her body up, slip-sliding, stirring a wave that sloshed the bathroom tiles. She gripped the slick sides of the tub, climbing out, sloshing yet more water. A flood unleashed. Watery red streaked her inner thighs.

Sarah spun toward the closed bathroom door. Sarah's mother had appeared in her childhood bathroom doorway in their Back Bay apartment when Sarah'd had an unstoppable nosebleed in her bath and prim

Mother burst out at the bloody water: What have you *done?*

Bloody show, bloody show; first stage of labor. Sarah wrestled the wet doorknob, shouldered open the door. God, she was nothing but a big leaking sack of flesh. Spitting up food, secreting milk, trailing blood. *Bloody show, early labor, hard labor, transition, delivery.*

The stages of birth she'd memorized ticked through her head through the rush of what happened next: Sarah slipping on her red-wet, bare-foot steps. Sarah freezing, her legs streaked with blood, but *trickles* of water and blood, not a stream. Premature labor maybe, but not—please God, not—Premature Rupture of Membrane? PROM?

Sarah stumbled into the darkened bedroom. Where the hell was Paul? She tripped, at the foot of the bed, on *What to Expect.* She kicked the damned book under the bed. Its cover spotted with red from that kick.

Sarah staggered her bloody way around the bed to her side. Paul was banging around in the kitchen. Making what, at this hour? Panting, Sarah gripped the slippery phone. Bloody show; early labor; hard labor; transition; delivery. She didn't need the damn book. She had memo-rized, too, the signs: how bloody show is light at first, a mere trace of blood signaling the start of labor.

"Is it bright red?" Sarah's maddeningly placid OB-GYN, Dr. Claire Lutz, asked when she answered, her question posed with a casual lilt.

"It's *red*-red!" Sarah all but shouted.

Paul appeared at last in the bedroom doorway. He snapped on the bedroom lights. In one unsurprised sizing-up, he faced bloody-legged Sarah like she was part of some nightmare he was already having.

"Well, see, Dr. Lutz, we were—like everyone does and nothing like this happens to *them*—we were having sex." Sarah's voice shook as hard as her hands.

Paul stepped forward, lifting something from the bed. He draped it like a cape over her shoulders: the Birds of Happiness with its new stains.

"Sarah?" Dr. Lutz asked coolly, "Take some deep breaths. Is the bright red blood *gushing* out or are you more spotting? Sarah, are you there?"

"So it *could* be Premature Rupture of Membrane? Or it's only that if it's— it isn't, I swear—gushing? It's . . . well actually there's all this water mixed in, and I . . . I'm not sure what-all it's doing, my blood. But I do feel these, sort of, cramps."

"Hate to say so this late, Sarah," Dr. Lutz's professionally soothing voice replied, a hospital elevator chiming in the background, "but you and your husband had best get down to the ER, just to check you out. Sarah? Sarah?"

"You were right, you bastard, you're always right," Sarah told Paul, shoving the still-talking phone at him. He took it and pulled Sarah against his chest. She soaked his shirt. He spoke to the doctor, his bearded chin bumping Sarah's head

"Yes," and, "I understand," and, "We will."

"Screwing this kid up, but good, and he's not even outta the womb!" Sarah pushed away from Paul, dropping the Birds of Happiness. "You were right, Paul, we can't *do* this! How'd we ever think *we* could *do* this?"

She was rummaging in the mass of sheets for her sweatpants. Paul was snatching up his rattly car keys. Sarah kept trying to suck in her sobs, pull on her inside-out clothes. Screwed up. She'd screwed up everything royally. Now would the baby come too early—would the baby even die—because she'd so guiltily, impulsively pushed for sex?

RUTTING COUPLE LOSES BABY TO LUST.

Paul was helping Sarah pull on her clothes. He led her through the pumpkin-colored living room. They thudded down the stairs together, Sarah clutching her survival satchel.

She'd packed it back in the fall during Hurricane Sandy, based on CNN's instructions, and she'd unearthed it again this week after the marathon bombings, just in case they had to flee the city. Batteries, transistor radio, bottled water, underwear. All wrong for now, except for the underwear, but all she had. Metal clanked inside the bulging canvas satchel, her hands shaking.

Back on the rainy, autumn afternoon when Paul had first sat beside her in the Center cafeteria, her soup spoon rattled against her teeth, her hands so shaky. Suddenly, gently, he took the spoon from her as if he were going to feed her himself. He held it between them, his own hand steady, and laid it on the table.

They both looked down at it, then, for the first time, up at each other. And they talked, first, about the rain. How much they both loved Boston's extreme weather. Real weather, they agreed. Manic-depressive weather.

Paul led Sarah carefully onto their stoop now, into the chill, spring night air. She bent over with a cramp. Was labor starting, ready or not? *Not if I can help it*, Sarah promised the baby as she followed Paul onto the shared gravel driveway, toward their trusty Toyota.

She clutched the too-heavy survival pack she shouldn't have grabbed. She and Paul should've called 911. Everything they should've done, they hadn't.

Everything they shouldn't have, they had.

Harsh TV news voices drifted into the spring night air from neighbor's windows.

THE NEW PHOTOS . . . POLICE AND FBI . . . MASSIVE MANHUNT . . .

As Sarah and Paul crunched toward the darkened car, she thought far back to 9/11. Two months after 9/11, a separate plane crash, one the government later claimed was merely a crash-crash not another terrorist crash. Incredulously Sarah had heard on their previous Toyota's radio that yet another jet had just crashed outside New York. She'd been driving to work and the oldies station DJ, his smooth, fatherly voice plainly shaken, cut into "Moon River" with the news. Sarah at the wheel had started sobbing as she hadn't done on 9/11.

Planes were falling right and left; grown-ups were falling apart. America in chaos, no place safe. Just what Sarah had been feeling again this week, only this time Sarah had been there. Boston's own ground zero.

As firmly as Evvy had led Sarah back to her car on marathon day, Paul led Sarah across the gravel to their usual parking spot on the ungardened side of the driveway. When Sarah glimpsed the man-sized figure sprawled in the backseat of their shut up car, she thought first: *The bomber. It's him.*

She screamed. Paul startled, dropping his keys in the gravel. Inside the car, a man-sized, dark-haired boy sat up with a jerk.

Paul yanked open the unlocked driver's door. He leaned in as if about to lunge. Then he gasped, recognizing him at the same time as Sarah, saying hoarsely: "PJ? Is that . . . *you?*"

Spring, 2010

See, I might be pregnant, Sarah almost blurted out, refusing her usual wine at their usual Greek restaurant. Their corner table felt crowded. Sixteen-year-old, spiky-haired PJ sat between her and Paul with his SOLDIER OF FORTUNE *T-shirt and brand new broad shoulders, jiggling his knee so hard the small table shook. He kept fidgeting with the olive oil saucer, the candle, squeezing the flame between his fingertips, bragging he felt no burn. Sarah kept urging him to take a sample karate lesson with her new friend Evvy, see if he liked it.*

Their usual waiter paused at Sarah's refusal of wine. PJ raised his oversized, candlelit eyes. "Yo, stepmommy, you can drink 'round me."

Sarah hesitated, flushed.

"Ah . . ." The Dukakis-lookalike waiter who doted on her arched his greying caterpillar eyebrows. He studied her giveaway face. "Can it be you are . . . ?"

"No," Sarah rushed to say as subtle disappointment, maybe even disapproval, creased the waiter's face. Though he was the shorter man, the Dukakis waiter seemed to tower above Paul, who sat slumped over his placemat, eyes fixed on the menu he knew by heart. "Or anyhow I don't, don't think I . . ." Sarah found herself adding to her waiter in a foolishly lowered voice.

Paul and PJ stiffened in their different ways, the tabletop stilled.

"Ah, I see." Dukakis gave a nod, a flash of the fatherly approval Sarah craved. His warm gaze flickered between flustered Sarah and stone-silent Paul. Sympathy in those wry, moist eyes, just what Paul hated most. Was her heated flush a sign? Had those LHRH injections done something besides clear her infection-blocked Fallopian tubes and raise her cancer risk?

Sarah shifted in her seat, the injection bruises on her thighs finally faded, her tubes finally clear. It was Paul's turn, if he would agree to have his sperm tested. Sarah slid her gaze from Paul to PJ, his eyes frankly bulged.

"So you guys're, like, trying?" PJ asked, so loud the table behind Dukakis stilled its silverware. PJ rubbed his no-doubt burnt fingers together.

"No. Well . . . yes. But, I mean, nothing's happened," Sarah stumbled out, not daring to look Paul's way. The waiter nodded, the sympathetic glints in his eyes threatened to spill over. Sarah and Paul had been coming here to what Paul called his Watertown Watering Hole since they were dating.

Straight-backed Paul rose so abruptly the candle quaked. Dukakis stepped aside, nodded at Paul with his unwelcome sympathy. Paul muttered, "Excuse me."

He and the waiter turned their separate ways: Duke ducked toward the kitchen, Paul strode toward the Men's Room. Grape leaves stapled on the walls flapped in his wake.

At the table, Sarah felt her flush deepen, doubly spotlit by the candle, by PJ's widened, glittery eyes. It was the first time she'd acknowledged in front of her stepson what he must have instinctively known for years from her clingy step-mom hugs, her anything-to-please manner with him.

PJ, more than anyone, must know how badly she wanted a baby.

A new complicity flickered between them. PJ leaned toward her, table wobbling and candle flame flaring. PJ puffed up his lips, and blew it out.

"Yo, Sarah," PJ stage-whispered into the hush of intimate dimness he'd made between them, the candle smoking. "You want to, I could get you—"

"What? A drink?" Sarah kept her shadowed face blank, and pretended she didn't know PJ meant—he couldn't have really meant—I could get you pregnant.

Chapter Three

April 18, 2013; 9:50 p.m.

Pre-Labor Pains

"*PJ?*" Paul called louder into the dark car when his crouching son didn't answer.

"Paul," came PJ's muffled, belligerent shout back at him. "It's *Paul!*"

Everything—crickets and news voices and distant traffic and sirens and even Paul's panicky pulse beat—seemed to stop. It all froze: the whole zany scene in which he'd felt like an inept Ricky Ricardo bumbling his attempt to get his wife to the hospital. Paul pictured hugely, genuinely pregnant Lucille Ball with her red-even-in-black-and-white hair, and her eyes ping-ponged like she felt both too happy and too scared.

Beside Paul, Sarah was peering into the car's backseat window with that same pop-eyed stare. Almost like she was *acting* surprised.

"Where you two *go*-ing?" From the backseat PJ tensed up as if ready to leap into action, his gaze bright and shifty. Had he broken into the damn car? *No,* Paul reminded himself, *PJ has keys from last summer.* He'd left so abruptly in August he hadn't given them back.

"The hospital, Peej. Look, I wanna know why the hell you're sleeping in my car, but we can't talk now. We gotta get *her* checked out." Paul jerked his head sideways toward Sarah as if there were any other her. Sarah stood waiting, her head bowed like she was praying.

"But . . ." PJ sputtered. "I . . . she . . . isn't it too soon?"

"She's still in her seventh month, almost eighth. But she's . . . having some *pain*, some *blood*—"

"*Blood?*" PJ's shout overpowered Paul's. The kid got it; he could take over if Paul, with his thumping heart, collapsed.

"We gotta get her in the car," Paul was saying to his son, though Sarah was already making her shuffly, hunched-over way to the passenger side.

PJ scrambled out to open the door for her just as she rounded the bumper. A good kid at heart. Wasn't he? Pride thumped along with fear in Paul's overloaded heart, panic dancing in PJ's over-bright eyes. As he stepped back for Sarah, he closed his lips in a manly line of determination.

Could it be PJ had grown up in his mysterious time away? What in all hell had he meant about having bombs to drop? And why was he hiding out in this car like a crook—or worse? No time to ask any of this now. It would upset Sarah even more than she already was, Paul thought as he settled in the driver's seat. PJ climbed into the backseat like an overgrown kid.

"We can do this," Paul told both PJ behind him and Sarah beside him as he slammed the door. He revved the engine and flipped on the lights.

Give the kid a chance, Paul told Sarah silently, backing the car up. "So what the hell *are* you doing hiding in here?" Paul couldn't stop himself from asking PJ, meeting PJ's panicky eyes in the rearview.

"Think they'll think I'm him? The bomber?" PJ asked in a strained version of his same old caustic teen voice. Not so grown-up after all. "*You* think it's me?"

God, was the kid high on God-knew-what? *Was* he somehow caught up in the bombing, in something that bad? Paul eased the car backwards.

"Jesus Christ, of course we'd never think that," Paul lied. "And look, we've got no time to be playing games now," Paul added in his best dad voice.

"*I'm* not playing no games," PJ muttered.

"Stop it you two," Sarah pleaded weakly. Beside Paul, she was rocking in pain. As the car bumped down their gravel driveway, Paul remembered a much different kind of rocking with Sarah in a different front seat, years ago.

Sweet Sarah, Paul reminded himself as he twisted the steering wheel too hard at the driveway's end. The first woman he ever trusted.

⚉

The afternoon Sarah McCall resumed work after her fever, Paul watched her from his office window. Because they'd chatted briefly about their mutual, illogical love of Boston weather, Paul stepped out into the cold November afternoon to "inspect" the playground activities.

Sarah was wearing red mittens and a red scarf that sparked those dark red glints Paul always saw in her brown braid. He teased her, falling into step beside her as she pushed Maritza's wheelchair.

Why had she dressed up for a snowfall no weathermen predicted? Sarah halted the wheelchair. Spooky Maritza inside her helmet and plastic torso-suit stopped rocking. Maritza's black hair shone with the cold; her flat black eyes fixed on Paul. A hex stare, he thought, but Sarah chattered excitedly as a child about the year's first snow.

"It's coming. I can taste it." Sarah McCall licked soft-looking lips, and she gave Paul a startling, wide smile.

At the late shift's end, 11 p.m., Paul offered Sarah another ride home. This time she sat in the front seat beside him. She'd grown up, she told him, in a Back Bay apartment with a terrace. That was all her mother had salvaged from her divorce, so Sarah vowed to always live within her own means. As Paul drove toward her apartment building in Brighton and exited the highway, he slowed. Sarah chatted on sleepily, defending her mittens. How they kept her hands warmer than—her groggy words—grown-up gloves. How she didn't know why.

Paul mumbled, "Because your fingers press together in mittens. The best way to stay warm is always skin-to-skin."

She replied in a voice softened like she was drifting into sleep. "That's the way you explain things to our kids . . ." She meant—he slowed his rattletrap car further to quiet it, to delay the final drop-off—the kids at the Center. ". . . talking to them no differently than you talk to us staff."

"The difference," he found himself saying as the car crawled forward, "is that I like those kids better'n I like some of the—this is off the record—staff."

"Me too." Sarah leaned sideways. He felt her warm breath inside his ear. "I like the Autistics. The way they space out so much. The way they're so nervous but also so peaceful. I feel like here are, you know, my own kind . . ."

Paul was nodding, still curt. "It's not that I dislike . . . that I don't like . . ." silly, girlish like; her word, "for instance, you," he was stupidly saying.

"There!" Sarah shouted as if at something long awaited. Paul jerked onto a

side street he thought might be hers, though it came sooner than he'd remembered. Sudden snowflakes whirled like swarming insects in his headlights.

"This it?" he demanded, playing up his gruff supervisor tone, stopping on the deserted street. Sheepishly, she explained it was just the snow that made her shout.

He had halted by a lot full of darkened bushes, bedecked in trash.

"Let's watch," Sarah urged. In his headlights, falling snowflakes lit up like fireflies. Paul's engine hummed; the car under him pulled against its brake.

"Must be nice, when it's this cold, to have one of these." Sarah leaned on him, companionable and bold, running one mittened hand over his beard.

He chuckled, Mr. Avuncular, like it merely tickled. Her youth had infected him like the twenty-four-hour fever she'd given him, his head and body still lightened by its lingering effects. He tugged off her red mitten.

He kissed, first, her warm bare hand. A strong hand, strong arm. Sarah McCall was almost as good as him at lifting and rolling profoundly disabled adults onto changing mats. A whiff of talcum powder and soap scented her short-nailed fingertips. Intently, she felt his dense, black beard, his pride.

"Must be great to hide in that," she whispered, a breathless, inexpert flirt. "Like having . . . when I was little, I wanted to be an animal so I could have fur."

She pressed her weight against him. A strapping girl, he found himself thinking like an old man. Her face looked rosy, both from the cold and his car heater. Her braided hair crackled with stray strands. Paul searched, as he leaned into her, for those secret reddish glints that had first made him want her, want to reach back and slip her old-fashioned clip free, to bury his face in her wonderfully lush and warm hair.

Hours later, by snowy pink dawn light, he woke in Sarah's apartment bed with her curled up against him, naked. Paul noticed by the window's frosted light that, like the unbraided hair on her head, the kinky dark hair at her crotch gave off glints of reddish gold.

They were two animals bedded down. All they'd promised each other before that first sex was that they would keep each other warm this winter.

As Sarah finally stirred and shifted, Paul saw a stain on the white sheet. He hadn't seen blood last night in the rush of their bodies colliding. Real, he knew, though she'd sounded like she might be joking when she'd murmured she'd never done this before. Never done it so soon, he'd let himself think.

Her waking words, as she fingered that stain herself, echoed the words Paul first said about her fever. "See? You can tell I wasn't faking."

God, Paul was going to find out. He was going to find out everything she should have told him, only now it was too late. Too late, and this baby too early.

Sarah hunched lower in her seat as if hiding. If only she could. Paul sped the car too fast past the tall trees she loved on their pricey side street, the stately, renovated homes, one bearing an 1840 historic building placard. How hidden and undeservedly safe Sarah had felt in this quiet, well-kept neighborhood. She'd blown all the money her guilty, no-show dad had left, buying her and Paul's own slice of suburban security.

Their wheels hissed on the damp asphalt. Paul would find out any minute now that PJ had come to the house today and Sarah hadn't told him. And would he find out from PJ—in whatever twisted version PJ might concoct—*why* Sarah hadn't told?

God, everything was going to come out tonight—the baby, the lies— and none of it in the way Sarah had planned. *Trying to stage-manage life*, Paul always scoffed. *No,* she prayed to herself as she stiffened with the beginnings of another cramp, Paul and PJ both tense but silent in their respective seats. Sarah cranked down her window and breathed the chill, misty air. Almost 10 p.m. by the glowing numbers of the car clock.

Maybe twenty minutes from the last clear, full-sized cramp she'd felt as she'd dressed. A heated, tightened sensation like PMS, only bigger. A whole-body menstrual cramp.

"But I can still talk," Sarah gasped out loud, though she'd meant only to think it. The hospital won't declare you officially in labor, she'd read, until the cramps are so bad you can't talk. Before that the pains are— what were they called?—Practice Pains? Pre-Labor?

"Wha'd you say, Sarah?" Paul flipped his blinker to turn onto Com- mon Avenue.

"Sorry. Sorry," Sarah whispered only to her baby, her fledgling cramp subsiding. *It's too soon, you've got to hold on,* Sarah told her son. Maybe the baby was obeying her stage manager directions after all?

Paul shot her a look like a no-nonsense traffic cop. You stake your life on such urgent commanding glances. *Not now,* Sarah could feel him commanding her silently too. *You can't lose it yet; you can't have this baby in this damn car.*

Paul swung round the big curve on Common too fast, the twin Revolutionary War canons in the turnabout's central island lit up at night. WELCOME TO HISTORIC BELMONT. Their car skidded for a second, bumping the quaint, low stone fence that circled the island. Sarah let out half a scream.

"You OK?" Paul and PJ both demanded at her from separate sides.

No, I'm not OK, you idiots, she wanted to shout, *and it's all because of you two!*

"Just *go,*" Sarah managed. Paul was driving too fast past the historic, red-brick town hall and the white-pillared Belmont Womens' Club, founded 1843.

"Hey, God, Sarah." Behind her, Sarah felt smoky-breathed PJ lean forward. "Hey, God, damn. *Sorry.*"

She stiffened again in her seat, helpless to stop what he might say.

"You know. For what the fuck's . . . happening. 'Cause I *know* I kinda . . . didn't I kinda . . . cause it and all? I kinda upset you, showing up so sudden after, after—"

"No, no . . ." Sarah cut in, shaking her head, the wavy tangled dampness of her hair brushing her face. "You didn't . . . cause *this* . . ."

"What the hell do you mean, Peej? You showed up?" Paul seemed to grip the wheel harder. He was looking at the rearview, at his suddenly dumbstruck son.

Caught in a lie.

"Hungry," PJ proclaimed, his voice manly deep. His eyes still fixed on her breasts. Sarah took a step back from PJ. Was he going to go off?

"I'm hungry for two, like you," PJ told her nonsensically. Then he backed up so fast he knocked Paul's latest book, *The Mind's 'I'*, off the couch arm.

"Hungry for two? Like me?" Sarah turned and plodded toward the kitchen, switching into her best, brisk Stepmom voice. "Sure, OK, Peej, we need to talk. But first let's find you something to eat. Let's raid the fridge like . . ."

"Always," PJ filled in, close behind her.

"Always hungry, that's you," Sarah babbled, pulling open the fridge door with a suck sound like a kiss. A chill hum she bent into gratefully, cooling her flush. She blinked at fridge shelves crowded with her twin cravings, lemon yogurt and lemonade. "Hey, let's think outside this box. I've got soup on the stove I can heat up. It's one of Evvy's recipes, but no tofu, I promise . . ." Sarah swung the door shut. She faced the stove, and twisted its knobs. "I've been dipping into it all morning . . ."

"So you just chillin' 'round here, Sare? 'Member when I used to call you, um, Dad's trophy wife?"

"Vhat?" Sarah flung back her hair, rallying her Ivana Trump accent. Another old joke of theirs. "You sink I am zpoiled by 'Zee Paul'?"

PJ gave the brief bark of a laugh she used to love to win.

"Naw, Dad's too tight-wad," PJ confided. "But me, I'd spoil you if you were, like, mine."

Sarah faced PJ, shaking her head. "Don't, OK? Don't joke—or not-joke or whatever you're doing—about all that." PJ didn't blink. "About that card you sent, or about that day at Spy Pond. What I've w-wanted to talk to you about . . ."

"You've *w-wanted* to talk? Even if all that was a *j-joke*?"

Sarah turned her back on deadpan PJ. Shakily, she stirred the tomato soup. *Had* it all somehow been PJ's warped idea of a joke? Even the knife?

"'Cept," PJ added, shaky too, "bet Dad wouldn't, didn't think it was a *j-joke* . . ."

"Is that why you stayed away?" Sarah turned back around to face PJ, his eyes evasive. "You were scared I'd told Paul? Well maybe I should've, but I didn't."

"For real?" PJ stepped closer, sounding relieved, conspiratorial. His elbow bumped hers; he seized the warming saucepan. "Man, am I glad to hear that. I'll drink to that!" He lifted the pan and slurped a sloppy swallow. "Not hot enough."

He set down the pan. A sizzling slosh shot onto the bright orange burner. PJ faced Sarah with a tomato mustache above his pouty boy's lips.

"'Member that book you used to read about blended families?" PJ stared into the soup. "Wha'd you think went wrong in ours? Too much, like, stirring? Our modern family . . ."

Sarah remembered PJ telling her—mockingly, but he did everything mockingly—that he liked *Modern Family*. With the overblown, ridiculously sexy new young wife played by Sofia something. Weren't there sons in that sitcom attracted to their stepmom? Or were they gay?

"PJ, what're you trying to say? I never watched *Modern Family*. I'm living it. Talk to me."

He continued staring at the soup. What if he told Paul some screwy version of what happened last summer? Why had she been so foolishly secretive?

"Look, I *should've* told your dad about everything we need to talk about, Peej—starting with that crazy card you sent." Sarah edged back a step, mustering her firm Mom tone. "Seriously, PJ, we need to talk when you can be serious." PJ shrugged and slurped again from the soup pan, tomato dripping on his chin. "God, PJ, what is with you? Are you *on* something?"

"Like, on fire?" PJ clanked down the half-drained pan. He cracked a drippy grin. "Think I turned to drugs this week, what with the Bombers on the loose?" Then he was sing-songing again, his own version of lyrics from a CD he used to play. "'Won't you send me a Nur-sery Rhyme / to keep me safe / while I'm on fire?'"

"'On fire?' You're not saying you were . . . at the marathon?"

"You're not sayin' you think I blew up that finish line?" PJ shot back, widening his eyes theatrically. "Think I'm the Bomber, Stepmom? That why you so scared o' me you won't even gimme a freaking hug?"

"Oh Peej, I've been *wanting* to . . ." Sarah stepped clumsily closer. Her belly brushed PJ's old denim jacket. She took hold of his shoulders and pulled him to her. He held her stiffly, not too close, but she could feel the metallic bulge in the zipped front pocket of his jacket. The jack-knife he'd slipped from his shorts pocket back in August? She pulled away, took one wobbly step back.

"Look PJ, we have to—to talk about that, first." She picked up her wooden spoon like some lame weapon and pointed it at his pocket.

"What? My one true pal, little ol' Captain Jack?" PJ bared his teeth, his fakest smile. He reached for his zipped, bulging pocket.

"Don't you *dare* pull that knife on me again!" Sarah half raised the wooden spoon. "Not now." God, she never should have let PJ up here. "I mean it, PJ; you don't pull that knife on me again. Ever—"

"I didn't pull it *on* you," PJ whined, stumbling back one step himself. "I just pulled it *out*. I just—fuck, I barely remember what I did that day. I was on these . . . these pills and shit I stole at the Center. *You* know—"

You know I never would have hurt you, he was saying.

"I know, I guess," Sarah muttered, lowering the spoon. "I gotta—we both gotta—calm down. Paul and me, we want to help you, Peej. We always do. Your dad kept trying to reach you all fall and winter, calling your cell. He knew you were with Nana. Then after the holidays and all, he knew from Nana you'd moved, but you never let us know yourself."

"Oh yeah? Well *some*-one managed to find me . . ." PJ's eyes turned sly.

"Who? Find you when? What are you talking about? PJ, just sit down and tell me—"

"Wait—yo, *I* know!" PJ jiggled his knee so hard he was bouncing. "Let's make Snickerdoodle dough! Let's eat a bowl of *just* the dough, just like—"

"Like I never should've let you do." Sarah finished flatly. She swept away the old anything-goes stepmom with a wave of her spoon.

PJ stomped his boot. "You're no fun no more." He spun and grabbed the fridge handle. Would he pull out all the food again, all over the floor? Like, Sarah pictured in a sickening flash, the Center girl PJ had recklessly brought here last summer. The one with the eating disorder where she couldn't stop.

"You don't give a flying fuck no more about your STEP-son." PJ yanked open the fridge, his profile stony, like when he'd hold back tears as a kid.

"PJ, God, don't say that. You know how much I care about you, worry about you. Your Dad and I, we've been sick with worry for months now . . ."

PJ shrugged brusquely, bending into the fridge. "Yeah, right. That why you guys couldn't bother to track us—track me—down? In my new pad in Cleveland? Scared I'd turn psycho bomber-or-whatever on you? Now you won't even gimme a freaking bite to eat . . ."

He straightened from the fridge, brandishing a carton of eggs, keeping his stubborn, black-browed profile to her.

Sarah touched his shoulder. "PJ, c'mon. You know that Paul wanted to drive out in October, that Nana told him he shouldn't? Paul really wanted to see you after the cow tongue thing. He would've driven down there for the holidays, too. I wanted him to, but he didn't want to leave me alone like this . . ."

PJ shrugged off her touch. He shoved the egg carton in her hands and stomped to the kitchen doorway. "I gotta pee. Fix me some eggs like I like, OK?"

Sarah slumped as he stomped out, relieved just to have him gone. Would she ever be able to relax around him again? Ever be able to talk to him, really? Admit to him how sorry she was about any signals she might've sent him the summer before—not meaning to, not consciously. What would Dr. Phil say?

Sarah turned dumbly to the stove. Someone had tracked PJ down. He was part of some *us*. She cracked three eggs straight into a pan. PJ *had* stayed away because of what had happened with her. Because she'd handled it all wrong. He'd run off and gotten into that crazy cow tongue trouble in Cleveland, plus God-knew-what else, because of all that.

The mess she hadn't meant to make. What made her think she'd be a better mom than stepmom?

She sloshed in some milk, scrambling PJ's eggs over such sizzling heat she couldn't hear what he was doing outside the kitchen.

❦

"I . . . you . . . Shit, Dad, I'm kinda con-fused 'bout to-day," PJ muttered to Paul's question. Almost like, Sarah hoped, he didn't quite remember this afternoon or was game to lie about it. Sarah pressed her hands harder over her belly in the dark, speeding car. Wishing she could press a hand over PJ's mouth, to stop it from talking on.

"I mean, like, I been . . . been on the road and I . . . I haven't been sleeping too good, see—and Dad, you hear all them cops? What the hell's going on?"

Multiple distant sirens were suddenly spiraling away in the night, most coming, it seemed to Sarah, from Cambridge. Coming closer?

"Maybe . . . they caught 'em?" Sarah reached for the radio dial. News voices came on extra loud, like they'd been waiting for the derelict car to tune in.

—AWAITING MORE REPORTS FROM A CHAOTIC SCENE IN CAMBRIDGE AND SURROUNDING AREAS, AS PO-LICE AND FBI FIELD HUNDREDS OF TIPS ON THE TWO SUSPECTS WANTED IN THE BOSTON MARATHON BOMB-ING. WE WILL KEEP OUR LISTENERS POSTED AS NEW REPORTS COME IN—

"Yo, guess I better keep out of sight," PJ muttered from the backseat. Sarah lowered the volume to hear what on earth he was saying now. "Y'know, Dad? I mean, you looked ready to shoot me on sight when you saw me in your car."

"I didn't know it was *you*," Paul protested above the distantly swell-ing sirens.

"Guys, please, not now." Sarah clicked off the radio, then wished she'd left it on. Was one siren closing in? *No*, Sarah thought with her thighs clenched. She would not let this turn into PROM or full-scale prema-ture labor, not let things get totally out of control. One siren seemed to be separating out now, yes.

"Don't worry, Sare. Hang on." Paul hunched lower over the wheel, passing a slow sedan. "Killers on the loose, Christ. Just our luck . . ."

"Don't you start with that Stratidakis luck stuff," Sarah shot back. "I was . . . damn lucky to get out of that . . . marathon crowd unharmed. God, slow *down*!" The lone close-by siren swelled up behind them.

Paul whizzed under a yellow-turning-red light.

"C'mon Dad!" PJ commanded from the backseat, his voice muffled like he was ducking his head. "Go faster! Don't let 'em catch up!"

"What the hell? You don't really think they're after you, Peej?" Paul whipped onto the Route 2 exit toward Alewife and Mount Auburn Hospital.

"Paul," PJ corrected from behind Paul. His curly dark head definitely ducked down. "Call me Paul, now, Dad."

The siren wailed on behind them, having whipped through the same now-red light. Sarah looked up anxiously in the rearview as Paul expertly merged onto Route 2. There was a stream of traffic between them and the cop car now. Surely that officer was not targeting them? How fast was Paul going? Sarah kept her gaze glued to the rearview, scared to look at the speedometer.

"You're not really telling me to run from those cops?" Paul was demanding. "Tell me *now*, son. Look, we'll help you, no matter what kind of . . . of trouble you might be in."

"Kind of trouble?" PJ repeated behind them in a stiff small voice.

"What in all hell you been up to, son?" Paul swung hard into the right turn onto Alewife Brook Parkway. The siren, or maybe a new siren, still yelping away along Route 2. *Good*, Sarah dared to think, clutching her belly in the turn.

"Great move, Dad." PJ poked his head up again.

"What, I'm your getaway driver?" Paul had to slow for the usual Alewife line of traffic, even this late. "Wha'd you mean about scaring Sarah today? Look son, you've got some 'splainin' to do."

Wincing not only from pain, Sarah recognized his Ricky Ricardo imitation from *I Love Lucy*—the TV show even Sarah was too young to really remember; the one Paul had watched as a boy. *It's just a dumb joke*, Sarah thought toward the ominous backseat silence of PJ.

"Ha," Sarah forced out, finding herself, even now, in a familiar role. The one who got the jokes Paul and PJ would make to the other. Paul took PJ's edgy, song-lyric non sequiturs as evidence of instability; PJ took Paul's 1950s references as impending senility. Sarah's "ha" came out like a grunt of pain.

Her insides were—*no no; stop stop*—tightening up again. That snake coil steadily widening its reach. 10:05 p.m.; would they ever get there?

"Some ex-*splaining*?" PJ croaked. "About, like, to-*day*?" His deepened voice gave its old adolescent squeak. Caught in the traffic, Paul was inching their Toyota past the looming Alewife Subway Station. Sarah squeezed her door handle, half wanting to jump out and grab a train.

"Look I . . . didn't mean to, Dad. Didn't want to up-set Sarah or any-thing. I never meant any of *this* to happen or I swear to God, I never would've come *by!*"

"Come by?" Paul shot a glance from the traffic-jammed Alewife Brook Bridge to Sarah. "Sare? PJ came by and upset you some way? Why didn't you tell me?"

Their car was rumbling, all but halted in traffic on the top curve of the bridge. When they crested that curve, Sarah found herself think-ing, would they plummet? The iron and concrete bridge giving way beneath them. Sarah's whole year's worth of mistakes crashing down all around them.

"PJ, you hear me?" Paul shifted his dark stare to the rearview. "Did you *threaten* her or something? Bully her about coming to live with us? That email you sent sounded like it was written by a goddamn gangsta." Paul jolted the car's gears. Their vehicle crested the bridge. The lit-up line of night traffic led straight toward what Paul always called the Rotary of Doom. "What's going on with you two? Son, *did* you scare Sarah somehow today?"

"*No*," PJ and Sarah protested in unison. Sounding, Sarah thought as she shut her dry-lipped mouth, like kids in cahoots.

"But," PJ pushed on desperately before Sarah could cut in, "No matter what I say, you're gonna think *I* did this! Made Sarah so up-*set* and all."

"So upset *how*?" Paul demanded, his baffled gaze still fixed on the rearview.

"You *didn't* do this, Peej," Sarah cut in. The new tightness expanded its circle inside her. Her already swollen insides were swelling further to make room for this pain. The doctors had to do something to stop this snaking ache in its tracks. "You didn't make this happen. No one did. 'Cause this, this isn't going to happen. Nothing's going to happen if you just *get* me there fast enough . . ."

A siren startled them again, only a few cars behind theirs. The same one? A new one? Blue lights were spinning in their rearview, PJ duck-ing down again. Was any of this really happening?

"Yeah, pump it Dad! Let's move!" PJ insisted.

Paul clenched his jaw and floored the gas. Their Toyota lunged into the left lane. It almost bumped a new-style VW Bug with an absurd, jaunty bumper sticker.

MAYBE THE HOKEY POKEY *IS* WHAT IT'S ALL ABOUT.

Sarah stared at the sticker, that song in her head. *You put your right foot in. You put your right foot out. You put your right foot in and you shake it all about—*

The siren behind them whooped angrily, stuck too, surely heading off toward chaotic Cambridge, surely not after them, Paul not even speeding now.

"Don't worry, Sare. We're moving," Paul assured her, sounding like his teeth were clenched like hers. They careened toward the notorious Alewife Rotary. Tank-like SUVs zoomed in from Cambridge, no signs except To Boston to tell anyone what to do, horns honking in unison. At them?

A Honda knifed in, too close to Paul.

"Go Dad. *Now!*" PJ begged behind the seat, their car shuddering.

You do the Hokey Pokey, Sarah chanted to herself, *and you turn yourself around. That's what it's all about.*

Their car—jolting forward as Paul tried to pass the Honda to gain entry into spinning rotary traffic—skidded sideways. Sarah screamed, drowned out. Horns blared in air-splitting unison. The siren sounded its hyper cry above it all.

"Jesus God," Paul called as Sarah squeezed her eyes shut.

"Whoa!" PJ called out from behind, gripping the top of Sarah's seat.

Sarah snapped open her eyes to face the central island of the rotary. To Boston. Paul seemed to steer toward that sign. Sarah remembered, *you must relax your body in a crash. Go with the motion, not fight it.*

But I can't, Sarah thought. Her whole hopelessly-tensed, seat-belted body jerked forward as their car ploughed up onto the grassy rotary island.

The To Boston signpost split Sarah's windshield view in two.

"Eggs're ready!" Sarah called from the kitchen, turning down the heat. The excessive, reckless sizzle died. The eggs smelled burnt.

"PJ?" Sarah poked her head into the empty living room, then startled to hear the downstairs door thump shut with wall-shuddering slam. Where was PJ running off to? Sarah knew she should hurry down and call to him, stop him.

Instead, she found herself following his faint, muddy boot prints across the living room toward the bedroom, the door wide open— wider than she'd left it.

She hugged her belly hard, the way she used to hold young PJ. She'd hoped in his time away he'd get used to the idea of her and Paul's baby; she'd hoped with the baby coming, everything could be made safe and simple again between her and PJ.

She halted in the bedroom doorway and faced her flung-open portfolio. PJ had dragged it from the closet, spread it out on the bed: her old charcoal sketches of Paul; of young PJ; of the cat; the bright, cartoonized animals and flat masks she'd painted for her art therapy patients. She stepped toward her colorful mess, sensing what PJ must have taken, what he might have glimpsed in there before.

How could she have been so stupid to have kept that card hidden in there? PJ had known she hid the birthday cards she made for Paul in her portfolio; he'd known just where to look.

Sarah stepped up to the bed, grunting as she bent. She shuffled through the papers, that oversized manila envelope gone. Of course it was gone. She shoved back the portfolio and sank onto the bed. Why had PJ taken it and run off? The birthday card he'd sent in February, that offer he'd made to father her baby . . . was he planning—what? To blackmail her somehow? She stuffed the loose papers and pictures back into the portfolio, but they didn't fit right.

So many small secrets had built up inside Sarah these past months, growing along with the baby, ready to burst out—today?

Moving slowly, carefully, as if driving drunk, Sarah lugged the portfolio back into the closet. She panted, glancing toward the window. Was PJ outside now, watching for Paul to come home? Waiting to brandish that silly card?

Stop, Sarah commanded her manic mind. Her hands caressed her baby, his body clenched the way *What to Expect* described—in anxious stillness.

Got to calm down for him, Sarah told herself. She shuffled back to bed. Her face flushing fiercely. She pulled off her sweatshirt, sat on the mattress edge, and rocked in place. She used to rock for blissful, tranced-out hours listening to LPs as a kid, a teen. She loved her mom's scratchy, dreamy Joni Mitchell and Ella Fitzgerald records. "Stars Fell on Alabama."

"Oversexed," Mom had decreed once, her hand on Sarah's shoulder, breaking her trance. Sarah spent too much time fantasizing, Mother had explained in her crisp, lady executive manner.

If she fantasized too much, Mother warned, she'd get oversexed. *And did I?* Sarah wondered now. Was that what was wrong with her, what made her into: PREGNANT STEPMOM DRIVES STEPSON TO—what? What next?

Leafy branches shuddered outside the window, sunlit now, the misty day clearing, warming up. PJ could be watching from the sidewalk again, but she couldn't stop him. Exhausted, she lay back against her piled pillows, scared to even turn on the TV, scared to see the photos they were babbling about releasing.

What in all hell had PJ meant by calling himself "Da Bomber?" *Please stay away*, Sarah prayed to her stepson as if he were trouble itself. She pressed her unborn son, curled up under her folded hands where she had to keep him safe. *Please.*

✦

Christ, a crash. How the hell had he—the driver, the dad—let this happen?

Sarah was sobbing beside him, letting go of the padded dashboard. Her fingers left gouge marks on the dash. Paul gripped her hand as she sank against her tilted-back seat. Her face, at least, looked unhurt.

"Sarah OK?" PJ poked his head up. *Like the gunman who shot that pregnant woman years ago*, Paul found himself thinking. As he touched Sarah's heaving shoulder he remembered: no, that masked gunman story turned out to be a lie. It was the goddamned husband himself who killed her.

"Sare? Sare? Christ . . . God, Sare. Are you OK?" Paul bumped his son's chin while shaking Sarah's shoulder.

She shook her head, saying, "Sorry. Sorry," like it was her fault. She was lying back in her angled seat as if in a dentist chair, holding her belly with both hands.

Paul pressed his big hand over hers, holding it together, holding the baby in.

A hail of horns surrounded them. Their Toyota had rammed the To Boston sign planted near the center of the island. Their crash had been slowed, thank God, by the grassy island itself. The car was tilted, so that Paul and Sarah were pitched backwards in their seats, while PJ gripped Sarah's seatback, holding himself up. The Toyota's rear bumper stuck out into rotary traffic.

And still—amidst the hostile honking, cars rerouting themselves, inching around Paul's protruding bumper—the stubborn siren that had seemed to follow them yelped, too loud to ignore. Blue and white lights flashed in a coded pattern.

"Go-*oh*," Sarah moaned, raising one hand to the single spidery crack on the windshield. The car bumper crunched against that sign. "God Paul, we gotta *go!*"

"Like, now," PJ whined, and Paul shot a gaze to the rearview—to see a Belmont squad car halting, two traffic-jammed lanes away.

"We are. We will." Paul revved the engine. "But it won't . . . move."

"We *got*-ta—" PJ insisted, his voice muffled as he ducked down again behind Paul. Then the flashlight hit spotlight-bright, straight into Sarah's passenger side window. A lanky policeman materialized, edging between cars in the rotary jam. Somehow the Belmont Police car had halted on the road's shoulder, its blue and white lights blazing. The tall, shadowed cop was striding around to Paul's window.

"Sir? Sir! Shut off your engine. Remain in your vehicle. Remain in your vehicle."

Why was this Frankenstein-sized officer saying everything twice? Head squarish—or no, that was the cop cap. Paul switched off the engine and squinted into the light—caught.

"Sir, we're heading for the hospital," Paul began, pulling his supervisor face. PJ stayed foolishly ducked down. Beside Paul, Sarah moaned to remind them all what mattered most.

"Sir? You didn't hear our siren a while back? Clockin' you over speed limit, with erratic driving on Route 2 and—"

"My wife—" Paul cut in, leaning back in his seat so the flashlight hit Sarah's belly. "My wife, she's in premature labor!"

Sarah turned her pale, sweat-glazed face into the light, squinting and moaning again, belly on full display. "Please . . . get me to . . . the *hos*-pital!"

The cop bent closer, red-faced and red-haired, younger than he sounded, narrowing his eyes warily. Paul felt other drivers in the slow-motion rotary merry-go-round staring too, taking in this whole mini-drama—minus PJ, unseen as of yet.

The cop shifted his narrowed gaze from Sarah back to Paul. Had Paul morphed from criminal to mere hapless husband in his eyes?

"What I'm trying to do is get to Mount Auburn Hospital, is all. Sorry for the speeding—and the crashing. With all the sirens out tonight I didn't know if one was after me. I mean, I do know you've got a real crisis on your hands tonight, and if we could just—if you could just help get my car out—"

"This car's not goin' nowhere, sir," the cop informed Paul. "Gonna need a tow. But we're gonna get ya to Mount Auburn, sir. You're gonna be gettin' yourself a ticket. But yeah, you are right. We are in an emergency situation here."

"*I'm* an emergency situation!" Sarah turned to her own window where a second, older, Hispanic cop had materialized, his flashlight politely lowered. As he bent to Sarah's window, his manner seemed fatherly, *or what a father should be*, Paul chided himself. Calm, steady, commanding.

"Hospital, you say? We'll get you there, ma'am."

He opened the passenger-side door and helped Sarah out, steadying her on the grassy island. So, they'd take her in the cop car? The line of cars slowed to a stop as the older cop held up one hand. He parted the small sea of traffic.

Just as Paul started to climb out himself, half forgetting in his daze of hope PJ cowering behind him, the young Frankenstein cop's flashlight caught something in the rear seat. PJ's curly black hair? Paul froze in his own seat.

"Hold on here. Who's *that?* Who's back there?"

Suddenly, red-faced Frankenstein was aiming his flashlight like a weapon behind Paul. Paul felt PJ awkwardly shifting, straightening from his criminal crouch, raising his pop-eyed face.

"Just my son. He's . . ." Paul began but didn't know how to finish.

"*Hidin'* back there? What you *doin'* hiding back there? You stay in the car. Remain *in* the vehicle!"

"Me?" PJ blurted, his words coming out loud and fast. "Me? Oh, see, I'm just hiding here so, you know, so you won't see me and think I'm, like, like—"

No, Paul pleaded silently, bright, light-shocked floaters in his eyes.

From behind Paul, PJ slowed his stagy voice. "Won't think I'm him. Y'know, the bomber."

⸙

Sarah clung to the beefy Belmont Policeman, who muttered he was Officer Cruz—her Spanish-accented savior. She held his bent arm hard, like an old lady, bracing herself for the next abdomen-clenching cramp. Would her baby be delivered in a Belmont Police car? Cleaner, maybe, than Boston cop cars?

"We'll get you there, ma'am," Officer Cruz reassured her as they stepped between the momentarily halted traffic. Horns stilled to let the pregnant lady, in visible distress, pass.

"Stay *in* the *vehicle!*" the other, younger cop was shouting behind her. Shouting that line again? God, he'd found PJ. Of course he'd found him hiding.

She couldn't twist 'round to look back. She had to keep walking forward, stiff-legged, leaning on the husky, sweat-and-cigarette smelling policeman. She had to pee so bad. Maybe that was intensifying these cramps? Maybe it was pee plus nervous tension? Anything but PROM.

"Here, you get into the back and—them? They coming too?" Officer Cruz halted Sarah at the Belmont Police car, parked askew on the side of the rotary road. POLICE INTERCEPTOR, proclaimed small metal lettering on its rear bumper. Was she—were they—being intercepted? Sarah stepped closer, the squad car's blue and white lights blinking frantically, blinding her.

"Yes," Sarah said in a flashbulb daze as Cruz opened the rear door for her. She heaved herself in, sinking into the black, vinyl, weak-springed seat like a caught criminal. The door slammed. That was when Sarah saw the bars—three actual metal bars running vertically across the backseat windows. Did all cop cars have these, and she'd never noticed?

"Yes, they'll come," Sarah made herself tell Officer Cruz as he climbed heavily into the driver seat. She drew a breath of the sealed-in air: vomit and lame disinfectant; Belmont crooks were no cleaner than any others. Metal mesh separated her from the front seat. Who knew how many crazed criminals had sat where Sarah was sitting. Somehow, she'd made her husband and stepson crazy, too.

"My husband," Sarah managed above the rev of his engine. Pain catching up with her again. "He—they both—need to come, too. My husband and my son, stepson."

"Lucky we came a-long." Cruz stuck his arm out his open window, signaling the traffic to make way. Parting that angry Red Sea for her again. "Keep gettin' all kinds of calls tonight. Everyone an' their mother thinks they've seen those two bomber brothers . . ."

"Brothers? They're brothers, the white hat and black hat?"

Barely glancing in the rearview, Cruz confidently backed up. "Nothin' confirmed yet. Just lotta calls comin' in, lotta calls."

Sarah nodded, though the whole Boston Marathon bombing manhunt felt distant and beside the point to her right now. She was the point. No, her baby.

"Sorry to make you do this on this night and all." Her throat was tightening, the next cramp taking hold. "But you *can* take me . . . get me to . . . Mount Auburn?"

"You are not the problem," Cruz told her above an urgent-sounding voice on radio—"ALERT, TWELVE LOCATION, REPORT OF SHARP, QUICK NOISES—"

Cruz flipped a switch and turned on a siren. It yelped like a mechanical dog overhead. Sarah fumbled with a hopelessly stretched out seatbelt. No one cared if criminals were strapped in safely. She gripped the door handle as Cruz backed into the rotary traffic with a no-nonsense tire shriek.

This was going to be a hell of a ride.

Sarah's pulse thumped her throat to the siren beats above. Suddenly, through the forced break in the traffic, she saw the Rotary of Doom Island all too clearly. Their familiar Toyota smashed against the sign, the hood and front bumper bent-up. The taller, younger cop was leaning into the rear window of their car, seemingly shouting something at the shadowy, tensed-up young man Sarah knew to be PJ.

The young man with the Boston Bomber hair. God, what now? Would they find PJ's knife? Officer Cruz pulled up beside the island, the over eager young cop straightening as if annoyed to be interrupted. *Can't anyone see,* Sarah thought, *I'm the emergency?* Unwisely, she gripped the metal bars—a chill clammy feel from many sweaty hands before hers—and peered out at the scene. The angry gawky-tall cop, no doubt, about to frisk PJ. Sarah's baby, no doubt, about to be born prematurely.

Sarah thought clearly, *I can't let that, any of that, happen.*

Above the piercing yelper, into the blinking, blue-white night, Sarah shrieked through the bars, loud as a real mom, "Everyone get in! *Now!*"

Winter, 2012

Cracking an egg for Paul's birthday cake, Sarah spread her thumb and index finger so the white stretched; the yolk plopped into the bowl. Her doctor had spread her gloved fingers that way, only wider, Sarah watching from between her own knees, to demonstrate the thickness and stretchiness of Sarah's mucus.

No reason anymore, Dr. Lutz decreed months ago, for no baby. At least not from what she called "Sarah's end."

Deftly, Sarah whisked the egg into a golden froth. She raised her wrists like a magician, pouring in milk and canola oil, both low-fat for Paul's heart. Then she lifted the whole bowl of wet ingredients. These she dribbled in extravagant, satiny streams over the dry.

"One, two, three—" She counted the strokes of her wooden spoon, not wanting to count and light Paul's fifty-two candles. Each year, Sarah dreaded this day.

Especially this year, what with Paul's new sperm count and PJ sending that card to her. Should she have pretended never to have gotten it, read it? At one hundred, Sarah stopped her spoon. Then she added a hundred and first stroke, for luck.

She wiped her eggy hands on her flour-powdered denim shorts. She unscrewed the maraschino cherry jar. Popping her cherry—had it really felt like that? She should ask Paul. From, she'd specify, his end.

After all they've been through, couldn't she—shouldn't she—have told Paul about PJ's outrageous offer? PJ's craziest-yet gambit, written as a taunt of a poem, meant as some sick PJ joke? Sarah mixed the cherry juice with milk. Bright red streaked the white, blending into an aggressively cheerful pink.

No, no, no, she told herself with each stroke of the spoon. No, PJ wasn't— was he?—joking. And no, she wouldn't show Paul PJ's bombshell card from the day's mail. Just as she'd chosen not to show Paul the second sperm count that had arrived the day before—yet. Still "borderline low." Sarah felt, as she lifted the heavy bowl, overfull of secrets.

Her hands shook, tipping out a spill of white powder. That might be all the baking soda, her mom, the reflex-pessimist, would have decreed. As sloppy compensation for any baking mistakes, Sarah stirred in an extra handful of walnuts. Carefully, she slid her overfilled pans into the oven.

Her braid swinging, she strode back to her bedroom. She fished the birthday card addressed to her, not Paul, out of her nightstand drawer. Shakily, she slid out the card she'd first opened hours before. The shock of it still fresh.

The glossy Hallmark cover showed a close-up of a birthday candle. Maybe meant to remind her of the candle PJ blew out at that Greek restaurant two years before? She'd wondered if she only imagined that he'd been more tense and awkward around her in his visits since. Sometimes she and PJ would joke around, and their eyes would meet a beat too long, then ricochet away with a flare that felt visible.

The "hope all your wishes come true" card trembled in her hand. His message inked inside in block letters, like a ransom note. Slowly, Sarah reread.

> STEPMOM SARAH
> I CAN GET U, GIVE U
> WHAT U—& ME 2—
> WANT—
> U KNOW I CAN
> U KNOW WHAT I AM SAYING
> U AND ME
> AND BABY MAKES—
> YOUR
> DR. PJ

Sarah folded the card, crackling, in half. She listened to the stillness she loved to pace and contemplate. Her and Paul's quiet nest. She carried PJ's card into the kitchen, and held it with her fingertips, looking only at the soft-focused, creased photo of the candle. Determinedly, she struck a match from the matchbook she took out along with Paul's birthday candles.

As she held up the flame, she blew it out, resisted making her usual wish. Hasn't it warped her, wishing so badly to be—that word that's always haunted her—pregnant? The match smoked in her hand. She can't burn it, and she can't throw it away, either. This card is like a ticket for some forbidden trip.

Sarah stepped back to the bedroom. She slipped the card deep into her jam-packed artist portfolio. Thinking of her own mom, who always wrote formal thank-you notes, Sarah got out blank paper, and addressed it to PJ. She printed in her mother's small, careful hand. She thanked PJ for his card and for his "poem;" she told him that she didn't know what to make of his "strange song lyrics," but she appreciated him sending them, and she hoped he was OK, that she and Paul loved him.

She sealed the letter and washed her hands, done with all that. They shook, but she couldn't stop herself wondering if this might somehow be her last chance. She padded back to the kitchen, opened the window, let in chill air to dissolve the faint, waxy scent of smoke.

Sarah shut the window. She got out her paints, acted calm and competent, like her mom. As she smelled her cake solidifying, Sarah sketched Paul's birthday card, one of their many cozy couple traditions. Microscopic newsprint shreds stuck to her finger; she pasted this year's joke headline onto her own cartoon.

The oven buzzed. Quarter 'til four. Fifteen minutes left to dress then pick up Paul, take him home for their traditional little celebration. Sarah shut off the buzzer, her gluey fingers sticking to its knob. She flung open the oven. The cake layers bulged with walnuts, bumpy like two halves of a cherry-speckled brain.

Bent into the sweet heat, Sarah vowed to make Paul's birthday—no matter the number of candles or sperm—perfectly damn happy.

Chapter Four

April 18, 2013; 10:15 p.m.

Early Labor

They were whizzing down the middle of Alewife Brook Parkway. The world, Paul felt, turned inside out. The siren—sounding like it was all around them—howled then stopped then howled again, louder, longer. Cars on either side nosed up against the curbs and onto the sidewalks, parting for the cruiser as if mowed down. All of it seen through the weird metal bars over the backseat windows.

Drivers, no doubt, thinking these cops were chasing down the Bombers.

Christ, Paul thought in the rattling backset, crammed against his stiff-legged, maybe-suspect son. They really were an emergency; Sarah really must be in danger the way the mellow older cop was driving. Sarah and her baby belly: crammed up against the far door. Big shouldered PJ in the middle because the red haired, hotheaded cop had hustled PJ over to the squad car first. Pushing him in like he might make a break for it. How Paul wished he'd spoken up, insisted on sitting by Sarah. She hunched lower than before, her face clenched as if in more concentrated pain.

Hang in there, Sare. We'll get you there, Sare. A childish chant in Paul's mind.

Wasn't PJ a full-fledged emergency now too? Junior Cop shouting at PJ to stay in the vehicle. Then firing off questions as Sarah was led away, with the harsh flashlight spotlighting PJ's dazed face.

PJ managed slow, low-voiced answers to his name, to where he had spent this evening. "Asleep in this vehicle," PJ had insisted, adding, "and I don't have any white hat."

"You think this is a joke, son?" the young policeman had demanded.

Paul had babbled a defense of PJ, unconvincing even to his own ears. His son was overtired, overstressed. He wasn't aware of what he was saying.

"And why was that?" The young Frankenstein had turned his light on Paul to demand.

Because I've been a bad dad, Paul had half wanted to reply, wondering wildly if maybe these cops might consent to arrest him instead of PJ.

Could you be arrested or held just for saying *the bomber*? Tonight you could, Paul had felt grimly sure.

Then as if to save them all—at least for the moment—the Belmont Police car had pulled up and Sarah in the backseat had shouted. The last loud sound she'd made, poor Sare. Her pain now something she could barely talk through. Meaning real labor had begun?

"GET ON IT! . . . Get me twelve location, MIT . . ." Staticy voices crackled on the cop car's radio. "Sarge, we got everything going—" Paul sat dumbly, holding Sarah's bulky Hurricane Sandy satchel, craning his neck to see past his shell-shocked son—whose eyes were shut, either in prayer or drug-induced daze—to Sarah. Her own head turned toward the window, resting on the seatback, bouncing with the cruiser's illegal speed.

Had Paul ever in his long life gone this fast, felt this scared? At least the younger cop was delaying questioning PJ any further—maybe in deference to Sarah. Or maybe because he was listening so intently to the crackling commands on the cops' radio.

Had they caught those bomber bastards? At MIT, of all places?

"Mount her bun," the accented, fatherly cop announced into the two-way radio.

"Mount her *what*?" Paul croaked back, thinking for another crazed second he was being arrested—he should be arrested!—for mounting his pregnant wife. *But I didn't mount her,* Paul silently explained, the siren hiccupping with robotic, cosmic laughter. *She was on top. We thought she was safe.*

"Mount Au-*burn*," the Dad Cop shouted above his siren. "Car six seven on route to Mount Auburn *Hospital*—"

"Oh yes, yeah." Paul hacked to clear his throat. "That's the one we were gonna . . . Well, just go wherever's closest but that's, that's—"

"*Yes,*" Sarah called out as if in climax, the exact throaty pitch. "Just *fast!*"

Paul reached his long arm over PJ's lap. He managed to pat Sarah's stiffened knee, his son keeping his eyes shut like some sort of yogi. Like his leotarded mom, Adina Mazanian, back when Paul met her.

"GodPaul," Sarah started saying in a strained, intimate voice Paul wished only he could hear. She shook her head, her hanging, tangled hair. "GodPaul, *another!*"

She hunched so suddenly Paul's hand fell onto his son's denim thigh. Muscular, tensed thigh; a knee twitch might kick Paul aside. Paul yanked his hand back, and held on to their useless emergency bag with both.

The cruiser vibrated with its rising speed, whipping past the staid brick walls of Harvard professor homes. Those walls so snooty and unscalable to Paul back when he'd been a student at BU. New to big, chilly Beantown from the dingy double-decker apartment he'd shared with his mother in Waltham. He'd never wanted to move to bosky Belmont where Sarah said the crime rate was so low and the public schools so good. Christ, would their already unlucky kid ever make it to any sort of school?

Boston Police radio voices were issuing commands that the younger, taller cop leaned forward to hear. Too tall for this squad car, his square hat brushing the ceiling. His neck tensed. Maybe he resented being the junior officer, stuck with punks like PJ; he wanted to be out catching the real Bombers.

Paul glanced again at Sarah, wishing he could catch her eye. Paul wondered if she was remembering their own wild ride to Mount Auburn. Paul speeding round these same Alewife Brook curves. Sarah clutching the plastic cup of still warm semen they had to deliver to the Mount Auburn's Urology lab within one hour of ejaculation. Paul's sperm count, as they'd suspected, turned out low—borderline low. After his painful, invasive, yet technically minor surgery, Paul's count inched up only into the borderline medium range. So their baby, Sarah joked though Paul never laughed, was a borderline miracle.

PJ's knee jiggled up and down, jackhammer hard.

"Guess you gonna *be* there, Dad. To see this freaking *one*, this freaking *son*," PJ sing-songed. Paul patted the knee that PJ wasn't jiggling.

Paul had missed PJ's birth; PJ early too, but only by a week. Paul and

Adina had married when she was just beginning to show, when Paul was still doubting whether he was the father at all. Adina, with her flashing Armenian eyes like cut diamonds, purple lipstick, and waist length hair, had worked at the Waltham Wet Shelter Paul managed, the only shelter in the Boston area that took drinkers back then. Adina threw herself into the hectic atmosphere so intensely in her lavender leotard leading the entranced floppy-limbed drunks in yoga. Adina in her round, wire glasses reading their scrawled journals. Paul knew the first night she'd be a quick burnout. Their affair would've flamed out fast too, had it not been for the unexpected, and at first, unbelievable baby. Then the wedding that Adina's canny, two-hundred-pound mother bulldozed into being. But it was Adina's mother who failed to notify him on his overnight shift that Adina was in labor. Adina's mother had already, by then, introduced her to the mustached Armenian businessman who would steal her and baby PJ away to Cleveland.

"Christ, you know I wanted to be there, Peej," Paul muttered by rote, glad to hear PJ say something sane. "I've told you that. I just, I couldn't be reached . . ."

"You can say that again," PJ muttered back, his knee hammering away.

Paul had never told PJ his grandmother hadn't phoned him on the birth night. He respected her day-to-day care of PJ, just as she respected Paul's monthly support checks, which Adina needed after the fancy Armenian guy vamoosed. So, they'd agreed not to badmouth each other.

"You OK over there, Sare?" Paul called across PJ. The cruiser was slowing, the driver eying an impossible illegal left turn. "You hanging in there?"

"Just *get* me . . . there," Sarah commanded through gritted teeth. She'd seemed, when Paul first met her, like a sturdier version of long-haired, manic-eyed Adina.

"Whoa," PJ cut in, his jackhammer knee suddenly stilled. He was watching the deadpan Dad Cop driver, transfixed. The cop spun the steering wheel decisively.

Then they were all leaning right, leaning on each other—Paul's shoulder ramming PJ's, whose other shoulder bumped into Sarah's head—as the cop casually swooped across four lanes of Alewife Brook in a daring left U-turn. The cruiser bounced. Christ, couldn't Belmont afford to give these guys shocks?

The brakes squealed, its siren triumphantly whooping.

EMERGENCY: the letters screamed red into the misty dark. At last they were speeding past the MOUNT AUBURN HOSPITAL sign, past the old-fashioned, gothic, brick outbuildings, up the long, curved drive to the giant, blazingly lit main building.

Christ, he would've driven this fast from Waltham Wet Shelter to PJ's birth, if only he'd known it was happening. If only—Paul leaned on his son in the final sharp curve—he hadn't handed over the kid so wholly to Nana, then spent his thirties bailing out his hapless old man again and again, all while supporting his depressive, needy mother—all while he should've been focusing more on his own son in Ohio.

Baby PJ: that hot-skinned bulldog bundle who struggled whenever Paul rarely got to hold him close. But it was PJ's ill-tempered squawking—plus the grown-together brow PJ showed even as an infant—that hooked Paul's heart. Yes, PJ was a damned, doomed Stratidakis, was *his.*

That bad Stratidakis luck catching up with the kid tonight? Would the wannabe badass junior cop up front really try to detain PJ, just for mouthing off?

"We're, like, here?" PJ demanded, sounding scared. Paul glanced at his sweaty-faced son. The cruiser slowed, swinging along the To EMERGENCY curve.

PJ slid his hand into the stuffed front pocket of his jean jacket. For his jackknife? The infamous knife he'd used to slice that damn cow tongue? Paul tensed up, ready to wrestle his uncontrollable son.

Don't, Paul was about to command. Incredibly, PJ slipped his hand from his pocket to his mouth, popping some sort of tablet onto his tongue. It looked like a stick of gum, only PJ didn't chew, he swallowed, hard. Paul wanted to jam his hand down his son's throat as PJ's Adam's apple bobbed. He swallowed again, harder. Paul clapped his hand on PJ's knee to hold him still.

"What the hell you doing back there, son?" the young Frankenstein cop demanded "I hear you movin' around back there."

"Just getting something. It's like, gum." PJ answered back in a whiny burst. "I mean it's, like, legal. Lethal dose of legal shit and who cares? I'm *not,* like, a *bomber.*"

Paul squeezed his son's knee so hard PJ shut up. But too late?

"We need to get your Stepmama to safety. Get the baby to safety," the more genial cop announced, putting on the brakes. Sarah must have gotten this guy on her side. But Paul wondered, with a chill of fear upon fear, what the hell his son had just swallowed. "You all got to get . . . ready for baby, right?"

"Yes—"

"No—"

Paul and Sarah answered in opposing unison, Sarah's *no* loudest and clearest. The cop rocked the cruiser to an impressive gentle stop against EMERGENCY's blindingly lit curb. A short patient drop off ramp stretched up to glass doors.

"Y'see," Sarah added breathlessly. "This's . . . too early. This's f-false labor . . ."

"Stay where you are, ma'am," the Dad Cop replied, sounding distracted. Ready to be done. He slammed out of his door, leaving his hyper partner leaning even closer to their radio.

"Officer down, MIT campus. Officer down—"

"They gonna call all units—" the impatient young cop burst out. His big chance, Paul realized. Surely they'd see PJ was small potatoes trouble?

Potbellied, yet light footed, the fatherly cop was jogging round the cruiser. Beside Paul, PJ reached again into his unzipped pocket. The younger cop was fixed on the urgent radioed commands. In the confusion, PJ slipped a bulky metal object from his pocket into Paul's hand.

Jackknife, Paul realized, closing his hand around the closed-up knife, palm-sized when folded up. Paul had pictured it bigger. Or maybe this was a different knife? Maybe the police— the other police, Ohio police—had another bigger PJ knife? Hurriedly, as the older cop reached Sarah's side of the squad car, Paul slipped the knife into his own khaki pants pocket.

He tried to meet PJ's eyes but PJ was turning earnestly to Sarah's side of the seat. The fatherly cop jerked open Sarah's side door.

"What's goin' *on, man?*" PJ asked, leaning forward. "Someone got *shot* at MIT? They think it's *them?*" PJ leaned further forward to better hear the radioed in reports.

"We don't know yet." The Dad cop leaned down to Sarah, her back to Paul—everyone's back to Paul.

"If it's *them* then they aren't *me,*" PJ insisted, talking too fast, but at least making sense now. "So lemme *go* with my Dad, my Stepmom! My half-brother's being born!"

"Yeah, we've gotta be with Sarah," Paul muttered loudly from his side. Nobody paid the slightest attention. The front-seat cop listened to a new voice barking a new order.

"All units respond—all units—GET ON IT—"

PJ took hold of Sarah's shoulders and helped ease her up to her feet, his own broad shoulders straining his denim jacket. His front pocket emptied now. Not only of the jackknife but hopefully of whatever drug or whatever PJ had just popped in his mouth. Not that the cops couldn't do blood tests and find out exactly what PJ was on. PJ twisted indifferently toward Paul; he pulled the clanking overnight bag off Paul's lap, starting to hand it over to Sarah.

At that clank, the young cop turned at last from the radio. "Wait. What in hell is in that bag?"

The bomb, Paul realized, had been packed in a duffel bag. The marathon bomb.

"Just, like, her *clothes* and shit!" PJ replied but then he raised the bag and it clanked louder—metal clanking. It sounded worse than it was, Paul knew, trying to remember what-all was packed in there. Batteries and canned goods and a can opener.

"Sorry, sorry." Sarah told the older officer, gripping the officer's arm like she might fall over. Paul fumbled with his own door handle, relieved to find it unlocked. So maybe they weren't under arrest yet? Paul scrambled out into the misty air before anyone could tell him, yet again, to stay in the vehicle.

He rushed around the rear bumper to Sarah, wanting to catch her if she fainted.

"Not you, ma'am. Not your fault," the older officer was saying to Sarah.

"Look, we really are sorry to cause any trouble," Paul cut in, breathless. "And now it—it sounds like the bomber suspects are off on a shooting spree at MIT?" Paul raised his own hoarse voice to supervisor level. The knife hung heavy in his pants pocket, hopefully hidden by the loose folds of khaki. He'd lost weight this year.

"We'll go see about that, sir." The older officer was stiffening as if ready to spring into action, but Sarah still had hold of his arm.

"Please," Sarah managed to interject beside him. "Please, our stepson, PJ. See, he just . . . He talks out of his head . . ."

"Yeah. I do," PJ called through the half-open car window, earnest as a groom. He looked as young as he was, nineteen, his bug-eyed, beetle-browed face abashed for once.

"You don't worry, ma'am. We'll take good care." The father cop nodded decisively, the one in charge. He turned and fixed his no-nonsense black stare over Paul's shoulder.

An equally no-nonsense steel wool-haired nurse with a wheelchair pulled up behind Sarah. Ignoring Paul, the cop and nurse eased Sarah into the chair.

As the nurse settled Sarah, the younger cop aimed his low voice out his front seat window. "We gotta check out the boy's bag."

"There's no *bomb* in this *bag*," PJ shouted. The nurse had already begun wheeling Sarah away. But Paul stood in frozen horror on the curb, watching as PJ in the squad car's backseat started unzipping that damn disaster bag. "Shit, what *is* in here?"

"Don't open that bag," the front seat cop commanded. The father cop shot his own firm nod at his partner. The two of them agreeing about PJ as he froze his hands mid-unzip, gazing up in wide-eyed confusion, the suspect bag half-open in his lap.

Officer Cruz faced Paul, telling him brusquely, "You are staying here, with her. Your wife. We'll let you. But we gotta check your son out. He been drinking? Need to check that bag o' his. Need to hold any one says anything 'bout bombs tonight. You get that, sir?"

"I—he," Paul began, shooting another nervous glance over his shoulder. Sarah was being wheeled through the hospital's vast glass doors.

Speechless, Paul turned back to the squad car. PJ stared up through the window bars at Paul, like his dad could fix this. Paul drew a breath, no idea what he could or should say.

"All units, we got all units," the hothead cop announced. From the passenger seat, he spoke into the squad car radio in a loud electrified voice. "Car sixty-seven Belmont responding. Car sixty-seven Belmont departing Mount Auburn. Departing Mount Auburn!"

"Wait. Please," Paul sputtered, bending down to meet his son's panicked, glassy gaze through the backseat window bars. Should Paul climb in with him?

"Stay with Sarah, Dad." PJ's words came out clear. "Sarah . . . It's all *my fault.*"

"*What's* all your fault?" Paul demanded, extra loud, too. Who cared who heard?

Quickly for a guy of his size, Officer Cruz had trotted 'round to the driver's side and was climbing in.

PJ widened his over-bright eyes, his next words lower and more muffled. "I fucked up her, both hers. You gotta stay with her, Dad. Gotta stay with the babies."

"*Babies?*" Paul gasped, wondering if he'd heard PJ's mixed-up words right.

"Stand clear of the vehicle," the Franken-cop commanded. "Vehicle" seemed to be his favorite word. And PJ—crazed though he was—was right. Paul had to stay here. He stepped back as the squad car engine revved.

What in hell had PJ meant by *both hers*? By the bomber talk that was getting him hauled in? Surely PJ wasn't caught up, on this night, in real trouble?

"I'll call Evvy. She'll get you out of this," Paul managed to shout to barred-in PJ, his face boyishly scared. As the squad car shuddered into gear, PJ faced front like a soldier on a mission. Like the red-haired cop, facing front, too.

They had Bombers to catch. The siren war-whooped into life. The Belmont Police car squealed away in blue-white flashing-light splendor, carrying away PJ, the suspect son. Paul gulped moist spring air. He heard other distant sirens. He had to find his other unborn son, and fast. Paul spun round, hurried toward the doors.

⌖

He had forgotten how huge Mt. Auburn Hospital was. A wide, windy expanse of brick and glass surrounded him. An ambulance pulled in with silently pulsing lights. Could it contain the MIT shooting victim? No, that had just happened, though the past few minutes felt like ages.

Paul halted at the doors, PJ's knife bumping in his pocket. Sarah had already disappeared into the lit-up hospital, its doors automatically opening now for Paul. A dead-looking old man strapped into his chair was wheeled out.

Paul entered the lobby at a near run and rushed up to the check-in desk. The jowly, sour-looking night nurse barely glanced at him. Her eyes, like all eyes, fixed on the emergency wait area TV, the thrilled-sounding news voices.

SHOOTING AT MIT, one was rushing to announce.

Christ, what in hell was PJ heading into? That cop car, like probably every cop car for miles, was heading right into what the hyper reporter was describing as A CHAOTIC CRIME SCENE.

A new and desperate family burst through the glass doors and approached the desk: a brown-haired girl clutching a bloody *Dora the Explorer* towel, wailing in her mother's arms. Befuddled brunette sisters or cousins surrounded the mother and girl.

Both *hers*? What could PJ possibly mean? How would Paul ever get a straight answer out of him or Sarah? And where *was* Sarah? He needed to be beside her, like a real husband, a real dad. Paul babbled to the distracted nurse that his wife was in labor. She replied curtly that Paul had to sign her in. Then she motioned Paul toward the glassed-in office behind her, another nurse typing away on a computer as one old lady answered questions and a second quavering oldster awaited their turn.

Paul backed away from the desk, nervously smoothing his dense beard, picturing PJ scratching his dark hair in the cab. Was the tablet PJ had taken kicking in? Was it making him itch? Paul tried to recall from his Wet Shelter days which pills made them itch.

He looked around the wait area. The check-in nurse had turned her surly attention to the *Dora the Explorer* family. Everyone else was facing the urgently talking news man on a big-screen TV. Fresh headlines scrolled on the crawl: SHOOTING CONFIRMED AT MIT.

God, PJ in a squad car heading right out there. It seemed unreal, impossible. Would PJ get shot? Get taken hostage by the crazed Bombers? Would Paul ever see his son alive again?

"Paul," a voice called out from behind him. Paul turned and faced a nurse with a clipboard. Surely she would take him to Sarah. Paul wanted to fall into her capable arms, but she waved him off. "No, no, sir. Wrong Paul."

Yet another horrifically old man, the right Paul, was hoisted off a plastic-cushioned couch. He raised his bloodless, yet alert, face to the nodding nurse.

I'm the wrong Paul, Paul told himself as he backed further away. PJ wanted to be Paul now. PJ had been listed as Paul in the brief Elyria *Free Press* article about the Cow Tongue Incident. Paul ducked his head to make his own illicit escape.

He strode away from check-in, remembering with an inner wince the article's snide headline. COPS DON'T LIKE THE TASTE OF INCIDENT: HIGH SCHOOL STUDENT CAUGHT IN COW TONGUE RITUAL. Christ Almighty, how could Paul have let those Belmont cops spirit PJ away? Paul had to call Evvy. She would do anything for Sarah. Evvy would bail PJ out if need be. Wouldn't she?

Paul slipped out his cell, exiting the ER area. How could the man-sized suspect the police were holding be the young son he knew? PJ pasty with sweat, like the hopeless drunks in Waltham Wet Shelter, the lushes who couldn't even follow the no drinking on premises rule, who'd down whole cheap bottles of mouthwash to get high. The mouthwash, the Shelter workers theorized, ate their brains.

"I gotta find my wife," Paul announced to no one in particular. He didn't dare ask directions to maternity or someone might detain him, too—him and his trusty knife. Paul stepped past a garish flyer on the wall, an inked face of a brooding man, like the faces Sarah sketched of Paul on his birthday cards.

Get to know mr. Stroke: time lost is brain lost.

And baby lost, Paul thought. He speed-dialed Evvy's number Sarah had given him, and got her voicemail. Paul followed the signs for Childbirth Center, his voice low.

"Evvy? It's Paul, Sarah's Paul. Sarah's at Mount Auburn, maybe, probably in labor. And PJ . . . he's in town, too. He's being held by the Belmont Police, if you can believe that, and he's . . . a mess. He's high on something and he said something to the cops about looking like the Boston Bomber. It's all crazy, everything tonight. Anyhow, any chance you can call the damn Belmont Police and see what you can do? Maybe you know something about what's making PJ so crazy? Anyhow, if you can track down PJ, Evvy, call me. Anyhow, I'm here at the hospital, and I'm heading up to my wife."

At that, Paul clicked off his cell. He picked up his pace, rushing as if he knew just where he was going in the hospital's corridor maze.

Once, over a year before, Paul had raced with Sarah and his damned semen cup down the same maze, forgetting which floor the Urology lab was on. The nurse they'd asked had smirked. Finally, he and Sarah had burst together through the lab doors.

Paul had resented, more than the smirking nurse, the slacker lab technician who'd recorded the exact time Paul had ejaculated.

He'd sensed even then what the sperm test would reveal, what Sarah would want him to do. *Led by the balls,* he'd thought the day they arrived for the outpatient varicosity surgery. When he woke from the anesthesia weeping, the nurse told him the depression he felt was a result of the drugs, that it would pass, but it lasted months, even after the pain in his groin had subsided and the stitches around his so called varicose veins dissolved.

Once the depression at last let up, the resentment remained. Led by the balls.

Emergency Treatment / Day Surgery / Childbirth

Paul veered toward the Childbirth arrow; he plodded along a

walkway, dodged into an elevator. What could PJ, serial liar, possibly mean by *I fucked up her, both hers?* And what was happening right now down at MIT? Paul was afraid to hear what the next TV might say.

The elevator *binged*. Childbirth opened up before Paul: the floor he and Sarah had visited with other parents-to-be in the single class she'd persuaded Paul to attend. Why had he been such a bastard about all that, sunk in his sore-balled depression? Why hadn't he taken the no doubt numbing Zoloft his know-it-all doctor advised?

Women were grunting, muffled by doors. A newborn, mewing like a sick kitten, wheeled past Paul. The pruney, blue-veined baby looked unnaturally tiny—a preemie like his and Sarah's might turn out to be? Like a number of the residents at the Center were? Paul knew the first question on special ed. forms: Was the child full-term? Were there any birth complications?

But there was still time to prevent all that. Drugs they could give to delay premature labor . . . right? Paul's cell beeped, startling him. A text from Evvy. He halted to read it hungrily: GOT MESSAGE& AM ON IT- TRAFFIC TERRBLE- MORESOON Ev

Paul thumb-texted back a THNKS, sure as he pressed send that traffic wasn't the only thing terrible out there. A young couple passed by Paul, chatting excitedly.

"—but I heard it was just the policeman, just the campus policeman, who got shot—"

Let that be true, Paul thought, stowing his phone in his pocket with the jackknife. Let it be true that it was the poor campus policeman, Rest In Peace, and no one else shot out there, yet. And—Paul continued his almost-prayer as he strode down the corridor—*Let Sarah be safe. Sarah and the baby.* As if in answer, Paul suddenly heard and followed Sarah's low, strained-by-pain voice. He headed toward the nearest half-open door.

"So we were . . . we never should've been . . ." Sarah was saying to someone.

"And after intercourse, the bleeding started," the nurse prompted, scratching on a clipboard. She was standing before Sarah, still in her wheelchair. Sarah was crying.

"But this c-can't be labor . . ." Sarah's dark, undone hair hid her face. She snuffled. She was shaking her head in a stubborn way that scared Paul, determined to hold onto this baby. Could she if their reckless fuck had jarred everything loose?

Sarah bowed her head, gazing with prayerful concentration at her belly. She'd always been determined not to have a Caesarean, not after the serious infection from her appendectomy had nearly made her infertile. She'd chosen her doctor based on the determination to do this birth her way. To stage manage it like she still tried to do with life in general, poor kid.

Paul wished, coughing dryly, that he could cry like he'd done after his surgery. Cry with Sarah.

"It happens, honey, it happens," the nurse murmured, more or less sympathetically. Then she turned to Paul in the doorway, her steel wool hair and hawkish nose reminding Paul of his own grim, dead mother. The nurse's narrowed gaze asked him, plain as day: *How could you, you old goat?*

❦

Numbers were jumping in Sarah's head. How many centimeters, how many weeks? At twenty-eight weeks, seventy-some percent of premature babies survived. This was almost thirty weeks. What was the survival rate at three days shy of thirty? Sarah wanted to ask the nurse with the clipboard who had turned away, disgusted maybe, by the story Sarah stammered out.

How she and Paul made love, then she'd started bleeding and now . . .

It all seemed incredible to Sarah, too. Down the corridor, Sarah could hear urgent news voices, but she wouldn't turn on the TV in her own—hers, dammit—birth room. She hunched over in her wheelchair, fighting another cramp.

The nurse was telling Paul that the doctor was coming, that he needed to sign Sarah in.

"Can I talk to her first? Sarah? Sare?" Paul called from the doorway. The nurse tightened her grip on her clipboard like she might swing it at Paul.

"What time is it?" Sarah gasped out. Her next cramp overpowered her. The ache in her lower back, the larger ache in her abdomen. The cramp coil strengthened like a belt inside her. Her baby and her gut both clenched. *Pretty good*, she thought grudgingly as she straightened, blinking back tears. Pretty bad, yes. But were these the legendary pains of hard labor?

Surely not. *Surely all this isn't yet unstoppable*, Sarah told herself. Finally, Paul shuffled into view. He already looked as wiped out as she felt. His face drained and stunned like after his sperm count surgery, when he'd been led out to Sarah. She'd kept asking the nurse if it really was OK for Paul to go home that same day.

He stood tall and unsteady before her. His face looked tensely expectant, as if she could explain all this. What was happening to their baby and, Sarah remembered with a jolt, to PJ, too. PJ blurting out so much in their own car to Paul. PJ saying God-knew-what to that hothead policeman. Reading her mind, Paul told her PJ was safe, told her Evvy was going to come and get PJ. Sarah nodded dazedly. Evvy. Yes, good old Evvy. Evvy coming here? Or was PJ somewhere else? Sarah couldn't focus on PJ now; she had to focus on the numbers. "What time, Paul, what *time?*"

Paul glanced at his watch, told her, half past eleven. Her cramps now less than ten minutes apart. God, it must be hard labor? Sarah pressed her thighs together through her sweatpants. She asked the nurse, "Can't you give me something, please? I mean . . . something to stop this f-false labor or whatever . . . before it's too late?"

What-all had she read about premature babies? Sarah tried to remember as the nurse explained again that Dr. Lutz would be here in minutes. Paul demanded to stay with Sarah until the doctor arrived. Possible complications for preemies, Sarah remembered, included breathing, vision, hearing, kidney damage. In some preemies: learning disabilities and darkening degrees of cerebral palsy.

Sarah repeated this ominous list to herself, surveying the small, sparsely furnished birth room, the flat-screen TV still blessedly blank.

Paul addressed the nurse. "My wife's cramps are coming closer. Shouldn't the damn doctor be here? Some doctor? Isn't it true you can still stop this? Isn't there some sort of drug?"

Sarah gripped the wheelchair arms again, her inner belt tightening.

"Such drugs," the nurse replied, "can harm the baby if labor is too far along. Such drugs can't be given at all once the mother's water has broken, or the baby is at risk for infection. And if a birth is premature, the use of even painkilling drugs could be risky."

"But it . . . her . . . the water hasn't broken yet, right Sare? Sare?"

Sarah managed a nod, suddenly unsure. There had been so much water streaming down her legs in the tub. Could her water have broken, and she didn't know it?

She gritted her teeth, willing this whole scene to change, rewind. She hadn't even yet completed the natural birth classes that Evvy was accompanying her to, since Paul disapproved of the natural birth plan. Too risky, he felt. *If you want to make the gods laugh,* Evvy liked to remind Sarah, *tell them your plans.*

I haven't finished the last classes, Sarah strained to keep from crying out.

A familiar, high school panic was overtaking her brain, freeze-drying it. Like when she'd snap out of her teenage daze to face a mystifying pop quiz.

But I didn't complete the natural, didn't study for the final!

Sweat was popping out on Sarah's forehead, moisture leaking from her breasts. Her body felt like a swollen water balloon, a flesh sack of fluids poised to burst.

Her face wet, her eyes blurred, she heard Dr. Claire Lutz's quick-clicking heels. Trim, efficient Dr. Lutz with her clipped hair and year-round tan, her reputation for pushing her patients through natural births. No-C. Dr. C, she was known as. Sarah had never warmed to her, but she'd sensed Claire Lutz was one of life's winners, ruthlessly cool. Sarah wanted that type on her baby's team.

Sarah wiped her eyes with a too thin hospital tissue. A new set of hands, an aide's, wheeled Sarah toward the room's daunting, elevated bed. Back when Sarah and Paul had glimpsed a sample birth room, Sarah thought it small but cozy with its gingham rocker. Now, as her wheelchair halted at the metal-railed bed, the gingham plaid struck her as phony, untrustworthy. Like the garish bright fabrics on airline seats designed to distract passengers from the fact that they are soaring through treacherous skies in a tin can, flammable and fragile.

"Yes, of course; Paul. We've met once. Dr. Claire Lutz."

Dr. Lutz was greeting Paul as if she'd just strode in off the tennis court. Too late for tennis, but maybe Dr. Lutz had a twenty-four hour indoor court lit by tanning lamps. Sarah wiped her hot face. She struggled, along with the soap-smelling aide, to rise.

A curtain screaked around its track, tenting the bed. Shakily, watching the aide's deft hands for cues, Sarah pulled off her inside-out sweatshirt and pants. She slipped on her hospital johnnie and allowed herself to be positioned on her back. Trying to pull herself together, trying to look, when sharp-eyed Dr. Lutz opened the curtain, like she was not already too far gone.

"Here a bit ahead of schedule, are we? And what a night, with everything going on." Dr. Lutz attempted the bedside-manner chitchat that seemed to bore her, too.

"No," Sarah announced. "No, Dr. Lutz, it's *not* gonna be early. We can still *stop* this. I—I've still got my waters and, and—"

"Feet apart, please. We need an internal, to see how far you're dilated." Dr. Lutz sounded now like the Lutz Sarah liked, the one who'd give the numbers straight.

Preemie babies over something—three pounds? Four?—had a something-percent better chance of survival. Sarah started panting. She braced her body against Dr. Lutz's cold, metal speculum, then against the cramp she felt gathering strength, triggered by Lutz.

"Almost seven centimeters already," Lutz reported as if this were a marathon race and Sarah would win by rushing her baby across the line nearly two months too soon.

Seven. God, she was fully dilated. She had entered hard labor already. As if distantly, she heard Dr. Lutz explain this to her and to Paul on the other side of the curtain. Inside the curtain, inside her body, Sarah felt all alone.

This is it, Sarah knew with her next cramp. The whole body, hard labor pain she'd been awaiting. The pain that would shake her awake from a lifelong trance. Mixed with her sinking fear, as she let loose a yowl: irrational happiness. At last, real labor.

Breathe, she reminded herself above the annoying voice of Lutz. Sarah had entered her own tunnel. There was only one way out. Go through the tunnel's full, twisted darkness.

Breathe in little hard puffs, Sarah told herself. *Like blowing out a candle*.

At least she remembered this much from the birth classes. Breathe so you won't push. Why weren't you supposed to push?

As she gathered her first puffy breath, it hit, full force.

The candle went out, everything went out. Sarah jerked her head back, arched her spine. An ocean wave knocked her flat, dragging her along gritty, murky bottom, her skin battered and ears roaring. Then Sarah was blinking, dripping sweat and tears together.

Her flesh ached, inside and out. She'd forgotten, as the class had instructed, to pick a focus point. To puff, to count.

"—so called Tocolytic agents to relax the uterus and delay labor," Dr. Lutz was explaining on the other side of the curtain. Everyone was on the other side.

"—but that would put the baby at risk of infection. Even an epidural might inflict damage with a baby at this stage. Frankly, the overall risk is less if we simply go with the premature delivery. You know with Sarah's previous history, we don't want a C-section. Hopefully the baby's small enough where a Caesarean won't be required."

Small? Whoever said—you never said—this baby was small.

"So we might be looking at a fast onset of labor. Sarah's already past seven months and near seven centimeters. My guess is we won't have a choice once her membranes go."

My membranes aren't *going to go, you bitch.* Sarah clenched her insides around her baby. The curtain opened. Paul again, his eyes dark as his beard. His face, like hers, tightly drawn. He, too, was trying to hold everything inside.

"Sare? She says you'll come through this fine. You and the baby . . ." Poor, hoarse Paul made a valiant effort to sound, as he never was, optimistic. "Did you hear what the doctor told me? About how the drugs might, at this stage, damage a premature baby—"

"But I didn't . . . we're not *ready,*" Sarah burst out. Yet she didn't want anyone thinking she wanted a Caesarean. The idea of a Caesarean—of cutting into her abdomen again when it almost killed her with her appendix—had always terrified Sarah. She'd chosen Dr. Lutz because of her reputation as a doctor who saw her patients through grueling vaginal deliveries. Like a drill sergeant, one nurse had confided of Lutz.

At the time, Sarah felt that might be exactly what she'd need because weren't vaginal deliveries, like breast milk, best in the end? Or did it work differently, did everything work differently, with preemies?

"The rules do not apply," Sarah heard PJ sing-songing from sometime last summer. She squeezed her eyes shut, braced again, warm and sweaty and leaky all over. The sheet covering her felt heavy, sticky, dirt mixed with sand.

A kiss on her forehead now, light and tender, only that Spy Pond day it was on her lips. *PJ?* Sarah had thought as she woke from her hot, groggy nap.

"PJ . . . that kiss . . ." Sarah blinked her damp-lashed eyes, still bracing for the cramp. Surprised, like at Spy Pond, by the face she saw hovering above her. Evvy, that day. Evvy smirking, already making a joke of the light kiss she'd planted on Sarah's lips.

And now, tonight, Paul, blurred by sweat and tears, not sun.

Yes, Sarah had felt Paul's dense beard just now. How could she not have known it was her husband who'd kissed her forehead, not her lips?

"That kiss, that PJ . . ."

That kiss that PJ saw. That summer day at Spy Pond. It was just—

What? What was she thinking, bringing that up now?

Sarah blinked harder, Paul's looming face above her out of focus. Some combination of liquids clouded her eyes, oozed from her skin.

"What kiss? What do you mean, that PJ?" Paul whispered, only to her. "You mean, Sare, today?"

"Today?" Sarah repeated, her lips dry. Today seemed far away. She swallowed; it hurt, her throat and mouth the only dry parts of her. "Water."

"I'll get you some," Paul mumbled. Sarah felt his relief at pulling back from her, hiding his own overloaded face, stepping behind the curtain.

"Y'know," a nurse voice was saying to Paul. "In labor, they . . . the moms . . . they say just anything." Liquid was pouring, ice cracking. "They talk outta their heads."

Out of my head, Sarah thought, swallowing nothing again. Just what she'd said about PJ to the police. But when? Out of her head: where she'd been longing to be. Out of her head and into—she grasped a cup from someone, not Paul—her body.

"Sir? Excuse me?" A new voice behind the curtain. Paul answered from behind, too. Sarah raised her head just enough to gulp the water. "Are you Paul Stratidakis?"

Sarah lay back again, sucking her ice. Paul muttered something.

"If you could come down to check in, sir. I hate to bother you here, but we do need to get your wife registered . . . So if you could just come down . . ."

Swallowing hard, ice sliding down like a chilled pill, she heard Paul protest that he had to stay here. She heard the nurse tell Paul that nothing was going to happen just yet. That they were in a long haul, a long labor, an early birth.

Had Paul been right that they should've had the risky amnio? Was this preemie going to be born with Down's or, the second most common nightmare defect, Edwards Syndrome? Teeny babies who had pixie-like ears, damaged kidneys, and no spines. Frail fairy babies who lived mere weeks.

But no, Sarah told herself and her baby. Her baby wasn't tiny like that, was he? How big now, how many pounds had they estimated her last checkup? Four and—what? Sarah shook her heavy, tangled hair back and forth.

She needed to rebraid her hair; needed to find a fucking focal point. She strained her arms and back, struggling to sit up, to follow Paul somehow. She needed him to time these contractions, rub her back between them, do his part.

But he had to deal with PJ—Paul and Evvy.

Where is PJ? Sarah formed words to call to the nurse. The one who'd known she was out of her head. As Sarah propped herself by her elbows, she felt a paralyzing tightness around her waist and legs.

Take them off, she'd begged her perpetually disappointed mother. She'd just tugged the leotards her mother had bought for ballet lessons over her solid, ten-year-old body.

Sarah plucked at her hospital johnnie, wondering if somehow some nurse had belted her to the bed. Sarah's hand fumbled through the cotton; she felt only her thickened, tightened skin. *My skin's too tight,* she wanted to call out. *My skin's too tight; he'll never get out!* She drew a big shuddery breath to shout it.

But she burst. The pressure in her abdomen released in one sudden gush. Warm wetness seeped from inside her, soaking her legs, her gown, the sheets, the pad beneath her. Sarah sat stiff-legged in it. Not sticky or smelly like pee, not a flow she'd controlled. Not a flood as she'd always imagined, a sea unleashed. One clumsy gush that left her wet but bloated as ever.

Was it all out? Was there not enough water because this baby was too early? Was this somehow *not*—but Sarah knew it was—her water breaking?

"Stop," Sarah moaned, knowing nothing could stop it now. The curtains screaked harshly, this time yanked wide, all the way.

That kiss; that PJ. That kiss; that PJ.

Paul barreled down the childbirth floor corridor, his feet making a hard beat to Sarah's soft, confused words. *That kiss that PJ . . . gave me?* Was that what Sarah was trying to say? Was that—or something even worse—the bombshell PJ had been threatening since his email to drop? Would he ever even get to ask PJ about all this?

NEW REPORTS ABOUT THE CARJACKING FOLLOWING THE MIT SHOOTING, a local TV news voice was breathlessly reporting from some other mother's birth room. MIT CAMPUS POLICE OFFICER LEFT DEAD IN THE SHOOTING. BOTH BOMBER SUSPECTS ALLEGEDLY INVOLVED IN BOTH INCIDENTS.

At least they were talking about the MIT shooting in past tense. Surely they'd say if someone other than the cop had died. Surely the Belmont Police would not drag PJ along with them to investigate this alleged carjacking? Paul whipped too fast past a young intern with acne dotting his sloppily shaven face, the wannabe doctor dawdling in the hall, trying to overhear the latest news update. As Paul brushed by, the intern wheeled round as if to admonish Paul, his coat flapping like white wings.

But Paul pushed on, bending into his strides. What if PJ bolted from the police and tried to make a run for it? What was PJ running from, what secrets? Christ, if PJ had either kissed Sarah or tried to kiss her today, *had* PJ triggered this premature labor? PJ messing with Sarah's already overstressed, post-marathon nerves. PJ would have to be crazy himself to do such a thing. And now he was out there, on this craziest ever night, God knew where.

"Excuse me." Like a blatantly rude Boston driver, Paul cut around a wheelchair bearing an exhausted, damp-haired new mother, fresh from her own delivery. How in hell could he be wondering about some kiss when his wife was sunk in that unimaginable pain? When his son was possibly under arrest or in danger? Or both? Paul tasted a whiff of mother blood in the wheelchair's wake.

He nearly rammed into the sealed elevator doors. He stabbed down. Then he rapped on the elevator doors, hard enough to hurt his knuckles. Damn Stratidakis temper. Paul's Dad kicking over the TV when a horse he'd bet on lost the derby, the fallen TV spitting and sparking. Paul's own outbursts were rarer and less spectacular, but still shameful. Paul slowed his foolish knuckle raps, lowered his fist.

Paul remembered hustling three-year-old PJ too roughly into a makeshift time-out corner. PJ swinging his own little fists at Paul, then hunching in the corner like a whipped puppy. Paul crouching beside him and hugging him and telling him he'd make it—though he knew he couldn't—better. Then just this past March: Paul biking up behind PJ when his son veered from the Lexington Green onto dangerous Massachusetts Avenue. Paul leaning from his own bike to seize PJ's shoulder, meaning to slow him, but PJ startled and his bike tipped, spilling him onto the sidewalk, pedestrians staring at Paul like he was a monster father.

Bing. Slow, metal doors unsucked. Paul edged onboard, crowded by a big meal cart. He breathed TV dinner fumes of flavorless, aluminum meat, exuded by a few picked-at, hours-old plates. Magenta beets— why always serve beets to the already ill?—bleeding onto soggy squares of cornbread. Still, Paul's nearly empty stomach stirred; his ashy mouth watered. Christ, what he really needed was a smoke.

The orderly commandeering the dish tray held the elevator open for one more passenger, an elated teenage boy. *Or no,* Paul thought as the boy bounced onboard, a guy in his twenties, a glazed, first time Daddy. *And Sarah's all alone,* Paul told himself as the doors sucked shut. Sarah alone except for a nurse in her birth room.

Down, down. The unstable beet-mobile wobbled, bumping Paul. The giddy new dad chuckled, his baby out and OK. Who could or should ask for more?

Paul coughed, gravelly throated, trying to remember what Lutz had said about how twenty-nine-and-a-half weeks was doable, how he and Sarah better get ready to—Dr. Lutz delivered the perky phrase flatly, unsmiling—meet their baby.

Like meet your Maker, Paul thought as the elevator touched down. *Only you are the maker, the one who's damn well responsible.*

Bing. Doors unsucked.

Paul burst from the beet debris into the dry, disinfected smell of the first floor corridor; he followed the ER arrow doggedly. *They said it would be a long haul for Sarah*, Paul reminded himself as he raced past a wheeled bed displaying piss-stained sheets, that familiar Center smell of yeasty adult pee and baby powder. Veering from it, Paul almost ran into the emergency girl, still clutching her *Dora the Explorer* towel in her wheelchair.

"'Take a step at a time,'" Paul told himself, slowing and panting. Words from the inane, defunct theme song of *Blue's Clues*. Paul plodded toward the main lobby, picturing the skinny *Blue's Clues* star who was rumored to be a cocaine addict, a boyish man dressed like a child, with an oversized, coked-out nose.

Paul hesitated in the phone/snack corner. He checked his cell. No new text. *You lost him*, Nana had told Paul of nineteen-year-old PJ, when really he'd lost him years before. How skeptically Paul had always regarded Center parents who doted over their kids while they were little and "at least cute," as one accidentally frank father put it. Liking children, Paul secretly scoffed, just meant liking a time of life. Who followed through and liked the screwed-up adults those kids became? Paul hadn't been there for PJ as a kid; at least he could try to be there for him now.

Paul quickly scanned the snack machine for cigarettes. Would the new baby have even worse problems than Peej? Would he be a helplessly sweet, slant-eyed baby with Down's syndrome? How had Paul-the-pessimist let Sarah talk him out of the amnio, even after her blood tests revealed a moderately high level of something called AFP? Alpha Feto something. Which meant, a tarted-up geneticist had explained to them, one of three things: either the baby was further along than had been thought, or the baby had a serious spinal-tube defect. Or it might mean, the white-coated blonde had finished with a sadistic lipstick grin, *nothing at all.*

"How do I sign in?" Paul practically threw himself against the information desk that overlooked the ER wait area.

"Shoulda done this sooner. Computers are down now with everything going on." The receptionist shoved a clipboard Paul's way, her jowls vibrating with contempt.

Paul bent over the clipboard, glad to have a task. SARAH MCCALL, he block-printed in ink as if they'd never married. No room left on the line for Stratidakis. What had he done? He should have put his name. His wife. His wife, his son.

He looked over his shoulder—as if he might catch a shot of PJ himself—to see the Shell Station on Memorial Drive, where Paul had often stopped for gas, emblazoned on the big TV. There, according to the newest CNN news crawl, the bombing suspects had carjacked a Mercedes SUV. Paul almost hoped they'd get away, just to keep PJ out of harm's way. Paul peeled his eyes from the TV, turned back to the check-in counter, to the hospital form he would've filled out two weeks before their due date, if this were a normal birth.

"Daddy?" a young voice called out trustingly. "Daddy, the Bombers stole a *car!*"

Christ, the Bombers careening around in some stolen SUV with PJ out there too? No one out of harm's way, not tonight. Paul scribbled out MCCALL. He block printed STRATIDAKIS outside the line. Who knew what Paul Stratidakis Jr. was babbling in that Belmont Police car? PJ: certifiable liar. A teacher had written those very words on his report card the year PJ kept telling everyone he was a certifiable CIA agent.

Paul copied out his insurance numbers, wondering how he could have let those cops drive away with his nutty son, then squinted at the numbers he'd copied all wrong.

Out of your head, Paul told himself as he recopied the numbers. The jowly receptionist lifted Sarah's check-in form without a glance, craning to see beyond Paul to the TV.

NEW INFORMATION EMERGES ABOUT THE LATEST FIREFIGHT WITH POLICE IN CAMBRIDGE, an amped-up TV voice announced, and Paul turned like everyone else toward the screen. FOLLOWING THE CARJACKING, SUSPECTS ALLEGEDLY ENGAGED IN A BRIEF SKIRMISH WITH ONE GROUP OF POLICE, HURLING HANDMADE EXPLOSIVES.

"Christ," Paul muttered aloud, stepping toward the TV to stare into the confusing footage of clustered police car lights, blinking their blue and white signals. Was PJ trapped in one of those cars?

"Christ, was anyone hurt?" Paul asked aloud. No one around him answered, everyone riveted to the screen. But maybe, with her witchy instincts, Evvy heard. Paul's phone vibrated. He sidestepped from the TV, fumbling to pull out his cell.

"Evvy," Paul gasped into his cell phone, stepping further away from the TV voices to hear, from her, the only news that counted to him. "PJ. Where is he?"

"I sprung him," Evvy's welcome, husky voice crackled into Paul's ear. He leaned against a sickly-green hospital wall in weak-kneed relief. One son safe, anyhow.

"Thanks, Evvy. Thank God. Christ, what happened? The police let him go?"

"Sounds like he had himself a little adventure. Got driven out to MIT after that poor young campus cop was shot. Don't sound like they got close to the action with half the cops in Boston there. Anyhow, them Belmont cops musta decided PJ wasn't worth their while. They dropped him at the Belmont station, gave him a breatho-thingy, which he passed. When I showed up a few minutes ago, they booted him out. No charges. We're on our way now. Be there in a bit. Call ya then."

Paul choked out more words of thanks. When the call cut off, he slumped for a moment—maybe more than a moment—against the wall. Then he staggered into the men's room, surprised to find his eyes teary. PJ safe. PJ on his way. Paul washed his hands extra-long after peeing. The men's room was blessedly empty and relatively quiet. Paul splashed cold water on his face, remembering young, exuberant PJ splashing water on him one day at Walden Pond. Paul and Sarah had taken him swimming there.

PJ had swum so far out at Walden that the lifeguard had shrilled his whistle. But Paul had felt proud of his energetic young son that day—PJ pushing the limits.

Paul shouldered through the bathroom door, wondering how soon Evvy would arrive. He pulled out his cell and phoned up to the birth floor. He was told his wife was unchanged. Paul was heading toward the elevators, toward Sarah, as his cell buzzed again. This time, Evvy sounded edgier, the old take-charge Evvy Paul had never much liked. She wanted to drop PJ at the front lobby entrance. Then she'd go park in visitor parking so she could see Sarah.

So would Paul come get PJ? Evvy asked as if he might actually refuse.

"Sure, of course, I'm coming," Paul told Evvy, turning in what he hoped was the right direction. "But Sarah's in labor. I've got to get back up to her—"

"I'll sit with Sarah for a bit," Evvy told Paul like he had no say. "You need to take care o' PJ. He's not drunk but the cops said he's been taking these . . . ephedrine tablets or some-such. Over-the-counter and he overdosed on 'em. PJ calls 'em mini-thins—"

"*What?*" Paul asked, not sure he'd heard right.

"You'll have to ask your son," Evvy replied, and cut him off.

✦

"GodDad, it was like . . . lights, lights all around us and we, the cops and me, in our, in their squad car . . . We were way in the back of this whole, like, *herd* of cop cars. So many lights flashing so fast you couldn't see. I couldn't see, but I could *hear* this cop up front on a bullhorn saying to clear the area. And these FBI guys ran right by our car carrying, like, A-K machine guns or whatever. Then the cop up front in *our* car, the older nicer one? He goes, 'get down!' So me and the other cop, we *do!*

"We duck down after the FBI guys run by and then our guy, the driver-cop guy, he like speed-backs-up and zooms 'round to Memorial Drive so he can—so we can secure the exit and shit. Then we sit there, all sitting up, all of us, me and the cops, watching for him. Them."

"The shooters. The Bombers," Paul filled in, facing PJ in a corner of the vast hospital lobby, trying to follow what his son was saying. He'd hugged PJ hard when Evvy in her Jetta had dropped him at the doors. Then he'd pulled PJ to a corner of the lobby while Evvy whizzed off to park, so, as Evvy had commanded, he and PJ could talk.

"Yeah, yeah. The shooters *are* the Bombers, Dad. That's what they all were saying there on the . . . the *scene!*" PJ grinned as if he'd captured those Bombers himself, his pupil-filled eyes vibrating with a different kind of high.

His ruddy, unshaven face lit up like he was describing a religious experience. *Or maybe*, Paul thought as PJ began pacing hyper circles around him, *PJ's still just mini-thin high.* Paul's relief at seeing PJ safe was shaded now with anger that PJ had put himself in danger in the first place, that Evvy was on her way up to see Sarah, up where Paul should be right now.

"Calm down, Peej. It wasn't some . . . some scene on a TV show. You know that, right?"

PJ halted his pacing steps and shot Paul a sour, offended look. His pumped-up face deflated. "'Course I know that! I'm trying to *tell* you it wasn't like TV. It *was*, like, for *real*. I was there for *real*, in the middle of it *all*."

Here PJ's glazed pop-eyes finally met Paul's, and Paul couldn't stop himself, couldn't not unload on PJ once he finally had the kid's attention.

"But Peej, you were keeping those cops *from* doing their job in the middle of it all. Didn't you know if you mentioned the bomber, they'd go ballistic? Is that *why* you said the bomber . . . to get us all, on this night of all nights with Sarah in labor, in danger, to get us all paying attention to *you?*"

PJ's face closed up into his usual, sullen frown. Paul regretted his own badgering words. *Just trying to get attention,* therapists at the Center were always saying of the patients, and Paul had always hated that reductive phrase. PJ had been trying to explain something bigger to Paul, but now he was whining in his old teenage way.

"Oh yeah, right. That's what *you'd* think of me, *Dad.*" Heavy sarcasm on the "Dad." Paul tried to interrupt, start over, but PJ was turning from him, stalking from the lobby corner, heading toward the lobby TV and the small, quiet group gathered 'round it. "Yeah, right. I'm always just trying to get attention." PJ raised his voice too loud as he approached the long lobby couches. A dozen or so spectators were there, some in orderlies' uniforms, fixed like everyone everywhere in Boston on a big-screen TV.

Paul hurried to catch up with his son. PJ was reaching in his denim jacket pocket. At least Paul still had the knife in his own pants pocket. Christ, he probably should have thrown that knife away. Did PJ even remember giving it to him?

PJ halted in front of the wildly brightened TV. Above him, onscreen, there was a blue-lit image of police cars herding together, just as PJ had described. A big-lettered news crawl headline announced: CAR-JACKING FOLLOWS MIT SHOOTING.

The lobby denizens leaned toward that TV, their eyes on the screen, not on PJ. Paul made himself step toward his son. *Paul,* Paul coached himself to call PJ as his darting glance snagged on his father. Other eyes began watching Paul, too, like Center residents watched him when he arrived to subdue someone going off.

"Hey, yo. I got something to say!" PJ hopped up on an oversized, rectangular coffee table under the TV, partly blocking the screen.

"Outta the way there, boy," an old man complained, other heads nodding in lobby solidarity. Oblivious, PJ yanked out and waved some sort of battered news clipping.

"Yo, lookie here. My claim to fame," PJ announced in his strange, stagey voice. All of the dozen distracted people arrayed around him craned their heads to see the TV.

—THE CARJACKING TOOK PLACE AT A GAS STATION ON MEMORIAL DRIVE, APPARENTLY PERPETRATED BY THE TWO BOMBING SUSPECTS—

With the elaborate care of a drunk, PJ unfolded his tattered clipping. Paul halted about two feet in front of his son, hesitating. He wanted to lunge at him and lift him down from that table like PJ was his old, hyper kid-self. As he cleared his throat, PJ towered on the table, temporarily taller than Paul—and permanently stronger.

He squared his big shoulders, and stiffly began to read. Maybe only Paul could hear PJ's words under the louder, surer TV voices going on and on about the carjacking.

"'Damaged gravestones, goalposts, and a raw cow's tongue were left in an Elyria High School student's wake Sunday night on the All Saints Cemetery grounds'."

"PJ, knock it off." Paul stepped closer. PJ kept reading, picking up speed.

"'In All Saints Cemetery, police found what they believe to be a shrine near a gravestone that had been knocked over. Officer Ron Palmer discovered the raw cow's tongue, half a bottle of vodka, candles, and a white, unidentified food substance on a plate. Palmer said the teen'—that's me, folks—'was armed with a jackknife and has been cooperating with police.'"

"PJ, get down. Now." Paul braced himself to grab PJ. The news voice cut off as taped footage involving explosions played onscreen. PJ raised his head to add an aside.

"Yeah, I cooperated, but I didn't rat out my witchy woman." He bowed his head over the clipping again, reading fast to get it all in. "'"It is a bizarre situation," Palmer stated. "We're trying to gather information on what type of folks would engage in that type of activity."'"

Paul snatched the flimsy clipping from PJ's hands. Muffled explosions continued on the TV screen the other impatient lobby waiters were now standing up to see.

"Me too!" PJ announced as if Paul had done nothing. He threw up his hands. "*I'm* trying to figure out what type o' folk . . ." He stared down at Paul, wobbling.

Paul clenched the clipping in his fist, crumpling it.

When he'd gotten the call at work in late October that PJ had been arrested for vandalism, Paul left his Center office, phoned Sarah, and drove off onto I-90, heading for Ohio. He'd heard on the radio as he drove how the truck driver father of the latest high school student gunman had unhooked his freight truck load when he'd gotten his own call. He'd driven straight to his murderer son in only his truck cab. When Paul reached Nana by phone, she insisted he turn back. She said PJ didn't want to see him, said PJ was fine. Exhausted, Paul nearly wept with relief to hear her say that PJ had not mutilated an actual cow in some psycho-killer rage, but had bought the raw tongue at a damn Cleveland deli.

For some sort of spell he and some girl tried to cast, was all PJ had admitted.

"Outta our way," the unofficial lobby spokesman demanded. About to call security? Paul took hold of PJ's arm, a strong arm. He glared up at PJ, haloed by the big, blurry, bright TV screen, still showing night footage of a firefight. HOMEMADE GRENADES HURLED AT CAMBRIDGE POLICE, a newsman was explaining.

Everyone was standing up and stepping closer to see it all, closing in on PJ and Paul.

"What was that spell?" Paul asked, low-voiced, trying the old trick of getting the crazy talking about something, anything. PJ shook off Paul's hold.

"Antifertility," PJ mumbled, swaying like he might fall. "But man, it backfired. Like, *double*." PJ jumped down from the table, bumping Paul.

Half-catching him, staggering with PJ's weight, Paul hauled PJ off to the side, away from the big-screen. A lone pair of hands gave a few flat, sarcastic claps.

PJ pawed at Paul's fist, tearing the crumpled clipping. "Now gimme that—"

"Wait, son." Paul gripped PJ's denim jacket arm again, harder.

—POLICE APPARENTLY ENGAGED IN A BRIEF FIRE-FIGHT AS SUSPECTS FLED IN THE CARJACKED SUV, HURLING WHAT ARE DESCRIBED AS HOMEMADE GRENADES IN THEIR WAKE—

Paul half-dragged PJ through the lobby toward a phone/snacks nook. He practically shoved PJ round the corner. "First off, what're you *on*?" Paul demanded low-voiced, keeping hold of both PJ and the clipping, wishing he could be both upstairs with Sarah and down here. "What're these mini-thin things?"

"Relax. They're, like, legal." PJ shook off Paul and turned to the soda machines. He hadn't been caught doing drugs since he was twelve and stole his mom's Valium. "That's how come the cops let me go, I guess. No weapon and no illegal substance. Plus I played nice when they asked their questions. Like, they really thought I might be, like, this dangerous dude."

Was PJ dangerous? Paul could feel the knife still hanging heavy in his pants pocket. Was PJ going to try to seize it?

"The tablets you took, the mini-thins? That what's making you itch?"

"Took lotsa mini-thins. Just took some more they didn't find, see. I hid the mini-thins in gum wrappers, see. Yeah, they make me itch. Lotsa things makin' me itch." PJ nodded spastically toward a To ELEVATOR sign. "Yo, you gotta get back to Sarah, right? Evvy's up with her now, right?" PJ's dilated eyes finally met Paul's with alarming directness. PJ scratched his face, the scruffy beginnings of his own beard.

Paul squeezed PJ's crumpled clipping. "Christ, is *Evvy* your witchy woman? Not some girl? I always suspected Evvy had something to do with . . . with *this*." Paul raised his fist, the ridiculous Cow Tongue Incident inside. "What do you mean by antifertility? By it backfiring?"

"Hey, yo. No comment." PJ scratched his unshaven chin, a sound like sandpaper.

Paul cleared his unclearable throat, holding PJ's deranged gaze. Maybe PJ's brain was so addled by the Ephedrine or whatever that he didn't remember kissing Sarah. Or maybe there had been no kiss at all? Paul held out the balled-up clipping, just to get PJ to stop scratching.

PJ snatched the clipping back.

Paul drew a deep breath to steady his voice. Christ, he smelled cigarettes. He'd done this for years with his dad, with patients at the Shelter then at the Center. His one true talent: talking calm to crazies. "What happened today when you visited Sarah? Something happened that's upsetting her. I want to know what."

"I—I need a drink." PJ sounded suddenly whiny. "You got a dollar, Dad, for a Dr. Pepper?" Then he was singing falsetto style: "'Dr. Pepper, so misunderstood. If anyone would *try* him, they'd find he taste goo-oo-ood.'"

Paul shoved PJ against the soda machine. The whole thing shuddered.

—SUSPECTS ON THE RUN, the faint lobby TV voices announced from far away. A MASSIVE MANHUNT UNDERWAY—

Paul and PJ stood toe to toe, Paul still, and always, taller. PJ gaped up at Paul from under his thicker-than-ever Stratidakis brow. His back pressed the Plexiglas that shielded the subtly vibrating bottles inside.

PJ didn't blink. "You think it *is* my fault she's here."

"No, no." Paul struggled to keep his voice steady. "Whatever happened with Sarah today is not your fault, not only yours." PJ's dilated eyes stayed so maddeningly blank and black that Paul pushed on, if only to get the kid to listen. "Sarah and me, right before she started bleeding, we were in bed—"

"Having, like, sex?" PJ's stare glinted with dim dismay, belying his calmly mocking tone. "Last summer, Dad, seems like you didn't hardly even, like, look at her . . ."

An elevator *binged*; A doctor was paged, a tensely calm voice, "Stat. Four."

"Last summer?" Paul took hold of PJ's firm, newly muscular shoulders. The kid could take him in a fight if it came to that. "What's last summer got to do with anything? I was tending to your dying granddad, someone had to, and working my butt off trying to earn my new salary. That's what I was doing last summer. And what were you doing, besides screwing up your Center job and hanging round Spy Pond with Sarah and Evvy?" PJ tilted his head sideways, rubbing, itching against his denim collar. Was he even listening? "Look, yeah, I've gotta get back up to Sarah, but you know Sarah's upset, and I need to know why. She said something about PJ and a kiss . . ."

PJ blinked. He managed, despite Paul's grip, a two-shouldered shrug.

"*What kiss?*" Paul shook PJ. The jackknife shook inside Paul's pants pocket, too.

PJ's head bobbed, then snapped upright. His pupil-filled eyes briefly focused.

"Y'know, you guys keep acting like I'm, like, the least important person here. But maybe I'm . . ." PJ's eyes shifted as if in a dream, under closed lids, "the most."

"What in hell do you mean?" Paul seized PJ's denim collar. Someone in white was passing by, slowing down. Paul felt foolish, conspicuous, but kept hold. "What'd you mean, most important?" Paul cleared his throat, trying to follow the wild implications of PJ's words. "What'd you mean before when you kept saying you *did* this to her?"

PJ heaved another effortful shrug. He stunk of sweat and sour breath.

"That maybe . . ." PJ half-closed his wholly dilated eyes, talking in a dreamy, musing voice. "She and me. Maybe the baby, it's, like . . ." He finished with a teasing question, his voice high and boyish, "mine?"

Spring, 2012

Sarah pumped her bike pedals passionately, zoomed along the Minuteman Trail in Lexington, straining to keep up with PJ. On his sleek, rented bike, he had shot ahead of her and Paul, his broad back hunched. His legs pumped hard, working off unburnable energy. He disappeared around a leafy green bend. Sarah upped her own shaky speed; her spokes whirred.

Ahead of her, Paul pedaled hard on his creaky, older bike, too, maybe afraid to let wired-up, eighteen-year-old PJ out of his sight. This whole, tense first weekend of PJ's week-long March visit, Sarah had been braced for Paul's son to blow up in some new way.

How will she survive this PJ week without him confronting her over that damn card he sent in February? She gulped in cool, mid-March air; her ponytail streamed behind her. It was a relief to be out of the condo. PJ sulked behind his iPhone, barely meeting her eyes. It was freeing to be on this trail again.

"Feels good," Paul called over his shoulder, "if the kid doesn't kill us!"

Sarah and Paul used to bike the Minuteman nearly every weekend: the trail wound from Cambridge through Belmont and Lexington to Bedford. Then Sarah read that regular biking, for men, can further lower sperm counts, the balls pressed too close to the body when riding.

Today, she surprised Paul and PJ both when she broke the tense computer game-bleeping silence in their condo with her suggestion.

"Guess he was serious 'bout racing us," Sarah panted to Paul, catching up to him. Her legs pumped so fast her red bike shuddered.

"Guess you're the only one . . . who can tell when . . . he's serious . . ." Paul panted back.

Sarah hunched her head like PJ's, leaning around the bushy bend. She didn't think Paul suspected anything odd between her and PJ—not that there's anything real to suspect. That's what made this visit so—PJ might say—freaky.

PJ whizzed onto the turn to Lexington, led Sarah and Paul toward the

Battle Green. He knew the way from the times they'd biked here in previous springs; Sarah was always happy to bring Paul's boy to this Green where other families parade their perfect, sunlit offspring.

Today, PJ slung his shiny bike down beside their usual bench. Still wearing his rented helmet, he stalked from the bench toward the tallest park monument. Usually he and Sarah visited it together, tossing their pennies at its copper-cluttered base, making their separate wishes.

Does this mean, *Sarah wondered as she pedaled past Paul*, PJ wants to talk to me alone? *Sarah wobbled to a stop ahead of Paul, and leaned her bike against their bench.*

"Hey Peej, wait up," she called out breathlessly, hearing Paul roll up behind her.

She strode toward the tall, granite memorial to the Green's fallen dead, the Sons of Liberty. Yes, her Blended Family *book would advise getting hidden tensions out in the open. They would sagely say PJ was just testing boundaries, but didn't he push those boundaries way further than the upbeat book could imagine?*

Sunlight hit Sarah's flushed face and helmet. Sarah's mother, if she could still speak coherently, would advise restraint. Sarah hiked the long, grassy slope, past the golden-haired children gamboling in the sun, up toward her stepson brooding in the monument's shadow. Would her mother be right? Had she been right to pretend PJ's card lines were—and maybe they were—a provocative poem, an over-the-top joke? An impulse he now regreted?

Sarah halted beside PJ. She slipped off her helmet and shook back her mussed ponytail. She fixed her eyes, like his, on the monument's carved words.

BLESSED BE THE BLOOD OF MARTYRS!!

PJ muttered between the iron bars, flatly, "It's you, exclamation point."

An old joke between them: how the longwinded 1700's inscription used two, and even three exclamation points. Sarah set down her helmet. Straightening, she took hold of two cool, rusted bars. She kept a careful pair of bars between her and stony-profiled PJ. He still had on his helmet, his coarse, black hair sticking up under the straps.

Abruptly, PJ butted his head forward. His helmet clanked the bars.

"Talk to me, Peej," Sarah said as the bars vibrated.

"Thanks," he answered through clenched teeth. "Thanks for your thank you note, exclamation point. Glad you liked my so-called poem, exclamation point, exclamation point."

Sarah's face burned. "I-I've been wanting to talk to you about that, that birthday card. Peej, you know you shouldn't have sent it. That-that poem you—"

"It wasn't a quote poem unquote, exclamation, exclamation, exclamation!" PJ butted his helmeted head on the bars: clank, clank, clank.

Iron vibrated; sun-kissed families stared. Had Paul on the far bench seen or heard?

"Yes, OK. Believe me, Peej, I do know that." Sarah gripped the bars; her hands ached. Clustered wish-pennies scattered in the grass at the monument's base.

PJ let go of his bars. He began digging in his jeans' pocket.

"But you know," Sarah added, "you just shouldn't have sent it. I'm your stepmother . . ."

"Wish you weren't." PJ pitched his penny hard. It pinged, bounced off the monument base, flashed then fell. PJ turned and thrust a penny at Sarah.

"So wha'do you wish?" From under his astronaut helmet, PJ shot her his old "dare you" stare. Their eyes collided; she clutched the penny.

"PJ, listen." Sarah kicked her helmet in the grass, an emptied half egg. "I haven't been thinking straight, or-or acting straight. I'm sorry if I've given you the wrong idea, and I want you to know I-I've stopped wanting, stopped wishing for a baby."

"Yeah, right, exclamation point." PJ tore at his chin strap, yanking off his helmet. "You talk about thinking straight or whatever. Can't you say anything straight to me anymore?"

With both hands, with a basketball whoosh, PJ hurled his helmet over the spiked fence top. It cracked hard against the granite, rolled into the grass. It rocked; pennies glinted all around it.

PJ leaned close to whisper, his breath hot in her ear, "Dad might buy your story, but I know how bad you still want a baby . . ."

Sarah shut her eyes hard, her tears as hot as his breath. PJ did know. PJ, with his own secret and unburnable passion.

"I know you know," she found herself saying, but he pulled away fast.

"PJ, wait," Sarah called, blinking, her throat tight. He'd gone. He brushed past the wobbly toddlers on the sloping stretch of green, and marched toward the bench where his father sat and his bike lay.

PJ mounted the bike, riding off without a nod to Paul, without his helmet. Standing, Paul shot a distant, questioning gaze at Sarah. She raised her hands as if—she is—at a loss. With a shake of his head, without his own helmet, Paul mounted his bike. He pedaled off after PJ in the direction of Lexington Center, the teeming Massachusetts Avenue traffic.

Stop! Sarah wanted to shout, but she sunk to her knees in the shadowed grass. She lifted her helmet, gazing through the bars at PJ's white helmet, the unreachable second half to a whole egg. It's true she'd never stop wanting a baby. Copper wish-pennies blurred with her tears.

And something else may be true. Sarah couldn't stop this crazy thought, cradling her empty helmet. She may be losing, with PJ, her last chance to get pregnant.

Chapter Five

April 18, 2013: 11:20 p.m.

Hard Labor

Sarah surfaced, hoarse and gasping. The suffocating pain wave had subsided enough so she could breathe. She blinked. Her vision blurred, but that familiar face was real.

Evvy Elfman. Evvy hovered over her like that summer Spy Pond day: Evvy's feathery hair wavering into a fuzzy halo tonight from tears, not heat. No kiss had woken Sarah this time. Evvy's skin was not tanned, but winter white and lined with concern.

She was trying to meet Sarah's unfocussed gaze.

"You're—here?" Sarah croaked, needing more water. Beyond Evvy, she heard her rubber-soled nurse padding away. The nurse who had—it seemed long ago but must've been only minutes— told Sarah that Paul would be back soon and not to push yet.

Pushing too soon would swell up her cervix and make it all harder, the nurse had said. She had urged Sarah to try what she called a Pelvic Rock. *Oh shut up*, Sarah had longed to answer. *Don't go*, Sarah wanted to call now.

The room door thumped, sealing Sarah and Evvy in together.

"I just picked up PJ at—well, never mind all that. Paul's got PJ now, and I just had to check up on you, kiddo. Been sitting here . . ." Evvy bent closer in her black E. E.'S KARATE & KICKBOXING T-shirt. The scent of her aloe soap and dried sweat cleared Sarah's head. "Lucky I knew a shortcut here. I got a friend who lives nearby. Works in the lab. Lord, half of Memorial Drive was shut off after those crazy Bombers carjacked an SUV or some such. PJ was totally zonked out, and we listened to the radio news in the car all the way here . . ."

"Wha—?" Sarah felt a dim flutter of panic. "Where's PJ now? Where's Paul?"

"No place bad, sweets. Down in the lobby. I brought your overnight bag with me. PJ said it was yours. Wha'd you pack in there, rocks? Lookie, I'll go down in a minute and take over with PJ. He's gonna be all right. I just wanted to give him and Paul a chance to talk . . ."

"Talk?" Sarah managed, the very word giving her pain. She tensed her aching lower back and tried to pull herself upright, but she felt the tug of wires. Wires taped to her belly, under her gown. The Pelvic Rock nurse had done it. Jelly on Sarah's belly then the subtle tug of wires, the *blip blip* above her head like sounds from an aquarium.

"Look PJ—he got sprung from them police. The ones who, sounds like, drove you to the hospital? You been through plenty already tonight. You don't need to be worrying over PJ. Whatever's goin' on with PJ, I'm guessing Paul can handle it, hon. At least 'til I get down there. Just had to see you first. Here, I brought you a bloodstone—for protection."

Evvy opened her palm, a polished, reddish brown stone gleaming there, small and shiny. Sarah couldn't rally a thank you, her belief in witchcraft evaporating.

"Just gimme some ice," she rasped.

"Sure thing, sweetie." Evvy hopped up, blocking the TV-sized monitor screen on a metal cart, blips and jagged electric lines Sarah couldn't read.

The real TV screen was on without sound. Sarah shut her eyes against its light. With a mouthwatering, crackling sound, Evvy reappeared holding a cup of ice. Sarah kept her head on the pillow; she opened only her lips. Evvy, bless her, slipped ice chips in her mouth. Sarah sucked, bracing herself against a coming contraction. She glanced at the clock by the bed. Almost midnight. When had the last cramp taken hold?

"Five," Sarah burst out before she lost the ability to speak. Evvy frowned at her, not understanding. *You idiot!* Sarah wanted to shriek. But Evvy slipped another soothing chip between Sarah's lips. She sucked hard against her re-tightening muscles.

My contractions—I think they're about five minutes apart, she couldn't say.

Bleep, bleep, the baby through its monitor replied. *I'm here, I'm here.*

The only one who matters, Sarah thought. *But where is everyone else?* She threw back her head, transported into another black tunnel. She puffed breathlessly, trying not to push.

She focused on Evvy's T-shirt, KARATE & KICKBOXING: the second K faded so it looked through Sarah's blur like ICKBOXING.

Ick, Ick. Sarah chanted to herself instead of counting. Ice crackled in the cup Evvy thrust forward. It bumped Sarah's chin. She had drool on her chin, but she had no strength to wipe it.

"So . . . PJ . . . talk?" Sarah managed as the ice slipped down her throat.

"Yep, PJ talked to me in the car on the way here," Evvy answered distantly, "after I picked him up when the Belmont Police was done babysitting him. PJ said he'd shot off his mouth to those cops and wound up being driven out to MIT and the whole crime scene and all. PJ said it all made him wish he was a cop himself, if you can believe that. Anywho, the cops searched PJ and gave him a breath-o-thingy. Found nothing. But listen, you tell me. What on earth happened with you an' that boy today?" She slipped Sarah another ice sliver: the ice as clear as Evvy's bluish-grey eyes. Sharp eyes that Sarah always sensed saw right through her.

"He, PJ? He acted so crazy. He steal, the, the . . ." Sarah swallowed, straining to stay lucid, to remember even Evvy didn't know about the card. "PJ and Paul, they . . . t-talking?"

"Well, PJ's probably talking, babbling away. Police said he was high on this drugstore-cowboy over-the-counter asthma thingy. Ephedrine. Maybe he still is high, that boy . . ."

"Stop them," Sarah keened, her voice strained with the tightness gathering again, relentless below her wired-up belly. "PJ . . . outta his head."

"And this little Mama's outta hers," the Pelvic Rock nurse called through the curtain, sneaking up on them. "You keep her calm now. All this TV talk and manhunt business is riling everyone up tonight. An' don't you listen to what-all she says. Her oxygen's falling from her brain to the, y'know, the site of the birth . . ."

"Pussy?" Sarah broke in, a word she'd rarely spoken. "Brain's in my pussy?"

Evvy snorted her old Evvy laugh. Sarah halfway laughed, too, then she choked. What had she been trying so hard to tell Evvy? She was coughing, gripping hold of Evvy's T-shirt, crumpling up the ICKBOXING. "God, Evvy, PJ . . . you gotta go keep watch on him . . ."

"Why, sweetie? Wha'd that boy do today? Wha'd he steal?"

Sarah shook her head, not strong enough to explain the card she'd so stupidly kept secret. She drew a big breath, her breasts straining the maternity bra she'd worn all day.

Bleep, bleep: Those baby blips, maybe quicker. Panicked now, too? Wasn't it panic over PJ's visit that had made Sarah push Paul for sex? Now, Sarah wished she could tell Evvy that the baby would pay the price for every reckless, needy thing she'd done.

"Look, Sarah, sweetie," Evvy gently eased Sarah's grip from her shirt. "I'll take care o' PJ. You've gotta forget 'bout PJ for now." The shirt uncrumpled. Sarah fixed intently on Evvy's ICK, Evvy's sure voice. "You can't dwell on all PJ's nonsense now. You can't think straight, sweets, so don't try. Just remember, whatever ol' PJ has been feeling 'bout you, nothing really happened between you two . . ."

Sarah shook her head harder. *Yes*, but she wanted to say no, too. She wanted to tell Evvy about that last Spy Pond day, the day Sarah had strained not to think about or dwell upon, only there was no stopping anything inside her now.

"Sarah?" Evvy asked insistently. "Sarah, you even hearing me?"

"You hearing me?" Pelvic Rock opened the curtain. She scolded Evvy, telling her to stop upsetting this mother. *I'm this mother*, Sarah reminded herself, the tunnel blackness closing in again. "Go find the father," the nurse ordered Evvy. "We need that damn father up here now."

"Yes, sure. I'll fetch him," Evvy was saying, jumping up as if eager to leave, the Pelvic Rock nurse telling Sarah yet again not to push—not yet.

Bleep, bleep, the baby was agreeing, pleading. *Not now. Not yet.*

Sarah stiffened her body, all her muscles clenched around her baby. All of Sarah's skin felt stretched, her body swollen with everything she was trying to hold inside, everything that was just about to—Sarah's last thought before the black—burst out.

⚫

Her eyes were shut but vibrated with red. She half-wakened, half-buried in gritty, sun-heated sand, so her eyes behind her shut lids could see. Seeing red: August afternoon sun pulse.

I should get up, Sarah told her sleepy self. Lately, she hadn't been sleep-ing well.

Spy Pond splashed; kids not her own laughed. She stirred her legs, but heavy, damp sand pinned them in place. PJ's hands had patted the sand onto her body, his and Evvy's hands, and laughs. It was almost the first time he'd touched her all summer, except for a few awkward hugs.

Usually, PJ would just show up at the pond and practice his karate moves with Evvy or swim laps around Sarah. Usually, it was easy to chat with PJ over picnic lunches as long as Evvy was there, chat almost like old times. Sarah kept her eyes shut, lying still as a mummy.

It had seemed a good sign, playful, when Evvy started burying Sarah in sand and PJ joined in, goofing around like they used to do when PJ was younger, like they could still do—maybe.

PJ is supposed to call Paul, Sarah reminded herself. Sun pulsed on her lids; her brain filled with facts: How PJ had promised he'd call Paul at the Center and make sure what time his afternoon shift began; how last week, PJ had virtually kidnapped a Center kid, not signing her out. Just because, PJ claimed, the kid wanted to see her old, favorite staffer Sarah. "Maria Z. needs to see you," PJ had announced as he and Maria burst into Sarah's kitchen. "Just like me."

A half-smile curved Sarah's lips. Although it had been all wrong for PJ to go AWOL with that kid, she loved to be needed that way. Maybe she'd never have a baby of her own, but she had her stepson and her art therapy students. She widened her smile to think of spreading her arms so wide to hug both PJ and plump, bouncy Maria Z.

One safe way to hug PJ, feeling like mom of the whole world.

As Sarah smiled widest, her eyes still shut, she felt it. First, the cooling shadow from the sun; then, the kiss on her lips. Warm and light.

"PJ?" Sarah mumbled, alarmed. She blinked her sandy-lashed eyes.

"Naw, just little ol' me." Evvy's shadowed face and glittery wet hair hovered above Sarah. Evvy's smirk mocked the lip-to-lip kiss she'd just bestowed.

"God . . ." Sarah squinted in sun. "H-how long've I been—?"

"In love with me? Or no, sweet Sarah, me in love with you?" Evvy laughed in her flip way, shaking her head hard. Chill droplets speckled Sarah's sunburnt face, delicious nips of wet. Sarah needed that like she'd needed the brightness of Evvy's, of PJ's, eyes upon her all summer. Private antidotes to Paul's dutiful but distracted gaze, this summer.

Just for the summer, Sarah told herself sternly now, lowering her eyes from Evvy's, not getting drawn into any love talk with Evvy.

"Listen, where's PJ?" Sarah shifted under her packed sand, cracking the sun-dried crust. Beneath that crust, the sand against her skin felt damp and heavy as cement. "What've you two done to me?"

"What've you done to us, sugar?" Evvy drawled, still jokey. "PJ's gone to call his dad about his shift today. Poor kid's scared Paul'll somehow've found out about last week, him taking that Maria Z. girl without permission and all. And I told PJ—" Evvy shook her head again, "you won't tell on him."

"But." Sarah summoned her strength and sat. Chunks of sand, dry mixed with damp, crumbled off her upper body. Sticky sand lodged under her T-shirt and inside her swimsuit, grains itchy between her breasts. "Look, Evvy, I did tell. I felt like I had to. I told Paul this morning. But Paul—" she added fast as Evvy tensed her tan face so its lines showed. "Paul promised he wouldn't punish PJ, wouldn't even tell PJ that I told. Paul would never've forgiven me if I hadn't. I mean, Paul's in charge down there. He needs to know so he can keep better watch over PJ, so PJ won't do something worse. Plus, you know . . ." Sarah brushed off more sand chunks, looking away from Evvy's disapproving frown. "He's my husband. It's corny and all, but I've always told Paul . . . well, everything . . ."

"Oh yeah?" Evvy scrambled up off her knees. She peered down at Sarah from the jagged sunlit halo of her hair. "'So you gonna tell big ol' Paul that little ol' me kissed you?"

Sarah managed a sheepish grin, though Evvy's tone was no longer quite so joking.

"Yo, Sarah—" PJ's shout; startlingly loud and near. "Sar-ahh!"

The small cluster of moms down the beach stopped chatting. Mom heads turned. Beyond Evvy, shirtless PJ strode up the stretch of dirty sand, stepping over a sprawled out teenage girl. His broad, tattooed shoulders moved with his strides. His black-haired head lowered like a bull's.

"You gonna tell Paul everything about," Evvy lowered her drawl, "your terrific, terrible mid-life talent? For making everyone fall in love with you?"

At that, Evvy Elfman spun on her heel. She jogged in her boyish tank-top swimsuit to the water's edge. She kept jogging and splashed in.

Sarah longed to follow. She hoisted up her knees, breaking through layered sand. PJ stampeded toward her so fast she thought he wouldn't stop. He'd run her down.

"Yo Sarah. Where's your girlfriend?" PJ halted, with a mad skid of sand.

"My what?" Sarah brushed crust from her knees, the dampest sand caked between her thighs. "You mean Evvy? C'mon, she was kidding around. She just dove in again to cool off."

"Cool off is right, Stepmommy. I saw that kiss or whatever she planted on you." PJ switched to mock singsong. Sarah stopped trying to clean off her dirt and sand. "How 'bout I tell on Stepmom-mee, just like she tell on mee?"

"What're you saying, Peej?" Sarah squinted up. "You mean Paul, he—?"

"He fuckin' busted me." PJ folded his arms over his hairy, bared chest. His eyes glinted in the sun, purplish black like the slashing Chinese characters tattooed on his shoulders. Symbols PJ had refused to decipher. Now I'll never find out what they mean, *Sarah thought dumbly as PJ pushed on.* "I call in to check what time I'm due, an' I find out I'm already late. Then dad, he goes ballistic, saying he can't let me keep pulling this crap, and I'm like, wha'd you mean 'keep' and he's like, you think I don't know things? He knows all about how I—he says it could be called this—kidnapped Maria Z."

Sarah drew a shaky breath to speak, but PJ shifted back to singsong, narrowing his eyes in a Paul-style glare. "Dad won't say how he knew, but I see it written all over you."

Sarah shook her head to his quick, bitter rhythm. "OK, PJ. I'm really sorry, but I did tell. I should've told you I was going to tell. I never thought he'd—"

"Fire me?" *PJ cut in.* "Anyhow, Dad seemed like he was about to fire me, so I up and quit."

"Oh no. Oh, PJ, let's talk about this . . ." *Sarah heaved herself onto her knees, more sand crumbling off her, a mini avalanche, a hopeless mess.* "You knew breaking any Center rule would piss off Paul, Peej. He's got your temper, or you've got his. But you know, too, Paul's always fair, willing to talk things out—"

"Out is right." *PJ's stiff karate chop nearly sliced her nose. His hand dropped.* "OK, whatever. I'm out—outta here. I just wanna say . . . bye."

"Bye?" *Sarah stared up from her knees, lightheaded.* "PJ, don't leave like this, mad like this. Where will you go? Back to Ohio?"

"Maybe." *PJ shrugged like it didn't matter where. Abruptly, he dropped down on his knees, facing Sarah. He took hold of her sandy shoulders. He steadied her, eye to eye.*

PJ's black Paul eyes glittered. He told Sarah in a harsh, smoky whisper, "Yo, I won't tell Dad 'bout you kissing Evvy if you . . . kiss me goodbye."

His gaze stayed "dare you" steady. So close, his black-eyed, bristly face looked more than ever like Paul. Her Paul, only younger than Sarah had ever seen him.

"Kiss you?" *Sarah saw her own tiny face waver in PJ's inky eyes. She was melting in the heat.* "Oh Peej, don't ask that." *She swayed on her knees.* Maybe, *she thought,* I'm fainting. Maybe I'm pregnant. *PJ pulled her toward him, hugging her hard like she hadn't let him do all summer. PJ's heart thumped with hers.*

"You know I can't do that," *Sarah mumbled, trying to push him away, but his stronger, younger arms tightened.*

PJ hugged her harder, mumbling in her ear, "You know I want way more than a freaking kiss . . . Want to give you . . . what you want . . ."

"'Course I know." *Sarah shook her sandy-haired head no and started to pull away again.*

"So quit acting like you don't!" PJ smoothed her braid, its gritty twisted bumps. Sarah shook her head harder, no and no, pushing at him harder.

"You quit." Sarah thrust PJ away decisively, her hands braced on his damp-haired chest. His nipples standing up, darkest brown like Paul's. His heart under her hands thudded. Sarah yanked her hands back and heaved herself to her feet, her heart thudding as heedlessly as his. "No. I'm saying no. I mean, yes, I do know what you want. You know I do. And you understand, maybe more than anyone else, how much I want a baby. But look, I shouldn't've let you want me like you did—like you do. I shouldn't have let any of this happen inside you."

"Oh right, it's only in me. Sicko me." PJ scrambled to his feet, too. Sarah backed away from him and toward the woods edging the pond. She found herself stepping behind green-leaved forsythia bushes. She halted there, away from eyes she could feel watching from down the beach.

PJ followed her, facing her.

"Peej, look, I'm not saying it's just you. It's my fault, really . . ." Sarah hugged her hot, sandy skin. PJ stepped closer. "I should've been discouraging it. Your attention. I mean," she reminded herself and him, her voice cracking in exasperation, "I'm your mom."

"You're not." PJ dropped onto his knees again in front of her. This time, unsteadily, she stayed standing. "Wish you were," he mumbled, his voice suddenly shaky like hers. He was a little boy again on the wobbly verge of tears. "Wish I coulda been . . ." PJ embraced Sarah, wrapping his arms around her solid hips. "Your baby . . ."

"Peej . . ." Sarah stiffened up, her hands frozen at her sides. She stood stupidly still in the heat, feeling PJ's black-haired head press against her sandy T-shirt, her stomach, her belly that might never hold a baby of her own. "I wish that too . . ."

Was it OK for her to admit that?

PJ pulled himself upright, so he stood taller on his knees. He hugged her waist now. "Prove it," he mumbled, gazing up at her, daring her again. "Prove you love me . . . as much as a real mom . . ."

"Peej, what're you—?" Sarah straightened, raising her hands to push him back again.

"I'm hungry," PJ moaned, closing in, muffled by her T-shirt. He nuzzled between her breasts. She froze and gripped his big, unmovable shoulders.

"Feed me," PJ singsonged. His damp mouth pressed her shirt. He was kissing her stiff nippled breast through layers of cloth and bra.

"Stop!" Sarah shoved PJ back with both hands, with her full strength.

He staggered on his knees and stumbled up to his feet. He looked as stunned as she felt, his slack lips sandy, his face sweaty, his eyes blank and panicky. He shoved his hand into his cargo shorts pocket.

"Don't—" He told her as he brought it out fast, a metal gleam. At first Sarah blinked, not believing it. Her stepson shakily unfolded a compact knife.

He clicked the serious-looking blade open. PJ had bragged boyishly about his real jackknife. It was smaller than Sarah'd imagined, but its blade glinted, sharp. Sarah blinked in the sun haze, incredulous. Yes, PJ held a real knife, blade pointed to the sand.

"Don't you tell Dad," PJ mumbled to the sand, not to Sarah. "Don't you dare tell him. I mean it. Or, or . . ."

His hand holding the knife shook hard. God, would he stab her? No. He'd stab himself. Sarah stood frozen too, her thoughts whirling. She managed only to say, "Peej—"

"I gotta get away from here, from you," PJ muttered, still to the sand. He took a hurried, barefoot step back from her. He spun around on his bare heel in the sand, still holding the knife. "Gotta get away, or I don't know what I'll do."

These last words were louder. Not directed over his shoulder, but again at the dirty sand.

"No, Peej. Don't go now, like this." Sarah made her voice loud, too. Don't run with that thing, she wanted to say like a real mom.

As if hearing her unspoken words, PJ snapped his knife shut. Sarah stepped toward him, fumbling in her mind to find real words, the right words. Her heart thumped with delayed fear at the click of that knife. She knew she should tell him again not to go.

But PJ was already running. He ducked around the bush, stomping off down the beach. Sarah stepped from behind the bush, its leaves feverishly green in the sun, her head swimming. She swayed, gazing down the Spy Pond beach after rapidly retreating PJ. He started singing, loud enough for all the real moms to hear.

"New York City is the place where—"

Walk on the Wild Side; Sarah recognized its beat. Was PJ saying he'd run off to New York? Why wasn't she trying to stop him? She staggered toward the water, sand-cement cracking all over her skin. PJ disappeared down the beach.

Sarah waded into Spy Pond, up to her knees. Evvy swam obliviously, far out. God, she should call Paul right now, tell him everything. But wouldn't telling drive Paul and his son apart for good? The one son he might ever have? Wouldn't it drive her and Paul further apart, too? Sarah bent to splash water on her sticky, dirty skin, the Spy Pond sand not really sand, but sand mixed with dirt.

Sandy soil not meant, Sarah thought as she splashed her sun-heated skin, for play.

Paul sat guarding the men's room door, PJ inside. After he had blurted out his incredible claim—that this baby, Sarah's baby, might somehow be his—PJ had wrenched free of Paul and bolted for the bathroom, mumbling that he'd be right back. How many minutes had it been? Ten? Paul should go in there, he knew, but he couldn't move, couldn't face PJ again. Not yet.

Elevator floor tones were beeping around the corner. Inside Paul's head, unbidden, other numbers were spinning and taking on a fresh, ominous meaning. How Sarah's raised AFP level might've meant a baby further along than had been assumed. How maybe Sarah wasn't early today, but on time if she'd gotten pregnant sometime before they'd thought? Before she'd led him to believe? He'd suspected it with Adina, with reason. Maybe this time, somehow or other, it was true? But it couldn't be with Sarah. Paul's sperm count had risen only to what the doctors had deemed a borderline acceptable level after his surgery.

Hadn't Paul the pessimist instinctively doubted their so-called borderline miracle baby? But all that didn't add up to his son fucking his wife.

Anyhow, numbers weren't really what nagged at him now. Not numbers, no, but feelings he'd picked up on these last few years. Teenage PJ always watching Sarah, always drawing out his hugs. PJ cooking beside her, hip to hip, in the kitchen. A crush on her, Paul had joked with Sarah. An innocent, mother-hungry crush.

Paul stared blankly at the men's door. PJ was a man now. Paul looked down at his own large, older man hands, his dulled gold wedding band. He cracked his knuckles.

"There you be! You're harder to find than the damn Bombers!"

Paul startled at the southern-fried voice and the spidery touch on his shoulder. There she was, backing up with one light, combative step: Evvy Elfman. The middle-aged so-called witch who'd rescued PJ from the police; who'd inserted herself into his and Sarah's infertility treatments; who'd possibly inspired PJ into his cow tongue craziness; who'd so foolishly taken Sarah to watch her run the doomed marathon.

Yes, Paul sensed as he met Evvy's knowing blue grey gaze. She was somehow involved in whatever the hell was happening between his son and his wife. Yet, Evvy stood with her mussed, boy cut hair and her black martial arts uniform, facing him down like he was the criminal and she the cop.

"Glad you're back," he made himself say, finding it partway true. It was a relief to hand over PJ, at least. He could trust Evvy, who'd already come through for them tonight. "How's Sarah?"

"She's hanging in there. Her contractions are coming closer, but they're still telling her not to push. Look, I know you need to be up there. I can take over with PJ. How's he doing?"

"Not so good." Paul nodded toward the closed men's bathroom. Evvy sat beside Paul on the second of two welded-together plastic seats. "It's been a hell of a night, with the Bombers and police and all. You were just with PJ. You know how wound-up he is." Paul leaned toward Evvy, feeling like he was playing private dick. "PJ and I," Paul began awkwardly, "had quite the talk here few minutes ago."

"Quite the time to have 'quite the talk.'"

"Look, Evvy, you're the one who told us to talk. Now you and me need to talk. What in hell—you tell me this, and fast—what's been going on between my wife and you and PJ? What-all went on last summer? PJ keeps bringing it up."

"You wouldn't know, would you now, Paul? You were so out of it, so doggone depressed. So doggone bent on stopping Sarah from having your baby, which was all she ever wanted. What was going on? It woulda been pretty clear if you'd opened your eyes. Your kid, PJ, he had a big fat crush on Sarah. Hell, I had a crush on her. Seems like everyone last summer had a crush on Sarah—except you."

"Me? Look, what in all holy hell . . . ? This is my wife we're talking about. My wife and my baby. Only now my son's telling me this baby of hers may be—he said this—his."

"What? That lying shit said that? Where is he?" Evvy marched over toward the Men's. "In here?" Evvy sidestepped the door as it opened, and a bandaged boy, not PJ, limped out. The door swung shut. Evvy rapped on it, shouting: "PJ? You in there? PJ, you come out now!" Her strident voice echoed in the snack machine alcove. Paul stood and glanced back toward the lobby where PJ had already created one disturbance.

"Quiet; I'll get him." Paul stepped up and touched Evvy's arm to elbow her aside. She spun around karate quick.

She faced him with snapping eyes. "You get this first." Evvy had the sense to lower her voice as a nurse passed by. "Sarah busted her butt to have your baby, and you know it. I gave her that first god-awful shot myself. Then she had to beg you to have that lil' ol' outpatient surgery that got your count up."

"Got it borderline . . ."

"Whatever!" Evvy burst out in PJ-pitched exasperation. PJ himself pushed out of the Men's, so fast both Evvy and Paul stumbled sideways.

"Whoa there." Evvy caught her balance, half raising her hands as if to seize hold of him.

PJ faced Evvy and Paul, looking ready to lunge, too, his own half raised hands wet from the bathroom sink. His black, curly hair stuck up, like he'd scratched it all the wrong way. His doubly black, dilated gaze met Paul's glare.

"Are you still high?" Paul asked over Evvy's head, glad for this wiry, strong woman planted between him and PJ. "What's with these mini-thins? Did you take more in there?"

"Me, Dad-dee? I'm high on life. But I wanna get high on—" PJ took two zig-zag steps around Evvy to stand before Paul, "mommy milk."

PJ scratched at his bristly face with both hands. A passing doctor slowed his steps and fingered the pager strapped to his belt. The button for security emergency? Paul wished he could press such a button and eject himself.

"Mommy milk?" Paul repeated, his own tongue slow. He'd tasted, only hours ago, Sarah's warm, oystery breast milk. *What was PJ the bomb thrower claiming now?* PJ straightened up like a kid awaiting praise. Paul folded his arms, gripping his own elbows, fighting the urge to seize and shake PJ. "You stop talking about Sarah and making up crazy lies. Look at me. Sarah said something about a kiss."

"Kiss, schmiss." PJ snort laughed. "Didn't never kiss her, dad. Didn't want that. Thought I did, but didn't. Got down in front o' her like this . . ." PJ puckered his lips and dropped to his knees. He swayed on his knees, facing his father's crotch.

Paul stepped back fast, dumbstruck. A grandfatherly man by the soda machines watched disapprovingly, punching buttons extra hard. Was PJ going crazy for real? Right here on this craziest-ever night? Had some gear inside him slipped? A soda can thunked.

"Stop all this." Evvy tugged PJ's arm, forcing him to stand, murmuring to him.

As he stood frozenly staring, Paul recalled his first full day at the Waltham Wet Shelter: a hardy, old drunk throwing a chair out the upper window and trying to jump down after it. Paul and a muscleman staffer wrestled the poor guy back; a thumb jabbed Paul's eyeball. Paul knew as he sat in the smoke-choked staff room pressing an ice pack to his throbbing eye that he'd entered some new level of hell, but an official, professional hell. Freeing in a way, after years in unofficial Stratidakis family hell in a cramped apartment with his depressive mom, where you couldn't punch a time clock out.

"What's with him?" Paul directed his question at Evvy, grateful for her calm, brisk manner. Making himself step up to her and PJ. Evvy, who wouldn't make a bad Center staffer, took one of PJ's arms. Paul took the other. They led rubbery-limbed PJ to the chairs.

"He surely is high, for starters," Evvy told Paul. "Lookie, I'm gonna take him up to the cafeteria and dunk this boy's head in black coffee." Paul nodded gratefully, then he released PJ's loose, denim arm. PJ sank back in the plastic seat, maybe relieved, too, by Evvy's take charge manner. She clapped a hand on PJ's shoulder. "I'm used to his nonsense. Don't worry 'bout him, 'bout this new craziness he's talking. You get on up to Sarah. She's the one needing you now. So, dammit, get moving." Evvy pointed with her thumb to the elevator.

"Thanks." Paul nodded again. But he wondered, stepping numbly over to the elevator, if the southern charm Evvy was ladling out wasn't meant to distract him from what PJ was saying. PJ's supposed crazy talk—or was it?

At the elevator, Paul glanced back at Evvy and PJ. His son already sat up straighter, his drained, unshaven face so impassive Paul wondered if his outburst had been some act.

"Don't leave the hospital," Paul called out to Evvy. "Peej, you stay with Evvy. Evvy, you get him fed, and keep him calm. I'll come back down as soon as I can . . ."

Paul thumb-pressed the elevator button hard, thinking what real fathers surely never thought. *Get me the hell outta here.* Of course, what was he escaping to but another son, already in trouble?

A cheery *bing.* The oversized elevator doors sucked open.

"She's just jealous," PJ called as Paul stepped inside the empty elevator. PJ stood up. Tall for once beside small, startled Evvy. PJ pointed to Evvy with his thumb. "She jus' wishes the baby was Sarah's and her baby. Like I wish my baby was Sarah's and mine . . ."

Hadn't PJ just claimed the baby *was* Sarah's and his? What did he mean by "my baby?"

"What total bullshit," Evvy burst out indignantly. Paul pressed three urgently, his getaway ride.

But PJ called out as the doors shuddered, "Yo, whoa, I forgot. I got a card for you—"

The elevator doors sucked shut, sealing in Paul and his own

unstoppable thoughts. A card? The card PJ had mentioned long ago, by phone? Why was Evvy so defensive just then? Paul shook his head hard, like he was the drugged one. Evvy had given Sarah those first fertility treatment shots. Had she somehow also—God, who knew?—shot Sarah up with a turkey baster thing full of PJ's sperm? This completely whacked-out scenario made a twisted kind of sense as the elevator started its slow-motion climb.

Number one went out; number two lit up.

And what about those damn AFP levels? They had been high in Sarah's four-month blood tests; they could indicate a baby further along than expected. Had Sarah known that was the case with her? Was that why she had been so strangely adamant about refusing the recommended amnio? Hadn't he wondered about that at the time? And why had PJ cut his summer visit short in early August? Because he and Sarah had done the deed?

Either via insemination or, even more unimaginable, sex. Which might make this baby one or two months earlier than Paul had been led to believe? Led by the balls, into all of this?

The elevator halted with a bump at two. A burly aide maneuvered a grey metal cart on board, coffin-sized. A body inside? But didn't bodies ride on a special elevator? Paul flattened himself against the elevator wall, as far away from the death cart as possible. He held his breath, trying to hold back the absurd, paranoid thoughts crowding his mind.

The doors sucked shut again. Which was worse? Would Paul rather have PJ demented enough to tell such outrageous lies or depraved enough to have somehow slept with Sarah? Had she been crazy enough, baby-crazy, to let that happen? But she wasn't. Paul knew crazies, and Sarah wasn't one. The whole elevator shuddered. The death cart jiggled.

But hadn't PJ left a particularly strange phone message on his birthday in 2012, Paul remembered helplessly as the elevator climbed again. A message mentioning, in fact, a card. Hadn't Sarah's reaction been as strange as PJ's message? All this on the same night Sarah so surprisingly backed off on pushing for more infertility treatments, as if knowing somehow they weren't needed. Then later, in a phone call on PJ's own birthday, when Paul had asked him about his phone message, the kid hadn't seemed to remember any birthday card or message at all. Yet, he was shouting about a card tonight.

Paul startled; the elevator thumped to its stop. The big metal death cart clanked the elevator wall, sounding hollow. Paul half wished he could crawl inside its hidden coffin and simply sleep, but the reflective, metal doors sucked open onto the walkway to other wings. Paul stepped out, hesitated.

Which way was his wife?

⟡

"Wake up, mister supervisor. It's party time."

Paul blinked reluctantly. Sarah, dressed for the 2012 birthday he'd just as soon have slept through, shook him awake from his nap. Damn; she'd shut off his serene Schumann. He stretched on the couch. "But I love those little slices of death . . ."

A line about sleep from a vampire movie they'd stayed up late watching.

"Yeah," Sarah answered wryly, "it's those big slices of life that give you trouble. You didn't think I'd forget your fifty-second birthday, did you?"

"I had my hopes," Paul grumbled, but it was his playful, put-on grumble. He pulled himself upright, glad to see Sarah, down so often lately, awaiting his sperm count results, standing above him, bright-eyed and smiling. Ruefully, he scanned her new dress: olive green, low cut. "My time is up, huh?"

"Foolish mortal, you cannot escape me."

"What'll you do if I resist?" Paul switched to his mock supervisor voice. "Wrestle me into a four point restraint?"

"Whatever you want." Sarah bent over him. She kissed him, burrowing into his beard, her lips tasting of vanilla cake icing.

"I'm shocked, doll," Paul told her, Bogart style. "It's not fertility week."

She made her voice half mocking like his. "Fuck fertility."

Ceremonially, she lifted the stack of cardboard birthday cards she added to each year: ink cartoon drawings of him and her. First she showed him the blank cardboard square she'd already cut for next year, which she slipped on the bottom of the stack for luck.

Then she set the stack before him and stepped back into the kitchen. Cherry nut cake: his lifelong favorite. One thing that made his mom, Rest In Peace, happy too, for one meal. Paul reached across the couch and pressed the answering machine, lit up with two messages.

"Not sure you'll wanna hear that message," Sarah called from the kitchen, her joking tone less relaxed. "I mean, it's from your dad . . ."

"I can take it," Paul called back more jauntily than he felt.

"Happy one, Saint Paul. It is today, isn't it?" Paul drew a deep cake scented breath, listening to the long distance rasp of his sickly Dad.

"Found myself back down here in Florida. Friend of mine from my old Pimlico Track days has a horse here at the Gulf Stream Track he wants me to size up . . . and now I'm hoping my Saint Paul might wire me some cash to . . . see

me on home, son. 'Course I'm hoping you two"—A crackly pause, implying there should be three or more— "make yourselves as big a celebration as you can." His dad heaved a rough exhale and hung up.

During his last visit, Paul's dad had filched money from Paul's wallet. Tall as Paul, he'd paced their home restlessly in his big-shouldered sports jacket, sizing up their condo, asking Sarah when he'd "get" his grandson.

As if PJ didn't count, wasn't good enough. Paul's dad still couldn't understand Paul losing PJ and giving up custody. Maybe dad had been right for once, Paul thought. *PJ's ever deeper young man voice materialized on a second message.*

"Yo, Dad?"

Paul re braced himself. Why hadn't Sarah warned him about this one, too? Was Peej in trouble again? *In the kitchen, Sarah's plate clinks halted.*

"Hiya Dad, hiya Sarah. Happy B-day and all. Hope you get what you want. Hope Sarah, like, got my birthday card. Ol' Dr. PJ, maybe he can help . . . Sorry, Dad; I'm high on life. Just don't forget son number one . . ."

"What in hell?" Paul muttered at PJ's fumbled hang-up. "What's this about some birthday card to you? About Dr. PJ?" Paul raised his voice, recalling the Greek Restaurant night when PJ'd found out he and Sarah were trying. Had Sarah somehow told the kid about Paul's surgery? How he'd gone under the knife a month before; how he and Sarah were awaiting his post-op sperm count.

"I–I hadn't heard that message . . ." Sarah sounded shaken. "He must've left it when I was picking you up . . ." She stepped from the kitchen holding Paul's present, a beribboned bottle of darkest Merlot. *"I don't know what card he could-could mean . . ."* She fiddled with the ribbon. *"What's he mean by 'high on life?' that's what we oughta worry about . . ."*

"Let's call him up, find out what he means." Paul reached for the phone.

"No." Sarah smiled determinedly from across the living room. *"No, listen, please. You know how I like to do up your birthday. Can't we just . . . focus on that now?"*

Humming "Happy Birthday," loudly as if onstage, Sarah started walking toward him. Why is she so flustered by PJ's message? *Paul asked himself as she halted.*

"Just for tonight, OK?" Sarah set the wine down beside the stack of birthday cards, staying bent so he'd see her breasts, no bra on under that new dress.

"Like your birthday clothes," he murmured. Sarah settled close beside him. He shot her a 'let's take this slow look,' pouring the wine. "Can't believe that PJ."

"Yeah." She took a big first sip. "Your dad, too. Can't believe he's off on some racetrack trip. God, won't he ever retire?"

"From being manic depressive? It's a life sentence. For PJ, too, maybe . . ."

"Manic depressive? Peej isn't that." Hurriedly, Sarah corrected herself, eyes on her wine. "I mean, I don't know what he is. I just . . . he's just . . ." She took a big sip and swallowed. "Can we not talk about PJ for once?"

"You're the one who always wants to talk about him, worry about him . . ."

"Not today." Sarah slid to her knees onto the floor. She reached for her stack of cards. Paul took his own sip of wine, not wanting to dwell on "Dr. PJ" either.

"I don't suppose, Sare, we could skip laying our life across the floor?"

She stared up, doe eyes wide, sounding hurt. "You don't like 'This's Our Life?'"

"Sure I like it. I always like your drawings, but Christ, Sarah. I'd just as soon ignore this birthday, so let's not make such a big production out of it."

"OK then, Saint Paul. We'll forget all about 2008—" She flashed her cartoon sketch of her and Paul with a Castro-esque beard, captioned by a cut-out headline: MAY-DECEMBER ROMANCE BLOSSOMS FOR RUTHLESS DICTATOR.

"And 2009—" A silly headline playing on their newlywed sex-talk: PEAK YEAR FOR VOLVOS. "2010, too." Sarah flashed him that year: RIVAL TWITS. From RIVAL TWITS NEW CHAMPION; with a scissor slice she'd made the verb a noun. "Forget especially—" She flashed the 2011 head-line that referred to their fertility treatment plans: PROSPECT OF ALIEN INVADER THREATENS SMALL TOWN PEACE. She tossed that card hardest over her shoulder, whizzing the wobbly square Frisbee. It clunked against their stereo. "I mean, does the world need one more of us?"

With a flourish, Sarah raised the new 2012 card. Her usual ink cartoon of them, the cartoon-colored USA Today headline pasted above it: U.S. IS #1

"Number one what?" Paul asked, gamely grinning.

"That's what I wondered. There was something specifying whatever the bar graph thingy showed. But at first I thought USA TODAY was simply declaring the U.S. to be the best, period." Sarah met Paul's gaze. "Only on my card, U.S. is us, you twit. Us two."

"We two," he corrected, mock scholarly, but he eyed her more closely. "What's up with you tonight, Sare?"

"I'm just . . ." She set the 2012 card over the blank 2013 card. "Just up. Up for no reason, like a Down's kid." She rose to her feet and smoothed her dress over her curvy hips.

Breathlessly, her braless breasts jiggling, Sarah fetched his cherry nut cake. Its fifty-two unlit candles flickered as she carried it out, humming again. She set the cake plate on the couch end table. "So what're you gonna wish for?"

"Nothing," Paul answered firmly, like he expected a fight. "Just . . . for things to go on as they are. I'm feeling too old to want anything more."

"Oh?" Sarah bent and kissed him, slipping in her icing-flavored tongue. "Last thing I want you to feel tonight, Saint Paul . . ." Reaching down, she unzipped his pants, "is old."

Paul closed his heavy hand over both her poised hands. "Look. Of course I'm feeling old this week, what with today, with waiting to hear my goddamn—"

"Count." Sarah straightened up. Paul raised one brow. Before he could ask, she burst out, "Listen, OK; your sperm count came yesterday. It is . . . well, despite the surgery, still low. Only borderline-low now, the letter said. So, the doctor says we oughta come in again and discuss further treatment options . . ."

Sucked into the damned infertility industry. Paul sighed an old-man sigh. After her shots, his surgery, was Sarah going to push for something even more extreme? Christ, it'd kill him. IVFs and surrogate babies.

"But y'know what I wish?" Sarah pushed on. Paul shook his head, bracing himself for her earnest arguments. "That we just—not."

He waited a beat. Her face waited, too.

He spoke cautiously. "C'mon now, Sare. You don't have to pretend you're not disappointed in this, in me . . ."

"I'm not." Unsteadily, she stepped back. She fished a matchbook from her pocket. She struck one match, its tiny heat pulsing and bent over his cake.

"Maybe you're right. Maybe we've had so much trouble making a baby because we shouldn't." She dipped the pulsing light: wick to dry wick. "Maybe it's all a sign from the odds Gods." His dad's term. She shook out the match. Fifty-two bright, hyper flames quivered. "Anyhow, borderline's not no. It could still happen; it's possible." Sarah knelt again before Paul. "But, it's not the end of the world if it doesn't . . ."

By cake light, her eyes gleamed with some different hope, like she really did want to not want a baby so desperately, to not put them through more desperate, doomed procedures. He smoothed Sarah's hair behind her ears schoolgirl style.

She reached into his pants. "I'm gonna make your birthday happy whether you like it or not." Keeping her eyes on his face, she moved her fingers in slow, sure circles. Paul felt his face relaxing, creases disappearing from his forehead, from everywhere. His cock was hardening fast, like the old, pre-fertility timing days. Christ, he was turning younger by the second.

"Shouldn't I . . . blow that out?" Paul managed to ask, half choked.

"Not if we're both wishing for nothing."

His cake pulsated, fitful candles sinking into lush icing. Did Sarah actually mean all this? Paul wondered. More slowly than she, he sank to his knees. He kissed Sarah, eased her onto the floor. She kissed back hard, burrowing deep into his beard. His spine tightened.

Would his damn back give out? Too old, he thought, to fuck on the floor.

Above them, his cake vibrated wildly: its remaining brightness doubled by *the wax and sugar glaze puddled on its top, oozing down its sides. As Sarah wrapped her thighs around his hips, Paul felt his big feet disrupt his new cards. He glimpsed the blank 2013 card. He stretched his leg, calibrating his movement so Sarah didn't feel it.*

He nuzzled her neck and her long, fragrant hair. Blindly, Paul kicked the blank card that would be filled next year by who-knew-what far under the couch.

❧

Paul pulled aside her closed bed curtain. He found Sarah lying with her face pressed into the hospital pillow. Her hair, ripply and tangly, spilled all over the starched pillowcase. She always liked her heavy hair off her face. *I should push it off her face*, Paul told himself.

But he stood still a moment more, breathless.

She was in transition, the nurse had murmured to him, as if his wife were transforming into some new creature. Was she? Under the hospital sheet, Sarah lay on her side with her big belly resting like a too-heavy sack. Her legs under the sheets were bent, and her ass curved the way he'd always loved. The line of her spine looked strong. Her whole curled-up body seemed poised for action.

"She doesn't want the TV sound on," the nurse had added to Paul before letting him approach the bed. She sounded more amazed by that than by Sarah being in transition. Through Sarah's birth room's open door, Paul heard other TVs in other birth rooms tuned unusually loud for a hospital.

News voices babbling about the manhunt, about possible "bomber brothers." At least PJ wasn't out there with them anymore. Soon bomb-shell-dropping PJ would have his own little half-brother to corrupt. Paul appreciated Sarah tuning out all else but that still innocent baby.

He inched closer to her. The force field of her concentration, her pain; Paul could feel it, admire it. But it was keeping him back. Behind the curtain, the nurse cracked more ice.

Paul stood uselessly still, studying Sarah's spine, willing himself to stop thinking—overthinking. He stepped closer. How had he believed Sarah was really giving up her push for this baby back in February? What was true? The baby monitor beeped in rebuke.

Don't, don't, Paul told himself to its beat. He was tired and hungry. He couldn't even imagine how Sarah felt by now. Paul stepped up close. She was making loud, panting breaths: more desperate versions of the neat, puffy ones he'd heard her practice.

Paul stood above her. Sarah whipped her head around, facing him with her eyes shut. She twisted her head in the opposite direction, her hair falling over her mouth. Paul reached for her hair and pushed it back from her face.

Her lips moved with mumbled numbers. "Ten, 'leven, telve—"

"Telve" without the *w*: she was counting like a child. His child bride, they'd always joked. His personal virgin. His wife of thirteen—unlucky thirteen?—years. They'd married in the new millennium. Sarah: his new hope.

The nurse slipped behind Paul, setting down a water pitcher she'd refilled. Her skin was coffee and milk, her hair gelled into tight curls, her voice slurry but sure. "I've been here much as I can. We've been looking for you, sir." This nurse gave a contemptuous edge to that "sir." She eyed him suspiciously, backing away. What in hell was showing in his face? Paul tried to compose it, to neutralize his expression, before Sarah saw.

"Six–six–teen." Sarah's numbers stopped. She let out a throaty groan.

Paul took Sarah's stiff hand. He felt the scene with PJ by the soda machines begin to recede. Everything seemed small compared to Sarah's mound of belly and the shifting, sharp-peaked mountains of electronic blips on her monitor.

Paul wiped his forehead, sweating now like PJ, overwhelmed by a familiar sense of having been derelict, in the wrong place doing and thinking wrong things while he should've been up here with Sarah, totally focused on the baby, like her.

He sank into the chair by Sarah's bed. "Sare?"

She snapped open her wet-lashed eyes. Still on her side, she raised her head like she was coming up for air from underwater, gasping.

"Y-you?" Her voice sounded thick like she was sleepy. Only her olive eyes seemed shocked and wider awake than ever. "I-In trans-trans—"

Transexual from Transylvania, Paul found himself thinking. Words Adina used to sing to him, quoting *The Rocky Horror Picture Show*. Swaying seductively, theatrically, like she wanted to be out dancing. Wasn't Paul taking his genuine paternity doubts about Adina and grafting them onto Sarah?

"Transition," Paul said, squeezed Sarah's hand. A solid, strong-fingered woman hand, whereas Adina's had been a silken little sack of bones—a restless hand that never lingered long in his.

Adina had been lovely, mercurial, and flighty. She'd given PJ her looks and her temperament, too, her addiction to risk and melodrama.

PJ had been, as he might say, pushing that to the max today. So Paul told himself, and he told Sarah how sure the nurse had sounded when she'd told him the labor was too far along to stop. The baby was coming, ready or not.

"Mom'd–be mad . . ." Sarah muttered. Mad if she wasn't senile, Paul knew she meant. "She'd 'Oh Sarah' . . . for screwing up . . . baby too soon . . ."

Paul nodded. Sarah's brittle, hypercritical mother: yes, she would see a preemie baby as a failure. Yes, she would 'Oh Sarah' Sarah. Paul pictured her squinting up from her wheelchair in the posh Providence retirement home Sarah felt guilty for not visiting enough.

"C'mon now, Sare," Paul made himself say. Dutifully defending Sarah's mom even though the woman looked down on him. Even though Sarah's cold fish mom had indeed 'Oh Sarah'd' her choice of art therapy over a grander major, of a husband in the helping professions. Paul couldn't fault the snooty old bird on that one. Sure, he'd risen to Regional Center Director and a respectable salary, but what kind of husband had he made for Sarah?

He tilted Sarah's cup of melted ice chips while she sipped, swallowed.

"W-where . . . Peej?" Sarah demanded lower-voiced. "W-what he . . . say?"

Paul set down her hollow, Styrofoam cup. It was a strain to set it down and not fling it at the wall.

"Sare, not now. Stay calm." It was his own voice he struggled to keep calm. "PJ's fine. The police, they let him go. PJ's with Evvy. We don't have to—you don't have to—think about PJ now . . ." Paul smoothed back her heavy, sweaty hair.

"God Paul, PJ . . . can't believe he was . . . really with the police. God, God."

Sarah flopped onto her back. Her belly jutted higher than ever under the sheet. Paul pressed his spread-open hand onto her belly to the warm, live mass of body inside her body. Not moving like it had done other times under Paul's hand, but clenched up inside Sarah, ready to spring. Unmistakably, right under Paul's cupped hand, alive.

"You're strong," Paul told both the baby and Sarah. He pressed Sarah's baby gently, signaling to it that he was there, that he wanted his son to come through strong and healthy.

As long as it's healthy; wasn't that what real, unscrewed-up parents say?

Sarah began her ragged panting again. She bucked under her sheet, possessed by some pain too big for her one body. *Where in holy hell is the doctor?* Paul smoothed back Sarah's dense, damp hair. Her brownish-green eyes showed a swampy mix of pain, hope, guilt.

"PJ . . . talk . . . crazy." Sarah gulped more deep breaths, alarming, raspy breaths. Paul heard the nurse step back into the room. He heard the steady *blips* of the baby monitor.

He carefully said nothing. Sarah coughed. Paul lifted her ice cup too fast; it spilled on her mattress edge. He fumbled to gather the slippery cubes.

Sarah watched his hands, saying insistently: "Suck. Wanna suck."

He slipped ice between her lips. She sucked his fingertips with the cubes.

"Peej." Sarah pushed on once she'd swallowed her sucked-down ice. "Wha' say?"

"A kiss?" Paul dared to fill in, whispering so the nurse wouldn't stop him. He leaned closer to Sarah. He breathed a scent of pee, of damp padding beneath Sarah. He should call the nurse in, but Sarah's stare held his so intently. She never could stand to keep any secret inside her. What if what she was hiding was, in fact, the biggest, most excruciating of secrets? Killing her now, upsetting her enough to throw off her risky, early labor?

Then again, if this somehow was PJ's baby, this labor might not be early. Christ, Paul couldn't keep up with his own mixed up thoughts, but he'd swear something in Sarah's stirred up stare was pleading for relief, confession.

"A kiss, is that what PJ did to you, or tried to do or something today?"

"N-not kiss . . ." Sarah twisted her head back and forth.

"Sare," Paul made himself say, "It doesn't matter now. I—I don't want you upset . . ."

"Upset? I'll show you upset." The guard nurse called through the curtain behind Paul, her voice no longer mellow. "You let her be with all your questions, you hear me?"

Paul felt the broad-bodied nurse standing behind the curtain, poised to hustle him out.

Sarah twisted her head again, still murmuring. "It a . . . a—m-mother thing . . ."

Paul leaned closer to Sarah, whispering. "Look, I know what you're saying. A mother thing. For years, I know how badly you wanted a baby . . ."

"Want-ed a—?" Sarah sounded bewildered by those last words.

"Sir." A firm nurse hand on his shoulder. "You gonna to have to step away. I smell something here I gotta clean up for this mother."

"Yes, sure. Thank you." Paul backed away. "Concentrate on the baby, Sare. This baby is coming today." *Our baby*, he should've said, wondering if she'd heard at all.

Sarah twisted her head hard, grinding it into the pillow. "No—too soon. Oh GodPaul, shoulda had am-nio . . . What if—like Lit-tle Rich-ie?"

Richie from the Center, Paul knew she meant. Little Richie, they all called him, though he was twenty-nine years old. Backing away, Paul pictured Richie's undersized head, his oversized ears spreading out wide and keen as a cat's, his mouth slack soft.

"He won't," Paul told Sarah through the curtain. The nurse took his place at Sarah's bedside, holding a pan of soapy water, shaking her head.

"Wha's wrong with Little Richie?" She chuckled, bending over Sarah. "One of the hardest working men in showbiz, hon, and you're gonna be the hardest working woman tonight . . ."

"First gotta—gotta pee," Paul heard Sarah answer back, weak voiced.

"You not only gotta pee, you did. We're gonna get you cleaned up. But you're gonna have to roll for me, hon. Try my Pelvic Rock . . ."

Paul ducked into the room's bathroom, his own bladder full, and his head overfull of words. Sarah saying in such an anguished, confessional tone, "It's a mother thing." PJ saying his antifertility backfired, double. PJ saying: "both hers." Saying: "my baby."

Paul fumbled with his zipper. Christ, he needed coffee to clear his muddled head, needed a smoke. He pulled out his cock, still tender from today's sex. Wasn't that lovemaking all the proof he should need that he and Sarah were as connected as ever? His piss streamed heavily; he felt relieved as he flushed the toilet. *It can wait*, Paul warned himself, scrubbing his hands with the oozy, pink soap they used at the Center. *It all can wait.*

He couldn't afford to lose his head when PJ and Sarah were both out of theirs.

Through the bathroom door, as he dried his hands on the paper towel, Paul heard soothing sloshes, the growly beginnings of more moans. A mother thing. A marathon only mothers could run. God knew Sarah had already run a marathon just to get to this point. This night.

Late night now and no end in sight. Of course in the Boston Marathon the finish line had proved to be the most dangerous part of the whole race. Unlucky 2013. Hadn't Paul known, when Sarah had claimed she'd put off further infertility treatments, that it was too good to be true? The sick scenarios planted in his head by his certifiable liar son, they were too bad to be true. Paul hurled his balled up towel into the trash. He stepped out of the bathroom and heard more sloshing. A bed bath: what Little Richie had to have since he was paralyzed as well as developmentally disabled—a double whammy.

Paul gazed out the room's single window into a quiet sky. No more mist, just cool, uncompromising black. Paul's breaths fogged the windowpane: fast vanishing ghost fears.

"There," the nurse murmured to his hidden, frightened wife. "All clean."

Let it be anyone's, Paul found himself thinking. *Just let it be a big and healthy baby.*

Summer, 2012

Sarah swayed, up to her neck, buoyed yet unbalanced by bright, sloshing water. And by PJ swimming sloppy circles around her, splattering her face. Below the surface, her breasts felt tenderly swollen. Could that tenderness mean she was pregnant at last, against odds? Her heart thumped, double strength. But no, it probably only meant her period was coming.

Could she stop hoping for a miracle pregnancy, ever?

PJ—suddenly man-sized this June visit—circled closer. His tattooed arms slashed water, his kicks splashed her harder.

What is he up to? What new nineteen-year-old PJ game, this first weekend of his visit? His first summer-long visit. Unexpectedly, he'd found roommates and a cheap apartment in Somerville. Sarah gave an uneasy laugh, barely keeping her balance, her toes curled into Spy Pond's silt bottom.

"Hiii–" she called out to Paul onshore, her Stepmom voice gay and shaky. Through his son's rising splashes, Sarah waved at distant Paul.

He sat on their blanket by their packed picnic basket, talking on his cell phone. Another long-distance call to the Florida home he was trying to get his uninsured, seriously ailing Dad into. Sarah was wearing a red swimsuit Paul used to like. He used to eye her on the beach, then keep watch over her like a lifeguard as she waded and swam.

Only he wasn't watching now, never seemed to see her lately.

She waved her upraised hand harder at Paul as if signaling for help. He didn't notice, or didn't wave back. Talking away, long distance. Sarah couldn't help but notice how PJ had watched her today more closely than Paul. Sarah always looked best in summer, her skin glowing and tan, her full-figured body trimmed down from swimming.

She basked for a moment, her face titled towards the sun, happy her husband and stepson were both here. A family; imperfectly blended, but still a family. Could they get back to normal, even after PJ's wild card?

PJ kept circling closer, splashing harder. He'd been so silent in the days since he arrived for his summer sojourn, since that distant-seeming March day at the Battle Green.

PJ's splashes spouted plumes, dampened Sarah's sunheated hair. "PJ!" She shook back her heavy braid, still gamely smiling. But PJ swam so close his elbow bumped her submerged shoulder. Sarah almost lost her footing, her chin and half open mouth dunked.

Paul finally stood onshore. Sarah tensed her whole body protectively as she steadied herself again. She blinked to clear her eyes. Goldenrod spears along the Spy Pond banks wavered, their bold, festive yellow doubled.

"Hey PJ, slow down," Sarah commanded, but shakily.

Beyond PJ's wake, Paul strode to the edge of the sunny, buzzing pond. His supervisor-strength shout overpowered hers. "PJ, STOP!"

PJ wouldn't hear or halt. Sarah wobbled again with PJ's rising waves. More water splashed into her mouth. She never could tell when PJ was playing and when not.

Her voice strained like a real mom's. "Your Dad said stop!"

Sarah had been determined to start over with PJ this summer. But how to even start starting over? Anything was possible with PJ, who kept swimming his crazy-close circles. PICNIC PANIC: STEPSON DROWNS STEP-MOM IN GAME GONE WRONG.

Sarah tried to splash out of PJ's orbit, picturing a Boston Herald *headline, the kind she clipped. The infinite ways families fuck up. PJ cut in front of her again.*

His arms and legs were slashing faster; his black hair glittered. He was circling her determinedly as if trying to trap her out here, where she could barely reach bottom.

"No," Sarah commanded more harshly than she'd ever done with PJ.

"PJ, you hear me?" Paul waded in from the distant shore, his shirt still on. His voice boomed out to PJ as if to a Center kid who was going off. "What in hell are you doing?*"*

PJ's vigorous, digging arm bumped Sarah's stiffened shoulder, harder than before. She lost her foothold in the stirred-up silt. A wave slapped her face, swamped her.

As her head slipped underwater, Sarah squeezed shut her eyes. She hugged herself, shielding her belly, thinking in the murky churned-up silence, as if this would make everything stop: But I might be pregnant!

Things kept right on moving. Sarah bobbed back up, gasping and treading water now, the sandy bottom suddenly out of reach. Swimming up beside her,

PJ grabbed Sarah's arm. Dazedly, she let him help her splash forward into the lower water, back on her feet now.

PJ began laughing, but Sarah cut him short, jerking her arm away.

"Don't scare me like that," she told PJ sternly as he met her wet-lashed eyes.

PJ heaved a big, wet-shouldered shrug. "Didn't even know you—saw me there."

Sarah lowered her eyes from his unblinking gaze. She'd avoided holding his gaze ever since she'd confronted him about his card back at the Battle Green. Pushing PJ away then. Would he now push back? Literally? Would PJ ever actually try to hurt her? What kind of game was this older, angrier PJ playing today?

"It's OK," PJ shouted to distant, bewildered-looking Paul, standing knee deep as he stared across the water at them. "It's OK, Dad—I got her!"

Chapter Six

April 18, 2013; 11:45 p.m.

Pushing

"Don' go . . ." Sarah gasped as the Pelvic Rock nurse started to stand with her sloshing pan of water. Paul stood hovering behind the curtain; he looked stiff in shadow. He was holding back so much, Sarah could tell. PJ and Evvy and Paul gathered down in the lobby, saying and doing who-knew-what to each other.

Why had all that been so important? With Bombers on the loose and her baby on the way?

"Bath," Sarah found herself murmuring. Shabath, she was thinking, a long-lost word.

Shabaths: her and her mother's name for Sarah's hair-washing sessions, a combination of shower and bath. Water streamed over young Sarah sitting in the tub. Her mother, still dressed in nylons and skirt, knelt next to it. Mom, smaller and closer, off her high heels at last, would sink her strong fingers into Sarah's thick, reddish-brown hair.

"Your father's hair," Mom had told her; the one part of Sarah's long-gone, Scottish father that Mom seemed to admire. Mom scrubbed Sarah's lush hair slowly, sweet green Herbal Essence shampoo bubbling.

Rich foam dripped down Sarah's face, filling and tickling her ears. Every sound—everything in the world—blocked by the roar of the shower, the rhythmic scrubbing of Mom's hands.

"More Shabath," Sarah would beg when Mom tipped her head to rinse. Foam rolled down her bare back like a princess's cape, but the water was shifting from lukewarm to lukecool. Mom was standing up in her brisk way, saying the hot water had run out. Saying, as she wiped her hands on a towel, "There's only so much, Sarah."

"More bath," Sarah mumbled as Pelvic Rock wiped her hands on a hospital towel.

Sarah lay on her back on her new, clean pad with her knees raised, her gown bunched up over the wires taped to her belly. You can push now, she'd been told—an hour ago, minutes ago? Sometime near midnight? She had to somehow use the same muscles she used to tighten herself around Paul's cock—but that wasn't pushing. More like pulling, sucking deeper and deeper.

"More bath?" Pelvic Rock asked in her annoyingly placid voice. "You can have 'more bath' later. We gotta get you working. Gotta get you to *use gravity*, you hear me?"

Curtain rings jingled. Paul and Pelvic took hold of her arms, hoisted her upright by her armpits. Sarah, stunned to be suddenly sitting, could barely follow Pelvic's words.

"—called a supported squat," Pelvic was telling Paul.

Pelvic, with her smell of antiseptic soap and Dorito breath, was supporting Sarah on one side. Paul, with his smell of scared sweat and smoke, on the other. Somehow, Sarah had her arm slung around Paul's sturdy shoulder. Paul wrapped his strong arm around her back, holding her in place. How she always loved the weight of his big arm encircling her.

"C'mon hon. Bear down." Pelvic cupped her hand over Sarah's bent knee. Paul cupped his heavier hand over her other knee. Both of them told her to push when she already *was* pushing, but her inner muscles seized up, stopped.

She'd stopped that push too soon, Pelvic muttered, and Sarah resented her again. "Try hands an' knees," Pelvic advised supervisor Paul, like Sarah had no say.

"Bend forward," Pelvic Rock told Sarah, but really the four hands on her were forcing her forward, on her knees, on all fours. Her breasts and belly hung down and her bared ass stuck out into the air, her hands braced on the firm hospital mattress.

Dog position, Sarah wanted to whisper to Paul.

Sarah, on her knees with the heels of her hands digging into the mattress like this, Paul on his knees, too, thrusting in from behind her. Sarah's head bowing down, and her hair spilling forward like a waterfall. They shuddered together, fell sideways in slow motion, curled up together. Then twisted around, panting and laughing, finding the next new position.

"Sorry," Sarah gasped, falling sideways alone, those four hands losing hold of her. She lay heavy and limp again, breathing hard.

"Back on her back," Pelvic grumbled like Sarah had flunked some test.

Can we not do this right now? Sarah wanted to ask.

"Can you roll over, hon? On your back again? Now you do want to *meet* him, don't you? Only one way you're gonna *meet* this baby, hon. You know that?"

Lying flat on her back, her throat tightened up. Sarah didn't answer.

A hard-knuckled *rap* on her hospital room door. *Rap, rap* above the *bleep, bleep* of the monitor. *I hear you,* Sarah thought behind her shut eyes. That knock, so loud and sure—it must be him, her baby. Wanting, demanding, to be let in.

❧

Can't be him, Paul told himself at the *rat-a-tat* knock.

No, PJ was with Evvy getting fed and hopefully sober. The guard nurse edged out as the door squeaked open. What if it *were* PJ behind that curtain, PJ escaped from Evvy?

Paul watched Sarah grind her head into her pillow with a look of brute, inner concentration. Her eyes squeezed shut like a girl's, her face screwed up like an old woman's.

"Yeah, that's it," Paul told her, but he sounded unconvincing, unsure.

"How far along are we?" Dr. Lutz poked her smoothly coiffed head into the curtain, her white coat spotless. So, where had she been all this time? "ICU Neonatal is all set once this little one makes his appearance," she announced. Paul's heart sank.

"Dr. Lutz, wait. Are you sure intensive care's going to be . . . necessary? Look, we want to take every precaution, but . . . are you sure this baby is . . . *that* premature?"

Paul blurted out these words. Sarah kept twisting her head and grimacing, seeming not to hear. Dr. Lutz settled herself on a metal, wheeled stool at the foot of Sarah's bed.

The nurse was spreading Sarah's knees so Lutz could ogle her cervix. "What are you saying, Mr. Stratidakis?" Lutz glanced up at him, gloved hands poised. Was he actually half wishing for the wildest, worst-case scenario to be true, for this baby to be full-term? If Sarah somehow conceived while Paul was gone in Florida in late August? Or early August, when Paul was still there? But then she'd have missed her period in September, something she would only keep a secret for extreme reasons. Waiting until October to tell Paul, the patsy? The baby a bastard; his own son's, but, on the plus side, full-term?

Paul shook his head hard. "Nothing. I'm just . . . confused."

"Seven months is doable." Lutz hunched over his wife. She fixed on Sarah's cervix; she was through with this befuddled husband. "Many babies come early, for many reasons . . ."

"Yeah, many . . ." Paul backed through the curtains. He poured himself some of Sarah's icy water. Ice trembled and cracked as he raised the cup.

ICU Neonatal. That special nursery Paul had glimpsed on tour. TWENTY-FOUR-HOUR VIDEO SURVEILLANCE posted above the archway like the mini graffiti scratched above the Waltham Wet Shelter door: ABANDON HOPE ALL YE WHO ENTER HERE.

Paul crunched a chunk of ice.

"They say they're brothers," a voice in the hall announced. "The bomber guys. They're out there, out here in Cambridge God-knows-where, and they're brothers—"

Like PJ and this poor kid, Paul thought woozily. The older bomber brother, the one in the black hat, no doubt the ringleader, corrupting his kid brother. Where the hell had the father been in all this? They ought to string up the father, too, in the end.

Paul felt lightheaded; he needed food and coffee, but he couldn't leave Sarah, couldn't risk running into PJ again in the cafeteria.

PJ was probably passing out cigars down there, claiming this kid is his. Paul set down his hollow cup hard, another unbidden memory surfacing.

Just over a month ago, on PJ's birthday in early March, Paul and Sarah were at their off-season beach hotel. PJ still off in Ohio then; Sarah so oddly rattled when Paul had phoned him. Paul and Sarah having, that day, their biggest fight of Sarah's pregnancy.

Why did that memory nag at Paul now? Because he sensed, even if it wasn't a bastard baby, there was something secret going on between PJ and Sarah. Why else would Sarah keep PJ's visit today a secret?

"Any time now," Lutz was decreeing. Paul could practically hear her check her watch through the curtain, maybe wondering if she could fit in a quickie work-out, watching the latest Boston Bomber update from a treadmill, before attending to this premature birth, before socking his newborn son away in Neonatal ICU. *Had* PJ, his visit, somehow triggered all this? What-all *had* Sarah said that stormy March day?

"Paul?" Sarah called from behind the curtain, her voice weak and pleading like she believed, like she had reason to believe, he might leave.

❧

Awaiting another downpour, Paul and Sarah faced storm clouds roiling over the ocean. It was late afternoon, early March. They had gotten a room at their usual beach hotel, off-season, for the week their condo was being deleaded. Usually, they loved the view of "their" beach: the curved cove their balcony faced, the perfect length for walking together. Usually they loved a cloudy beach day, but today they'd stayed planted in their chairs on their chilly deck. Paul had taken out his cell phone and sat holding it, bracing himself to give PJ a birthday call, not that PJ had answered any of his recent messages.

"Hey—" Sarah raised her puffy-fingered hand as if to halt him. "Hey, aren't swollen hands listed in What to Expect *as a sign of something bad?"*

"Like what?" Paul sat straighter in his deck chair. He and Sarah were bundled in sweaters in the damp ocean air. Better than the dank closed-in air of the room.

"God knows. GodPaul, your hands look even worse than mine . . ."

Paul glanced down, his hands still blistered from all the furniture he'd moved to prepare their condo, renovated from a stately 1950s era home, to have its lead paint stripped off.

"Guess you're gonna try PJ again." Sarah sounded edgy. Paul nodded toward the vast, darkening ocean. Breakers rolled in relentlessly, a single wetsuit-clad surfer floundering. On the balcony beside theirs, the unabashedly fat, sweat-suit-clad mom strode up to her wood rail. She yelled at her son in the evenings, and she was possibly the hotel's only other guest.

"Todd!" the mom called down to her morose-looking son, digging in the sand.

"'Course I'm gonna try again." Paul replied, edgy, too. "Haven't talked to the kid since my birthday. Remember, weird PJ phone call number one hundred? All he said then was that this year he hadn't sent me 'another card.' When he never did send me a card, or any that I got . . ."

"Well don't bring that up!" Suddenly Sarah went on alert. "I mean, just keep the talk, you know, positive . . . if he even will talk to me—I mean, to you."

"Why wouldn't he talk to you?" Paul asked. Sometimes he felt the unborn baby had erased PJ for her. PJ must feel that, too, Paul thought grimly, punching Contacts.

"It's gonna storm!" the mom hollered at little Todd as if it were his fault. Paul pressed the cell phone to his ear, vowing to at least be a better parent, please, than Todd's mom.

As if in reply to this unspoken, almost-prayer, PJ answered, far off, somewhere in Ohio. Paul stiffened in his deck chair and felt Sarah do the same beside him.

"Yo, Dad? You, like, remember your ol' number one son?"

PJ sounded slurry, drunk maybe? Paul barked out a too-hearty happy birthday.

When that was met with silence and then a slurping, a probable beer-guzzle on the other end, Paul asked awkwardly, "Where are ya, son? Out partying or . . . ?"

"Like you care." A belch. "And . . . like I care . . . where are you? You two, you three . . ."

"Uh, at our old beach, if you can believe it. Remember the beach in Gloucester we used to take you to? Good Harbor Beach? We got off-season rates at the hotel for a week while Sarah— while we—get the condo deleaded. The paint, y'know . . ."

Another slurping pause. Sarah sat frozen beside Paul.

"Ha. Doin' it all the right way this time, huh Dad?"

"Peej, listen, and I mean this—Sarah means it, too." Paul darted a glance to frozen-faced Sarah, but he plunged on ahead with words he was inventing on the spot. "We want you to come out here. It's been way too long. Come before the baby—your half-brother—gets born. I'll pay for the train ticket, whatever you want . . . Sarah'd love to see you, too," Paul added when more heavy-breathing silence greeted his impulsive offer. "Want to, uh, talk to her?"

"She doesn't want to talk to me," PJ stated flatly, and he cut off the call. The phone buzzed in Paul's ear, making buried bells go off inside Paul. Paul pressed off.

"He says you wouldn't want to talk to him." He breathed brackish air. "Why not, Sarah?"

Sarah looked at her hands, clasped over her belly, a fight gathering as surely as the storm clouds. "GodPaul, how should I know? I can't explain anything PJ does or says. He's . . . jealous of the new baby is why, I guess. What I want to know is why you didn't talk to me first before inviting PJ out here?"

"Since when is PJ not welcome?" Paul stuffed his phone in his pocket. "He missed the damn holidays, and yeah, he did sound jealous of this new baby and the damn deleading and everything this baby is getting that he never had. You're the one who used to go on about everything PJ never had. Now it does seem like you don't . . . want him around anymore."

"Me? I'm fine with PJ coming out here. I just want a little warning! What worries me is . . . how much you're feeling threatened by this baby, too!"

"What in all hell?" Paul burst out, gripping the arms of his deck chair. "I've done every last thing you've asked. Jerked off into a fucking cup, let laser-surgeons have at my balls, let those deleaders take over our home! I went along with you when you refused the amnio . . ."

"Me?" Sarah raised her dark, flashing eyes. "I thought we decided not to do that, not to stick a dangerous needle in my belly, in our baby, not to go there . . ."

Paul squinted toward the fogged-over Atlantic. This morning's sparkly water had been replaced by a choppy, olive-grey surface—the ocean's true color, minus its gloss of sun.

"GodPaul," Sarah pushed on, ginning up her old arguments. "Why find out bad news on our baby when we're going to have him no matter what? And love him no matter what?"

"Like we gotta love PJ no matter what," Paul put in, trying to steer this out-of-control discussion back to the question—his questions—about his existing son.

"I mean, those genetics testers . . . You said yourself it's a racket! Recommending that amnio just because my AP-whatever level was up . . . Which could mean, that lady told us, nothing at all!" Sarah seized from their folding table her most dog-eared pregnancy book. She flipped the pages aggressively. "What I'm worried about is right now. Here." She read aloud into the wind. "'If your hands become puffy, notify your doctor. Such swelling may be insignificant or, if accompanied by a rise in blood pressure, may signify the onset of a dangerous condition: pregnancy-induced hypertension.'" She slapped the book shut and raised one puffy hand. "Doesn't that sound like me, Paul? Hypertense?"

"Sounds like both of us," Paul muttered, studying Sarah's hand. "My last visit with Dad, back in August, only days before his heart attack? I noticed his hands seemed swollen. Seemed, for the first time in years, bigger than my hands, but I didn't say anything, didn't think of it again 'til now . . ."

"So maybe it's, my hands are . . ." Sarah set the book on the table, "really something?"

"Look, Sare." Paul pulled out his cell phone again, intending to give Sarah's doctor a call. "You lie down and I'll . . ."

"Call PJ again?" Electric, pre-storm wind blew Sarah's hair. She met Paul's wearily patient stare. She looked as wicked as Medusa, snake tendrils flying around her head. "Tell him to come down right away, so we can all be hypertense together?"

"I was gonna call your doctor, but maybe I oughta be calling a shrink instead. One of those family counselors you used to want to drag me and Peej to." Paul pulled himself up, catching a glint of fear in Sarah's giveaway eyes. "What in all hell do you know about PJ? Why, for all these months, the damn kid would barely even take my calls?"

Sarah heaved herself up, too, her belly sticking out between them.

"Just like you wouldn't take your Dad's calls for years," Sarah answered. "God, maybe you've been right about bad things passing down through the doomed Stratidakis genes."

"You're saying you think PJ's doomed?" Paul shook his cell phone. A lame weapon.

"I'm talking about our baby!" Sarah pivoted, jolted the sliding glass door open. "GodPaul, you never did want this baby!" She lurched into the dark hotel room. With a clack meant to be heard, she locked the door.

Dr. Lutz opened Sarah's curtain wide. She told Paul, in a clipped voice, that Sarah was fully dilated. Paul nodded numbly, wondering if Sarah could last through much more.

"Isn't this drug-free labor dangerous?" Paul asked aloud.

"What's dangerous would be to try any drug with a preemie birth. One benefit to preemies is that their smaller size makes for, usually, a quicker delivery. Though that may not prove true in your case . . ."

What did she mean, "may not prove true?" That this baby wouldn't prove to be preemie-sized? Dr. Lutz turned away, clicking out the door, leaving it open behind her. The guard nurse sat scribbling on her clipboard. Paul shut Sarah's curtain behind him. Sarah, still on her back, shot him a look of gratitude, glad he was back.

Ridiculous, Paul told himself as he sat in the chair by Sarah's bed. How could he keep entertaining such ridiculous, paranoid PJ-thoughts when his wife lay here in such pain? Sarah gazed up at Paul with drained, unseeing eyes. Her hand groped for his; he caught it up, held it.

Her hand always fit his, not too small like Adina's. Paul squeezed it. A woman's hand—his woman's—his ring on her finger.

Yes, Yes, Yes. The baby monitor made its small, pulse-like *beeps.*

Someone stepped toward the open door outside. Lutz again? He'd make her stay put this time. He'd get a grip on this situation, Paul vowed as he heard the boot steps.

Can't be him, Paul foolishly told himself again.

"Who're you?" the guard nurse asked.

Paul squeezed Sarah's hand hard as they both heard it—him.

"You gotta lemme in." PJ, maybe standing in the room's doorway, his hoarse voice lowered. "The baby. My baby. A baby's, like, *mine.*"

Paul released Sarah's limp hand, her face still blank. The metal-legged chair *scrawked* the floor as Paul stood. Sarah twisted her head back and forth, maybe willfully not listening.

"Who are you?" the nurse was demanding, sounding almost scared.

"*Her* son, *their* son, and the baby's, maybe, *my*—"

"Stop." The metal-ringed curtains *screaked* open. Paul stepped out, turned his back on PJ, *screaked* the curtains shut again. Then he faced his son.

"Mr. Straddy-duck-us, you know this boy?" Guard nurse glared at Paul, her middle-aged moon face stirred at last from its bemused calm. "He's saying . . . what is it you're saying?"

Big-shouldered PJ filled the doorway. His dark-browed, unshaven face no longer shone with sweat. Had his feverish high broken?

"He knows me. I'm his number one son. And see, the baby, this baby—"

"He's my son, all right." Paul stepped up to the door, standing tall beside the plump nurse. They'd make a good team if they had to hustle PJ out. "But listen, he shouldn't be here now. He might upset her, see, my wife."

All this Paul said only to the nurse. He felt unready to meet his son's gaze.

"Jesus God, PJ!"

Evvy, calling from the hall, charging up behind PJ in her black karate uniform.

"Sorry, y'all," she apologized to Paul and the nurse. "He slipped me while I was in Ladies'. PJ, I swear, you're in deep shit. Don't you go messing with Sarah."

PJ ducked his head. With his linebacker shoulders, he bulled past the nurse. She and Evvy looked at Paul like Center staffers look to him when someone starts going off. Paul felt his pants pocket for the folded knife. *Male staff,* Paul wanted to call out.

Behind the curtain, Sarah began another groan. Paul stepped up to PJ fast, gripping his denim sleeve. Like a dog, PJ strained toward Sarah's curtain.

"I gotta—" PJ twisted to glare at Paul, his bulgy eyes black. "I gotta . . . I *get* to . . . see Sarah."

"Not like this you don't."

PJ wrenched his arm free. He lunged straight into the curtains without parting them, flailing his arms, searching for the opening. His voice rose, stagey yet shaky. "But this baby . . . *I* got a baby!"

From her bed, as PJ stumbled free, Sarah whimpered. Curtain rings *screaked* loud.

"Whoa!" PJ halted his own eager step, jumped backwards. Staggered on his feet, stunned. "Whoa," PJ repeated hoarsely, letting Paul pull him away.

Through the opened curtain, Paul saw what PJ had seen: Sarah on her back with her belly and knees sticking up, her hospital johnnie bunched around her crotch. Her pubic hair, with its secret tint of auburn. Her belly heaved in panicky breaths.

Grunting, Sarah lowered her legs and half-raised her head. For a second she gaped straight at PJ over the hump of her belly. Her widened eyes glinted with shock and warning.

"You," Sarah choked out. Her olive eyes flashing in her sweat-glossed face. She looked scared, looked PJ's age. PJ with his beard bristle and bulky shoulders felt like a man more clearly than ever in Paul's grip. A tense current hummed between this man and Sarah.

"*You* ba-by?" Her head collapsed on her pillow. Her voice sounded so thick and intense she might've been talking in her sleep.

"He's talking nonsense," Paul answered weakly, echoing Evvy. He reached past dumbstruck PJ for the curtain. Sarah was tugging at her johnny, wincing, covering herself.

Paul whipped the curtain shut. "Don't worry. I'll take care of PJ," Paul told the closed swaying curtain, glad Sarah couldn't see his own out-of-control face, heating up.

The baby monitor *bleeped* on, a teeny voice saying *Me, Me, Me*—the room's only sound. Paul hustled PJ roughly toward the door.

"Me too, Sarah Sweetie!" Evvy materialized at PJ's side, grabbing PJ's other arm. PJ gazed behind him at the bed curtains like he couldn't believe what he'd just seen, done.

He opened then shut his mouth, dumbstruck as an actor who'd forgotten his lines. Sarah, from behind the curtain, groaned again, no louder than before, back at her work.

Paul tightened his grip on his son's arm, feeling PJ's muscles tense-up in answer through the denim. Ready, like Paul, to fight.

"Outta here," Paul managed gruffly, pulling PJ forward. "I've gotta stay with Sarah," he added to the whole room, the only words he wanted Sarah to hear. He and PJ and Evvy began moving as one, like a crack Center team. The guard nurse by the door stared frankly.

"Wait, I got a *card* for her, for you—" PJ strained again against Paul's grip.

"Don't know what's going on with you all," the nurse told Paul. "But you better get him outta here, and you better not leave your wife again,

Mr. Straddy-duck-us." Paul and Evvy halted PJ at the doorway. The nurse marched over to Sarah's closed bed curtain. Sarah's moan rose as if in pained agreement. "We don't wanna come looking for you again, sir."

"You won't. I'll . . . be right back." Paul led PJ and Evvy out the open doorway, into the wide, empty, clean-smelling hospital corridor. Outside Sarah's room, maybe relieved to be out, PJ struggled harder. He shook loose Evvy's grip and sent her stumbling sideways.

"Stepmom never answered my card," PJ proclaimed, at least keeping his voice low. "Not really, she didn't. I want someone to answer my card!"

With his freed hand, PJ dug into his jacket pocket. Evvy beside him looked fed up, a teacher pushed too far, her lips tightened. She seized PJ's elbow.

"Whatever it is can wait." Paul kept hold of PJ's tensed left arm, kept his own voice steady. "I gotta get back to Sarah, her and the baby . . ."

Sarah's room door shut loudly, the guard nurse fed up, too. Paul wouldn't blame her if she locked that door, but hospital doors had no locks. From an open, nearby birth room, Paul heard a relentless news voice, still hyper at midnight or whatever-the-hell time it was.

—MASSIVE MANHUNT CONTINUES IN CAMBRIDGE-WATERTOWN AREA: CAR-JACKING VICTIM CLAIMS HIS ASSAILANTS CLAIMED RESPONSABILTY FOR THE MARATHON BOMBING—

A loud cry, not-Sarah's, and the news door shut. So many screwed up birth nights converging. At least, Paul hoped, the multiple, muffled TV voices might keep everyone on this Birth Floor from hearing the smaller-scale crisis unfolding in their hallway.

"Here!" PJ jerked his hand from his pocket, breaking Evvy's hold. He waved a torn envelope.

"PJ, whatever that is . . ." Evvy reached on tiptoe for the envelope that PJ jacked high up above his head. "PJ, you give me that thing!"

"What you got there, Peej?" Paul demanded in his own tensely lowered voice.

"Birthday card," PJ told Paul. "Sarah never, like, answered. But she kept it, see? Kept this card hidden with her art stuff. I found it there last summer, see? I just had to check today . . . see if it was still there. It was, so then I stole it, like. So lemme just give it back to her. Signed, sealed, delivered—" PJ flapped the envelope. "I'm yours!"

A bald head poked out from a nearby birth room door. "What's going on out here?"

"Don't pay him no mind," Evvy called gamely.

Paul was fixed only on PJ. He leaned closer to PJ, arms half raised.

"Sarah, she wouldn't have kept this card, my card, if she hadn't at least *want*-ed . . ."

"You shut up about Sarah!" Evvy cut in hotly. "What she wants now is you gone!"

"Oh, OK . . . maybe *I* want that, too! That's what we all want, right? Me to shut up . . . for good. OK, OK, then gimme it back." PJ glared at Paul. His dark "dare you" glare. "Never was gonna hurt anyone but lil' ol' *me* with it, so give my knife back, Dad!"

"No," Paul managed to answer, picturing his son plunging the jack-knife in his own throat. PJ lunged at Paul, stuffing his hand into his father's pants pocket. Paul gripped his son hard to stop him. Locked in a bear hug, the two staggered.

"Nurse, we need help," the bald dad-or-someone shouted.

"Gimme it, Dad!" PJ bulled his full weight against Paul, shoving him backwards. Paul bumped hard against the corridor wall.

PJ had gotten hold of the knife; he was fumbling to snap it open.

"No," Paul commanded with desperate steadiness. Never startle a crazy with a weapon, he'd learned at the wet shelter. Paul took one small, stiff step toward PJ.

"What's going on down there?" A new voice, a woman's deep as a man's, called from far up the hallway.

Before PJ could point the knife anywhere—at his father, at himself— Evvy jumped PJ from behind, seizing both his elbows and trying to pin them back. Some damn karate move? PJ and Evvy struggled. A blur of bumbling movement, and the two of them fell sideways. Evvy cried out. The knife clanked on the floor. PJ landed on his butt.

From the floor, he gaped up at paralyzed Paul.

"What's going *on?*" the nurse demanded, closing in.

PJ's booted legs stuck out straight. The jackknife lay askew beside him, someone's blood dotting the floor. His back to the nurse, Paul bent fast and reached, seizing the knife.

"I . . . I hurt my ankle," Evvy called out, drawing the nurse's attention. Paul twisted round to face the stocky, middle-aged nurse marching up to them, her eyes on Evvy.

"Call security," the nurse commanded to someone, bending beside Evvy. Paul quietly snapped the knife shut. He stuffed it back in his pants pocket, his hands always so steady.

"Your ankle?" PJ on the floor leaned toward Evvy. "Wow, God. I . . . I'm *sorry*."

"Shush now," Evvy hissed, her voice tightened by pain, her sock red with blood.

The bulldog nurse was reaching into her pocket and pulling out plastic gloves, seeming not to have noticed, Paul hoped, him hiding the knife—but PJ had noticed.

PJ stared from the blood spots up to his father. He shot Paul an abashed and maybe grateful, or maybe merely pleading, dark-eyed gaze. Then PJ turned back to Evvy, who was hunched over, clutching her bleeding ankle.

"I . . . I twisted it . . ." Evvy gave a moan that sounded lame compared to Sarah's.

"But how did you get this cut?" the nurse asked. So, she hadn't seen PJ's knife?

"These people don't belong here," the bald dad-to-be complained from the nearest doorway. *You're right*, Paul thought as he met the glare of the nurse. His shoulder ached from hitting the wall; his heart thumped though he kept his face expertly calm.

"This boy . . . he's your son?" the desk nurse demanded. "We have no disturbances on the birth floor, you hear me? What's this all about?"

I sure as hell don't know, Paul didn't answer, bending for the card envelope PJ had dropped. Lifting that briskly, like the knife, like it was his own. Then telling the confused nurse, "Just a little disagreement here. Everything's fine now. If we could just get help for Evvy and her ankle. She just, in the tussle she must've . . . cut herself or something."

"Cut herself? On *what?*" the nurse demanded of Evvy, but she was, maybe fakely, moaning again, holding her ankle, bright blood oozing under her hands.

PJ beside her sat watching the whole scene in dazed dismay.

"I did it. I'm the, the . . ." PJ began loudly, shakily.

"The *son*," Paul cut in, louder and faster. "He's the . . . my . . . son." He shot PJ a Dad look that said *No*, that said, *you joke about the bomber one more time, it'll be your last joke.*

PJ lowered his dirty-haired head like a kid, ashamed.

"My son . . . he . . . he came here to see me, me and my wife," Paul declared in his false calm, glad that the nurse only had eyes for Evvy. With her gloved hands, she began loosening the ties on Evvy's sneakers. Not looking up as PJ protested Paul's words.

"No I'm not! I'm not with no one!" PJ declared, red-faced, scrambling to his feet.

"We need a wheelchair to ER! And we need security up here, pronto," the nurse called to another older nurse shuffling toward the scene.

"My dad, he's gotta get back to my stepmom," PJ added as the matronly, white-haired nurse halted beside him. "But, see. I'm a daddy! Daddy, too! But not here, not her . . ."

The nurse was still crouched by Evvy, asking her to wiggle her toes.

Clutching PJ's envelope, Paul edged sideways. He took hold of the handle to Sarah's closed birth room. Sarah was moaning away full force behind the door, as if calling to him.

"Go! Go back to her, Paul," Evvy told him raggedly. "I'll handle Peej! Go to Sarah! Oh God, my fucking *foot*!"

"Not here, not her," PJ repeated nonsensically, as the kind-looking, white-haired nurse took hold of his arm. PJ shut up, gazing at her lined, patient face like she'd stepped out of a dream. Christ, all the poor kid ever wanted was a mom.

"Sorry," Paul told everyone, meaning it. He heard the elevator *beep*, security arriving on the scene, the professionals taking over with the son Paul had hopelessly failed. "Sorry, I gotta . . . gotta be here, in here." With that, Paul opened the door.

He stepped into the doorway, and hesitated, surveying the scene ongoing without him.

"Yeah, you go to her, Dad," PJ mumbled to the floor, not shaking off the firm hold of the older nurse. Ready to surrender—but to what? To a real arrest this time?

"Over here," the nurse beside Evvy shouted down the hall, TV voices still talking away, all the hospital staff keyed-up, on alert. At least PJ hadn't claimed, again, to be the bomber.

With this final thought, with everyone looking away, Paul seized his chance and backed into the birth room. He shut its door on them all, hard. "Christ almighty."

He heard Sarah panting behind her curtain as if running a race, the homestretch. Paul still held PJ's raggedy envelope; he was still standing by the door, outside the closed curtain where Sarah couldn't see him, so he yanked out the birthday card PJ had kept mentioning. Maybe it held some clue to what had gone so wrong in his messed-up family? PJ said he'd found it in Sarah's art supplies last summer. Why had she hidden it there? Paul's big hands stayed steady as he opened it.

She wouldn't have saved it if she hadn't at least wanted . . .

What? What further words had Evvy been so anxious to cut short? *Not here, not her.*

Outside in the hall, Paul heard a man's voice demanding, "Come with me."

"Just took a fall," Evvy was claiming to security in the hall. "Just a little tussle here."

"You're all coming downstairs," the man's voice replied, no-nonsense. He wasn't going to take any chances tonight. Who could blame him? Through the door, Paul heard PJ saying something in a lower voice, calmer now that his brute of a dad was gone, maybe glad to be caught at last, told "No." With a small, shameful rush of relief, Paul heard the bustle of purposeful movement, everyone following orders. God knew what would happen to PJ. Evvy or someone would call Paul if they needed him. Right?

"Mr. Straddy. What're you doin'?" the guard nurse called warily from behind the curtain, at Sarah's side. "What on earth's goin' on out there? This is no night for family fights!"

"You're right," Paul agreed readily, yanking the card out. "Everything's fine, Sarah. I'm here, Sarah. Just gimme a second . . ."

Paul knew he shouldn't look, but he couldn't not. He held the shiny birthday card, a soft-focus close-up of a candle. Paul had never wanted a cigarette so badly. He raised the Hallmark card closer, catching a whiff of Sarah's tempera paints. The golden, photographed flame blurred as if, in Paul's too-tight grip, it was burning.

The room door had thumped; Sarah had heard that. She'd heard the raised voices and scuffling in the hall. All of it seemed far away. She was about to bear down on another cramp, to push harder than ever. Pelvic Rock called to Paul again. Sarah wanted to call out, too. There was something important she needed to say, to deny, but her throat tightened.

Only an *eeee* sound squeezed out. She was, her body was, pushing again. Her legs scissored on the mattress. When the push died down, too soon again, Pelvic Rock rested one hand on Sarah's ankle.

"We need to change things up. I know what you need, hon." You need to kick, and hard. I know who." Pelvic raised her voice. From behind her shut eyes, Sarah heard Pelvic shout what she herself wanted to shout. "Mis-ter Strad-dy! You get *in* here!"

Was Paul out there at all? Was PJ still saying—had Sarah heard him right?—her baby was his baby? *No*, she wanted to shout back, but no one was there. Sarah panted.

Something to kick, yes. Someone to kick.

"Sorry," Paul mumbled, and he stepped through the curtain looking as deeply dazed as Sarah felt. His dark eyes avoided hers. What had happened with PJ in the hall? What on earth? Sarah wished she could ask Pelvic or someone exactly what had just happened in this room, what her crazed young stepson had claimed.

"Over here, Mr. Straddy. Your wife, she needs someone to kick around. That'll be you and me, you hear? You take one foot, sir, and I'll take the other. Sarah, you getting ready? You gonna kick us both to kingdom come?"

"King come," Sarah muttered, her throat parched. Paul had come. He took his place beside Pelvic Rock. He lifted Sarah's foot in his strong, familiar hand.

"You keep holda that one foot an' me this one," Pelvic Rock was instructing Paul. "Keep hold no matter how hard she kicks you, kicks us. You hear?"

Paul jerked his bearded chin.

You here? You here? Sarah braced herself to kick, to push. Her foot pressed flat against Paul's firm thigh and, on the other side, against Pelvic Rock's, softer.

"Hard now, honey. You kick just as hard as you need to . . ."

Sarah couldn't waste energy in words or nods. She'd wasted more than enough already today on all her wild worries. Paul was here, her husband, standing tall as ever at the foot of her bed. Paul furrowed the black brows that her baby would inherit.

Let him be the one to worry. Sarah tensed her extended legs. Why in hell couldn't Paul look her in the eye? She shot her feet forward, like Evvy and PJ karate kicking. Inside herself, much more mightily, Sarah pushed.

"Ugh," she grunted as she kicked Paul and Pelvic. Their solid, standing bodies absorbed each kick. Pelvic Rock swayed with it; Paul stayed straight like a soldier.

"*Ugh*," Sarah grunted harder, pushing hard. Picturing PJ and Evvy antically kicking up dirty sand on the Spy Pond beach, that memory distracting, disturbing.

"Push *through* it, hon. Stay *with* it, hon."

"Push *through* it, Sare," Paul echoed, sounding less sure.

"Don't," Sarah snapped as her head collapsed back. *Don't tell me what to do.* Her body slackened. Her legs hung limp, her feet still grasped in their hands, four-point restraint, in Center terms. Sarah panted in defeat, her body exhausted, the baby exhausted. Did its monitor *bleep* softer?

"Don't you tell us. You *show* us," Pelvic, the only not-tired person in the room, urged. "Your doctor's on her way. She's caught up in an emergency."

But I'm an emergency, thought Sarah on her back, hoarsely panting. Paul, on his side, nodded along with Pelvic's unstoppable scold.

"This next push, don't you waste no breath on no words, no sound, none of that. You still *fighting* the pain. You gotta let that pain do its work."

Let it, let it, Sarah thought silently through her next push-kick. The same maddening advice all the fertility books gave—stop trying so hard, and it will happen. Hadn't that been true, for her? Sarah flopped backwards again; her ballooned face and cheeks deflated.

She'd quit the push too soon yet again. Pelvic Rock subtly shook her head. Paul looked down at Sarah like a judge, like he was trying to figure out who this woman, swollen with this baby, was. This baby, his baby—*her* baby, really, from the start.

"I—I . . ." Sarah croaked, meaning "ice," and meaning *I can't do this. I'm innocent. No, guilty. No, both. Please God, don't make this baby pay for my mistakes.*

"Ice?" Pelvic Rock asked, mellow-voiced again, and Sarah loved her again. Pelvic's shiny curls vibrated with her coaxing nod. "You want ice, hon?"

She opened the curtain. Distantly in the hall, voices were talking about a manhunt. The manhunt for the Bombers still somehow going on—marathon manhunt. *What I've been on,* Sarah told herself. *Marathon hunt for my baby, my own son—son hunt.* When would she ever, finally capture him? Paul, as if she'd spoken aloud, stepped over with her cup. *Had* she spoken aloud? Who knew what she'd said tonight?

Still Paul, like a faithful servant, bent to hold the cup under her chin. Sarah slurped ice chips from the tilted cup, the nurse behind him with a white handkerchief. No, a white washcloth, like a handkerchief she'd seen onstage. Hands in gloves like OJ's, about to strangle a wife. Where had Sarah seen that? Boston Symphony Hall, one of her and Paul's first and only fancy dates.

"I want to strangle *him*," Sarah, with her hair piled on her head, had whispered at the end of the opera when Othello strangled Desdemona over a handkerchief. A spotlit square of white cloth.

Sarah swallowed cool, soothing ice and whispered to Paul fast, "PJ . . . it not true . . ."

"Shh, shh," Paul answered like she was the baby. "I know that. I know."

His *I know*s sounded rushed, too, untrue. "All that's gotta wait, Sare. Everything but this."

He rested his hand on her taut, riled-up, wired-up belly, her baby only a giant push away. The giant push her aching, sprung muscles were bracing to attempt again.

"Yes," Pelvic Rock echoed, like they finally got it. "This's gonna be *the* Push." She nodded hard, her coiled curls springy. She motioned Paul impatiently into his place. Sarah thrust up her foot so Paul had to take hold of it. He braced it against his thigh.

Sarah wanted to push so hard, kick so hard, she'd knock both him and Pelvic flat. Knock Paul and PJ and everyone out of her way. Her and her baby's way.

I CAN GIVE U—

"Push, now, hon. Give us that biggest push. You know that push I mean?"

I CAN GIVE U—

Paul patted Sarah's ankle, rubbed her calf. He was looking at Pelvic Rock, asking low-voiced, like Sarah shouldn't hear, where in hell was Dr. Lutz?

"Where *you?*" Sarah demanded in a strained voice, straight to her husband.

"Right here, Sare. I'm right—"

"You're *not*, you're *not!*"

She thrust her foot forward with each not. She was pumping herself up, glad to feel Paul stiffen with each kick. Like he *was* there, was feeling it, too.

I CAN GIVE U—

WHAT U—& ME TOO—WANT

Did Paul ever want this too? Sarah wondered as she kicked, hard, two-legged frog kicks against Paul and Pelvic and everyone.

"Bad," she found herself croaking like the girl in *The Exorcist*, that horribly strained voice from hell, "How bad . . . son hunt? How bad? I *want* . . ."

"The baby. I know, Sare. I know how bad, how you'd have done anything. But listen, listen. That, none of that—"

"Makes no sense at all," Pelvic Rock put in, cutting Paul short, patting Sarah's foot. "None of this talk, no more. This mommy's just way, *way* outta her head . . ."

I'm not, Sarah wanted to protest from her tornado's-eye center. *Not outta my head now, but I was then, before the baby.* She pushed again, screwing up her face, puffing her cheeks.

"*Eeee*—" escaped her throat like steam from a kettle. *Eeee*, a train screeching and shuddering to a halt, too damned soon.

"Just outta her head," Pelvic Rock repeated distantly like Sarah's latest push wasn't big enough to notice, to count. Pelvic lowered Sarah's limp foot and stepped up to her holding the white cloth.

"No," Sarah whispered raw-throated at sight of that handkerchief. Desdemona died for a handkerchief, a foolish misunderstanding. Wet handkerchief—no, washcloth—pressed her forehead. Lukecool, like Spy Pond always felt. Little ripples, not waves; perfect for wading.

"Thought . . . safe . . ." Sarah gasped, trying to hear the baby monitor above her own breaths, to feel the tug of those wires. Were they still attached?

"Safe?" Paul was repeating, far away at the foot of her bed. "You thought what was safe, Sare?" Then, hurriedly, like he didn't want to know, "You are safe, Sare, the baby, too. You're safe now . . ."

"Not *me*," she gasped back, exasperated. It shouldn't have mattered whether she felt safe. Not when she was supposed to be the adult, the mother. Not when she should've been protecting him, both him's. Her sons—her stepson and son-son.

"Not me . . . safe," she insisted, thick-tongued, meaning it only mattered—only should matter—if the baby was safe. But she shouldn't be speaking, stealing breath from her next push.

The push that had to be *the* push.

Winter, 2012

After an almost perfect Christmas Day for two spent in bed, just Sarah and Paul, and—they both joked—Sarah's new second-trimester breasts; after gorging on undercooked sugar cookies and overheated 1940s melodramas on DVD; after Paul had tried repeatedly to phone PJ and received no answer; after Paul had gotten "drunk for two" watching It's a Wonderful Life *beside weepy Sarah and fallen into a snoring, sated sleep, Sarah made herself phone her mother.*

"Yes, we're having a happy *one," Sarah shouted into the receiver to her half-deaf, semi-senile mother in her Providence rest home. "Because you know—" Sarah knew she had to re-state though she had told Mother repeatedly and even showed her during her most recent, dutiful visit, "I'm finally, you know,* pregnant, *Mom."*

"Oh, Sarah," her mother sighed impatiently from her permanent daze of disappointment, "No you are not. You are still just a little girl."

After she ended the call awkwardly, and brushed sugar-cookie glitter from the sheets, Sarah lay awake beside vigorously snoring Paul and felt the guilt she'd held at bay all day wash over her. It was her fault PJ didn't answer his father's calls. Paul thought it was because he'd fired PJ back in August, because he'd been a bad Dad. But wasn't it Sarah—the secretly wicked stepmom, the child bride who'd never really grown up—who was to blame? Sarah, who even after getting what she'd always wanted still wasn't grown-up enough to tell her husband the truth and ruin their pretend-perfect Christmas?

Chapter Seven

April 19, 2013: 12:15 a.m.

Delivery

"That big push, biggest push," The guard nurse kept relentlessly repeating to Sarah, a code between females Paul wasn't supposed to hear. "That push you're most scared of, girl . . ."

The nurse was holding a washcloth to Sarah's forehead. Sarah's dark, damp hair was wild on the pillow. Paul stood tall and dumb at the foot of the bed, waiting to be kicked again. But Sarah lay flat now, her legs limp. Her belly seemed an unmovable mountain.

"The push you think'll tear you in two—"

Tear it in two; what he ought to have done. After he'd read it, Paul had hurriedly stuffed PJ's bizarre card, along with the folded up jackknife, into Sarah's emergency overnight bag by the door. He couldn't throw the card away when he'd barely skimmed the words his son had block printed there, PJ so blatantly stating that he could give Sarah a baby.

But would Sarah have kept such a card if PJ really had? No, Paul felt sure as Sarah's fierce, pain-blinded stare pulled him closer. He let his fingertips brush her mound of belly.

Hadn't PJ all but admitted he'd lied when he'd said that Sarah keeping his card showed 'at least' she'd wanted what he offered? PJ had wanted to see if she still had the card today where he'd found it last summer. PJ had grown up to be as melodramatic as his mom. Poor PJ, practically threatening to stab himself with his damn knife.

Had all that really just happened, right outside the door? Had PJ been serious about stabbing himself, hurting himself? Adina had seemed manic-depressive to Paul. Had PJ inherited some lethal combination of the Stratidakis gloom and Adina's diva mania?

"Breathe, honey; you gotta get your strength up, hon—"

Was PJ still breathing down at security? Two strikes and you're out, arrested for real? Paul rubbed his eyes. The guard nurse wiped Sarah's sweat-slicked forehead with the hospital washcloth. Paul slipped out his cell phone and checked his texts.

One from Evvy, bless her interfering heart.

AM IN E.R. W/ STITCHES & PJ PASSED 2nd BREATHO-TEST BUT SECURITY HOLDING HIM FOR QUESTIONS BUT HVE NO WEAPON—WILL MAKE STATEMENT & HOPE 2 CLEAR MESS UP—KEEP THE YOUKNOWWHAT OUTTA SIGHT & KEEP SARAH IN.

The text ended there—keep Sarah in sight, and the knife out. Jesus, like they didn't have anything better to do tonight than question this kid of his, who was surely not a danger, really, to anyone but himself. Would PJ have stabbed himself in the hall?

Paul texted back a quick THANKS, I WILL. KEEP ME POSTED.

Then he pressed send and, feeling he was letting everyone down at once, in different ways, sank back into the chair at Sarah's bedside.

Sarah lay limply, as if defeated, against the pillows.

"Gonna go fetch Dr. Lutz," the guard nurse said to Paul. He nodded, hearing from somewhere outside the sealed hospital windows sirens busily spiraling away.

Could they have caught them at last, the bomber brothers? Paul groped for the remote on Sarah's bed stand. She hadn't wanted the TV sound on, but she might not even notice at this point. Maybe she needed the distraction, as he did. Didn't he, as the father of a possible person of interest, need to know what the hell was happening out there?

Paul aimed the remote at the flat-screen TV suspended above the foot of Sarah's bed. He turned the sound on low, so not to startle Sarah. But her eyes snapped open. Like Paul, she fixed on a blurry, blown-up photo floating onscreen—the younger brother. The white hat boy who did look, in the sullen sideways shot, slightly like PJ.

—MARATHON MANHUNT CONTINUES, the CNN voices informed them. BOMBING SUSPECTS HURLED HANDMADE GRENADES AT POLICE IN CAMBRIDGE SHOWDOWN. POLICE ARE PURSUING SUSPECTS INTO CAMBRIDGE/ WATERTOWN AREA, NEW I.D. INFORMATION EMERGING . . .

The blurred yet intense close up showed the dark-haired white-hat suspect in long-nosed profile, his fierce straight-ahead stare. Paul and Sarah both fixed on his face.

Sarah muttered something, counting maybe, under her breath. Counting her breaths as she'd been taught to do?

"Bomber Boy," she seemed to mutter. Was that what she'd said? Or maybe Paul was hearing things?

"Dr. Lutz is coming," Paul told Sarah. "Bomber Boy," she mouthed again. Paul nodded dumbly, sensing this might be his last chance to check again on his own boy bomber—the older brother. *Our own black hat brother*, Paul thought grimly as he stepped outside the curtain, and slipped out his cell again. Sarah oblivious, mumbling her numbers. No new texts from Evvy. Because everything had settled down, or because Evvy and PJ were en route to police headquarters? Surely not. Not on this night? Paul peeked in at Sarah.

"Bomber Boy," Sarah muttered again, staring fixedly at the blurry Bomber Boy face on TV. Then, as if making a wish, clenching her eyes shut again against yet another wave of pain.

"I'm turning off the damn TV," Paul announced. The nurse was setting another cup of ice on the nightstand. "It's upsetting my wife . . ."

The nurse nodded distractedly, her own eyes glued to the TV screen. But she stepped away again fast, a beeper going off on her belt. Paul stepped back, pulled open the curtain, lifted the remote, and clicked off the Bomber Boy.

"No," Sarah moaned when her eyes opened, pointing shakily at the TV. "I—I need him . . ."

Which him? Was Sarah thinking that boy was somehow PJ? PJ, who might be under arrest for real by now? And why would Sarah need PJ anyway? Wasn't the "he" she needed her own baby?

"He's fine. He's going to be fine," Paul made himself mutter to Sarah, meaning PJ, meaning their baby boy. His attempt at a reassuring voice sounded hollow to him, but Paul grasped Sarah's hand, which she grasped avidly back. More swollen than ever this night, or so her hand felt to Paul. He felt, too, the hard metal of the wedding ring embedded in her finger.

Their rings pressed painfully together. Bones and gold. Sarah had always said she could read his thoughts when their heads were close together. From her pillow, Sarah met Paul's gaze. She held it as she'd done hours ago when the Belmont cop car had pulled up beside them, both of them bracing themselves for disaster; Paul felt it, then and now.

Both of them wondering—Paul practically heard Sarah wonder this too, as grimly as him—what the hell next?

"'The best way out is always through,'" Paul found himself reciting to Sarah. A line from some Frost poem he'd been made to memorize lifetimes ago.

"Through," Sarah murmured, her voice so far away.

"No matter what," Paul added, quoting the tiny engraving on the inside of their wedding rings. He squeezed her hand again. Her flushed, stripped-down face winced. It was hurting her, Paul knew: their wedding ring on her thickened finger. "Sare? Is that ring hurting you with your finger so swollen? Should we do like we did when I was in the hospital?"

Paul jabbed his pinkie straight out, pointing at her. Sarah slipped her hand from his loosened grip. She managed to point her ring finger. He pressed the tip of his pinkie to her trembling fingertip.

When he'd had the surgical procedure intended to alter his sperm count, he'd been asked to remove all jewelry, but he'd never taken off his wedding ring. He and Sarah hadn't wanted the ring to leave their own fingers, so they'd joined fingertips and slid his ring onto her. Then, after the outpatient surgery, they'd slid the ring back onto him.

"Let me," Paul told her now, twisting and sliding Sarah's tight ring. He eased it up over their shakily joined fingertips. He slid and forced it onto his own left pinkie.

"Lemme—" Sarah squeezed his extended pinkie. "Like–his . . ."

Paul knew what she meant by his. In her few babyhood visits with her father, before he flew the coop to his well-fixed family in Europe, Sarah had gripped her father's big pinkie. Her mother had told her she'd gripped so hard his pinkie turned bright red.

Paul held his own pinkie steady in Sarah's manic grip. He wished that baby Sarah had lopped a finger off that coldblooded, auburn-haired Scotsman bastard, that father who'd left her. Another simple, bracingly clear thought. Men who left babies were bastards. No doubt those damn bombing suspect brothers had been dumped by some deadbeat dad.

Just like Paul had dumped PJ in a sense last summer—or that's how it must have felt—when PJ screwed up his Center job and left town so abruptly in August. Shouldn't Paul have chased him down and driven on out to Ohio right away before PJ ran into police trouble and was arrested for a misdemeanor? And tonight, maybe something more serious. Especially if PJ acted up downstairs? If he dared another bomber quip?

THINK HE'S ME, DAD-EE? Paul remembered PJ's last email from hours before. WAIT&SEE WHAT I'M UP 2

WHAT BOMBS I GOT TO DROP ON U

Christ, Paul should have torn up his printed copy of that email—like Sarah should have torn up that card, should've shown him that card first. Then Paul would've—what? Torn into PJ? Sarah's hand gripped harder, as if to calm Paul down. Reading his thoughts, as always?

"Any," Sarah managed, her mouth sounding dry, "Any word . . . from, from—"

"No news from PJ," Paul lied. "Not since he busted in here and . . . and Evvy took him away, took him back downstairs," he added, making it not quite a lie. Security and the ER were both in the giant hospital's lower level, right? "She'll take care of him," Paul finished.

Hoping that, at least, was true. Sarah nodded, then caught her breath. She squeezed Paul's pinkie so hard she set off a small shock of pain. Her blotchily flushed face screwed up again like a little girl's or an old lady's—like both.

Paul breathed in a welcome, familiar smell: fresh hot coffee. A steamy, Styrofoam cup. The guard nurse or some other angel had set it on Sarah's nightstand.

Paul lifted his free right hand. Coffee, at last; the next best thing to a smoke. He gulped it, scalding his tongue and clearing his befogged brain. Sometime in the unimaginable future, when their baby was safe, Paul would find out exactly what had gone on between PJ and Sarah.

But not now. Paul set down the half-drained cup. Determinedly, he rested his coffee-warmed right hand against Sarah's big belly, pressing through the sheet. He felt the baby curled up so still and firm inside. Sarah's belly still seemed so big to Paul. His caffeinated brain clicked forward, no stopping it.

A preemie would surely be Paul's baby because PJ had been in Ohio all September and October. Paul had been gone for so much of August, had been distracted and depressed. Yet, he and Sarah had made love during early August. A full-term baby didn't have to be suspect.

The main point, Paul told his temporarily clearheaded self, was this: if the baby was full-term, there might be no reason the doctor couldn't give hopelessly moaning Sarah some damn drugs. Paul lifted his free hand from Sarah's belly.

"Too hard," Sarah mumbled. Was that what she was saying? Though his hand was aching, Paul kept his pinkie extended like a bird perch for Sarah. She squeezed.

No matter what, Paul reminded himself. No matter what she might have done, she was his. Her wedding ring pressed into his skin; its gold cut to bone.

"Too hard," Sarah repeated, meaning the pain—meaning Paul sitting so far away, it seemed. And herself—too far to go to get to this baby at the marathon's end, the pain spiraling like sirens. Were those real sirens somewhere outside? Sarah kept squeezing Paul's pinkie.

What had he been telling her? Something important, but she couldn't keep hold of it. Something about PJ? Ocean roar was rising in Sarah's ears. She pushed against the roar, pushed from her deepest aching insides. She bucked her back against the mattress. The mattress throbbed like the washer at home.

Blood, egg, milk. Blood, egg, milk.

Sarah leaning on the washer. The washer throbbing at her back, spray bottle in her hand.

Removes protein stains, the label tells her, instructs her.

Blood, egg, milk.

"Push. Push harder hon—"

Two voices from behind her squeezed-shut eyes are instructing her; two voices too loud. *Removes protein stains,* and then in parenthesis, *blood, egg, milk.*

Sarah breathed a wet breath, tasting it all: blood and egg and milk. She re-gripped Paul's pinkie with her whole, sweaty hand.

"Stay," she managed to command Paul. Away for too long with his dad last summer. Leaving her for long minutes out in the shouting hall to contend with PJ—because of her. Sarah wanted to open her mouth to speak, apologize, but she couldn't even open her eyes. She sensed a missing light through her eyelids, the TV turned off.

The Bomber Boy gone, missing in this endless night, out there some-where, like PJ. Eyes flat, yet sad, needing help, needing a real mother and father.

Like PJ—as Sarah knew even better than Paul—capable of God-knew-what.

"I'm here," Paul told her again.

"I need to talk to the husband," another voice said, brisk like Mom's, like she needed to tell Paul something bad and drop some bombshell, like PJ.

What had PJ blurted out in this room?

God knows, Sarah was thinking, pushing. Pushing it all away, every-thing that was too hard to think about now. She pushed even harder, losing hold of Paul's pinkie.

"OK, talk," Paul told Dr. Lutz. Though Sarah had released his finger at last, he stayed seated. He kept his eyes fixed on that monitor like the *bleep* might stop if he looked away. No more checking for texts; no more nothing until this baby was delivered. "But I need to be, Sarah needs me to be, here."

Dr. Lutz was nodding, flipping clipboard pages, Sarah zoning out into her pain again.

"All right." Lutz set down her clipboard with a brusque clack. "I'll talk to you both."

"Is it," Paul asked the monitor screen, "the baby? Is the baby in . . . in trouble?"

"Well, any premature baby is at risk, but there are few signs of—" Dr. Lutz checked the jumping electric green line, "fetal distress. Not severe. Not yet. Often in a premature delivery, the baby is so small the labor is relatively brief, but that doesn't seem to be the case with your baby . . ."

Paul nodded uneasily. He still tasted the coffee, but his caffeinated clarity had blurred, his thoughts jumbling again with his panicky pulse. *No*, he told himself sternly.

This baby was conceived, as they'd assumed all along, in the rush of lovemaking he and Sarah had thrown themselves into in September after Paul had finally returned from Dad's funeral week in Florida. His dad's terrible, freeing death had triggered this baby despite Paul's low sperm count. Right?

". . . and now with the baby so long in the birth canal, positioned there for hours, you see, the baby may be getting a bit . . ."

Paul held his breath for both himself and panting Sarah.

Lutz finished with the first warmth Paul had heard in her voice: "a bit puzzled."

"Puzzled?" Paul asked back, his voice cracking with hope.

He shot a glance from the monitor to Sarah. In her normal state she would've smiled, too, would've savored the notion of their son in his birth canal being merely puzzled. But Sarah's glazed gaze remained fixed on the beeping monitor.

"However," Lutz continued crisply, "if he, the baby, remains in place like this much longer, especially with his lungs not fully developed, he's at risk for infection or respiratory distress. So, we need to change the dynamic here . . ."

By a Caesarean? Paul wondered with an inner lurch of dread and relief.

Would Dr. No-C. Lutz permit that? Or would she, as her reputation suggested, push Sarah through what his wife romantically called real births? Sarah was growling low in her throat. Prelude, Paul was learning, to deep pain. A wave of pain that would carry her off so far he'd have to do the thinking and the deciding for both of them. All three of them.

❧

Sarah had lost hold of Paul's pinkie, but Paul was still here, despite whatever it was the doctor was telling him.

Sarah blinked open her burning eyes, gasping and half gagging. She'd pushed her guts out; yet the two faces on either side of her both looked disappointed.

And where was PJ? Where was the boy bomber? Someone had turned him in. No, off.

"We're not where we should be at this stage," Dr. Lutz told Paul in mommy's eternally disappointed-in-Sarah tone. *More, more,* demanded the bleeping baby monitor.

Sarah was letting everyone down. She was sagging back against her damp pillows.

"Can you get me more coffee?" Paul asked someone. He shot Sarah a wry glance, knowing she knew he needed a smoke, really. But he wouldn't leave her side.

Didn't she and Paul always get back in sync, no matter what? Why had she been worried about disappointing him?

Sarah wiped her wet face. A rainy day, she found herself remembering. Back in March; at the beach. After they fought, in the car to the doctor, hadn't Paul said something beautiful to her? Something about a beautiful room? The beautiful room inside her?

In the car, in the rain, with the two wipers making one pulse, making one silvery mass—what the baby, with its pulse-sized heartbeat, must see in her beautiful room, beautiful womb.

Sarah breathed the steam of Paul's coffee. What had he said about the beautiful room? She wanted to ask him, but she couldn't speak. She couldn't give up, give out. She gulped another breath of coffee steam. She had to do this without drugs. The doctor had explained that the labor was too far along now. The labor too far along and the baby not far enough along and Sarah damn well had to be strong, stronger than she'd ever been. Now, at her weakest.

Dr. Lutz touched Paul's shoulder, speaking straight into his ear. "So, Mr. Stratidakis, with a full-term birth I'd advise a picotin drip at this point to ease the pain and speed the contractions. With a thirty-weeker, however, I still don't want to risk infection . . ."

"But," Paul blurted out. Knowing it was crazy to say even as he set down his fresh coffee to speak. "What if this baby may not be thirty weeks, may not be all that premature . . ."

"What?" Lutz bent closer to him, her sculpted hair unmoving.

"Wha—?" Sarah echoed from her pillow, weakly but sharply, too. Paul had been assuming Sarah might not understand his words.

"Look." Paul hesitated with those two pairs of cool and hot and fierce female eyes upon him. "If there's any possibility," Paul told Sarah alone, testing her stricken face for some sign of recognition, "that there might be a . . . a confusion as to who, to when—" he quickly corrected himself. What in all hell was he saying, his head buzzy from coffee and hunger and terror? "However it may've happened, if there's a . . . a confusion as to when this baby was conceived; maybe then—" He turned from Sarah's wide, outraged stare to Dr. Lutz's narrowed, sizing-up one, "then maybe you can give Sarah some damn drugs to help it all along . . ."

"No—" Sarah erupted, a sound from deep in her throat. The way she sometimes shouted "Yes!" in sex.

Paul faced his wife, willing her to understand. No matter how unimaginably she might have screwed up, he wanted her to know that he was still and always here. He raised his aching hand again, holding out his ringed pinkie to her.

"I—I'm just saying if there's any possibility—"

Paul's eyes darted between Sarah and Lutz. "Look, Doc." Paul turned from Sarah, whose olive eyes burned with righteous anger or craven shame or both. "If the baby might be full-term, if Sarah might be helped by any kind of drug—"

Sarah seized Paul's pinkie, wrenched it backward. Pinpoint pain shot through his finger bone. He drew a harsh, startled breath.

"No," Sarah told him and Lutz, loud and clear. She gave a deeper more guttural moan. Paul held his stung, strained pinkie. "No drugs. No-ohh!"

Sarah arched her back determinedly, grinding her head into her pillow. The force of her push sent Paul to his feet. It sent him backing up fast as an "*eee*" of anguish escaped between her clenched teeth. But no other sound.

Paul was standing at the foot of her bed with Lutz, so he saw it: the first flash of the baby's head, cresting from between Sarah's widely spread legs, her bloody stretched vagina. One flash: bluish white skull slicked with wet, black hair.

Then it—the baby's black-haired head—was sucked back in.

"Oooh, he's got him some hair," Guard Nurse, who'd materialized beside Lutz, breathed.

Lutz decreed, approvingly for once, "Well, if Sarah can do that much with one push . . ."

"Then he's coming?" Paul demanded, still seeing that black, Stratidakis hair.

"Oh, he's coming," Lutz and the nurse murmured as one.

<hr>

Finally smiling: Paul and mommy doctor, both staring between Sarah's legs. Both saying words Sarah barely heard through the diminishing roar in her ears. The push and the baby were receding back into her body—she felt it.

Everyone watched between her legs now, expecting another push like that, when that one took everything out of her—everything but him. *Out, out,* she told her baby in time to his *bleep bleep.* If she couldn't get him out now, she knew in a post-pain flash, they really would resort to drugs.

They would hurt this baby even more than he'd already been hurt. All because she and Paul had sex too late and labor came too soon. The boy bomber floated over them all like a curse, an unloved baby boy. A PJ whose fuse of fury had blown. Would PJ's, too, tonight? With Paul believing, saying—what?

"One more," Paul urged, his hand gripping her tensed ankle. What had Paul been saying before? About when, about who. About giving her drugs because of when and who.

Tears and sweat blurred Sarah's eyes so she saw only his dark beard and brow. Her Paul.

You, Sarah wanted to scream at her husband, who even now stood too far away, but she couldn't shout how angry she was at him, couldn't find the words or facts for why she was so angry. *You, you,* she was thinking again, this time to the baby's *bleep bleep.*

This time to the baby. A final urge to push formed. Not from her. Not her body pushing but the baby's body pushing, opening her. The biggest wave yet was gathering. It was curling all around her, lifting and dropping her.

Her head snapped back; her spine electrified. Her body strained so hard her head almost burst. Her pain louder and louder until it was a roar she couldn't hear. Her teeth clenched, holding in all sound. Her hand, or some other hand pressed her side through this push, pressed her womb, her beautiful room. Pearly sea light filtered through her eyelids, a pulse of silence inside the roar. She and the baby shared that silent inner space one more moment.

"One more like that! One more!" Someone was shouting.

All their faces blurred together as Sarah blinked her eyes, not wanting to see them. Wanting to see, instead, what it was they were so raptly watching.

"Me see," Sarah croaked. But Mommy—no, doctor—stayed hunched over, glossy head bowed between Sarah's knees. Only Daddy—no; her baby's daddy—only Paul heard her.

"A mirror or something," he requested in his deepest, steadiest voice that made people listen and obey. Then the nurse was pulling one down somehow, one suspended by metal from the ceiling. A round, suspended mirror that Paul stabilized, holding it, centering it for Sarah.

A shiny circle: everything inside. Her spread open thighs, her stretched open vagina. A bluish-white curve like an egg, black hair slicked and slimy. Crowning, it was called. One fish-smelling flash, then the baby's head disappeared, sucked back into her yet again.

"One more, just one more—"

She was pulling back into herself, too, sucking back into that silvery, silent space she and the baby still shared. Only she didn't shut her eyes this time, didn't dare take her eyes from it, the shiny circle of light her husband held steady. Circle of her.

Sarah heaved back, open-eyed and open-mouthed: no clenched teeth halting her howl. Her roar ripped her throat, louder and louder, too big to hold in.

"Ohh—" she was crying like "No," but it was "yes." It was coming. She was moving with it, shiny circle shaking. Her slit in the circle spreading incredibly wider, opening. The head, like a blue egg with black hair, pushed further this time then, maddeningly, Sarah's breath exhaled—back inside.

"Out," Paul urged, his hand on her spread knee, holding her so wide.

Out, out, baby bleeped but more slowly. Dr. Lutz murmured that the heartbeat was slowing. The baby's oxygen level was dropping.

Sarah saw Paul shoot a glance at Dr. Lutz, the doctor's face hidden by Sarah's other knee.

"One more try," Lutz decreed from behind Sarah's knee. "And then we will need to—"

No, Sarah wanted to shout again, but she didn't shout. In silent, head bursting fury, Sarah pushed. With an aching tear of her flesh, an audible, bloody splurt, his head squeezed through. His nose popped up. A new nose!

His face filled the circle, heart-stoppingly human. Her son's pasty, blue-tinged face frozen in wince like a dead warrior's, carved from wet clay.

Just the head; the body somehow still inside Sarah, though it felt like nothing was left. Everything, even pain, had vanished into this sealed-shut head. This baby Sarah faced through her wide, apart knees, telling her emptied self: *He's beautiful and he's dead.*

God he's dead; Christ Almighty God.

Paul stood stunned at the foot of the birth bed, still holding the round mirror. A good job for him, the doctor or nurse had maintained: both doctor and nurse faded into background. Everything faded now but this baby's radiantly pale head, a stripe of Paul's own dense hair.

Some pair of hands—brown, white, nurse, doctor?—was pressing Sarah's belly, pushing out something slippery and limp, too small to be the body. But it squirmed. It moved, those stunted legs and arms. Paul saw, through hazy tears of joy and fear, his son's eyes unseal.

Black hair; blue-black eyes.

"He's—" Sarah managed to gasp, "here."

Alive, Paul knew she meant. He nodded so hard his tears spilled, but he didn't lower his numbed hand or her mirror.

"Oh, he's here," the doctor and nurse murmured as one.

Dr. Lutz, bless her cold-blooded calm, had caught the body in her hands. The baby amazed Paul by moving his slit-open eyes suspiciously once around the room, casing the joint.

Tears streaked Paul's face. A paranoid, like his papa! This baby so tiny and—Paul's brain told him though he no longer knew why—*so mine.*

Just as Paul thought this, sure the baby was his at last, many hands lifted his and Sarah's tiny-bodied, big-headed baby. *Happy birthday*, Paul had meant to say this moment. His throat, his whole self, was too full. Paul's vision blurred, but he was still seeing his son.

His head, his body. His face like no other.

"My baby," Sarah called out. She raised her arms with tremulous effort.

The baby had been swept away; he was being wiped off. Sarah wanted to jump up and follow, but Paul gripped Sarah's bare foot like he was wildly shaking her hand. Squeezing it and meeting Sarah's teeming gaze, his eyes ashine with pride.

Paul released her foot and stumbled toward the front of the bed. She kept reaching for her baby, reaching past Paul and everyone.

"Gotta get you warm, little one. You causin' so much trouble with that big head o' yours . . ." The nurse stepped to Sarah with the swaddled baby. No nipples had formed yet on his tiny, rib ridged chest. Webs of blue veins showed through his thin skin.

Sarah took shaky hold of her bundled son. She and Paul were both laughing and crying. Sarah heard Dr. Lutz issuing a low-voiced order to the nurse, something about tests and NICU, the dreaded four letters.

"My baby," was all Sarah answered, saying it straight to the baby she held, a bloody cord trailing from the baby's tiny body, still connecting his body to Sarah's.

"You wanna cut the cord?" the nurse demanded of Paul.

"S-sure," Paul stammered: his first word in front of the kid, and he sounded anything but.

He took hold of what the nurse handed him, what looked disconcertingly like rubber handled, everyday scissors.

"Cut that cord," guard nurse told him impatiently. Her capable hands directed his big ones to the rubbery, bloody stalk. *But I'll screw it up,* Paul wanted to say, PJ flashing in his mind. The son Paul had failed.

"Just cut, and fast; we gotta get this little fella into NICU," the nurse told Paul alone. Sarah kept crooning "perfect" to the baby alone.

NICU, Christ. Paul touched his son for the first time. The cord was slimy and warm, alive, a bloody lifeline.

"I got it," Paul told the nurse as she reached for the scissors.

He may not be the best one to do this, but he was the one who damn well should. He cut the cord like sausage. A foul yet sweetish smell: Sarah's blood, the baby's blood. Sarah and the baby's blood was still one, until Paul's clumsy, muffled snap.

At that snap, the kid cut loose, a small yet piercing wail, a kitten's yowl. Sarah whispered something Paul could not hear, Sarah's and the baby's voices mixing like their blood. Paul bent over them both. He rested one blood-stained hand on Sarah's slack shoulder and curved one around his baby's back. All too plainly, through the blanket, he felt the tiny, precise bones of the baby's spine, his son's skin more like membrane. So small, too small. Yet, as Sarah had said, perfect.

Paul squeezed Sarah's shoulder, and his sore pinkie twinged. His wife; his baby. How in hell had he doubted it? What help had he been in this birth room except to—a dad's real role? —enrage his wife so much she finally pushed the baby free.

Sarah hugged the baby closer, lying on the bloody padding of her birth bed. My wife, Paul repeated to himself, their two wedding rings on his one hand glinting. Sarah's fingers, like her whole body, still swollen. Sarah's forehead gleamed with sweat like the baby's. Who knew what was going on in either head? Paul stared, straining to take them both in.

With the last gasp of his paranoid brain, he wondered again, but calmly, how he could have doubted Sarah. That seemed ages ago now, another life. Not his—*their* new life.

"My baby," Sarah keened, this time in protest.

"Your baby needs an oxygen boost, hon." The guard nurse bent stoutly over Sarah. She lifted the baby away from Sarah's weakened arms, cruelly fast, it seemed to Paul.

"Oxygen boost?" Paul straightened, shaky on his legs. The nurse turned and pressed the shockingly light baby bundle into Paul's unready arms. As Paul struggled for hold of his weakly squirming son, the nurse clamped a plastic mask over the baby's nose and mouth. Suddenly, Paul himself was holding the lightweight oxygen mask and tube in place. In her voice pitched only for Paul, the nurse told him, "You can only hold your son a minute more, you hear? We gotta get him into his incubator; we gotta run his preemie tests."

Keeping the mini mask in place, Paul balanced his baby who weighed no more than a doll. In the bulky blanket, only his purplish forehead showed. Purple better than blue? Or not? Christ, Paul thought, he should've bent heaven and earth to see PJ born and to keep him close. He pressed the light, yet alive, body of his new son to his own body, a part of him.

❦

"My baby," Sarah found herself saying again, though she knew as Paul held their son she should say "our baby." She made herself thank Dr. Lutz and the nurse, yet as she mumbled those words she couldn't help feeling she'd done the whole thing by herself.

She reached for her baby again. "I've gotta let him nurse. How can he nurse in that mask?" Sarah's tongue felt thick, and no one seemed to hear her. She could see how small her baby's body was inside the blanket as Paul held him, but his head was perfectly rounded, not the bullet shape of a Down's baby. His black hair grew in a strip, like a mohawk. He'll be OK, Sarah told herself shakily, taking stock, babbling to Paul. "Your hair, my nose—did you see that little nose pop up?"

Paul nodded, breathing hard above Sarah. It sounded like he'd stopped crying. "Sarah, we've got to let them take him now . . ." He knelt carefully with the baby. Paul's head pressed Sarah's, his beard damp against her damp face, her own tears just starting to flow.

We can cry in shifts and hold the baby in shifts, Sarah thought. She swallowed her salt tears and a taste, too, of blood. The nurse was spritzing warm water between Sarah's blood crusted thighs, but Sarah felt numbed below from something stronger than drugs.

What was Dr. Lutz murmuring so urgently? And what exactly was this plastic mask that Paul was holding over the baby's mouth and nose? Sarah dipped her head so she met the baby's eyes—her own, in their almond shape.

"Want to . . . nurse." Sarah longed to open her gown, her breasts achingly swollen.

"No, no, hon." Nurse Pelvic Rock stepped over, coming into focus again. "No, you can't nurse with the baby. Not yet," Pelvic told her, bending to take the baby from Paul. "He can't swallow. He might choke. They'll feed him by NG tube, hon."

Nurse Pelvic took firm hold of Sarah's baby. Paul let her ease him— their baby—up and away. Sarah gasped, the baby gone. Paul pulled himself up as Pelvic edged past.

"But he'll be OK?" Paul demanded, doing the talking for both of them. Sarah's mouth stuck half-open; her tongue as numbed as her lower body.

"They're ready for him in NICU." Dr. Lutz reappeared at the foot of the bed, her face drained of make-up yet as composed as ever. "The Birth Center's ICU; the Neonatal Intensive Care Unit," Dr. Lutz was explaining. "Just one floor up. An incubator is indicated for any thir-ty-weeker with an Apgar wellness rating of 4, as well as Cyanosis, that blue you see in his skin, and a probable sepsis, or infection risk. Breast milk can be expressed for him and fed with a dropper. We need tests right away . . ."

Sarah made herself nod. She hugged herself, already missing his warmth.

"Better safe than sorry, I'm sure you'd both agree. All indications suggest he must be tested for possible neurological and physiological complications ASAP."

"A-S-A—?" Sarah found herself repeating stupidly. These letters had meant something in her other life, so had *neurological*.

"Go along—" Sarah tugged Paul's untucked shirt. "The mix-up thing," she added, reminding him of the one plan they'd made: that Paul would accompany their newborn baby from the birth room to the nursery. To make sure, despite finger and footprints, their baby was not, as the Boston Herald exclaimed in a headline Sarah had clipped: SWITCHED AT BIRTH!

"I will, Sare, but I already know I'd never mistake that face."

"Me neither," she told Paul, managing a half-smile. Paul sent Sarah his own pained smile, his hands hanging at his sides. Yes, they had to give over their boy to the doctors, for now. Nurse Pelvic started to carry the baby bundle away. From behind his plastic mask, Sarah heard a muffled, imperious yowl of protest. Sarah felt her breasts leak in answer.

She blinked back her tears and held them back for one last glimpse of him, even just the mottled curve of his forehead already unmistakable. Her him, her son.

Spring, 2013

At the beach in March, in the storm, in the car on the way to the urgent care center. The day of their big fight over PJ and his birthday call, over Paul inviting PJ to come visit: the first time Sarah felt it. That maybe Paul did want this baby, their baby.

Despite all the awful things she'd said, Paul had banged on their hotel door and insisted on taking her to the local urgent care center to have her swollen hands—it turned out to be merely water retention—checked. Both of them apologized to each other in the car, in their rain-blinded ride to who-knew-what. Paul saying—this was the part Sarah remembered at last—that he didn't regret canceling the amnio. That he agreed no matter what an amnio might have showed, they were having this baby, their baby.

"Yeah, we could never tear this baby from inside you," Paul had said in his slowest, lowest voice. "Could never tear him from his beautiful room."

Rain streaming on the window and headlights melted like candle lights, Sarah nodding and staring teary-eyed into the wipers and water and silvery mass, knowing this must be what her baby sees. Two wipers making one pulse. Two people loving you no matter what. No matter what they might have done to each other. Wasn't that enough to live on?

Chapter Eight

April 19, 2013; 12:40 a.m.

Recovery

"My son," Paul gasped at the closed double doors leading to security. He barely knew which son he was talking about at that point, though he'd just accompanied his infant son to the glass-windowed doors of the Neonatal ICU and abandoned him to his first battery of tests. "My son, I think he's . . . here. Being . . . held? Paul Stratidakis Junior?"

The name felt strange to say aloud. The blank-faced, uniformed young punk who seemed to be guarding the security offices, or maybe just taking a break, showed no flicker of recognition. Was he standing there asleep on his feet, too?

Paul smoothed his coarse, unbrushed hair with a shaky hand. Without pause to track down cigarettes or coffee, Paul had stumbled his way down the hospital corridors, silenced except for late-night crisis TV voices claiming that police and FBI were converging in the Watertown area. He made his way back to the elevator where Paul nearly fell asleep leaning on the metal wall going down.

"Look, my wife just had a baby," Paul told the young, unblinking security guard, his impassive, dark brown face and zoned-out black eyes.

Was he wearing invisible ear-buds? Listening to the latest bomber man-hunt update instead of frazzled, sour-breathed Paul? "And my son, my grown son, PJ—Paul Stratidakis Junior, he got into a, a scuffle upstairs and got hauled down here . . . oh, a while ago now, and I know he's being . . . held?"

The young man neatly sidestepped, opened the door marked SECURITY: STAFF ONLY. He called into the empty hallway, "Mr. Strat-ti-dick. He's here for his son?"

TV news voices echoed in the narrow security hallway, then paused, maybe muted. An older man barked out something that Paul, older by the minute himself, couldn't hear.

Suddenly Paul was stepping through the door the robotic younger guard held open as if for some dignitary instead of some Stratti-dick dad. *The one to blame for everything,* Paul felt as he followed the guard to the modest security chief office, its open, wooden door.

A large-screened computer on the chief's metal desk had in fact been muted—the screen showing live TV feed of night darkness and mul-tiple flashing police-car lights. The security chief, with a deeply lined, basset-hound face and grey hair in a military buzz-cut, lifted his wary gaze reluctantly from the screen.

"My son," Paul began politely, knowing what it was like to sit behind the boss desk. He met the chief's distracted stare, this ordinary office seeming strange, on the other side of his new son's birth.

"You the father?" the chief asked gruffly. Paul nodded. He sure was PJ's father, and the new baby's, too. The baby they had yet to name. That was the last thing Sarah had reminded him of before surrendering their baby to the nurse and collapsing into a coma-like sleep. Sarah and her earnest lists of possible names, the least of their worries now. Paul stepped toward the chief cautiously.

He sat on the chair by the chief's desk, feeling like a kid facing the prin-cipal. The chief launched into a flat-voiced, uninterruptible monologue.

Paul's son was in trouble. He was being held on a possible disor-derly conduct or even assault charge. Due to the emergency situation in the city of Boston, hospital security had been advised to hold any person of interest. Paul Jr. had been seen by a nurse wrestling with one Evelyn Elfman, currently asleep in ER with a sprained ankle and four stitches in her calf from what appeared to be a knife wound. Yet Ms. Elfman was insisting that PJ hadn't stabbed her, and she did not want to press charges, but she had offered no plausible explanation for her wound. Paul nodded gravely and tried to cut in, tried to second Ms.

Elfman's improbable statement.

No knife, Paul was ready to claim.

But then, he thought as the chief paused to slurp from a super-sized coffee, *what if they marched upstairs and searched the damn dumb Hurricane Emergency bag in Sarah's birth room? What if someone was already up there?* Finding among the canned goods the weapon in question, possibly even stained with Evvy's blood?

The chief didn't believe Ms. Elfman, he told Paul. Paul Junior claimed he wasn't sure or couldn't recall what-all had happened, exactly. He had been searched and had passed a breathalyzer test; his blood had been taken, and toxicology results were pending.

"Good thing you came down here on your own steam, Mr. Strati-dick-us. We were going to send for you soon as your wife delivered." The chief fixed his seen-it-all stare on Paul.

"You want him?" a voice interrupted from the still-open doorway. The younger guard poked his head in, unperturbed by the chief's annoyed sigh.

The chief did not seem to want this him.

"Dad?" PJ's hoarse voice croaked, as if sure that nobody did want him. PJ shuffled into the office; the guard, with a subtle twitch of a shrug, backed away.

"Peej!" Paul blurted out like his son was five. PJ wiped his sweaty face, looking like he might burst into tears. His curly dark hair stuck out all over, so oily Paul wanted to scrub it himself. He still wore his worn denim jacket, minus the knife bulge in its pocket, but his face had lost the sullen, defiant Bomber Boy look he'd worn earlier in the night. He gaped at Paul, his bloodshot pop-eyes frankly scared.

"Dad?" PJ actually cracked a crooked, hopeful smile. "You're . . . here?" PJ asked, like he'd truly thought Paul wouldn't come. "So, like, Sarah, she—"

"Had the baby. Your brother, Peej. He's got some problems but they're taking care of him and . . . we think he's gonna be OK." Paul rallied his old, sure supervisor voice. He nodded at the chair beside his, and for once, PJ obeyed, sitting beside his father mutely.

Paul gave PJ's knee a firm pat. He *was* the father, for better or worse, and he had to get his son out of this no matter what that son had said or done—Or said he'd done.

"I can explain what happened," Paul began, turning back to the chief and his unamused don't-bullshit-me face. PJ, too, faced Paul, counting on him.

"It was me," Paul announced in his own hoarse, loud voice, relieved to say something that felt totally true. "It's all on me. All of this, everything bad that happened tonight. Chief, see, I . . . I had a knife, the knife. I still got it, upstairs in a bag in my wife's birth room. I . . . Evvy—Evelyn Elfman and me——we were having a fight in the hall, wrestling or whatever you'd call it. Completely wrong of us, I know. PJ tried to break us up, so it might've looked from a distance like he was fighting, too, but it was me. Evvy, she might've been confused before, but she'll back me up on this. We . . . we've never liked each other!"

Paul felt inspired, running on empty but putting on speed. It all felt so true. A relief to confess it to PJ and this canny old guy who could've been one of his own dad's racetrack pals.

"She wanted to be in the birth room with my wife, and I didn't want her there. I've never wanted her near my wife. She'd say that herself. So we were fighting, and PJ here, he was just caught in the muddle—in the middle, I mean. He's been traveling. He hasn't been sleeping. We haven't been . . . I haven't been . . . keeping track of him like I should. So PJ, he was just letting off steam. He was talking out of his head, like the nurse said, like I am, now. My wife and the baby and the Bombers and all—we're all pretty damn stressed out. Hey, mind if I grab some of that coffee?"

The chief barely nodded. Paul reached over the desk for the Styrofoam McCoffee cup, nearly empty. One lukewarm, bittersweet sip, soothing to Paul's dry throat, all he needed to push through to the end, whatever ends he had to go to, to spring his number one son.

"Anyhow, believe me." Paul wiped his mouth, his beard. "It's me. Arrest-or-whatever me." His fingertips tingled like he was beyond exhausted. The chief looked dog-tired, too.

It all felt like the end of a mandatory double shift, back in Paul's supervisor days when, sometimes, the second shift super wouldn't show up and he had to stay on, dead tired. Those dreaded mandatory doubles. Two sons now; Paul's life was one long mandatory double.

"If you need to arrest *anyone*, I mean. I'd think the police are busy with bigger things tonight. The mandatory—I mean, the Marathon Bombers . . . all that. It got PJ all riled up, like all of us." Paul nodded at the muted computer, a newsman looking worn out himself but talking on. "Anyhow, I can give an official statement. Happy to. Evvy and I were scuffling, and I had a knife in my pocket and . . . as we struggled, she and I, we wrestled for the knife, and it accidentally did cut her, but PJ had nothing to do with all that. I should have come forward before, but, but . . . See what a . . . a bad dad I am? I mean to PJ. I'm going to try to be better to my baby son, to PJ, too, but anyhow . . . it's all on me."

"Dad come *on,*" PJ blurted out into the awkward pause. "Dad, this isn't gonna—" he began in his teenage whine, his bloodshot eyes glittery. "*Help,*" he finished, and his voice broke.

PJ bowed his curly, dirty-haired head and scratched hard with both hands. Then he rubbed his eyes hard, choking back tears. "I . . . I never should've . . . never should've said—"

"I know, Peej." Paul clapped his hand again onto his son's square knee. Hard. "I know. And you don't need to say anything more now, son."

Paul clammed up, too, feeling the unreadable chief study them. Sensing he just wanted to get back to the TV and the massive manhunt, wanted to be done with this puny family drama.

"Look, chief, you can see PJ here is under a lot of strain." Paul stood up beside PJ. He rested his hand on PJ's hunched, muscular shoulder. "—coming back into Boston with all hell breaking loose . . ." Paul nodded toward the computer screen, the images there shifting to live coverage, explosive bursts of light. PJ stood up, too, he and Paul edging closer to the screen.

REPORTED FIREFIGHT IN WATERTOWN: POLICE CONFRONT SUSPECTS IN FIERY SHOWDOWN, the news crawl proclaimed below the flashing onscreen scene.

"They got 'em?" Paul all but shouted. The chief didn't waste words. He un-muted the computer.

Shakily filmed gunshot and God-knew-what flashes lit the screen and the faces of the chief plus Paul plus PJ, the three men leaning close together.

So it was that Paul and Paul Jr. and the Mount Auburn Hospital's Security Chief watched together the report: POLICE CONVERGE IN WATERTOWN? Huddled around the Chief's computer, they stared into the blurred light bursts—footage from the previous night's 'firefight'? Sounds of gunshots and homemade explosives. News voices stumbled over themselves to narrate UNFOLDING EVENTS.

Christ, Paul thought in horror, leaning forward with his son. PJ could have been caught up in this, but for a few hours difference. Or Sarah could have been, Paul realized as he recognized the darkened buildings on the public street where the firefight was unfolding. There was the

Arsenal Center for the Arts, where Sarah regularly did art therapy classes. Only blocks away from their favorite Greek restaurant, the Aegean. Only miles away, fifteen minutes or so, from their home. WATERTOWN RESIDENTS ADVISED TO SHELTER IN PLACE.

Paul could hardly believe it as he sipped more cold coffee, keeping one hand planted on his son's strong, tensed-up shoulder. Waltham High used to cream Watertown High in hockey back when Paul was a swarthy Waltham teen. Now prim little Watertown was in the national spotlight. PJ should've played hockey, would've if Paul had been given any say.

PJ was bent forward now like he wanted to jump into the computer screen, seize an FBI AK-rifle and blast away at those terrorist Bombers.

BOMBER BROTHERS, the news voices kept repeating, emphasizing. "Brother?" was the one question PJ asked, maybe silently absorbing the fact that he now had a brother, too.

"I got a half-brother in the Cambridge force," the chief muttered during a break in the action while the newsmen attempted to verify the brother detail, "and he might be out there right now," the chief added. Then, as if the hospital lab were also taking advantage of the break in the TV action, the chief's phone beeped. He took a call from the lab informing him that PJ's blood sample contained no illegal drugs, but that PJ had, in fact—as he'd bragged to Paul, so at least he'd been truthful—somehow ingested more of the over-the-counter Ephedrine tablets, so called mini-thins.

At this flat-voiced report from the chief, PJ nodded stiffly, not denying anything.

"Like you said, you need to be keeping better watch on your son, sir," the chief concluded to Paul under the news voices he'd kept on while talking. The "sir" stated coldly, lest Paul think any buddy-buddy bonding was taking place in this screen-lit, post-midnight office.

Paul nodded hard, in unison with his sobered-up son.

Then Paul rallied his best gravitas. He told the chief that he and his family regretted the trouble they'd caused, especially on this night, that they'd all just been overwhelmed by Sarah going into labor at seven months.

"A preemie, huh?" The chief shook his head, the lines around his mouth deepening. "Yeah, that can be rough. Used to be those babies didn't make it."

Then he turned back to the computer screen. As he re-faced the bright screen, too, Paul sensed that the chief had turned a corner, had decided to go easy on PJ.

He hadn't said so yet, but Paul felt the premature birth of PJ's brother, and maybe a baby who hadn't made it in the chief's past, might have tipped the balance. *But my baby made it,* Paul reminded himself. *My new baby son and my wife.* Whatever had gone on last summer between Sarah and the older son Paul hadn't kept watch on, Sarah was still his Sarah.

"Guess I got a half-brother now, too," PJ muttered after a long pause in which they'd watched a vehicle bearing the wounded MBTA officer making its way through the night.

"Half-brother, brother," the chief muttered, giving a square-shouldered shrug as if such distinctions were meaningless. Then the chief rubbed his buzz-cut head and turned to PJ like Paul himself wasn't worth any more words. "Oughta be callin' my brother now, 'cept I'm sitting here babysitting you. You see what's goin' on out there, boy? Got men out there facing nuts with bombs. You pick this night to fight your old man or whatever in hell you up to, boy?"

PJ and Paul both nodded, both abashed in the face of this fatherly tirade, the kind of dad rant Paul should be able to deliver himself by now in his advancing years. *So maybe the chief wasn't going to go easy on Peej after all,* Paul would remember thinking later when the chief's phone buzzed.

Red buttons on his phone console lighting up; the chief answering fast.

"Here?" he barked into the receiver, his heavily lined, hound-dog face suddenly lighting up. The chief was half standing in his seat. "Bleeding out? Jesus, how long before they—*Now?*— Yeah, yeah, we got it. We're on it." He slammed down the phone, shoved past Paul and PJ.

"Code red, code red!" He called into the hallway from his office doorway. Paul heard footsteps scuffling. Maybe there was a break room down there? All break-time broken now, ended. Someone—the cop who'd been shot?—was bleeding out, arriving NOW at the ER.

PJ straightened in his seat, listening as raptly to the chief as Paul.

"Wounded officer arriving at ER. Gotta put out an all-security call, and where the hell's my—"

"Here!" PJ exclaimed in a voice of urgent joy. He stumbled up to his feet.

Paul turned, startled to see his son seize hold of a large, rectangular radio-beeper, slung aside on the chief's cluttered desk. "This what you need?" PJ rushed to the office doorway, rewarded by a curt nod from the chief, who snatched the radio beeper.

PJ nodded back, his face ablaze with purpose, like the face of the younger, red-haired officer in the Belmont Police car Paul remembered as if from long ago. He stepped up beside PJ. The chief turned his broad back on both of them. The radio beeper PJ had handed him crackled to life.

Paul dared to rest his hand on PJ's tensed shoulder as the chief spoke into his beeper setting his whole security staff in motion. "Code red, code red. All officers to ER, ER main entrance."

In the hall, the young officer who'd let Paul in strode purposefully past the door, trailing yellow police tape. Sirens were sounding outside, audible even in this windowless office. The wounded officer from the firefight was at Mount Auburn, the chief told someone in the hall— bleeding out. They all had to hurry, the chief commanded.

PJ didn't shrug off Paul's hand, but Paul could feel in his son's shoulder, more strongly than before, how much PJ wanted to spring forward and follow the officers.

"You two." The chief turned abruptly to say to Paul and PJ. *Stay here*, Paul was bracing himself to hear. *Stay here and await arrest*, but the chief, with his own old face alight, shook his head hard, gave a dismissive wave with the hand not holding the beeper. "Stay outta our way," he told Paul. "And," he added to PJ, fast before he charged like a freed bull through the doorway, "stay outta trouble. Stay with your father. Go meet your brother."

❧

So Paul and PJ fell apart, together, in the Neonatal ICU.

Once they'd staggered out of the SECURITY: STAFF ONLY door together, PJ, bless his bad boy heart, slid his hand into his deepest denim pocket and pulled out a pack of Kools. He'd filched it, he confided to Paul, in the ER while Evvy got stitched.

PJ and Paul headed past a doctor in his winged, white coat trotting officiously down the corridor, no doubt toward the ER. No one noticed Paul and PJ slipping into a stairwell, stomping down to a side exit onto a deserted patio area with a sand urn for butts that PJ had noticed the security guards using.

Paul and PJ lit up hungrily, in bracingly chill pre-dawn air. Paul's lips were too numbed to do anything but savor the smoke he'd craved. Plus, PJ kept shooting him such anxious glances. He didn't speak at first. Then, as if the cigarette were a stronger drug, Paul found himself blurting out to PJ between puffs the secret he'd kept all of his son's life.

"She didn't call me, y'know. Your Nana. The night you were born. I swear, PJ. I had no damn idea. She just chose not to call me." Paul exhaled a giant breath of smoke, blurring PJ's dazedly amazed face. "It's true, but don't ask her. She'd deny it. Then she'd . . . kill me."

Paul drew in another long drag as PJ thoughtfully nodded and muttered, "Yeah, she would."

But he didn't say he didn't believe Paul.

"Don't get me wrong," Paul added. "I owe her, Nana. We all do. She raised you. She did what she thought was best for you, but she didn't call me that night. You gotta take my word for it."

PJ nodded again, and he said in a flat, yet satisfied-sounding voice, "OK, Dad."

Paul drew more deep drags, momentarily satisfied, too, wondering how the hell he could bring up all the bizarre questions he had to ask PJ soon, all the answers he had to demand. Wondering what to say next, feeling PJ wonder it, too.

Then they didn't have to say anything. Rescued by a sudden, rising din of sirens from behind the brick wall enclosing the patio area. The muffled, but unmistakably excited, voices of a group gathering round the giant hospital building corner at emergency where Sarah had been dropped off, seemingly ages ago. Would this wake her up on the birth floor? She'd looked, when she'd finally closed her eyes, like she'd sleep for weeks. Sarah tended to sleep—like she did everything—deeply, intently.

Paul held in a mouthful of smoke. Shoulder to shoulder with PJ, he was relieved to be listening to the loud and resonant sounds of history in the making with him. One tiny side effect of it all, Paul thought as bigger sirens approached, was to give PJ some breathing room. Paul and PJ stood together in the pre-dawn dark.

"It's coming! They're coming!" someone shouted above the rest.

"Stand back! Everyone back!" a bull-horned voice proclaimed. The chief himself?

Then a symphonic blare of giant, night-vibrating sirens. Brightest blue lights seemed to shine through the brick wall itself. In the flurry of overheard movement and shouting voices, PJ smashed his cigarette butt in the sand urn, like a thief knowing when he must leave or be caught.

Reluctantly, leaving half the smoke, Paul smashed his butt, too, in solidarity with his son.

He and PJ were edging back to the side entrance when two uniformed cops ducked into the patio from around the brick wall through some entrance Paul could not see. He and PJ froze unnoticed by the side door, staring across the patio as the two men in uniform lit up. Paul noticed the face of one man was so filthy it was hard to tell his race; his face was smeared with ashy black. A smell, along with the cigarette smoke, wafted in the spring night air across the patio—serious smoke, sulfuric smoke with a faint, soured, rotted-egg taste.

The news voices had said the bomber brothers hurled homemade explosives at the assembled cops in Watertown. PJ, beside Paul, was standing soldier straight, watching these men, breathing in, Paul thought as he touched PJ's shoulder, their whiff of history.

One officer coughed. The other mumbled something that sounded like "Holy shit, holy shit." Paul nudged PJ, steering him toward the door, their heads bowed as if leaving a sacred place.

"Holy shit," PJ repeated in hoarse awe when they'd slipped back into the hospital stairwell.

Climbing the stairs behind broad-shouldered PJ, setting a fast pace that left Paul panting, Paul reassembled all the reasons he was angry at his son. PJ halfway ran up the stairs on his toes, a kid again, dreading the reckoning he knew was coming. But the world outside was a war zone. A police officer was bleeding out in the ER, and Paul was too tired and too relieved to reckon with anyone just yet.

Boston was under siege, yes, but Paul's baby had been born and might be OK. His first son might get away, too, unscathed. The chief hadn't officially lifted a threat of charges but hadn't not. He'd sent PJ and Paul away, out of the way, commanding them only to visit Baby Boy Stratidakis.

Once they reached the birth floor, Paul led the way. He checked with the desk nurse, mercifully a different nurse from the bulldog who had helped Evvy, and he and PJ were directed to the upper nursery. In the halls and elevator, Paul, with his temporarily fortified mind, overheard solemn, low-voiced talk that the MBTA police officer was still clinging to life in the larger, lower-level ICU. Paul and PJ entered the Neonatal ICU all but unnoticed, the nurses inside watching the news on TV. Paul didn't want to know what was happening anywhere but here, his own ground zero. Paul and PJ stood outside the Plexiglas window.

They scanned the terrarium-like incubators and found STRATIDAKIS 4/19/13. PJ was the one to spot his tiny brother, to point him out to Paul with a flash of the same proud, lit-up look he'd had when handing the beeper to the chief. Paul wanted to pat PJ on the back but didn't dare press his luck. It was enough to stand shoulder to shoulder again with him, both of them smelling of smoke.

They stared together at the tiny, big-headed creature with the tubes taped to his nose, at his scrunched-up warrior face. Baby Boy Stratidakis, arrayed in his plastic torture-chamber incubator. Breathing, if fitfully. Alive.

PJ choked up beside Paul. He coughed, too hard for a kid his age, a cough too much like his Grandad's lifetime-smoker cough. Paul did dare to touch PJ's arm, to guide him to some welded-together plastic chairs. There PJ gasped to Paul with smoky, funky boy breaths that it was his fault, that he hadn't meant to freak out Sarah today.

He'd been high on these freaky mini-thins he'd gobbled to jazz him up enough to face her, those tablets that made him so itchy and twitchy. He never should've barged in on Sarah today. And now look. Look what he'd done to his brother. PJ jerked his scruffy tear-streaked face toward the doubly glassed-in baby.

Christ, what could Paul do? He draped his arm around PJ's big, shuddery shoulders. A majestic NICU nurse Paul would later get to know well marched out, a finger to her lips, her dark brows arched, and her hair piled in a fearsome bun. She led Paul and PJ to a narrow lounge, dimly lit and stocked with Kleenex boxes, no doubt the room where they led parents who actually lost their babies.

Paul said this to PJ after the door closed on them. Everything Paul said in his exhausted state seemed muffled to him, unreal. "Everything's falling apart all around us," he told his son. "But our baby's alive. He's going to be OK. We're hoping he's going to be OK." Paul told himself and PJ these reassuring words dutifully trying, like a good dad, to sound sure.

Then Paul told PJ, or tried to tell him, how he'd been horrified to see him holding that damn knife, talking like he was going to hurt himself. Paul asked PJ what in holy hell he'd meant by that? And by claiming the baby was his?

"You believed all that shit?" PJ asked, with a worn-out trace of his usual cockiness. "I never woulda used that knife—I mean, *on* anyone. Not even me."

"You think," Paul countered, "I believe *that* shit . . . after the way you pulled that thing out? Think I'm gonna let you out of my sight anytime soon?" Paul demanded, his own voice even more hoarsely ragged than PJ's. He could see the plain surprise in PJ's bulgy, bloodshot frog-eyes.

"Didn't know you'd even wanna lay eyes on me or whatever after all that shit I said. Didn't think you and Sarah would want to anyhow, once you had your real son. And—see, ya gotta believe this part, Dad—I never meant any of that shit I was spouting to you and Sarah . . ."

The part about not meaning the shit he'd been spouting sounded less convincing to Paul than the part about never using his knife, and all their words still felt like sleep talk.

"You *are* my real son," Paul began. "All too real sometimes, but you are. But that shit you spouted," Paul pointed out, "fit in with lotsa other shit I've been picking up on . . . between you and Sarah." He added after a pause, "for I don't know how long . . ."

PJ shrugged roughly, snuffling and swallowing, recomposing his cool. Then he mumbled, "OK, yeah, I had a thing for Sarah. I was, like, scared she'd forget all about me if she got pregnant. So, the cow tongue cemetery thing," PJ went on. "It was, like, a dumb ass antifertility rite. This girl, Crystal, she talked me into it . . . Maybe she really is a witch," PJ added, shifting his eyes from Paul. "The way things worked out," he finished.

"What do you mean, the way things worked out?" Paul asked, startled from his sleep talk daze, feeling awake again, feeling they were getting at something now.

"Just . . . just Sarah getting pregnant and all. See, I was so mad after I sent Sarah that, that crazy ass card . . ." PJ was winding down, losing steam. He looked away from Paul, at the carpeted floor. "You saw that freaking card I sent. The one, I told you, she never . . ."

"Answered," Paul filled in, looking at the blank, vacuumed carpet like PJ. "Just like you're not answering me." But he sensed that PJ had given all the answers he was going to give for now. Or maybe that Paul had reached his own limit for revelations tonight. What revelation should Paul need other than Sarah "never?" That the seven-month baby behind those layers of glass was, he knew in his head and heart both, his.

Paul rubbed his ashy fingers together, "but what did you mean you freaked out Sarah 'way bad' last summer? And what did you mean when you said earlier that the spell you were casting backfired double?"

PJ pulled himself up, abruptly. He peered down at Paul, his face shadowed. His unshaven beard bristle had fully sprouted in their hours apart. His tears had dried. In this dim, solemnly silent room, he looked like a man Paul didn't know.

"'Nough of this shit, Dad," PJ muttered in his smoke-deepened voice. "We gotta find that nurse with the hair. She looks like she knows stuff. We gotta find out what the fuck's going on with—"

"Your brother," Paul finished flatly. As if ending a contentious Center meeting, he rose, too. Yet he felt—as he often felt at the ends of those exhausting meetings—that nothing really had been resolved, or resolved enough. He tried to pat PJ's shoulder, but he sidestepped him.

❦

The MBTA officer, Officer Donohue, Paul and PJ learned almost as soon as they stepped from the death room and the rarefied quiet of the Neonatal ICU, had not bled out.

He'd been saved, or at least kept alive for the night, by the ER staff who'd somehow pumped massive doses of blood into his system. For forty-five minutes, he'd hung on the edge of life and had now at four a.m. or so, been pulled back into a kind of coma in critical condition in the Mount Auburn Hospital ICU.

All this Paul and PJ had absorbed by half-conscious osmosis as they'd staggered past the babbling lobby TV into the quieter dawn clamor of the hospital cafeteria. Together, they wolfed down microwaved egg-and-bacon breakfast sandwiches. "Donohue," Paul repeated between bites. "One of Sarah's latest name ideas for your brother is Don after this nice uncle she had, her mom's brother, who kinda played father for her on holidays. They called him Donny." Paul slurped his coffee. "His full name was Don, not Donald, she said. I wasn't so sure about that, about just plain Don . . ."

"But it is like Donohue. Like, short for that." PJ startled Paul by looking up from his own plate and meeting Paul's bleary gaze more fully than he'd done all night. "You guys ought go for it. It'd be like . . . like naming him, my brother, after him, after Officer Donohue."

Had Paul ever heard PJ speak a name with such reverence? He nodded solemnly himself.

"Sarah will like that," Paul told his son.

Then he and Paul Jr. sleepwalked together back to the lobby TV and the fresh, frenetic blasts of breaking news. Paul cell phoned the birth floor and learned Sarah was still sleeping through it all.

BOSTON IN LOCKDOWN, he and PJ were informed. The younger bomber brother was still alive, still at large. Citizens in the Greater Boston area were advised to SHELTER IN PLACE as police and FBI hunted down ARMED AND DANGEROUS BOMBING SUSPECT DZHOKHAR TSARNAEV.

News anchor voices mangled that strange, newly infamous name.

"Sounds like 'Joker,'" PJ mumbled under his breath to Paul. "Wonder if he wore, like, green hair dye like that Joker movie theater shooter in Colorado . . ."

"This's no joke," Paul muttered under his own smoky breath, shooting PJ a Dad glare. PJ's old, whiny, teenage self answered back, too loudly from their lobby couch corner.

"I didn't *say* it was a *joke*. I *know* it's not a fucking *joke*."

Paul shot a glance around for watching security guards. A new crew of visibly armed police gathered outside the lobby's giant glass doors, on the watch.

"You better know," Paul whispered to his son. "No more bomber jokes. You got that?"

PJ gave a jerk of a nod, his mouth curling into the same sullen shape as Dzhokhar Tsarnaev in the fascinating, new in-focus shots of his UMass Student ID on TV. Luckily, in the clearer shots, the sharper, longer-nosed bones of Tsarnaev's face showed leaner and meaner than the fleshier, wider-eyed face of dark-browed PJ.

As the hospital came to life, and morning light filtered in from outside the giant glass doors and wall-sized windows, Paul alternated between watching the latest news beside PJ and checking in on sleeping Sarah. The first time he checked, he'd found sleepy Evvy, who despite her bandaged foot, had beat him to Sarah's bedside. She'd promised Paul she'd call him the minute Sarah woke. How could Paul object to the woman who his son had accidentally stabbed, and who'd stabbed his wife with the needles that had led, however haphazardly, to the new son asleep in NICU?

So, Paul sat half-dozing beside PJ in the lobby, noting a new, un-Bostonian comradery among the fellow TV-watchers who traded the latest rumors and stories about Officer Donohue in ICU.

PJ and Paul sat apart from the chatter but closer together than normal on the plastic- cushioned couch. *If crabby, dysfunctional Boston can pull together,* Paul thought as he slurped yet another black coffee, *my damn, ineptly blended family can do the same.*

Incredulous, Paul watched surreal shots of armored tanks rolling past double-decker, shingled homes, through the leafy streets of Watertown, MA.

"Because they were losers! Losers!" a refreshingly harsh-voiced Chechnyan uncle of the alleged suspects emerged from his Watertown residence to shout at reporters. Was he ashamed of the bombing brothers? The hatchet-faced, enraged-looking uncle was asked. "Of course we are ashamed," he fired back. "They have brought shame upon our family!"

"Ya wonder how those brothers could've gone so wrong," PJ muttered beside Paul. "With that kinda support system in place . . ."

"Where's the dad? That's what I want to know," Paul muttered back. "It's always all on the dad . . ."

"Least I haven't shamed you guys as bad as those guys." PJ drained his own black coffee.

"Least I've been around more than their dad." Paul set down his hollow cup. "Or I bet I have. Even though you might not always want me around . . ." Then he pulled himself up, stretching so his knuckles rudely cracked which drove Sarah crazy. PJ, in answer, did the same, popping his own knuckles hard and yawning wide, then blinking up at Paul as if waking from a shared dream.

"Think you can behave yourself here?" Paul asked flatly. PJ gave a curt man-to-man nod. He shut his eyes and leaned his head back as if he might sink, like Sarah, into coma-deep sleep.

Barely holding his own puffy eyes open—would he ever sleep again?—Paul made his sleepwalking way from the hysterical, yet oddly comforting, drone of the news back into the disorienting, never-dimming brightness of his new son's home, the NICU.

"Shelter in place," governor Deval Patrick had ordered all Bostonians. This was the place he and his sons happened to be, Paul told himself as the soap-scented nurse helped him into his medicinal-scented, papery mouth mask and scrub suit smock.

This was the place. Paul vowed, as he took a seat by his son's incubator, that he'd damn well better find, better make, shelter here. For both his sons.

Part Two

Release Day

Chapter Nine

May 4, 2013: 9:00 a.m.

Baby Safing

The more you express, the more you make.

Paul hauled his overstuffed CVS bags into the kitchen. Would this be the day Donny came home? Donny and Sarah? Trying not to focus on those as yet unanswerable questions, Paul sprawled the drugstore goods on the counter beside *Baby Safe Your Home.*

He'd consulted that broken-spined tome at dawn. Up early, determined to be prepared for whatever might go down today after the final evaluation report that Paul and Sarah both dreaded. Paul flipped on the kitchen light against the drizzly, midmorning gray outside.

"They might finally let me breastfeed him today," Sarah had told him last night by phone with a quaver of hope in her voice. "So I've gotta keep expressing my milk. See, the more you express, the more you make . . ."

Paul kept mixing up those words with some damn Beatles song. He would ask Sarah the title if she were here. If she were her old self. Would she ever be either: here or her old self? Paul opened one wilted, crackling bag. All the baby safe list items. Plus, of course, they'd need whatever meds and gadgets the hospital would send home for their particular preemie.

Their Don. If he came home today, at last. Don and Sarah. Or—this was the thought Paul had been trying all morning to keep at bay—would Sarah somehow surprise him and insist on taking the baby herself alone, insist on Paul and PJ both moving out?

A crazy thought, but the past ten days had been a post-crazy daze. He and Sarah had not had a chance to talk, really talk, since the birth night.

After staying in the hospital an extra week due to her post-birth infection, Sarah had wound up spending the last few days bunking with one of Evvy's endless supply of women friends, or who knew, maybe an ex of Evvy's. This woman, Marti, happened to live within blocks of the hospital. Sarah was officially staying there just to be near baby Don, but Paul knew it was to stay away from him and PJ too, for as long as possible.

Who could blame her? *Maybe me*, Paul thought. He fingered Sarah's wedding ring, still wedged on his pinkie. Somehow, in all the confusion and worry, they hadn't transferred that ring back onto Sarah's no longer swollen finger—not yet. No doubt Evvy had noticed the lack of ring. No doubt she and Evvy's pal were trying to talk Sarah into leaving her husband and his troublesome grown son. Not that Sarah would listen. Right?

Paul glanced outside at gathering clouds. Poor Don, born into a dangerous world, even with the marathon bombing suspect shipped off at last to a prison hospital. The MBTA cop whom Donny was halfway named after, whose story Paul and PJ had followed each day, even after he was transferred from Mount Auburn. Officer Donohue had been upgraded to serious from critical, making slow progress, like Don.

Methodically, Paul unloaded iodine-colored ipecac syrup in its tiny, stoppered bottle: FOR EMERGENCY USE TO CAUSE VOMITING IN CASE OF POISON; then packets of white plastic plugs to block electrical outlets. How long before Don was strong enough to electrocute his teeny fingers? The digital thermometer, for ear or rear, the cheery pharmacist told Paul. He squeezed the odd rubber ball of the last item from the bag experimentally. With one pointy horn designed, its label stated, to SUCK EXCESS MUCUS FROM MOUTH AND NOSE.

Paul crumpled the first deflated bag. The second bulged with breast-feeding gadgetry: bottles to store the milk Sarah had kept expressing, which Don licked from her fingertip but still couldn't suck, and the plastic disassembled hand pump that Sarah would use at home.

At the hospital, they'd hooked up Sarah—the new older Sarah with her hollowed face and stony, swollen breasts—to a double sucking contraption that chugged like a mix master, tubes running to funnels cupping both Sarah's breasts. Her tight, stretched breast skin puckered, as if that relentless pump would suck off her nipples. Her barely-white milk bubbled in little bottles.

Don only sucked small amounts at a time. God knew what the hospital had been doing with all Sarah's excess milk. Paul glanced behind him at the empty kitchen doorway. PJ had said he'd be home by nine after teaching early white belt class. But of course, thank God, he was late.

Maybe Paul had time for a smoke before he and PJ, as PJ ominously requested last night, talked. Paul was dreading that talk, as well as the one he'd probably have today with Sarah. The talk in which Sarah might insist PJ move out before she'd move back in.

Paul groped in the breast bag for the bottles first, intent on finishing this one task, on baby proofing their home. *Sterilize in boiling water before use.* Sarah was so proud of her milk. Proud that she'd kept it coming, or it would've dried up. Expressing breast milk had been the one concrete thing she could do in the tense post-birth week.

They'd taken turns sitting hunched beside Don's beeping incubator and sticking their hands through the circular holes to finger stroke his seemingly limp, boneless arm.

Paul had helped Sarah in and out of her own hospital bed, her steps slow and shuffly. Partly, the nurses told Paul, this was from Sarah's Chorioamnionitis, or infection of the amniotic fluid, and partly from her *postpartum,* they matter-of-factly labeled it. They didn't have to add the word depression, didn't have to explain that part to Paul.

So, Paul had no choice but to snap to. Hadn't this always been his and Sarah's rhythm? Be the sane one, the busy one.

He ripped open the sealed boxes and lined up four white plastic bottles along the stovetop. At least during the second week Sarah had stopped asking "how could we have?" and bemoaning how guilty she felt over everything she'd supposedly done to cause all this. Not that he'd pressed Sarah yet on what she meant by that. What exactly had happened between her and PJ? Was that what PJ wanted to talk about at last? Or were they going to talk about the even more pressing matter at hand: where and how PJ was going to live. How the four of them were going to live together if that was indeed the plan.

Christ, if Don was actually going to be released today, which Paul couldn't quite believe, they'd damn well better come up with an actual plan ASAP. Paul filled a metal pan with water, his hands moving stiffly. Was it early arthritis, his mom's curse, settling in? Arthritic old man hands fumbling to change diapers. How PJ would scoff.

If PJ is here, Paul thought as he switched on the burner. What in hell would Peej say to him today? Paul slipped a cigarette from the pack in the knife drawer. He lit up and drew a bracing, burning drag. Then he raised the kitchen window to the mild, rainy outdoors.

He exhaled and waved smoke out. *Sorry, Don.*

Paul always called the baby Don, his real name. Sarah kept calling him Donny. Paul couldn't deny bedridden, infected Sarah anything that would add a spark to her worried stare.

It could be worse, Paul had kept reminding Sarah as they'd peered in at Don in his plastic coffin of an incubator. His taped-on nasal cannula tubes distorted his nose so he seemed to always be flaring his nostrils in silent rage. His fierce, brownish-blue eyes, much more developed than most preemie eyes, the NICU nurses raved, regarded Sarah and Paul with understandable wariness.

Paul puffed and exhaled. He'd given up, struggling to assess the degree of blame they shared. Yes, Dr. Lutz had told him with her usual cool, the fact that they'd had sex had likely triggered the initial labor pains, but the infected amnio fluid they'd discovered after the birth indicated, Lutz's favorite word, the Chorioamnionitis that she claimed was a major source of many premature labors.

This mixed diagnosis had lifted Sarah from her initial, guilt-ridden angst. She'd had the strength to shuffle back and forth to the incubator, to croon Donny's name; to sing the interminable words to the "Mommy's Gonna Buy You a Diamond Ring" lullaby without—as Paul sometimes did, sitting in that damned NICU—dozing off.

Could be worse, he'd reminded himself and Sarah as they'd witnessed the convulsions and splattering diarrhea of Caitlin, the preemie in the neighboring incubator. Caitlin suffered, loudly, from Short Gut Syndrome.

Then, on a whole other level of NICU hell, there was the Belsanni baby. Paul had been rushed out of the NICU still in his face mask, and a priest rushed in to administer last rites to the suddenly blue-skinned Belsanni baby. Dying last week amidst reports that the Boston Bomber Boy would live after all; his life saved at Beth Israel Hospital, where he'd been treated for a self-inflicted wound in his neck.

What Paul had pictured PJ doing in a horrified flash when he'd pulled his knife long ago it seemed. Paul ashed into a saucer. Christ,

Mrs. Belsanni's wails carried through the walls.

The next day, when Sarah had mumbled from her incubator-side seat how inadequate she felt stroking Donny with one finger, when she'd complained it wasn't enough, Paul had snapped back, low voiced, "It's goddamn enough that Don's alive." Instead of retreating into tears, Sarah had glanced over to the emptied Belsanni incubator and nodded, slowly.

Awful as it had been, that Belsanni baby death had knocked Sarah from her deepest funk—that death plus Don's relatively positive test results. Knock on wood; as long as nothing new came up today. Paul rapped his free hand on the kitchen wall, then took another drag.

His smoky exhale wafted into pewter grey sunlight, faint but visible through the clouds.

The water was bubbling. Cigarette angled in his mouth, Paul dunked in two of the plastic bottles. They bobbed in roiling water like buoys. One major test still looming over Donny was a full screening by an audiologist. One in ten preemies suffer from some degree of hearing loss. Maybe exacerbated, the chattiest NICU nurse had confided to Paul, by the high noise level inside the incubator. "The motor and beeping and all," she'd added needlessly—the sounds that had driven Paul to a Walkman, headphones, and extended doses of Bruckner.

He flipped on the radio he'd moved to the kitchen during these two weeks of concocting makeshift meals with PJ. Or, anyway, meals for the often absent PJ.

A blare of heavy metal or death metal or grunge or whatever the new name was for the harshest possible rock blasted through the kitchen. Paul readjusted the dial to his all classical station. Chopin, he noted as he dragged, nodding his head to the still-startling beats. His favorite: the Prelude in E. The piece critics at the time trashed for sounding like the pianist was banging his head on the piano keyboard in despair.

Yeah, so what's the problem with that? Paul asked those 19th century critics in his head. He gazed into the day's delicate shades of grey with a watchful Zen equanimity he was trying to cultivate, a calm he'd need today. The door below banged followed by PJ's trademark boot thumps.

Hurriedly, Paul smashed his half-smoked cigarette. It was silly to try to hide it from PJ. Still, Paul sent the ashes and butt spiraling down the sink. Then he drowned Chopin and PJ's boot thuds by flipping on the grinding heavy metal trash disposal. Grind, grind, gone.

"Dad?" PJ called from the living room. Wary too, like his baby half-brother.

"In here." Paul flipped off the Chopin mid head-pound.

"Whatchya cooking?" PJ poked his head in the kitchen, his curly hair clean for a change. "I mean—" He took a deep breath, then added mock hopefully, "Whatchya smoking?"

Paul cracked a ha-ha smile. He fanned the leftover smoke out the window with his hands. As if he'd been shooed away, PJ ducked out, too.

"I gotta piss, then we gotta talk," he called from the living room.

"Sure," Paul called back, straining to sound game. Christ, this talk. Did he and PJ have to have it? Wasn't it enough that they were now civil and at peace?

Well, not at peace. Paul fumbled through the clanking cooking utensil drawer for tongs. Ever since PJ started helping Evvy out at her karate studio while she recovered from her injured ankle, hadn't things been better between him and PJ? Better since the afternoon they'd huddled together like a real family around Sarah's hospital room TV, watching the final capture of the bombing suspect. Their attempt to talk afterwards had been awkward and incomplete. Paul didn't want to think about that talk, didn't want to continue it today with PJ. But all of this was better, at least, than the two of them lunging at each other outside Sarah's birth room door.

Still, Paul reminded himself as he tong-lifted each boiled bottle, *that shouldn't be good enough.* One, two, three, four boiled bottles lined up on a paper towel.

Paul set down the dripping tongs. He used to boil syringes for his diabetic mom, the two of them listening to the all classical station she kept on all day in her cramped kitchen, her one comfort. Paul was a good son to her, she'd always tell him.

Maybe caring for a fragile newborn would turn out to be something stoic, hard-working Paul was good at. At least until the baby turned into a boy, a PJ.

Distantly, from the bedroom, the bathroom door thumped. Then two smaller thumps as PJ kicked off his boots. Paul dumped the water, still boiling, down the sink.

Since their epic length birth night, since the Boston lockdown day at the hospital and the tentative truce it had seemed to bring them, or at least the shared emotional exhaustion, Paul and PJ had lived here together carefully, tiptoed around each other, talked mainly about the baby. Not that they saw each other often. Paul was splitting his time between work and the hospital; PJ spent days at Evvy's karate studio then went out nights with a few kids he'd known last summer, or so he mumbled when Paul asked.

Why did you offer to father a baby with my wife? was what Paul really wanted to ask, to demand. *What did I ever do to you that you'd do that to me?*

From the living room, Paul heard the barefoot *shuffle-shuffle-thumps* of PJ practicing karate stances: PJ had names for each one. Rising Sun, the Knife Thrust? One good thing to have come from that fight in the hospital corridor: Evvy had convinced PJ to substitute teach her karate classes. Maybe the first job PJ had ever liked.

"Hey, Peej? I'll be there in a minute," Paul called out, noticing the green light on the answering machine. "Lemme just listen to these new messages . . ."

Paul stepped across the kitchen to the machine with a familiar mix of dread and hope. *Shuffle, shuffle, thump. Shuffle, shuffle, thump.* In the living room, in the space Paul and PJ had cleared by moving back the couch, PJ continued his stances.

Paul pressed play, keeping the volume low.

"It's me." Sarah, first. Paul leaned against the marble-topped counter. "Just wanted to check in before you come and meet me here. They're still saying if these last tests are OK, they might really let him go today. Knock on wood . . ." Paul actually heard Sarah rap something wooden, as he had done minutes before. "But I'm not sure I . . . believe that. Not sure, you know, how exactly we'd handle that, if it even happens. So if you can come a little early I-I'll be trying the nursing again and-and we can talk and all . . ."

Her message cut off. Christ, another talk today. And how *would* they handle the baby coming home? How exactly?

"Huh." PJ's live voice behind Paul startled him. PJ in his black E.E.'s KARATE & KICKBOXING uniform leaned in the kitchen doorway. "You two gonna talk, too?"

This manly, unshaven PJ seemed to be trying hard to sound cool, unconcerned. A second wrong number message of static played on the machine.

Bleep. The third message rolled. Nana's deep, commanding Armenian-accented voice.

"PJ? PJ, you are com-ing? It is set then? I sended you, wired it, like you say, your money for your train. Your Mama, she try to come, too, never so sure she come, and we make a dinner together, yes? That is what you say? You call. Call your Nana. I wait to hear you."

The machine *bleep*ed; the green light died.

"Train?" Paul asked. PJ shrugged, but his bare foot, hairy-toed like Paul's, jiggled so hard he seemed to be trying to shake something off it.

"You called Nana," Paul went on, cautiously neutral, "You said you'd go back out there? She's sent you money for the train? You could've asked me."

Another violent, big-shouldered shrug. "Evvy's gonna be back on the job next week. It's not like you and me and Sarah and all, like we have any big-family summer plans or whatever . . ."

Paul nodded, averting his eyes so not to show how disappointed and relieved he felt. How he'd dreaded trying to make it work: Sarah, infant Donny, PJ, and him living together here, like some TV reality show family, like the long-time tensions that had flared on birth night had simply dissipated and been worked through.

Will we ever be through with all that? Paul wondered. He made himself face his shifty eyed, jittery-footed son.

"So I . . . yeah. I kinda decided to ask Nana after, y'know, Providence . . ."

Paul nodded, scratching his beard though it didn't itch. Maybe the best thing he and PJ had gotten together to do, in these past two weeks, was visit Sarah's mother in her Providence nursing home. It was PJ's idea, unexpectedly. He had avoided visiting Sarah and the baby except for the one time on lockdown day. PJ avoided even mentioning Sarah, but then, last week, he suggested Sarah might like it if he and Paul could visit his other Grandma. PJ and frosty Grandma McCall had never been close, but the visit turned out surprisingly well.

In her semi-senile state, Sarah's mom surprised PJ and Paul with real, clinging hugs. She seemed to believe they'd been blown up by the Marathon Bombers. Paul held up the photos of Don in his incubator, shot through double panes of glass from outside the NICU window to avoid flashing bulbs into his son's supersensitive eyes. The old lady examined each shot, her blurry eyes dry but intent. She had clutched one photo to her sagging bosom to keep.

"I mean," PJ added, looking down at his jiggling foot, "that was such a trip. Seeing Grandma M. and having her act, like, halfway human. It kinda made me think how, even though Nana's been getting on my nerves for years, she can still talk and think and cook."

Paul nodded, breathing in as if smelling Nana's savory Armenian dishes. Lamb, green beans, and grape leaves simmered with tomatoes. The canned food had to be some certain brand, plus the spices she grew and ground down to powder herself.

Thank God for no-nonsense Nana, stepping in and raising his son.

"Sure, sure. Nana'd love that." Paul coughed, his throat thicker than ever. Two weeks of smoking on the front stoop with PJ—Something he'd miss when it would be just him, Sarah, and Don here. "Then you're planning to stay out there . . . or what?"

PJ heaved yet another of his oversized shrugs. He'd never run out of those. There was something heavy he kept trying to knock off his big shoulders. *The boulder-sized, fatherless boy chip that will always be there,* Paul thought with depressing clarity.

"Probably not, dad. I've got . . . some shit I gotta take care of in Ohio. So, like, relax; I'm outta here. I'm clearing out my stuff today, staying with, um . . . someone this week so's Sarah and the baby and you can . . . whatever, here. Alone and all."

"Staying with whom?"

"Like you care." PJ stilled his jiggling bare foot. He planted it hard on the floor. He started to turn his big, black-clad back.

"Hey, wait now." Paul stepped forward, but stopped short of touching PJ, holding him back. "I care. We care. You the-hell know that. Listen, we—you and me—might be able to bring home Sarah and Don later today. I told you that last night, we—"

"What *we*?" PJ did turn, stomping his bare feet like he was wearing his boots. "Yo, Dad. I'm not dumb, ya know. She doesn't want me there. I'm not part of any 'we' of yours."

PJ marched back into the living room.

Sure you are, Paul wanted to call out. *You and me will always be a we whether you like it or not.* Paul stepped into the doorway PJ had deserted. He was shoving the coffee table back further against the couch, preparing the room for—what now?

"You want to knock me down again?"

Maybe it was the right thing to ask, because at least PJ looked at Paul and nodded, deadpan. Paul walked in and stepped behind PJ. He stood in the position they'd practiced several times. Self-defense, PJ had explained. He needed to practice demonstrating moves for the karate kids. Or maybe, he'd added in his maybe joking tone, he just liked knocking dad flat.

Paul braced himself behind PJ, his legs spread and knees bent. PJ crouched, reaching through his own spread, bent legs. Deftly he gripped Paul's leg. He squeezed. Paul startled as his knees buckled and his balance slipped.

PJ tugged hard; the room reeled. Grunting, Paul fell heavily onto the couch. His back subtly popped.

"Guess I'm good for something," Paul muttered, wincing. He glanced up at his son, hoping for a grin. But PJ, arms folded, gazed down at him coolly. He heaved a shrug.

"What, I'm supposed to say, 'yeah dad, you're good. We're good . . .'"

Sprawled on the couch, Paul shook his head, but PJ shook his head harder. He pushed on, as if with a speech he'd long practiced. "Yeah, right. Just 'cause we've lived here together for two lousy weeks, that makes you an OK dad?"

"I didn't say that, Peej," Paul started to protest, sitting up straighter. He felt another shooting pang in his back. PJ glared down, his black brows knit.

"*Paul*. You can't even remember my name, and don't bother with the concerned dad act. You got what you want. I'm outta here. Matter of fact, I packed up this morning." PJ shot a nod over to a loaded duffle bag Paul hadn't noticed by the living room door.

Had PJ meant for him to notice? Had he failed another test?

"Look, P—Paul, you don't have to leave so soon. No one told you to. We can—"

PJ cut him short with a decisive karate chop. "We can what?" he asked. "Just settle in here like one big, happy whatever? Look." PJ glanced at the living room clock, shifting on his bare feet again. "I got things to do."

"What things?" Paul pulled himself up, stifling a wince at another back pang. "Christ, you're the one who said you wanted to talk. So, talk."

"You don't wanna hear it . . ." PJ began pacing and glancing at the clock again.

Paul stuck out one long arm. He gripped his son's strong upper arm and halted him. "What did you mean about shit you have to take care of in Ohio?"

PJ stood still, looked down at his own hairy toes. "This witch girl. This Crystal."

"Cow tongue girl? That girl?"

PJ nodded, eyes still on his toes. Paul released his arm, and PJ didn't move, except to shake his head. "Still can't hardly believe it, but. She, well . . . back in December, when I was so messed up, she called this friend of mine and tracked me down in Cleveland, y'know."

"No, I didn't know. It—it should've been me to track you down . . ."

At Paul's words, PJ looked up, locking Paul's gaze, agreeing without nodding, without a word. Paul was the one to nod, then PJ told the rest in one burst.

"She . . . see, Crystal, she found me in Cleveland in December when I was holed up not seeing anyone. She brought some cash from her tarot readings, and we took a room near Terminal Towers. And we, like . . . well now, Crystal's telling me we, like, got her pregnant."

Good Christ, a grandchild? Paul drew a shocked breath.

"Not even sure I believe her, dad. She's one wigged out, witchy chick, but she did really help me in December. Then she called me there 'bout this baby thing few weeks ago, said she was gonna get rid of it. But then a friend, she says Crystal didn't. Says Crystal hasn't gotten an abortion. It'd be more than three months now, which's too late—"

"—to get rid of a baby," Paul filled in numbly, unblinking. He reached out and patted PJ's stiff arm. PJ jerked back a step and turned toward his duffle bag. He shook his head, stepping over to the bag. "Crystal won't answer my calls. I'm not sure what the fuck I'd do." He turned to Paul, his dark eyes widened and abashed. "But I still kinda hope she hasn't."

PJ sat on the packed duffle bag; Paul stepped forward and stood above him.

"Good. What can I do to help you, Peej? I mean, Paul. Money, what?"

PJ was shaking his head again, pulling on his socks. "You don't wanna help me with this, just like you don't want me living here, Dad."

"Why not?" Paul asked unsteadily, still reeling from PJ's news and from his own fall.

PJ tugged on one boot. "Ask Sarah." His voice, deep though it was, came out slightly shaky. "You gotta ask Sarah. OK? Ask her how come I'd say that. Ask her what-all happened the day I left last summer. Then see if you feel like helping me."

Paul stepped back. PJ stood, facing him, his arms folded. His dark, direct stare was suddenly hard to meet. Paul made himself meet it; he made his face stay deadpan like PJ's. Inside he felt wakened from the daze he'd settled into in these post birth weeks.

His son a father? Was that what had knocked PJ so far off kilter?

"I will. I'll ask her. But—but one thing I've learned these past couple weeks. There are—out there, with all the craziness we've seen, we've been through—there are bigger things to worry about, son." Paul exhaled a smoky sigh, dissatisfied with his inept attempt at wisdom and perspective.

PJ waited for more, unblinking.

"But I will. Yep, I'll ask Sarah." Paul nodded once, curtly. "I'll talk to her. But you have to talk to me, to us. You have to tell us—call from Ohio and tell us—what in hell's going on with—"

"Her," PJ filled in. Her; both hers, he'd said. Within the mass of feelings churning inside him, Paul found room for relief that PJ did have another her, not just his own her.

PJ nodded. "Hey, you wanna flip me? I'll fall on the floor not the couch, myself. I need to practice fake falls for the kids. To make it look, like, real."

So they spread the couch cushions on the floor. Paul crouched gamely and took hold of PJ's knees. He yanked hard—that part felt good, blood rushing to his head—and flipped his son. PJ fell with a convincing, muffled thud on his back on the cushions.

He flopped his limbs, both booted feet thudding. His head was flung back, his eyes shut like he was knocked out, happy to be so.

"You OK?" Paul stood panting above PJ, his own spine aching again. Christ, had he blown his back, brained his kid? "PJ? Paul?"

At Paul, PJ snapped open his eyes. He fixed on the ceiling. "You got me where you want me," he told Paul, mock resigned, like he was inviting his father to plant his foot on his chest.

"We're gonna miss you," Paul made himself tell his flattened son.

"Yeah, well." PJ mumbled, sitting upright. "You'll see about that."

Then he sprang up to his feet. He was good at those gracefully abrupt karate moves. Paul dared to say that if PJ kept practicing, he could have himself a martial arts teaching career.

"I got another career in mind, Dad." PJ was heading back over to his duffle bag, all business. "But first, I gotta see what's up with Crystal. Not that she's my girlfriend or anything, but . . ."

"If the baby is born, you'll be a father to it."

"Least I'll try. Not that we got good genes for that . . ." PJ hoisted the duffle bag, no doubt full of the new, cheap clothes he'd bought with his paychecks from Evvy. He turned back to Paul, deadpan.

"I–I am sorry. You know that," Paul began haltingly. PJ cut him off.

"I gotta go," PJ announced with obvious relief, nodding toward the clock. Nearly 10 a.m. He stepped up to the front window and stared down at the rainy street. "This friend of Evvy's is picking me up. You won't see me for a while . . ." PJ shot one final, hard-eyed gaze over his shoulder. "Can't rush this one big family shit. You're the one who keeps saying, 'Take a step at a time,' right? That come from some head shrink book?"

"Nope." Paul shook his head; PJ refaced the window. "It's from that show, whatever-it-is. The damn kiddie show you used to watch, and they used to watch at the Center too. The one where the host turned out to be, in real life, a cokehead . . ."

"Oh yeah," PJ nodded at the window. "Used to like that show. Sometimes that song goes through my head, too. Drives me crazy."

"Me too." Paul gave a nod PJ might see in the window reflection. *"Blue's Clues."*

"Clues, right." Paul nodded again, glad in his new old man way to have that word supplied. Maybe PJ would know, too, what Beatles song said something like, only less corny: The more you give, the more you get.

Paul was gathering breath to ask when his son spun round on his boot heel.

"Good-bye," Paul called out instead, haplessly following PJ.

"Marines say so long." PJ marched toward the living room door, his duffle bag bouncing on his back. Down on the street, through steadily falling rain, Paul glimpsed a new looking SUV parked along the curb. A blonde middle-aged woman at the wheel.

"Hey Paul!" Paul managed to stop his son at the door with that name. PJ halted though he didn't turn, his shoulders tensed under his karate sweatshirt. "Where's your jacket?"

That battered denim jacket, which smelled like wet dog in rain. PJ's unprotected shoulders shrugged, his duffle bag bobbing. From below, through the downpour, the SUV's strident, cheery horn beeped.

PJ opened the door, explaining to Paul, "Oh yeah, my jacket. Guess I left it at, um, the house I'm gonna be staying in tonight . . . so she'll give it back . . ."

"Who?" Paul stepped into the open doorway; PJ was already thumping down the stairs. He stopped in the middle to look up, shoot Paul a sheepish grin.

"One of the karate moms. She's the one picking me up. She's got, see, a spare room. Hubby just left . . ."

"Oh?" Paul asked from half a flight above his blushing son. His strong, black-haired, black-browed son, crewcut and clean-shaven as a soldier.

PJ shrugged so hard his duffle bag dropped down. He re-shouldered it, balancing on the step. "Lots of the moms're hot for me. It's, like, a fringe benefit . . ."

Outside, the horn beeped even more stridently. Christ, Paul couldn't think what to say as PJ thundered down the last steps. 'Don't forget about Crystal?' Or 'Attaboy, kid?' 'Go For It?'

"Hey, take my rain jacket." Paul turned and seized his all-weather jacket from the rack by the door. "You can't go out like that."

He tossed the jacket down the stairwell. Its grey nylon ballooned like a parachute; it landed in a puffy heap at PJ's feet.

"Sure I can," PJ retorted, but then he did bend and snatch up the jacket.

PJ slammed the door below without a backwards glance. *He took the jacket*, Paul told his drained self. *It'll keep him warm. It and that blonde karate mom.*

Well, why not? Paul stepped back and shut the living room door. Why not a karate mom to comfort him before he faced Crystal? Weren't older women a logical next step since PJ had, Paul and Sarah used to joke, a mother complex the size of Texas.

From outside, Paul heard car doors slam. The SUV motor revved; tires whooshed in rain. Paul supposed he should counsel his son on possible fatherhood. Should warn his son against the older woman, but who was he to give advice on love? To advise against something that might hurt yet heal at the same time, like cigarettes? And God, Paul needed one.

"Marines say so long." PJ had made a point to say that. Christ, that could be PJ's plan. A way of paying for a baby without actually marrying this Crystal. Which was the scarier prospect: PJ signing up for the military or a shotgun marriage? Trying to outdistance his own thoughts, to stave off these new worries, Paul strode into the bedroom.

Outside the bedroom window, perched in the oak like a sign of bad luck was the black cat Sarah used to let in. The cat meowed pleadingly.

Paul turned his back on that cat, the whole notion of bad luck. He didn't have time for such nonsense, not anymore. He opened his closet and pulled on a tweed suit jacket he could wear to the hospital because PJ did take the damn raincoat.

It wasn't nearly enough. Nothing ever would be between him and the son he hadn't raised. *At least it's something*, Paul thought as he shut the dark closet. *Something I can give the kid.*

Chapter Ten

May 4, 2013; 10:10 a.m.

Baby Nursing

Sarah rocked cautiously, warming up the chair. The hospital rocker's squeaks marked off the minutes of this last, or hopefully last, hospital morning. At least she was finally sitting in one of the birth room's pristine wood rockers. For the first pain-dimmed week, she'd sat up in her bed in her own hospital room rocking in place, repeating to herself: *If we hadn't. If I hadn't.*

Then this week they'd let her have nursing sessions with Donny in the NICU, all too short, all with the help of the nurse with the bun, Ana, the one they liked best. Today, Ana had found an empty birth room for Sarah to nurse in. Sarah felt sure the NICU beeping sounds had distracted Donny, kept him from fully latching on, so this nicest nurse had agreed to let Sarah have this room to use for an hour or so, before they finally—but Sarah still couldn't believe it would happen—left the hospital for good.

Squeak, squeak. Any minute now, they'd bring Donny in. Sarah straightened her slump. Her stomach curved out, slack and padded. Her nursing bra stretched more than ever, her breasts achingly swollen with milk. Her limbs ached faintly, too, from the epic effort of having washed her hair earlier today in Evvy's friend's cramped shower. Her loose hair, always slow to dry, dampened her nursing shirt. She'd walked the blocks to the hospital in the drizzle with damp hair for Donny, her little man. Where *was* he?

For fourteen days, he lay like Snow White in his beeping box, stretched out. Tiny and big-headed but perfectly formed. Sarah's wrists chafed from sticking her hands through the incubator's plastic holes, fingertip stroking his curled-fern fist. At the start of the second week, Sarah had stiffly held her weightless bundle of baby as he licked droplets of her breast milk from her finger, his tongue cool and miraculously moist.

Twice a day, while Sarah still had her room, she sat stoically in her bed, hooked to the double-barrelled breast pump watching news of the Bomber Boy capture and fallout. The plastic suction cups and relentless mechanical suck made her overloaded breasts hurt like never before, yet that physical ache felt good to her overloaded heart.

It was a relief to grit her teeth in pain for the baby she'd already inadvertently hurt by making guilty love so recklessly and making him come out so small. The warped satisfaction Sarah took in breast-pump pain was one of many post birth feelings she could never explain to Paul.

Not that they'd had the time, energy, or privacy to discuss much beyond the baby basics—Donny's vitals, his gradual, precious signs of progress.

Evvy's gruff, kindly friend Marti worked nights at the hospital lab. Mercifully, Marti had been asleep most of the time Sarah was awake. Sarah had even avoided talking much to Evvy, despite all they owed her, since the birth night. The night Evvy had helped Sarah settle in with Marti, her friend had poured two glasses of wine, wanting to get the dirt on what-all had gone on between Sarah and PJ and Paul—all of which felt so distant to Sarah by then, compared to the reality of Donny, his endless tests.

Sarah had reminded Evvy she couldn't drink while nursing, and she'd tried to explain, as Evvy sipped the first wine, that she couldn't really discuss the whole PJ thing with her until she'd finally, belatedly, talked it all out with Paul. She'd added apologetically, leaving Evvy to down the second wine, that she had to get her sleep, to save her strength for Donny.

How could Evvy, caring though she was, fully understand that nothing was important anymore except Donny? Only Paul understood that, one bond they shared for sure, no matter what.

Sarah gripped the rocker arms as if the chair might lift off. She had to stave off thoughts of PJ, had to stay calm for Donny. She already knew how his little face screwed up in instinctive distress if she was feeling anxious or low. Why should she be feeling that on the day they might go home? To Paul and PJ.

Sarah drew deep breaths with the rocker squeaks. She would not miss the stale yet disinfected hospital air, the eggy, steamy trace of late breakfast trays being collected along the corridor. At least Sarah had gotten to eat real food, constant cold pizza, at Marti's.

Sarah arranged a pillow on the rocker's arm, nervous as if awaiting a date. Before the birth, Sarah had pictured nursing, the way she'd naively pictured birth itself, as something blissful and natural. Maybe it was a sign of progress that she now expected no such luck. Sarah braced herself, hearing the nice nurse bump through the door. "Mrs. Stratidakis?"

Sarah raised her damp-haired head at nurse Ana's throaty voice. "Yes, I'm ready . . ."

"He is too, looks like." Nurse Ana strode in through the curtains, tall and regal with her black bun, balancing the familiar baby bundle that still surprised Sarah by being so very small. Yet there was movement inside the hospital blanket—Donny's new, feeble kicks. "Doctor Eden agreed to meet with you and your husband in this room once he gets the all the results."

"Thanks for arranging that," Sarah told the nurse, who'd so often done them favors.

Little Donny kept kicking. *Good boy*, Sarah thought toward her baby as nurse Ana bent before her. Donny's radiantly pink forehead puckered in wordless worry.

"Such a serious face, this one has." The nurse transferred Donny into Sarah's tensed waiting arms. "Some of them, they open their eyes from napping and—*bam!*—begin to wail. This fella, he opens those big eyes and he's looking around, checking things out . . ."

Casing the joint, Paul liked to say, already seeing his own paranoid tendencies mirrored in Donny. Sarah drew his slight warmth to her chest, her bursting breasts.

"Yes, he's already a little man . . ." Sarah bent close to peek at his flushed, veiny face. Electric pink veins showed through his too-thin skin, webbing his high forehead. A Victorian boy's face, Sarah thought as she drank in a long look.

The petal lips pursed. The miniature nose flared, all nostrils, the wings of his nose chapped from tubes. The blue-brown eyes met her eager gaze, darker and clearer each day.

"My man," Sarah crooned, feeling Donny's feet prod her through his blanket.

"All right then," nurse Ana decreed, "we'll give it a shot. Hope he'll latch on good."

As matter-of-factly as she'd hooked Sarah up to the electronic breast pump, she spread open the slit of Sarah's cotton nursing shirt; her breast poked out.

"Let's get you two set here . . ." The nurse arranged baby Donny in the crook of Sarah's arm. Sarah bent forward cautiously, afraid she'd smother him with her heavy breast, her plenty— afraid she'd miss his mouth, stab her swollen nipple into one of his wide open eyes, afraid he simply wouldn't be able to take hold, like the times they'd tried before.

"Lemme help him out . . ." nurse Ana muttered. Her fingers felt cold, taking hold of Sarah's nipple. She crammed it into Donny's suddenly opened mouth. He burbled in surprise.

"He'll gag," Sarah managed to choke out, startling at his gummy nip, his mouth taking hold. Another muffled burble; he swallowed.

"Nope," the nurse proclaimed, straightening to her full, commanding height. "He's on."

Sarah bowed her head so her damp hair formed the tent of privacy she sensed her baby liked, too. "He's on," she repeated incredulously.

Inside their hair tent, Sarah savored Donny's gurgling gulps and swallows, the tug of his suck more irregular and infinitely more gentle than the pump's.

"You all set?" asked nurse Ana briskly, already backing away.

"Yes," Sarah murmured, the magic word that would let her be alone with him.

"Only give him a few minutes this first time. Maybe five or so on each side." The nurse was striding toward the open door. It shut.

Then Sarah and her baby were alone behind the closed bed curtains. Donny sucked, weakly but steadily. Sarah rocked, steadily, too. She relaxed into her rocking, his rhythm—his gurgles and swallows. He was draining her breast, thickening her heartbeat.

Filling her chest with warmth, relief, peace. He slipped off her right breast. She eased him to her other arm, a glimmer of milk on his lips. Clumsily, Sarah aimed her left breast into his widened mouth—a miss. Then Donny nipped her, took hold. The kid was a natural.

"Good little man," Sarah crooned, trying not to worry that he didn't seem to hear. How could she tell if he heard, when he was so busy nursing? Sarah didn't want to worry about the hearing tests, not now, as they finally rocked and nursed. They were just settling into a left-breast rhythm when a knock sounded on her room door.

Sarah drew a breath to answer but didn't dare startle Donny from his first real nursing trance. The door creaked wide.

"Sare?" Paul stepped into her room. He was early. His big, shadowy outline loomed through her drawn linen curtain. Donny squirmed in her arms but kept sucking.

"He . . . he's on. He's nursing," she called to Paul in a stage whisper, holding her determinedly sucking son steady. His nursing was tiring her yet strengthening her, too. "Come and *see*," she called softly. Then, fumbling to tug her slit nursing shirt down, she added, "Is, um, PJ with you?"

Paul had told Sarah they would try to come together to take her and Donny home. She'd wondered if PJ would get out of that as he'd gotten out of other planned visits.

"Nope," Paul answered, closer now. Sarah relaxed in relief.

"I don't want to scare Donny or anything," Paul muttered through the curtain, like he was a priest and she was about to confess.

"You won't." Sarah pulled Donny subtly closer. His suck resumed its rhythm. Sarah half shut her eyes, picturing Paul and PJ's two outlined man-bodies facing her through the bed curtains, crowding her room to watch her TV on lockdown day, the only real talk she'd had with the two of them, after the Bomber Boy capture.

"C'mon, Paul. He's almost done," Sarah stage-whispered. Donny's suck slowed again. Sarah reminded herself that the baby shouldn't have too much this first time.

"He's in a boat. They're shooting at him!"

Sarah had blurted this into her cell phone the afternoon of the lockdown day, when she'd finally wakened from her post birth on-and-off sleep. Other voices excitedly spreading the news of a late-breaking breakthrough in the manhunt had woken Sarah from her nightmare of black-jello blood and a mouse-sized baby sliming from between her unhinged legs.

"He's in a boat. The *Bomber Boy* is in a boat," a voice in the birth floor hall was announcing. *In a boat?* Sarah wondered groggily. *Where? On the Charles River?* With no one in her room to ask, she groped for her remote, saw onscreen the tanks and police cars converging on a street in Watertown that looked almost like their leafy street in Belmont.

She speed-dialed Paul, woke him from a nap in the NICU, where he and PJ were taking turns sitting near Donny.

"We're coming. We gotta see this." Paul told Sarah over the phone. He meant *we've gotta see this together.* Sarah was so raptly glued to the unfolding live scene on her flat-screen TV she had no time or energy to fret over seeing PJ.

Nothing mattered but capturing the damn Bomber Boy by the time Paul and PJ showed up together, un-showered and waking the sterile room with man-sweat. They crowded in behind Sarah's curtain to watch the showdown, the end game.

Like an ultrasound, Sarah murmured to Paul at the weird infrared photos taken from helicopters showing the shadow shape of a man, a boy—a boy-man sprawled under the tarp of a backyard boat in Watertown. The elderly owner of the boat had lifted the tarp to discover a bloody mess, but the mess in the infrared photos was moving.

Alive! The Bomber Boy was alive! Paul gripped Sarah's hand, and she forgot her aching breasts and her own infection tests as she and Paul—and quietly hunched PJ—watched the grand capture like any Boston family.

When the triumphant Tweet from Mayor Tom Menino was read aloud onscreen—WE GOT HIM—Sarah burst into tears and a hoarse cheer along with other ragged voices, other families up and down the birth floor. PJ and Paul clapped together in unison for once.

"'We got him,'" PJ repeated like he'd been part of the team.

We got him, Sarah was repeating in her mind, reminding herself. Our son—safe, for now.

The bombing suspect was in custody, was alive, the news voices kept emphasizing.

"Can we go see ... our boy?" Sarah dared to ask when the newsmen began the first in endless replays from the scene, the giant crowd of uniformed, armed men converged around the helpless-looking house with the boat.

The Bomber Boy had been made to lift his shirt, it was reported, to show he had no explosives strapped on. Then he'd fallen to the ground.

Someone's son, Sarah thought but didn't say aloud. *Someone, many someones, must have let him down, that boy. Him and his evil black hat brother, both of them. Someone's sons.*

The manhunt had been a son-hunt. *And it's over now,* Sarah told herself as she switched off the riveting TV, zapping them back to their own smaller scale showdown, or what might turn into a showdown if they really had to talk.

Blinking from the TV dream, she faced Paul and PJ. The room was dim with the TV turned off and the sky darkening outside. The son-hunt was truly over. She and Paul had their two sons, and they couldn't let them down—either of them.

"I want us to visit him together. I . . . I'm so glad, PJ," Sarah added, addressing him directly for the first time since the birth night, meeting his skittish, dark gaze. "I'm so glad we named him Don. I'm glad you had such a great idea. So, can we go see him? Donny?"

"Don," PJ and Paul corrected her as one, and they laughed together like a regular family, then sat for a moment awkwardly silent.

"Whoa, but Dad." PJ spoke up from his side of Paul. "I wanna see him again and all, but doesn't Sarah, like . . . she needs her sleep and all, right?"

Poor PJ still sounded anxious to get away from them, his un-blended family, but Sarah rallied, her med-numbed body still so fleshy. No one had told her a baby would leave behind so much heaviness. "We can do it. I can do it. I want to see Donny."

Paul cut in, maybe trying to strike a lighter note. "The nurses and Sarah call him Donny, so I guess we gotta put up with it—while he's little." Paul sat on the edge of Sarah's bed in his new doctor mode. "So, if Sarah feels up to the trip, let's . . . let's make it together." *Make it work,* Sarah heard him really saying to her and PJ. Still, PJ hung back, shifting his weight, ducking his dark head. Sarah glimpsed PJ's newly abashed, downcast gaze over Paul's shoulder. His big shoulders were hunched like her own shoulders. "But first, but PJ . . . was there something you wanted to say?" Paul was still running this meeting. Sarah braced herself for PJ's reply.

Out in the hall, someone was laughing, everyone relieved, upbeat for a change. *Even us,* Sarah thought woozily, though PJ looked so scared again. He jammed his hands in his pockets as if to immobilize them.

"Well?" Paul cleared his throat, faint smoke on his breath. He smoothed his beard. "Sare, see. We . . . PJ . . . we've both been wanting to talk to you. Can you, now?"

I can but I don't want to, she wanted to say. *Let's just celebrate like a real family.* Paul reached for her nightstand, handing her the cup of watery ginger ale. She sipped.

Mildly revived by the ginger ale's bubbly, comforting zip, she met

PJ's evasive gaze, his eyes as dark and unreadable as Paul's. He lowered his head further, like a bull, and began pacing her bed, halfway around, then back.

It was Paul who started talking, in his deepest no-nonsense voice. "Last night, PJ had been popping tablets," he told Sarah as if this explained everything. "Tablets containing ephedrine. The drug made PJ say anything that came to his head," Paul concluded.

Sarah nodded stiffly, thinking *was PJ on mini-thins when he wrote me that card asking to make me pregnant? Was I on mini-thins when I acted like that card hadn't happened?* She swallowed more ginger ale, a familiar, guilty heaviness gathering in her chest.

Paul took her hand, his strong as ever.

PJ didn't stop pacing but started talking. "All I wanna tell you is, like . . . sorry for saying all that shit last night when I was on those mini-thins and all . . ."

He kept pacing back and forth at the foot of her bed, making her dizzy.

"You're . . . you're not the only one who's sorry," Sarah gripped Paul's hand. "God, PJ . . . I mean, Paul. Both you Paul's. I . . . I wish I could say *I* was on some kinda drug this whole past year." She felt Paul squeeze her hand as if to stop her but she pushed on. "I know I . . . I handled everything all wrong, Peej. You getting way too attached to me and me kinda . . . kinda needing that . . . attention, thinking I needed it, but what I really needed . . ." She finished, sensing they all wanted her to stop short of Spy Pond, of their own showdown, "was, is . . . my baby, our baby. And I . . . I need to see him. Now. With you two."

Then Paul was fetching Sarah's robe, helping her to stand. PJ ran out and found a nurse with a wheelchair, he and the young nurse chattering excitedly about the Bomber Boy capture as they wheeled the chair in.

"Yeah, I'd just gotten back into town when it happened, the blast and all," PJ was telling this nurse so easily. Sarah realized as she was settled into the chair that she hadn't thought to ask PJ where he'd been during the bombing itself. One more mistake.

"It all happened the day my train pulled into town, y'know? All these armed guards at south station, and I kinda felt like trouble just, like, follows me, like I'd caused the whole damn thing."

"But you didn't," Paul finished in his deep, decisive voice.

He wheeled Sarah into the hall. PJ followed a few steps behind, like a kid.

They entered the NICU together; PJ was outfitted in his own

pale blue smock and face mask. *Good,* Sarah found her exhausted self thinking as she fitted her mask in place. *Now we can all put off talking any more.*

They gathered 'round the plastic, beeping incubator as if round an altar. PJ mumbled through his mask that Donny looked a little big. *Bigger, anyways.*

Sarah settled in the nearest chair. She stuck her hand through the hole nearest Donny's hands. Her huge fingertip stroked those walnut-sized fists, their slight heat. Donny's face was squeezed shut, fiercely sleeping, his nose still taped with tubes. His cloth cap had slipped and Sarah strained to reach it, but Paul on his side of the box was closer. His bigger hand barely fit through the wrist hole. He managed with a few deft fingertip touches to nudge the cap back in its place, so it covered the bumpy gap in Donny's skull, the pulsing soft spot.

"Oh, Peej," Sarah rallied to say, raising her voice through her mask. "We can't change what's happened . . . but we can give you a good start with your new little brother."

"Half-brother," PJ corrected behind her, though he bent closer.

"Half is better than none," Sarah told PJ. "Half is enough."

Awkwardly, PJ and Paul traded places. Paul stood behind Sarah's wheelchair. PJ sat in Paul's chair. He stuck his hand, bigger than hers but not as big as Paul's, inside the hole.

His stiff fingers prodded Donny's elbow. PJ seemed to hold his breath, studying his tiny half-brother. Watching, Sarah saw the love-hungry boy PJ had been for so many years.

PJ yanked out his hand after only a few moments. He pulled himself up and hovered behind his father. Sarah told him he could sit longer, touch Donny some more.

PJ's voice came out muffled by the mask and the *beeps,* so he not only looked but sounded smaller, younger. "N-no thanks. I'm scared I might, y'know, by accident . . . hurt him."

⊰⊱

"Just what you've been wanting," Paul murmured to her from the curtain opening. Sarah nodded, resisting the urge to demand *isn't it what you want too, by now?*

"Mmm," Sarah answered instead, cupping Donny's orange-sized head. "What Donny wants, too. Glad you could see it . . ."

Paul stepped closer, inside the curtain. He bent to lift Donny's blanket fold. He was still sucking, swallowing. Unlike others who addressed Donny, Paul never used a babyish voice.

"So you finally got your mom relaxed enough, huh?" he told Donny, matter-of-factly. "Maybe she's going to survive motherhood, after all . . ."

"Like a car crash," Sarah murmured. "That's something I flashed on when we crashed into the sign. I read somewhere that you gotta relax and move 'with' the crash, not fight it . . ."

Donny squirmed, his slackened mouth finally released Sarah's breast. His milky spit glinted then vanished. His sleepy body relaxed in her arms.

"We did it." Sarah pressed Donny close. "So where *is* PJ? Waiting for us at home or . . . ?"

"He's got his own plans." Paul straightened and stood tall above her. "It's . . . complicated. For starters, he's heading back to Ohio."

"So he's . . . left?" Sarah asked softly, bent over Donny. His head lolled back; his miniature, manly face looked slack and satisfied—a drunken sailor. "But for how long?"

"Your guess is as good as mine. No, your guess is probably better."

Sarah hoisted Donny on her shoulder, supporting his hot, downy head. She fingered his back, not daring to pat it, feeling inside him bubbles from the milk.

"Well," she told Paul cautiously, "Maybe that's . . . for the best, for now." She finger-tapped Donny's intricate, bony spine, afraid to tap too hard.

"You think?" Paul asked back, an edge to that *you*.

"I guess I do." Sarah lowered her voice so she could hear, could track, the bubbles inside her baby. *Shouldn't he be burping?* "Look, Paul," she made herself say. "You know how sorry I am about . . . how, how messed up things got with PJ."

"Just how messed up did they get?" Paul asked, his tone ominously flat.

Donny burbled, wriggled with effort. He coughed. Heaving his small body, he spit up on Sarah's shoulder. Warm milky spit wet her shirt, her damp hair.

"GodPaul, can you hand me a washcloth?" Sarah jiggled Donny to get it all out, spit-up milk clogging his tiny throat. Did she give him too much too soon?

"I got it." Paul had thumped into the bathroom; he charged out with a dry washcloth.

"Got him." Sarah jiggled Donny as she directed Paul: "Can you wipe his mouth?"

Paul dabbed the washcloth onto her shoulder. Then on Donny's chin. Donny was breathing in gurgly gasps. His tongue darted out.

"Hey, Sare. I think he wants more."

"Maybe . . ." Sarah reached her free hand into her nursing bra slit, touched her moist nipple. She drew her finger out, held it up to Paul. "He's used to it from my finger." She pressed her fingertip to Paul's like she'd done back when they'd transferred their wedding rings. Those rings both still on Paul's hand, Sarah noted, her own ring finger still feeling empty, odd. Yet she'd avoided bringing up her ring on his hand. They both had avoided it.

Lightly, Sarah smeared the warm white blob onto Paul's square fingertip.

"Here you go, son . . ." He nudged Donny with his wet fingertip, so much bigger than Donny's chin. Donny stuck out his pink, kittenish tongue. He licked milk from Paul's finger.

Paul stayed bent, watching his son swallow. Sarah smelled cigarettes in Paul's beard, on his held breath. Donny swallowed again, peacefully.

Sarah smoothed his back, whispering, "Want to hold him?"

Paul took hold of Donny. He pressed the baby to his chest and straightened slowly. Sarah stiffened in her rocker, gazing up past Paul's big, bent arms to Donny's widened eyes, appalled and alight. He'd rarely been held by his father, standing, so high up.

"Careful," Sarah couldn't not say. Paul patted Donny's back with four fingers, rhythmically. "Don't pat him too hard."

"You weren't patting him hard enough," Paul countered. A louder burble was rising inside Donny. Paul pat-patted his back; Donny let out a startling, startled baby belch.

Then, in unison with Sarah, an "Oh" of pure relief.

"Told you." Paul grinned within his beard. "The kid needed that."

"You were right," Sarah admitted. "You've got the touch with him, 'the kid.'"

"Well hell, he's mine." Paul bent, lowering Donny back into Sarah's arms. The baby felt limp now, half asleep. Sarah gathered Donny in gratefully, pressing him to her heart.

Paul stood tall again. Sarah rocked the rocker, its *squeak squeak* filling a pause between them, mixing with the metallic *squeak* of the NICU cart. A perfunctory rap on the half-open room door, and nurse Ana reappeared. She announced above Sarah's *squeaks* that she needed to take "the little one" once more, for that last weigh-in, last check by Dr. Eden.

"Really? The last?" Sarah asked uneasily. Without waking him, nurse Ana lifted Donny.

"For now, honey. Dr. E. will come and talk to you soon." The nurse reported this last, carefully reciting. A message from on high, Paul said when Dr. Eden was involved.

"But I'm sure," the nurse added unconvincingly over her shoulder as she wheeled their baby away, "everything will come out all right."

Chapter Eleven

May 4, 2013; 11:00 a.m.

Baby Examination

The door thumped shut, leaving Sarah and Paul alone for the first time in ages. *To examine each other,* Sarah wondered, *while Eden examines Donny?*

"So," Sarah began, "D'you think they'll really . . . let us take him? Today, like they said?"

"Like they said, they might." Paul met her determinedly hopeful gaze. Sarah rallied a smile. He answered with his own game attempt, a marriage mirror.

Could it really be that Paul's long-jawed face had aged in these two weeks, the way Sarah knew her own had aged? The lines in his forehead looked deeper, the grey in his black brows more pronounced. Sarah had noticed her own white hairs that seemed to have sprung up overnight. "Last I heard, Saint Paul, the official check-out time isn't 'til noon."

"Gives *us* a little time," Paul noted aloud, sounding as uneasy as she felt.

It was just after eleven a.m. by the bedside clock, Sarah noticed. Paul settled into the chair. Sarah walked over and sat on the bed made up for some other mother-to-be.

"So how about you?" Paul asked her. "You're relieved that PJ is leaving?"

"Not relieved, exactly. But yes, it feels right that I'm . . . going home with just you two, you and Donny." They both looked down beside the bed at the disaster survival bag that sat beside the bigger travel bag of clothes Paul had brought her. Sarah had taken both those bags to her crash-pad at Marti's. They'd used the disaster bag to hold Sarah's meds and pads and her pumping machine. The disaster bag still held, zipped inside it like an explosive, the card PJ had sent her. Sarah had found it there when she'd unpacked at Marti's. She'd been waiting, dreading, a chance to bring that up to Paul. Drawing a resigned breath now, she hauled the heavy, clanking bag up beside her. Then she looked again at the clock.

"Listen," she told Paul, lowering her voice though the room door was shut. "I sort of feel like this is our—you know the signs on highways?— our last rest stop for next one hundred miles."

"Huh?" Paul asked warily, but she sensed he knew what she meant.

"I mean, hopefully we're taking Donny with us today . . . So, this might be our last time really alone together for, for who knows how long and I . . . Well, you know that there's . . . things we need to talk about." She unzipped the bag, drawing out the card.

"Laying our cards on the table," she muttered as she set it on the nightstand. "Guess that's what we oughta do. Just to get it all, if we can even *start* to get it all, behind us . . ." She drew another big breath, keeping her eyes on the closed birthday card, its soft-focus flame. "This damn PJ card . . . you already know I never really answered it. I pretended I thought it was a poem. I kept it from you when I shouldn't have, but you know what?" She dared to look up at deadpan Paul, his gaze pained but steady. "In a warped way, this card helped bring us Donny. Because I knew when I got the damn thing, when it made me feel so, so—"

"Tempted?" Paul supplied, flatly.

Sarah let that word stand. "I knew then that this baby obsession of mine had gone too far, that it was messing with my mind, with our marriage, with PJ. So that's when I really did decide just to . . . stop. Stop *trying* so hard, stop pursuing the damn fertility treatments. And then it did turn out like the old wives say. The minute we stopped trying, it happened."

"Just like that," Paul muttered dryly, as if she were intending to wrap up everything as some kind of happy ending. *But I'm not*, she wanted to say.

Paul reached for PJ's card himself, lifted it. "Just like that and we're all OK, huh?" Paul gripped PJ's card, wishing he could jam the goddamn thing back in that bag.

He heaved a heavy sigh, sure Sarah caught the trace of smoke. He'd savored a cigarette in the hospital parking garage, pacing around their repaired, but still dented, car before coming up to her. "Glad it all turned out so well for you." He let the flimsy card fall open so PJ's crazed message faced Sarah. "But for PJ. Christ. Only thing I know is he's not gonna bomb Boston. He's not that crazy. But he's also not gonna . . ." Paul shut the card, "get well soon."

"I know that, *too*," Sarah answered too fast, sounding thick-throated. Christ, was she going to cry yet again? "Especially after," she pushed on, "after he disappeared for so long. GodPaul, I'll always feel responsible for him running away, him being out of touch too long, getting in that cemetery trouble. All of that triggering him to get so, so . . ."

"Out of control," Paul filled in. "So let's really lay out all the damn cards." He tossed PJ's card back onto the nightstand. "You did overhear what Peej said, what he claimed, on the birth night?"

"Enough." Sarah barely nodded, but her voice sounded steadier. "Yes, I know he was saying the baby was . . . his. What I don't know is, did you actually believe it?"

"A little. For a little." Paul sighed smoke again, shocked and relieved just to say that. He picked up the card again, re-creasing its stiff fold. "Y'know, *I* was out of my head too that night, and I'd been picking up on something strange between you and PJ for, for I don't know how long."

At this Sarah nodded hard, her gaze wavering.

"So did you . . . when you got this thing . . ." Paul waved PJ's card, wanting to throw it at her. Instead he took hold with both hands and ripped it in two. A loud satisfying tear severed the crease he'd sharpened. He dropped both halves onto the nightstand, not looking up at tense silenced Sarah. "*Did* you want what he—what PJ offered?"

Sarah's voice came out abashed, ashamed. But clear. "A little. For a little."

Paul swallowed a taste of ash. He made himself look up from the torn card. He held Sarah's bright, scared stare as she went on, shaky like him.

"Not that I . . . I ever would've acted on that, that screwed-up want. Not that *I* was ever *that* crazy. Not that wanting it, in a way, even lasted long . . . just long enough for me to see I was *going* crazy with wanting the baby so much with, with—"

"Wanting me to want the baby, too," Paul filled in.

"Yes. Yes that too." Sarah wiped at her eyes. Paul stood and started to pace a small, constrained circle at the foot of the bed, the same circle PJ had paced in a different room on lockdown day. Paul cleared his throat, feeling like a prosecuting attorney.

"Then it seemed like once you got your baby, Sare, you wanted PJ out of your whole . . . perfect picture."

Sarah shook her head, starting to protest, but Paul paced on and pushed on, inspired.

"Well, you almost got your wish. PJ almost held his knife to his throat, out in the hall on the birth night, like that crazy Bomber Boy in the boat, only he didn't do it—cut himself." Paul halted, digging into the disaster bag, pulling out the folded knife, maybe bits of Evvy's blood on the blade. Luckily no one had ever investigated. "I hid the damn knife in here so the security folks who hauled PJ away wouldn't frisk him and find it. Lucky for us, there were crazier boys than PJ on the loose that night."

Paul set the folded knife on the bed like evidence. He stared at it and not at Sarah, shaking his head and raising one hand to his own beard, his throat. "Christ, Sare. When Peej pulled that damn thing out, unfolding it, talking about hurting himself with it. When I think of that damn doomed Dzhokhar in that backyard boat, stabbing his own throat . . . Peej would never—or we think would never—but he talked about doing it, about how the only person he'd ever hurt with that knife was him."

Hearing Sarah start to sob, Paul finally looked up at her. Her face was in her hands, her damp dark hair swaying with her sobs.

"I know," Sarah gasped, choking out her words. "I . . . I know. I mean, I was scared of that t-too, with Peej. When he . . . he first pulled that knife at Spy Pond. Th-that last day. Not, like, aiming it at me or at him-self but, but . . . I didn't know *what* he might do."

"Look," Paul cut in. He sat down beside her on the bed. "Look, I've got things to tell you. Things Peej told me today, but you've gotta tell me one more thing, right now." Paul shot a glance at the clock. "I know it wasn't a baby, wasn't sex. But what *did* happen with you and PJ at Spy Pond? Peej said I should ask you."

Sarah sucked back her tears and swallowed. *Peej said.* God. Well, she deserved this. She made herself stand like she was facing a judge, a sentence. Her legs still felt weak, but each day walking got easier. She faced Paul sitting on the bed, his knees crowding her.

She drew a shuddery breath, looking down at folded knife and torn card. The soft-focus candlelight photo lay separate now from PJ's spiky, hand-printed words.

"It wasn't . . . like it'll sound. It's . . . so hard to explain."

"Try." Paul's command held his old supervisor edge.

Sarah inched closer to where he sat, bumping his knees. Would Paul walk out on her? *No,* she told herself as she reached down to him. If only because Paul would never walk out on his new son. She touched Paul's head, smoothed his coarse, curly hair.

"Last summer, with you so down about your dad and talking so little to me, looking so little at me . . . All that's no excuse, but all summer when I'd feel PJ watch me, you know the way he did. I . . . I missed being watched that way by you. I never should've let it happen, let any ideas like that grow inside Peej, but I felt like I *wasn't* letting anything happen with him. After that damn crazy card, I barely even let PJ *hug* me . . . you know those hard hugs he used to give me, which maybe was another mistake, me pulling back . . ."

She nervously smoothed Paul's hair, the same skull spot where Donny had his pulsing, soft skin. She wanted to halt this ridiculous, distant story, but it was like being queasy in early pregnancy and knowing she'd passed a point of no return. No way out but to spit it all up.

"A mistake because?" Paul prompted, his voice and neck tensing. He tilted his head, making her hand slip off. She let both her hands drop to her sides.

"Because then that day in August—the day PJ left. When he was so mad over losing his Center job, when he finally did hug me good-bye, PJ just . . . I just let him hang on so hard."

"And?" Paul breathed in rough commanding whisper. Then, louder, "Look, PJ said some weird shit—even for *him*—on the birth night. He said, when Evvy and I were asking him what in hell was wrong, he said he wanted to be high on mommy milk."

Sarah nodded frozenly; her throat closed.

"Just today, Sare, PJ told me I wouldn't want to help him out if I knew what had happened that Spy Pond day. And he did tell me I should . . . ask you."

"Ask me," Sarah repeated weakly. "Well, he's right. I'm the one who should tell you."

"So, goddammit, *tell.*"

Sarah pulled Paul toward her, pressing him to her, leaning forward so his chin poked her deflated belly, his head resting against her swollen breasts, so she couldn't see his eyes.

"OK. It all happened so fast, right after Peej had talked to you, and you'd . . . fired him and all. Peej was so upset. He was saying good-bye. He dropped on his knees in front of me. We were behind some bushes. Then he was hugging me, was . . . standing up on his knees and nuzzling me, my breasts, like he was trying, through my shirt and all, to . . . nurse. Of course I pushed him away, right away. And he didn't get under my shirt, get to my breasts, but he tried to. And m-maybe that's what he was after, a taste of b-breast milk."

"Like the taste you let me have," Paul mumbled into her sweatshirt, shaking his head, grinding it hard against her.

"On Donny's birth day," Sarah filled in, her voice cracking with familiar guilt, a relief at least to say all this out loud. All this crazy shit, as PJ would say. To share, at least, some portion of the guilt. Sarah swallowed back more tears. "One mommy milk taste, that night, and we went ahead and made love, made poor Donny come too soon."

Paul didn't nod, his head still pressed against Sarah's dense body. His own big body stayed rigidly bent forward as he balanced on the edge of the bed. He felt a warm dampness leaking from her breasts against his face. Christ, was Sarah falling apart all over again? Right now, when Paul was realizing just how far apart PJ had fallen.

Christ Almighty, his son trying to nurse his wife? They should all be on tabloid TV. Abruptly, Paul pulled back from Sarah. He sat straight, scooting back further onto the bed. He blinked up at her, not knowing what to do with her, his crying wife.

"Such a little thing, almost nothing," Sarah was managing to say. "But it almost made us lose *every*thing . . ."

Paul nodded, though he wasn't sure if she was talking about what happened with her and PJ or with, on Donny's birth night, her and him, his own taste of her milk.

Sarah began crying again, her face twisting up. Paul saw the damp crescents on her shirt where her breasts were leaking. He took her hands, holding on as her body, her new, thickened body, shuddered. From below, her clenched face looked distorted—a flushed, overflowing mother monster.

"S-sorry," Sarah gasped. Her mouth stretched back, exposing, from Paul's view below, the extra pink swell of muscle inside her upper lip that he'd always found sexy. Sexy and scary now; her mouth stretched wider as she sucked back her sobs. Its strained, gaping shape called to Paul's mind the word for hungry holes, for baby's open mouths. The word was the sound those mouths want to make.

Maw, Paul thought as he squeezed Sarah's hands. Baby's mouths so bottomless, hungry the way PJ always would be. Could anything ever satisfy that motherless, fatherless hunger, that hole in him?

Sarah squeezed back hard; Paul felt his wedding rings jam his finger bones. He felt Sarah pull against his grip, nodding toward a tissue box, so Paul released her, yanked out two tissues. She swiped at her face, then slipped her hand into the slits of her loose shirt.

Tears and breast milk, Paul thought as she wiped, as he handed her another wad of tissues. He swallowed hard, imagining, trying to, his older son nuzzling his wife, her breasts.

"Sorry," Sarah repeated, swallowing yet more tears. Paul saw how her warm, leaking milk soaked the flimsy hospital tissues, disintegrating them in Sarah's hand. She used the next tissues Paul handed her to wrap the wet mess. She dropped it all with a juicy plop into her trash can.

"Don't know what the hell to say, Sare. But, see, there's . . . more, too. Today." Paul looked at the clock—nearly 11:20 a.m. Was there some problem with Donny's tests, delaying the doctor? "No time to lay it on you . . . Except, like you say, there may not be . . . another time soon."

Sarah sat heavily on the bed beside Paul, not needing to be advised to sit down. Paul told her how the cow tongue girl may or may not be having PJ's baby. How PJ was going back to Ohio to find out.

"The cow tongue girl?" Sarah asked in drained sounding whisper. "She and PJ . . . have a baby? All along he's had this . . . *girl?*"

Paul looked at Sarah at last. He took in his wife's flushed giveaway face, and asked her: "Jealous?"

Sarah stiffened as she shook her head. "No, no. How can you *say* that to me? I mean, I *know* how you can, but I *can't* spend the rest of my life, the rest of our lives—"

"Wondering what I'm wondering?" Paul cut in. "OK, but we're not at the rest of our lives yet. I've gotta know what you . . . what you feel for our—for my—son."

Sarah bowed her head, her hair hiding her hot face. "He's mine too, Paul, my stepson. You know I'd have never . . . I never wanted him to have those feelings for me. And I . . . I'm glad he has a girl. I'm just so . . . I just always thought—"

"PJ'd spend the rest of his life pining over you?" Paul's words were harsh, but his voice sounded low and tired like hers. She looked up, meeting his eyes, letting him see her anger.

"No. It's not . . . not that I wanted that, I just—" She plunged on boldly. "This's why I couldn't tell you any of this. Because I knew if we started talking about it, you'd see through me, see everything I was . . . trying to keep down, to hide." She kept her gaze locked in Paul's see-all gaze. "I . . . I thought for a while it was *PJ* who could see into me, like he was the only one who really saw how badly I wanted our baby. Now here he is . . . with his own baby . . ." She shook her head, straining to take it all in. "Peej has a baby, or probably has a baby. Had or has one. Peej really said all that?"

What she was thinking was, *God, I really said all that, too?*

Paul nodded, his gaze on her holding steady. Yes, she knew he was seeing that ugly flare of jealousy she felt—and her selfish relief, too, to hear that PJ was so screwed up over more than just her, like when the doctor told her about her infected amnio fluid, how that and not just the sex triggered Donny's premature birth. Sarah let out a long-held breath.

At least Paul was still meeting her eyes. Seeing everything in her, but still looking. How could he stand to still look?

Paul's own face seemed today, to her, as drained and aged as hers felt. His eyes darker than ever, fixed on her as if weighing something. His breath smelled smoky stale. She felt him wanting to press her, to ask, no doubt someday he would, more.

About how much 'a little' meant, how much she'd been drawn to PJ as a younger version of him. He'd heard, Sarah could tell, enough for now.

"D-doctor'll be here any minute," she murmured to the clock. Paul nodded and Sarah sensed he was nodding at some other inner calculation. She stayed sitting on the edge of her bed, but Paul stood and settled back in the bedside chair.

Face to face again, Sarah matched Paul's dazed, wary gaze with her own. A cracked, but intact, marriage mirror.

Both of us, Sarah told herself, weighing it all. The wrongs they'd done each other. Too much to brush aside; but not enough, not on her side, to break them.

❦

The door *squeaked* officiously open, its sound startling Paul and shattering their shared, married-couple stare. Metal *squeaked*, too, the familiar NICU baby cart.

Paul blinked, still feeling he and Sarah hadn't finished. Would never finish? Dr. Eden nodded his stern, wordless greeting. The doctor wheeled the cart in by himself, Donny sound asleep. Paul stepped up to the cart first, bent over his son. Donny's mouth hung open with his new, sated slackness. Donny and Sarah both seemed relieved now that they'd finally nursed.

Sarah stepped up beside Paul and squeezed his hand, hers sweaty. They turned as one to Dr. Eden.

Paul's brain was overloaded with all that Sarah and PJ had told him. He was almost glad to focus on Dr. Eden's burnished, close-shaven face, his rimless glasses and coldly intelligent gaze—exacting, dispassionate Dr. Eden.

"Do you like Dr. Eden?" Paul had asked Sarah when the doctor had begun his round of tests.

She'd answered, "Dr. Eden isn't someone you like."

"The positive indications," Dr. Eden began with his usual lack of preface, slipping his clipboard from Donny's cart, "are as I previously outlined to Mrs. Stratidakis: that your son's RDS has in fact improved and of course his NC, Nasal Cannula, tubes have been discontinued. However," an imperious flip of a clipboard page, "our final tests today indicate strongly that additional tests by the audiologist I've recommended are imperative."

As the page flipped again, Paul's own hearing filled with a faint buzz. The earlier tests had determined that Donny wasn't deaf, but would the kid somehow be classified as legally deaf like some kids are legally blind? Would he need a hearing aid? Or worse, or more?

". . . and only further tests can determine the extent of the damage."

"What kind of tests? What kind of damage?" Paul felt he and Sarah were both speaking at once, but really, he realized as Dr. Eden addressed his answers only to Sarah, she was the one who had spoken aloud.

Though Sarah nodded as if Dr. Eden were giving vital, new information, from what Paul heard above his own inner buzz, it was mere repetition. No, even godly Dr. Eden couldn't yet tell the severity of the damage, only that Donny's hearing was clearly not in the normal range. And yes, Sarah was to phone tomorrow for an appointment for these further tests, to commence ASAP.

A-S-A-P, Paul repeated to himself like an unbreakable code as he sank back onto the bedside chair, the father chair. Announcing he was being paged, no doubt by a *beep* only doctors and dogs could hear, Dr. Eden turned his narrow, white-coated back. A-S-A-P, Paul thought to the brisk, retreating rhythm of Eden's footsteps. A-S-A-P, Sarah had repeated in apparent bewilderment and exhaustion on Donny's birth night ages ago.

The room door shut with a smart indifferent *click*.

*　　　*

"His *hearing*," Sarah exclaimed so loudly Paul feared she'd wake up peacefully sleeping Donny. "I mean, we knew that might be a problem, but hearing Dr. E. say it like that, like we just can't be allowed to get away free."

"We can't. So deal with it." Paul snapped himself out of his own panicked, buzzing trance. From Sarah's cracked voice, he guessed that she'd used up all her composure with Dr. Eden, that Paul must go 'on duty' now if they were going to get this baby home.

Paul pulled himself from the bedside chair; Sarah collapsed onto it, but as he laid his hand on her shoulder, Sarah didn't slump. Instead she straightened. Paul saw her stifle her tears in a way she might not have been able to do weeks ago.

She nodded, slowly. "Could be way worse."

"Donny will need a little extra care, that's all," Paul managed, his own voice thickened. "And yeah, could be so much worse," he reminded himself and her.

He swallowed hard, the taste of tears, the addictive tinge of ash. Who was he to think of Sarah as weak?

"It's because of us," Sarah was the one to say aloud, matter of fact. Paul squeezed her shoulder, not contradicting her. They both looked at the emergency bag open on the bed, the knife and torn card.

Sarah stood and faced the bed. She was the one to bend, to start cleaning up the mess.

"Let's at least put this damn stuff away." Sarah stuffed the knife, first, back in the open emergency bag. "GodPaul, if Dr. Eden was halfway human he would've noticed it all and declared us 'unfit' or something . . ." Then she lifted the two halves of the card that had caused such trouble, wanting to drop it all in the trash, but wasn't that her mistake in the first place, pretending it didn't exist? Wouldn't it be a mistake to think, to believe, they could put all this neatly behind them?

Sarah slipped the card halves back into the bag.

"Our disaster bag," Paul muttered. His voice gravelly as if with weeks' worth of smoke.

"Yeah, well there are big disasters and little ones," Sarah answered back. She zipped the bag. "One more thing," she added, looking at Paul's left hand. "My fingers aren't swollen anymore, you know . . ." Paul nodded, to her relief. He did know.

He unscrewed her wedding ring from his pinkie without ceremony this time. Over a year before, when they'd transferred the rings after his surgery, they'd pressed their fingertips together like teenagers and transferred his ring as if it had never left anyone's finger.

"No matter what," Paul said matter-of-factly: the engraving they both knew was on the inside of both rings—in teeny, unreadable print—but they knew. Sarah nodded.

He handed her back her ring. She screwed it back on her ring finger. "Still fits," she announced. Then she burst out, "GodPaul, can we at least agree that everything we've just laid out, it's nothing compared to him? To Donny."

She gazed over at swaddled Donny asleep in his cart, the cart they'd be leaving behind.

Paul nodded once, but hard, knitting his thick, graying brows as if impatient with that question. *Of course*, he seemed to say, though curtly. He was rubbing his freed pinkie.

"Donny and PJ," Paul added with a glance at the clock. "When I said good-bye to PJ, to Paul Jr, today . . . Christ, when he told me about the baby, he told me, too, about some plan, holding himself up straight like a soldier. Christ Almighty, I think the kid might really, like he's said he would—"

"Sign up," Sarah filled in. "Yeah, the way he's always been so into military and police stories, the way he got to see some of that up close, the bomber night. Yeah, I could picture him doing that. If he does have a baby, if he can't handle being a day-to-day dad to that baby . . . maybe running off and being a soldier seems easier? Better?"

Paul nodded, clamping his mouth shut. *Is he going to cry now, too?* Sarah wondered in alarm. But Paul pulled himself upright. He towered above her, as always and shook his head, raising his hands in a familiar, resigned *what can we do?* gesture. His dad's gesture.

Sarah heard footsteps through the door, the last damn nurse. They both faced the closed but unlockable door. "GodPaul, how will we keep them, either of them, safe?"

Before Paul could answer that unanswerable question about their sons, the door squeaked open.

Chapter Twelve

May 4, 2013: 12:00 p.m.

Baby Released

"You two ready?" The NICU nurse Ana, Paul's favorite too, bustled in, pushing an empty wheelchair. Then Sarah was saying she didn't need a chair, and the nurse was insisting Sarah needed the chair so she could hold her baby without waking him.

Because the hospital really was keeping Donny's little metal NICU cart. The hospital was just letting them take—incredible and ill-advised, it suddenly seemed—Donny himself.

Paul gathered Sarah's bags, remembering from another lifetime the overwhelming sense of responsibility he'd felt picking up Adina and baby PJ at the hospital. How relieved he had been when Adina's stolid mom had taken over and had let him back off, slip away.

Damn Nana, Paul thought, hefting Sarah's two stuffed bags. *Or no; Nana had done what she thought best. Damn myself for letting Nana take over, take PJ.*

"I can push her, push them." Paul rallied his old sure-sounding supervisor voice, which could serve, too, as a decent dad voice. "Just let me take them."

He half expected their bossy nurse to protest. But Donny was being released; the nurse's thoughts must already be with the steamy fried chicken lunch trays being served in the hall and the new mother-to-be waiting for this room. The nurse bent to carefully hug Sarah's shoulders without jarring the baby. She shook Paul's hand, firm but fast.

Then she was whooshing off down the hall, smoothing her black bun. Paul, with Sarah's travel bag slung over his shoulder and her clanky disaster bag hanging off his elbow, pushed the surprisingly heavy weight of his wife and son.

He bumped his knee on the wheelchair wheel, going too fast at first. More slowly yet more skillfully, he eased the loaded chair toward the elevators.

Faint strains of classical music—Mozart, some yuppie couple's birth room tape, aimed to educate their child from minute one—wafted behind a closed door. The Magic Flute, muffled the way all music might be for Donny. How in hell would Paul himself have survived this life without beautiful, clear music?

BOMBING SUSPECT DZHOKHAR TSARNAEV ALLEGED-LY CONFESSING FROM HIS HOSPITAL BED . . . THAT CONFESSION A SUBJECT OF CONTROVERSY REGARD-ING WHETHER TSARNAEV HAD BEEN READ HIS RIGHTS

From the open-doored room nearest the elevator, a grave news voice was ending a story about the ongoing marathon investigation. Then launching into an account of recent US military casualties among peacekeeping forces in Afghanistan.

PRIVATE FIRST CLASS . . .

Paul punched the elevator button with a rigid finger, tightening his lips. He maneuvered the wheelchair inside. The elevator doors sucked shut. Paul found himself closed in with his small family and a young Asian man, maybe too young to be a dad.

BOSTON STRONG, read this guy's T-shirt—already, T-shirts? Usually Paul scorned such slogans, but he had a sneaking fondness for this one, which had materialized seemingly hours after lockdown day. Paul had lived in the Boston area all his life, and it had given him a certain stoic, Yankee strength. All that bad weather has to be good for something.

Spring rain still falling now outside, Paul noticed along the walkway to the main lobby's elevator.

The younger man pressed L for lobby. Christ, would PJ really sign up and join the army? Become a Private First Class? SONS OF LIBERTY; PJ used to like that archaic engraving in the Lexington Green. It was true that he'd always loved playing soldier or spy.

Paul looked down at Sarah's hair, half dried but still damp, shampoo scented. Everything clean and ready for her and Donny back at the condo. At least Paul had done that part right.

The final doors *binged*; the lobby opened out. More BOSTON STRONG flyers decked the walls by the main elevator, advertising some rally or other.

Paul remembered as he maneuvered Sarah and Donny through the crowded lobby a moment he'd shared with PJ here on lockdown day. He and Peej overheard an impatient Brooklyn accented man say on his cell, "New York would not have shut down."

PJ had stiffened beside Paul on a lobby couch. Paul had met PJ's gaze in shared contempt. "Yeah," Paul had muttered under TV voices once the obnoxious New Yorker had hurried past.

"Yeah, those NY bastards would've kept their city open. Yeah," Paul had allowed, "they might be meaner and tougher than us. But we're smarter. And we've got a little more sense of right and wrong." PJ had nodded, he and Paul for once in total agreement.

You do us wrong, Paul thought now as he wheeled past more BOSTON STRONG flyers, *we will track you down within days. We will save your life at our fine hospitals. We give you a fair trial, then we will kill you.*

He felt a fatherly pang that PJ would not be around to watch the news of the upcoming trial. Paul pulled the wheelchair up to the smaller elevator, which he knew after his two weeks of hospital visits was the best one to take to the parking garage.

Paul pressed *up* and remembered a newspaper quote he'd read about how justice for the older black hat bomber was not possible in this world, but justice for the younger Dzhokhar would begin in the Middlesex County Courthouse. Paul re-gripped the wheelchair.

Parenting PJ might not be possible for Paul much more, in this life, but parenting Donny began here and now.

"It's raining out," Sarah murmured. "He's never breathed outdoor air ..."

He from here on in was and always would be Donny.

"That's why it's best if we take this way," Paul told Sarah. But he wondered as he pressed up again if even this small decision was right. Wouldn't it be better if he brought the car around, if Sarah and Donny waited in passenger pickup, if the baby breathed his first rainy-day air fresh, not parking garage dank?

The doors *binged* open; they had the elevator to themselves. Their ascent commenced. L and then P for Parking were blinking, on then off.

"Yes, good idea." Sarah was nodding. "We'll keep Donny inside a little longer. Then when we get home you can pull right up to our door . . ." She was babbling like she did when anxious, hugging the baby so close Paul behind her couldn't see his pink forehead anymore.

"You remember where you're parked?" Sarah asked just as Paul realized he didn't remember at all. The elevator doors to parking's upper level sucked open.

"Sure," Paul told Sarah. He'd been so damn distracted after talking to PJ, he hadn't scribbled down the parking space number from the vast garage as he usually did.

But Paul tried to push Sarah and Donny out like he knew what he was doing. At least he eased the wheelchair forward with less jostle this time. He was getting better at pushing the two of them. And that, Paul told himself as he started forward in the concrete and exhaust fumed dark, was all he could hope for.

That and finding, somehow, the goddamned car.

⚓

He doesn't know which way to turn, Sarah thought. She could sense it in the way Paul hesitated a second before pushing the wheelchair left or right. Donny stirred dazedly in her arms, maybe somehow sensing that same hesitation.

"It's OK," Sarah murmured to Donny as Paul randomly chose his path. Sarah tried to pitch her voice loud enough for her possibly hearing damaged baby to hear, but not loud enough to wake him up. Her voice felt lost anyway in this big, echoing garage.

An engine revved, so close Sarah half jumped in her wheelchair.

Paul pushed them steadily forward. But Sarah felt behind her the urgent craning of his neck as he searched among all the darkened vehicles for their dented fender. Donny's blanketed feet probed Sarah's stomach the way he used to probe her womb, seeking the exit.

"It's OK, we'll find it," Sarah murmured slightly louder to Donny. A non-nagging way, she hoped, of letting Paul know she knew he didn't know where he was going.

Outside the parking garage's concrete walls, Sarah heard Boston spring rain pouring down. Streaming and straining to get in and get them.

"Damn, I should've brought the car around," Paul answered back loudly. Almost a shout. He halted; Sarah felt him behind her fumble in his pants pocket. Then she heard the plaintive *beep* of his car key beeper. Unanswered.

"Remember Donny's beeping monitor that night?" Sarah dared to raise her voice almost as loud as his. She knew he'd know that night was Donny's birth night. She knew Paul would know she meant: let's just be thankful we're taking home this dear and live baby.

"Yeah, I kept thinking every second those beeps, those heartbeats, would stop," Paul answered behind her. And he *beep-beeped* the car key beeper again.

The *beeps* echoed plaintively, like a baby bird's *cheep*, still unanswered.

"But Donny's beeps didn't stop." Sarah pressed his tiny body to hers to keep him warm in the rainy-day chill. "We got away with it. With him."

Or almost, she amended to herself. She knew Paul shared it: a new specific guilt settling in his chest, as in hers. A baby who can't hear right, maybe would never hear right. All because of the baby's well-meaning but screwed-up—were there any other kind? —parents.

Sarah heaved a gusty, mother sized sigh. With a quieter answering fatherly sigh, Paul plodded forward down the next dark row of undamaged fenders, uncracked headlights.

AISLE C read an unhelpful, soupily-lit sign.

"Damn, I should've written down the letter or whatever," Paul muttered from above, pronouncing that *whatever* with PJ's exact angry edge. PJ here, even now.

"Shhh, he's waking up . . ." Sarah jiggled sleepy, wiggly Donny. Trying to convey to him with her arms that this damp, acrid air was nothing to fear. She turned her head, flashing on Paul's strong hands gripping the wheelchair handles, telling his hands: *Act like you know what we're doing . . .*

Paul maneuvered the chair into another blind turn. He sent out another unanswered *beep*. But, his footsteps stayed gritty and steady, pushing on. Donny's own feet groggily kicked Sarah. Donny didn't seem scared, not yet.

Sarah bowed her head over her baby. Her clean-smelling hair hung around him. Donny blinked. His miniature lips pinched shut. His nostrils widened. His darkened eyes widened too, alert, yet unalarmed.

Sarah nodded down at him. Donny's head bobbed with the motion of the wheelchair, like he was nodding back. His gaze stayed unbroken and unblinking. He trusted his mother and father, Donny was saying to Sarah with his wide, guileless eyes.

He trusted them to find their way through this big, cold dark and bring him home. ✍

Acknowledgments

Excerpts from this novel have appeared, in different forms, in the following magazines, with thanks to the editors:

> *Epoch, Solstice: a Magazine of Diverse Voices, Stonecoast Review, Words & Images* and *Michigan Quarterly Review* (story "Celebration" was the winner of MQR's Lawrence Foundation Prize for Fiction)

First THANKS to all First Responders in the Boston area who kept us safe the night of April 18, 2013. Special THANKS to Revere Police Chief Joe Cafarelli for kindly talking to me and sharing his firsthand knowledge of the manhunt.

THANKS to Alex Johnson for giving me a birth room notebook from Italy so beautiful I had to write in it; THANKS to my friends and soulmate scribes, who've been with me every step of the way: to Girl Groupers Ann Harleman and Gail Donovan (double thanks) and Debra Spark; to Lise Haines and to Mary Sullivan and to Jessica Treadway and to Suzanne Strempek Shea. THANKS to Al Davis, Nayt Rundquist, Samantha Albers, Ethan DeGree, and the whole terrific team at NRP; THANKS to John Talbot; THANKS to my entire ever-inspiring family; THANKS to my wise, wonderful husband of thirty years and counting, John Hodgkinson; finally, THANKS to and for Will.

About New Rivers Press

NEW RIVERS PRESS emerged from a drafty Massachusetts barn in winter 1968. Intent on publishing work by new and emerging poets, founder C. W. "Bill" Truesdale labored for weeks over an old Chandler & Price letterpress to publish three hundred fifty copies of Margaret Randall's collection, So Many Rooms Has a House But One Roof.

Nearly four hundred titles later, New Rivers, a non-profit and now teaching press based since 2001 at Minnesota State University Moorhead, has remained true to Bill's goal of publishing the best new literature—poetry and prose—from new, emerging, and established writers.

New Rivers Press authors range in age from twenty to eighty-nine. They include a silversmith, a carpenter, a geneticist, a monk, a tree-trimmer, and a rock musician. They hail from cities such as Christchurch, Honolulu, New Orleans, New York City, Northfield (Minnesota), and Prague.

Charles Baxter, one of the first authors with New Rivers, calls the press "the hidden backbone of the American literary tradition." Continuing this tradition, in 1981 New Rivers began to sponsor the Minnesota Voices Project (now called Many Voices Project) competition. It is one of the oldest literary competitions in the United States, bringing recognition and attention to emerging writers. Other New Rivers publications include the American Fiction Series, the American Poetry Series, New Rivers Abroad, and the Electronic Book Series.

Please visit our website **newriverspress.com** for more information.

About the Author

ELIZABETH SEARLE is the author of four books of fiction, most recently *Girl Held in Home*, and is the librettist of *Tonya & Nancy: The Rock Opera*, which has drawn major media coverage. Her previous books are: *Celebrities in Disgrace*, a finalist for the Paterson Fiction Prize; *A Four-Sided Bed*, a novel nominated for an American Library Association Book Award and released in 2011 in a new paperback and eBook edition; and *My Body to You*, a story collection that won the Iowa Short Fiction Prize. *A Four-Sided Bed* is now in development as a feature film. Over thirty of Elizabeth's stories have been published in magazines such as *Ploughshares*, *AGNI*, *Kenyon Review* and *Redbook*. Her nonfiction has appeared in over a dozen anthologies including *Don't You Forget About Me* (Simon & Schuster) and *Knitting Yarns* (Norton). Elizabeth's theater works have been featured in stories on *Good Morning America*, CBS, CNN, NPR, the AP, *People.com,* and more. Her *Tonya & Nancy: The Rock Opera* had a sold-out extended run at the New York Musical Festival (NYMF) in NYC in 2015. Elizabeth lives with her husband and son in Arlington, MA.

Elizabeth's website is: **www.elizabethsearle.net**.